D1109341

THE
HUMAN ZERO

The Science Fiction Stories of Erle Stanley Gardner

Edited by
Martin H. Greenberg
and Charles G. Waugh

WILLIAM MORROW AND COMPANY, INC.
New York   1981

LA GRANGE PUBLIC LIBRARY
10 WEST COSSITT
LA GRANGE, ILLINOIS 60525

Compilation, selection and introduction copyright © 1981 by Martin H. Greenberg and Charles G. Waugh

The stories in this collection were first published in *Argosy* magazine on the following dates:

Rain Magic   October 20, 1928
Monkey Eyes   Serialized, July 27–August 3, 1929
The Sky's the Limit   Serialized, December 7–December 14, 1929
A Year in a Day   July 19, 1930
The Man with Pin-Point Eyes   January 10, 1931
The Human Zero   December 19, 1931
New Worlds   December 17, 1932

All rights reserved. No part of this book may be reproduced or utilized in any form or by any means, electronic or mechanical, including photocopying, recording or by any information storage and retrieval system, without permission in writing from the Publisher. Inquiries should be addressed to William Morrow and Company, Inc., 105 Madison Ave., New York, N. Y. 10016.

Library of Congress Cataloging in Publication Data

Gardner, Erle Stanley, 1889–1970.
  The human zero.

  Stories originally appeared in Argosy magazine be-
tween 1928 and 1932.
  CONTENTS: The human zero.—Monkey eyes.—New worlds.
—Rain magic.—A year in a day.—The man with pin-point
eyes.—The sky's the limit.
  1. Science fiction, American. I. Greenberg, Martin
Harry. II. Waugh, Charles. III. Title.
PS3513.A6322H8   1981   813'.52   80-22494
ISBN 0-688-00122-X

Printed in the United States of America

First Edition

1 2 3 4 5 6 7 8 9 10

BOOK DESIGN BY MICHAEL MAUCERI

SF

CONTENTS

FOREWORD

Erle Stanley Gardner, author, lawyer, humanitarian, adventurer, was born in 1889. He did not begin writing until he was thirty-one, but in the next fifty years until his death in 1970, he averaged approximately one book every four months, one article every two months, and one novelette or short story every month. This is a remarkable record by itself, but it seems nothing short of astonishing when one considers Mr. Gardner's other activities: eleven years (1921 to 1931) of full-time law practice, twelve years (1943 to 1955) of attending to the Perry Mason radio show, nine years (1957 to 1966) of monitoring scripts for the Perry Mason TV series, fifteen years (1949 to 1964) of devoting most of his time to the functioning of the Court of Last Resort in an attempt to improve the criminal justice system in this country, and thirty-eight years (1933 to 1970) of almost constant travel.

As a person, Mr. Gardner was an interesting blend of New Englander and westerner. The first ten years of his life were spent in Massachusetts, and his parents' roots extended back to the *Mayflower* on his mother's side and to a long line of Yankee sea captains on his father's side. This heritage shaped his conservative personal habits (drinking little and gambling less), his competitive ambition to excel, and his tenacious persistence. In 1899 his father, Charles Gardner, moved to the West Coast to further his career as a civil engineer, and the young Erle took to many of the western ways. For example, from the frontier atmosphere came his love of the outdoors and his informality, his confidence in his ability to teach himself things, and his nomadic tendencies. For the rest of his days, he would consider himself a Californian. His lively personal style was in some conflict with his New England upbringing and was a source of annoyance, for instance, to his very proper mother.

Erle was a clever, puckish youth whose habit of outsmarting authority kept getting him thrown out of schools. Fortunately, however, his great curiosity and enormous energy led him into the study of law. He gained admission to the bar by the age of twenty-one and shortly thereafter began establishing a reputation in Oxnard, California, as a brilliant criminal lawyer. His strengths were an ability to outmaneuver his opponents prior to trial, a genius for utilizing obscure statutes in innovative ways, and an ability to draw the truth out of opposition witnesses through dramatic cross-examinations. These are traits which later, of course, appeared in his most famous creation, Perry Mason.

By 1917, however, he realized that being a successful attorney was not exactly what he wanted because he disliked being tied down in one place. So for the next four years he was president of a sales company, which provided a life-style that satisfied his needs for action and travel. But a recession led to business reverses and a decision to return to law.

Still he remained restless, and after investigating a few alternatives he decided to become a writer. Such a profession would permit him to travel while working, and at first he could bring in some extra money while still practicing law. He began to teach himself how to write by banging away at his typewriter each evening until two o'clock in the morning. A major breakthrough occurred as a result of a devastating criticism of "The Shrieking Skeleton" which the editors of *Black Mask* magazine had inadvertently enclosed with the rejected manuscript. This provided Mr. Gardner with clues about what he was doing wrong. He tore the story apart, and after three days of furious revision he produced a version good enough to be accepted. Other markets opened to him, and, by carefully analyzing the suggestions of editors, he learned to break down plots into component parts which he put on separate cardboard wheels. Some, for example, represented situations, characters, the lowest common denominators of public interest, and unexpected complications. By spinning these wheels and noting points of contact among spokes, he was usually able to generate a plot within thirty minutes. And since he wrote very quickly, he was able to produce a ten-thousand-word novelette every three days. Not all sold, of course, but enough did so that his income from writing increased from $974 in 1921 to $6,627 in 1926 and to more than $20,000 in the early thirties.

During 1932 he began reducing his legal work, and probably William Morrow's acceptance of his first two Perry Mason novels that year gave him the confidence to cease practicing law in 1933, except in a consulting capacity. For two years he had been promising his agent a novel, but other commitments had left no time. Then Mr. Gardner decided he could save time by using a dictating machine. He spent a half day thinking up a plot and dictated in three and a half days what was eventually to be called *The Case of the Velvet Claws*. Six weeks later he produced his second novel in the same fashion.

Now he could once again be free, and in the summer of 1933 he began the seminomadic existence he would follow for most of the rest of his life. When not traveling abroad, or staying at one of the several residences he eventually maintained, he could be found traveling around the desert with several secretaries, stopping wherever he pleased and dictating work that would be typed up on the spot.

As a writer, Erle Stanley Gardner is one of the most popular of all time. His books have been translated into 37 foreign languages. His paperback sales exceed every other author who has ever lived, and a current estimate of his total sales in all languages and editions would be well over 300 million copies. *The Case of the Velvet Claws* ultimately sold 4,000,000 copies, a stunning figure for any novel, not to speak of a first novel. Of the 151 mystery novels which appeared on the best-seller lists from 1895 to 1965, Mr. Gardner was responsible for ninety-one.

Like Shakespeare, Dumas, and Dickens, he was remarkably popular during his lifetime, but, of course, the truest test of literary merit is how well sales hold up over time. And in this regard, Mr. Gardner continues to do very well. In 1979, almost fifty years since the first, and nine years after the last, novel was written, he still averaged 2,400 sales a day, seven days a week, fifty-two weeks a year.

To those who know that he wrote rapidly and prolifically, that he thought of himself as a businessman/lawyer who wrote because of circumstances, and that he continually referred to himself as a fiction factory, such staying power in his readership may seem surprising. Study his career closely, however, and many reasons for his success become apparent. First, he had the ability to become an expert in any field of knowledge that interested him. Law and writing are just two examples from a large number which included astronomy, surveying, archery, salesmanship, forensic medicine, polygraph work, and criminal psychology. Second, he always had the drive and ambition to try to make himself the best in whatever field he went into.* Third, he possessed a mind which was both analytical and creative. As he did with the plot wheel, he was able to reduce complex matters to simple elements and then to utilize this information in innovative ways. He realized that to succeed in mass markets he had to appeal to the tired worker, the traveler looking to kill time, and the typical organization-bound individual. So he used rapid action, conflict, and drama to grip attention, and he sustained interest by appealing to his readers' desire to see

---

* A picturesque example: When he was revising "The Shrieking Skeleton," he pounded the skin off the ends of the two fingers he used for typing, covered the fingers with adhesive tape, and continued "hammering away on the blood-spattered keys" until the job was done.

ordinary guys with some extraordinary qualities achieve justice by successfully fighting crime, chicanery, or red tape. Fourth, he was not the type of person to turn down good advice about how to improve his work. He realized that continued sales would depend on his books being well crafted. Therefore, criticisms from his secretaries and editors were listened to attentively. He often groused about both the comments and the commenter, especially on questions of time element or pace in a story. But he usually recognized good advice and took it when it was offered. Finally, although his books were written swiftly, they were often rewritten several times before they appeared in final form. Besides being responsive to the suggestions of others, he often initiated rewrites himself. He wanted each book in a series to be better than the ones before, and, until a novel got into print, he would keep turning it over and over in his mind to see if he could think of how rewriting might improve it.[1]

As Freeman Lewis remarked about him in a letter to *The New York Times*:

Erle had a right to be proud of his skills as a writer. They were real and hard-earned. It often seemed to me that he operated as a professional in an area inhabited largely by amateurs. And it also often seemed to me that his books should have been reviewed by sports columnists rather than bookish people, for Erle had the kinds of learned and applied skills that sports fans understand and cherish but which book reviewers often are too pretentious to appreciate. . . .

He was mostly given bad marks or simply overlooked by "literary" critics and he resented it, though he seldom said so. But once, in a drive from Palm Springs to Temecula, he gave the most lucid lecture on how to write readable stories, how to plot, how to select and depict believable characters, etc., that I have ever heard. He was a very serious student of the craft of writing fiction and many of those who dismissed his talents would benefit from a serious study of his practices.[2]

Particularly interesting are the nearly six hundred novelettes and short stories Mr. Gardner produced early in his career. They were not only his training ground; they also display immediately his storytelling gift. The majority are series stories, featuring protagonists such as Ed Jenkins (a phantom crook), Lester Leith (a philanthropic type who fleeces crooks), Señor Lobo (a professional soldier of fortune), Bob Zane (an old prospector), Speed Dash (a human fly with a photographic memory), Bob Larkin (a juggler), and El Paisano (who can see in the dark). Both the Jenkins and Leith series comprise approximately seventy stories, and fourteen other series range from five to twenty-seven stories each. Most of this work is of the same quality that readers have come to expect from Mr. Gardner, and it often reveals additional dimensions of his writing ability. For example, besides rapid pace and crime, the Whispering Sand series weaves in romance and hauntingly lyrical descriptions of our western deserts. Surprisingly, however, only about six percent of these shorter works have ever been reprinted. *The Human Zero* collection is the first of what we hope will be a number of collections that will once again make this important work of Erle Stanley Gardner available to his millions of fans.

Mr. Gardner possessed many of the characteristics of the typical science-fiction fan: a feeling of not fitting in as an adolescent, an avid curiosity, a high intelligence, a great propensity for and enjoyment of arguing with people, and a tendency to alternate periods of solitude with periods of multiple companionship.[3] Who knows, had he been born fifteen years later, he might have encountered *Astounding*'s editorial genius, John W. Campbell, Jr., and ended up a science-fiction writer. But at the time Mr. Gardner began writing, no science-fiction magazines existed, and because of his background in law he quite naturally moved into producing detective fiction.

However, between the years of 1928 and 1932 he did produce seven science-fiction and fantasy stories for *Argosy*, and these provide us with a fascinating glimpse of the writer he might have chosen to be had circumstances been different.

The title story of this collection, "The Human Zero," is both a who-done-it and a locked-room mystery. A man is killed in a locked room, and both his body and his murderer disappear. So Sid Rodney, star detective, tries to avoid his own murder as he figures out who the criminal is and how the chilling crime was committed. The story exemplifies Mr. Gardner's philosophy of having "characters who start from scratch and sprint the whole darned way to a goal line."

"Rain Magic," the first to be published, is somewhat reminiscent of Edgar Rice Burroughs. It recounts the African adventures of a young shanghaied sailor who jumps ship. Told in very vivid first-person style, it involves love, intelligent ants, a monkey man, and a ledge of solid gold. The story is a strange one, but a prefatory note said that the essentials had been told to the author by an old desert prospector. Initially, Mr. Gardner thought "it was one gosh-awful lie," but upon subsequent checking on the locale, he found every fact given to him by the old man that could be verified was accurate.

"Monkey Eyes" is similar in flavor to some of Richard Harding Davis's work. Set in India, it centers around kidnapping, revenge, and a grotesque scientific experiment. An aerial dogfight, ceremonies at a lost temple, and an interestingly shaded villain are still other highlights of this story.

"The Sky's the Limit" is an interplanetary tale of a trip to Venus. Using the idea of an antigravity drive which H. G. Wells had popularized in *The First Men in the Moon*, Mr. Gardner mixes crime and adventure with a delightful narration of the spaceship's test run and an accurate description of what scientists thought Venus was like in the late 1920's.

"A Year in a Day" takes the idea of invisibility through

acceleration that H. G. Wells popularized in "The New Accelerator" and applies it to the framework of the crime story. The vivid descriptions of the invisibility effect compare favorably with similar attempts by Wells and by John D. MacDonald in *The Girl, The Gold Watch, and Everything.*

"The Man with Pin-Point Eyes" is a powerful adventure story of reincarnation and lost gold. As fresh as if it had just been ripped from the typewriter, its western setting is very similar to the Whispering Sand series which will be reprinted in a collection to follow soon after the present science-fiction volume.

"New Worlds" is an epic disaster story of a worldwide flood caused by a five-degree shift in the earth's poles. There is a marvelously descriptive scene of New York City being inundated by the rising waters. However, as Sam Moskowitz perceptively points out, yarns of this type are popular because catastrophes "vicariously release the individual from the responsibilities of family, law and conscience. They mark the demise of everything that binds, inhibits or restrains." And in this work, Moskowitz continues, Mr. Gardner uses the "cataclysm as a device for releasing a small group of individuals to unusual adventure."

By 1932, when "New Worlds" was published, Mr. Gardner had written his first two Perry Mason novels and was beginning to direct his major efforts into producing book-length manuscripts. As a businessman, he may have decided that the amount of time he had to put into researching a science-fiction story exceeded the amount he needed for a mystery or western. He was also concerned with the sale of reprintings of his works in the future and the need to avoid material which would date his stories. Now, science fiction, unless it is set far away in time, has a tendency to age rapidly as it is overtaken by scientific knowledge, and Mr. Gardner must have known that mysteries and westerns would age less. Faced with all these reasons, then, it is quite possible that he simply decided he could put his efforts to use more efficiently elsewhere.

In any case, those of us who love science fiction still have the following marvelous tales by which to remember him.

CHARLES G. WAUGH and
MARTIN H. GREENBERG

NOTES

1. For a summary of his life, including some of his methods of working, see Dorothy B. Hughes, *Erle Stanley Gardner: The Case of the Real Perry Mason* (New York: William Morrow and Company, 1978).
2. Such a study has now been published: Francis L. and Roberta B. Fugate, *Secrets of the World's Best-Selling Writer: The Storytelling Techniques of Erle Stanley Gardner* (New York: William Morrow and Company, 1980).
3. Charles G. Waugh and David Schroeder, "Here's Looking at You Kids: A Profile of Science Fiction Fans," *Anthro-Tech: A Journal of Speculative Anthropology*. Fall, 1978, pp. 12–19. Copies may be obtained from Dr. Darlene Thomas, Lockhaven State College, Lockhaven, PA 17745, for $1.00.

THE HUMAN ZERO

CHAPTER 1

A Mysterious Kidnaping

Bob Sands took the letter from the hands of the captain of police, read it, and pursed his lips in a whistle.

Four pairs of eyes studied the secretary of the kidnaped man as he read. Two pencils scribbled notes on pads of scratch paper, of the type used by newspaper reporters.

Bob Sands showed that he had been aroused from sleep, and had rushed to headquarters. His collar was soiled. His tie was awry. The eyes were still red from rubbing, and his chin was covered with a bristling stubble which awaited a razor.

"Good Heavens," he said, "the Old Man was sure given a scare when he wrote that!"

Captain Harder noted the sleep-reddened eyes of the secretary.

"Then it's his writing?"

"Undoubtedly."

Ruby Orman, "sob-sister" writer of the *Clarion*, added to her penciled notes. "Tears streamed down the cheeks of the loyal secretary as he identified the writing as being that of the man by whom he was employed."

Charles Ealy, reporter for the more conservative *Star*, scribbled sketchy notes. "Sands summoned—Identifies writing as being that of P. H. Dangerfield—Dramatic scene enacted in office of Captain Harder at an early hour this morning—Letter, written by kidnaped millionaire, urges police to drop case and bank to pay the half million demanded in cash as ransom—Letter hints at a scientist as being the captor and mentions fate 'so horrible I shudder to contemplate it.' "

Sid Rodney, the other occupant of the room, wrote nothing. He didn't believe in making notes. And, since he was the star detective of a nationally known agency, he was free to do pretty much as he pleased.

Rodney didn't make detailed reports. He got results. He had seen them come and seen them go. Ordinary circumstances found him cool and unexcited. It took something in the nature of a calamity to arouse him.

Now he teetered back on the two legs of his chair and his eyes scanned the faces of the others.

It was three o'clock in the morning. It was the second day following the mysterious abduction of P. H. Dangerfield, a millionaire member of the stock exchange. Demands had been made for a cool half million as ransom. The demands had been okayed by the millionaire himself, but the bank refused to honor the request. Dangerfield had not over two hundred thousand in his account. The bank was willing to loan the balance, but only when it should be absolutely satisfied that it was the wish of the millionaire, and that the police were powerless.

Rodney was employed by the bank as a special investigator. In addition, the bank had called in the police. The investigation had gone through all routine steps and arrived nowhere. Dangerfield had been at his house. He had vanished. There was no trace of him other than the demands of the kidnapers, and the penciled notations upon the bottom of those letters, purporting to be in the writing of the missing millionaire.

Then had come this last letter, completely written in pen and ink by Dangerfield himself. It was a letter addressed directly to Captain Harder, who was assuming charge of the case, and implored him to let the bank pay over the money.

Captain Harder turned to Rodney.

"How will the bank take this?" he asked.

Rodney took a deep drag at his cigarette. He spoke in a matter-of-fact tone, and, as he spoke, the smoke seeped out of the corners of his mouth, clothing the words in a smoky halo.

"Far as the newspapers are concerned," he said, "I have nothing to say. As a private tip, I have an idea the bank will regard this as sufficient authorization, and pay the money."

Captain Harder opened a drawer, took out photostatic copies of the other demands which had been received.

"They want five hundred thousand dollars in gold certificates, put in a suitcase, sent by the secretary of the kidnaped man, to the alley back of Quong Mow's place in Chinatown. It's to be deposited in an ash can that sits just in front of the back door of Quong Mow's place. Then Sands is to drive away.

"The condition is that the police must not try to shadow Sands or watch the barrel, that Sands must go alone, and that there must be no effort to trace the numbers of the bills. When that has been done, Dangerfield will go free. Otherwise he'll be murdered. The notes point out that, even if the money is deposited in the ash can, but the other conditions are violated, Dangerfield will die."

There was silence in the room when the captain finished speaking. All of those present knew the purport of those messages. The newspaper reporter had even gone so far as to photograph the ash can.

There was a knock at the door.

Captain Harder jerked it open.

The man who stood on the threshold of the room, surveying the occupants through clear, gray, emotionless eyes, was Arthur L. Soloman, the president of the bank.

He was freshly shaved, well dressed, cool, collected.

"I obeyed your summons, captain," he said in a dry, husky voice that was as devoid of moisture as a dead leaf scuttling across a cement sidewalk on the wings of a March wind.

Captain Harder grunted.

"*I* came without waiting to shave or change," said Sands, his voice showing a trace of contempt. "They said it was life or death."

The banker's fish-like eyes rested upon the flushed face of Bob Sands.

"I shaved," said Soloman. "I never go out in the morning without shaving. What is the trouble, Captain?"

Harder handed over the letter.

The banker took a vacant chair, took spectacles from his pocket, rubbed the lenses with a handkerchief, held them to the light, breathed upon the lenses and polished them again, then finally adjusted the spectacles and read the letter.

His face remained absolutely void of expression.

"Indeed," he said, when he had finished.

"What we want to know," said Captain Harder, "is whether the bank feels it should honor that request, make a loan upon the strength of it, and pay that ransom."

The banker put the tips of his fingers together and spoke coldly.

"One-half a million dollars is a very great deal of money. It is altogether too much to ask by way of ransom. It would, indeed, be a dangerous precedent for the more prominent business men of this community, were any such ransom to be paid."

"We've been all over that before, Mr. Soloman. What I want to know is what do you want the police to do? If we're to try and find this man, we'd better keep busy. If we're going to sit back and let you ransom him, and then try and catch the kidnapers afterward, we don't want to get our wires crossed."

The banker's tone dripped sarcasm.

"Your efforts so far have seemed to be futile enough. The

police system seems inadequate to cope with these criminals."

Captain Harder flushed. "We do the best we can with what we've got. Our salary allowances don't enable us to employ guys that have got the brains of bank presidents to pound our pavements."

Ruby Orman snickered.

The banker's face remained gray and impassive.

"Precisely," he said coldly.

"Nothin' personal," said Harder.

The banker turned to Sid Rodney.

"Has your firm anything to report, Mr. Rodney?"

Rodney continued to sit back in his chair, his thumbs hooked into the arm holes of his vest, his cigarette hanging at a drooping angle.

"Nothin' that I know of," he said, smoke seeping from his lips with the words.

"Well?" asked Charles Ealy.

Captain Harder looked at the banker meaningly.

"Well?" he said.

Ruby Orman held her pencil poised over her paper.

"The *Clarion* readers will be *so* much interested in your answer, Mr. Soloman."

The banker's mouth tightened.

"The answer," he said, still speaking in the same husky voice, "is *no!*"

The reporters scribbled.

Bob Sands, secretary of the missing man, got to his feet. His manner was belligerent. He seemed to be controlling himself with an effort.

"You admit Mr. Dangerfield could sell enough securities within half an hour of the time he got back on the job to liquidate the entire amount!" he said accusingly.

The banker's nod was casual.

"I believe he could."

"And this letter is in his handwriting?"

"Yes. I would say it was."

"And he authorizes you to do anything that needs to be done, gives you his power of attorney and all that, doesn't he?"

"Yes." Soloman nodded.

"Then why not trust his judgment in the matter and do what he says?"

The banker smiled, and the smile was cold, tight-lipped.

"Because the bank is under no obligations to do so. Mr. Dangerfield has a checking account of about two hundred thousand dollars. The bank would honor his check in that amount, provided our attorney could advise us that the information we have received through the press and the police would not be tantamount to knowledge that such check was obtained by duress and menace.

"But as far as loaning any such additional sum to be paid as ransom, the bank does not care to encourage kidnapings by establishing any such precedent. The demand, gentlemen, is unreasonable."

"What," yelled Sands, "has the bank got to say about how much kidnapers demand?"

"Nothing. Nothing at all, Mr. Sands. Mr. Rodney, I trust your firm will uncover some clue which will be of value. The bank values Mr. Dangerfield's account very much. We are leaving no stone unturned to assist the police. But we cannot subscribe to the payment of such an unheard-of ransom."

"A human life is at stake!" yelled Sands.

The banker paused, his hand on the door, and firmly said:

"The safety of the business world is also at stake, gentlemen. Good morning!"

CHAPTER 2

Who Is Albert Crome?

The door slammed shut.

Captain Harder sighed.

Sid Rodney tossed away the stub of his cigarette, groped for a fresh one.

"Such is life," mused Charles Ealy.

"The dirty pirate!" snapped Sands. "He's made thousands off the Dangerfield account. He doesn't care a fig what happens to Dangerfield. He's just afraid of establishing a precedent that will inspire other criminals."

Sid Rodney lit his fresh cigarette.

Ruby Orman's pencil scribbled across the paper.

"Scene one of greatest consternation," she wrote. "Men glanced at each other in an ecstasy of futility. Sands gave the impression of fighting back tears. Even strong men may weep when the life of a friend is at stake. Police promise renewed activity . . ."

Bob Sands reached for his hat.

"I'll go crazy if I hang around here. Is there anything I can do?"

Captain Harder shook his head.

"We'll have this letter gone over by the handwriting department," he said.

Sands walked from the room.

"Good morning," he said wearily.

Charles Ealy turned to the captain.

"Nothing new, Harry?"

"Not a thing, other than that letter," said Captain Harder. "This is one case where we can't get a toe-hold to work on."

Charles Ealy nodded sympathetically.

"Anything for publication?" he asked.

"Yes," snapped Captain Harder. "You can state that I am working on a brand-new lead, and that within the next twenty-four hours we feel certain we will have the criminals in custody. You may state that we already have a cordon of police guarding against an escape from the city, and that, momentarily, the dragnet is tightening . . . Oh, you folks know, say the usual thing that may put the fear of God into the kidnapers and make the public think we aren't sitting here with arms folded."

Charles Ealy scraped back his chair.

"Wait a minute," said Rodney, the cigarette in his mouth wabbling in a smoky zigzag as he talked. "I may have a hunch that's worth while. Will you give me a break on it, captain, if it's a lead?"

The police captain nodded wearily.

"Shoot," he said.

Rodney grinned at the two reporters.

"This stuff is off the record," he admonished. "You two can scoop it if anything comes of it. Right now it's on the q.t."

The reporters nodded.

They were there, in the first place, because the two papers were "in right" with the administration. And they kept in right with the police department by printing what the police were willing they should print, and by keeping that confidential which was given to them in confidence.

Sid Rodney went to the trouble of removing his cigarette from the corner of his mouth, sure sign of earnestness.

"I've got a funny angle on this thing. I didn't say anything before, because I think it's a whole lot more grave than many people think. I have a hunch we're doing business with a man who has a lot more sense than the average kidnaper. I have a hunch he's dangerous. And if there was any chance of the bank coming to the front, then letting us try to recover the money afterward, I wanted to play it that way.

"But the bank's out, so it's everything to gain and nothing to lose. Now here's the situation. I ran down every one I could find who might have a motive. One of the things the agency did, which the police also did, was to run down every one who might profit by the disappearance or death of P. H. Dangerfield.

"But one thing our agency did that the police didn't do, was to try and find out whether or not any person had been trying to interest Dangerfield in a business deal and been turned down.

"We found a dozen leads and ran 'em down. It happened I was to run down a list of three or four, and the fourth person on the list was a chap named Albert Crome. Ever hear of him?"

He paused.

Captain Harder shook his head.

Ruby Orman looked blank. Charles Ealy puckered his brows.

"You mean the scientist that claimed he had some sort of a radium method of disrupting ether waves and forming an etheric screen?"

Rodney nodded. "That's the chap."

"Sort of cuckoo, isn't he? He tried to peddle his invention to the government, but they never took any particular notice of him. Sent a man, I believe, and Crome claimed the man they sent didn't even know elemental physics."

Sid Rodney nodded again.

There was a rap at the door.

Captain Harder frowned, reached back a huge arm, twisted the knob, and opened the door a crack.

"I left orders . . ." He paused in mid-sentence as he saw the face of Bob Sands.

"Oh, come in, Sands. I left orders only five people could come in here, and then I didn't want to be disturbed. . . Lord, man, what's the matter? You look as though you'd seen a ghost!"

LA GRANGE PUBLIC LIBRARY
10 WEST COSSITT
LA GRANGE, ILLINOIS 60525

Sands nodded.

"Look what happened. I started for home. My roadster was parked out in front of headquarters. I got in and drove it out Claremont Street, and was just turning into Washington when another car came forging alongside of me.

"I thought it would go on past, but it kept crowding me over. Then I thought of all the talk I'd heard of gangsters, and I wondered if there was any chance I was going to be abducted, too.

"I slammed on the brakes. The other car pushed right in beside me. There was a man sitting next to the driver, sort of a foreign looking fellow, and he tossed something.

"I thought it was a bomb, and I yelled and put my hand over my eyes. The thing thudded right into the seat beside me. When I grabbed it to throw it out, I saw it was a leather sack, weighted, and that there was crumpled paper on the inside. I opened the sack and found—this!"

Dramatically he handed over the piece of typewritten paper.

"Read it aloud," begged Ealy.

"Take a look," invited Captain Harder, spreading the sheet of paper on the desk.

They clustered about in a compact group, read the contents of that single spaced sheet of typewriting.

Sands:

You are a damned fool. The banker would have given in if you hadn't been so hostile. And the police bungled the affair, as they nearly always do. I've got a method of hearing and seeing what goes on in Captain Harder's office. I'm going to tell you folks right now that you didn't do Dangerfield any good. When I showed him on the screen what was taking place, and he heard your words, he was beside himself with rage.

You've got one more chance to reach that banker. If he doesn't pay the sum within twelve hours there won't be any more Dangerfield.

And the next time I kidnap a man and hold him for ransom I don't want so much powwow about it. Just to show you my power, I am going to abduct you, Sands, after I kill Dangerfield, and then I'm going to get Arthur Soloman, the banker. Both of you will be held for a fair ransom. Soloman's ransom will be seven hundred and fifty thousand dollars. So he'd better get ready to pay.

This is the final and last warning.

X.

Captain Harder's eyes were wide.

"Good Lord, has that man got a dictograph running into this office?"

Sands made a helpless gesture with the palms of his hands. He was white, his teeth were chattering, and his knees seemed utterly devoid of strength.

"I don't know. He's a devil. He's always seemed to know just what was going on. And he surely must have known Dangerfield's habits from A to Z. I'm frightened."

Captain Harder walked to the door.

"Send in a couple of men to search this place for a dictograph," he said. Then he turned on his heel, gave a swing of his arm. "Come on in another room, you folks. We'll go into this thing."

The little group trooped into one of the other offices.

"All right, Rodney. You were mentioning a scientist. What of him?"

"I went to his office," said Rodney, "and tried to engage him in conversation. He wouldn't talk. I asked him what he knew about Dangerfield, and he all but frothed at the mouth. He said Dangerfield was a crook, a pirate, a robber. Then he slammed the door.

"But, here's the point. I got a peep at the inside of his office. There was a Royal portable in there, and these letters that were received demanding ransom were written on a Royal portable.

"It's not much of a lead, and it's one that the police will have to run down—now. If it's a matter of life and death, and working against time, then it's too big for our agency to handle. But my opinion is that Albert Crome was violently insane, at least upon the subject of Dangerfield."

The police captain whirled to Sands.

"What sort of a car were these men using?"

"You mean the men who tossed the letter?"

"Yes."

"I can't tell you. I know it's stupid of me, but I just got too rattled to notice. It was a big car, and it looked as though it might have been a Cadillac, or a Buick, or a Packard. It might even have been some other make. I was rattled."

The captain snorted.

"What do you know about Crome?"

Sands blinked.

"I know Mr. Dangerfield was negotiating for the purchase of some patent rights, or the financing of some formula or something, but that's about all. The deal fell through."

"Ever meet Crome?"

The secretary hesitated, knitted his brows.

"You'll have to let me think . . . Yes, yes, of course I did. I met him several times. Some of the negotiations were carried on through me."

"Impress you as being a little off?" asked Sid Rodney, drawling the question, his inevitable cigarette dangling loosely from the corner of his mouth as he talked.

"No. He impressed me as being a pretty wide awake sort of a chap, very much of a gentleman, with a high sense of honor."

*　*　*

Captain Harder pressed a button.

"Take these letters. Have 'em photographed," he told the man who answered the buzzer. "Check the typewriting with the others. Then get me everything you can get on Albert Crome. I want to know what he's been doing with his time the last few days, who he associates with, who's seen him lately, where he lives, what he's doing with his work, everything about him.

"And if you can get a man into his offices and laboratory, I want a specimen of the typewriting that comes from the portable machine he's got—a Royal."

The man nodded, withdrew.

Captain Harder grinned at the little group.

"Well, we might go down to T-Bone Frank's and have a cup of coffee and some eats. Maybe we'll have something new when we get back."

Sands fidgeted.

"I don't want anything to eat."

"Well, you'd better wait a little while, Sands. You know that threat may mean nothing. Then again, it may mean a lot."

Sands nodded.

"Are you going to tell Soloman?"

"Yes. I'll give him a ring, I guess. Maybe I'd better do it before he gets home and to bed. Let's see, I've got his number here. I'll give him a buzz and break the glad tidings and then put a couple of the boys on guard in front of the place. It'll make him think a little. Didn't like his attitude, myself . . . Oh, well!"

He gave the exchange operator the number, replaced the receiver, fished a cigar from his pocket, and scraped a noisy match along the sole of his shoe.

Ruby Orman scribbled on her pad of paper: "In tense silence, these men waited grimly for the dawn."

Charles Ealy put a matter-of-fact question.

"Can we get these letters for the noon editions, Harry?"

"What's the deadline?" asked the captain.

"We'd have to have them by eight o'clock in order to get the plates ready."

"I guess so. It ain't eight o'clock yet."

Ealy perked up his ears.

"You speak as though you had something up your sleeve," he said.

The officer nodded grimly.

"I have," he said.

The telephone rang. Captain Harder cupped his ear to the receiver.

"Funny," he said, "Soloman's residence says he's not home yet." Then: "Keep calling. Tell him I want to speak to him. It's important."

They went to the all-night restaurant, lingered over coffee and sandwiches. They were all nervous, with the exception of Sid Rodney. That individual seemed to be utterly relaxed, but it was the inactivity of a cat who is sprawled in the sun, keeping a lazy eye upon a fluttering bird, trying to locate the nest.

Charles Ealy watched Sid Rodney narrowly. Once he nodded slowly.

They finished their meal, returned to headquarters.

"Heard from Soloman?" asked Captain Harder.

Sergeant Green, at the desk, shook his head.

"They keep saying he hasn't returned. But we've unearthed some stuff about Crome from our department files. He wanted a permit to establish an experimenting station in a loft building downtown. Had the lease on the place and was all ready to go ahead when he found out he had to have a permit to operate the sort of a place he wanted.

"He was turned down on the permit after it appeared that his experiments were likely to increase the fire hazard, and he was bitter about it."

Captain Harder grunted.

"That doesn't help much."

"Did he send in any typewritten letters?" asked Sid Rodney.

"Maybe. I'll look in the files. Most of those things would be in another file."

"Got the address of the loft building?"

"Yes—632 Grant Street. That's down near the wholesale district, a little side street."

Sid nodded.

"Yeah. I know. What say we take a run down there, captain?"

"Why? He was turned down on his permit. There's nothing there for us."

Rodney lit a fresh cigarette and resumed.

"The man's a scientist. He hates Dangerfield. He impresses me as being very much unbalanced. He's got a loft that isn't being used. Now *if* he should happen to be mixed up in the kidnaping, where would be a better place to keep a prisoner than in an unused loft building, that had been taken over and fitted up as an experimental laboratory?"

Captain Harder grinned.

"You win," he said. "Get me half a dozen of the boys out, sergeant. I'm going down there myself and give it a once over. Better take along a bunch of keys."

"Do we go along?" asked Ealy, his eyes twinkling.

Captain Harder grinned.

"Certainly not," he said.

Sands took him seriously.

"I'm glad of that. I'm simply all in. I want to go and get some sleep, a bath, and a shave."

Captain Harder looked sympathetic.

"I know, Sands. Ealy and I were kidding. But if you feel all in, go home and get some sleep. We've got your number. We'll call you if there's anything there."

"How about an escort?" asked Rodney. "Those threats, you know . . ."

Sands vehemently shook his head.

"No. I don't want to advertise to the neighborhood that I'm afraid. I'll go on home and sleep. I'm safe for twelve hours yet, anyway. If you think there's any danger at the end of that time, I'll move into a hotel and you can give me a guard."

Captain Harder nodded in agreement.

"Okay."

CHAPTER 3

Into Thin Air

The two police cars slid smoothly to the curb before the loft building.

The first streaks of dawn were tingeing the buildings in the concrete cañon of loft buildings, wholesale houses and nondescript apartments.

Captain Harder jerked his thumb.

"This is the place. No use standin' on formality. Let's go up. He had the whole building leased. Looks vacant now."

The men moved across the echoing sidewalk in a compact group. There was the jingle of keys against the brass lock plate, and then the click of a bolt. The door opened. A flight of stairs, an automatic elevator, a small lobby, showed in the reddish light of early morning. There was a musty smell about the place.

"Take the elevator," said Captain Harder. "Then we won't have so much trouble . . . funny he leased the whole building in advance of a permit. This lease cost him money."

No one said anything. They opened the door of the elevator. Then they drew back with an exclamation.

"Look there!" said one of the men.

There was a stool in the elevator. Upon that stool was a tray, and upon the tray was some food, remnants of sandwiches, a cup of coffee, the sides stained where trickles of the liquid had slopped over the side of the cup.

Captain Harder smelled the cup, jabbed a finger into the crust of the sandwiches.

"Looks like it's less than twenty-four hours old," he said.

The men examined the tray.

Captain Harder snapped into swift activity. It was plainly apparent that the curiosity which had sent him down to the loft building for a "look around" merely because there were no other clues to run down, had given place to well-defined suspicion.

"Here, Bill. You take one of the boys with you and watch the steps. Frank, get out your gun and watch the fire escape. Go around the back way, through the alley. We'll keep quiet and give you three minutes to get stationed. Then we're going up.

"If you see any one, order him to stop. If he doesn't obey, shoot to kill. George, you go with Frank. The rest of us are going up in the elevator."

He took out his watch.

"Three minutes," he said.

The men snapped into action.

Captain Harder held a thumb nail upon the dial of his big watch, marking the time.

"Okay," he said, at length. "Let's go. You two birds on the stairs, make sure you don't get above the first floor without covering every inch of ground you pass. We don't want any one to duck out on us. If you hear any commotion, don't come unless I blow my whistle. Watch those stairs!"

He closed the door of the elevator, jabbed the button marked by the figure "1."

The elevator creaked and swayed upward at a snail's pace, came to the first floor, and stopped. Captain Harder propped the door open, emerged into a hallway, found himself facing two doors.

Both were unlocked. He opened first one, and then the other.

There were disclosed two empty lofts, littered with papers and rubbish. They were bare of furniture, untenanted. Even the closet doors were open, and they could see into the interiors of them.

"Nothing doing," said the officer. "Guess it's a false alarm, but we'll go on up."

They returned to the elevator, pressed the next button.

There were three floors, narrow, but deep.

The second floor was like the first as far as the doors were concerned. But as soon as Captain Harder opened the first door, it was at once apparent they were on a warm trail.

The place was fitted up with benches, with a few glass jars, test tubes, some rather complicated apparatus enclosed in a glass case. There were a few jars of chemical, and there were some more trays with food remnants upon them.

"Somebody," said Captain Harder grimly, making sure his service revolver was loose in its holster, "is living here. Wonder what's in that room on the corner. Door looks solid enough."

He pushed his way forward through the litter on the floor, twisted the knob of the door.

"Locked," he said, "and feels solid as stone."

And, at that moment, sounding weak and faint, as though coming from a great distance, came a cry, seeping through the door from the room beyond, giving some inkling of the thickness of the door.

"Help, help, help! This is Paul Dangerfield. Help me! Help me!"

Captain Harder threw his weight against the door. As well have thrown his weight against the solid masonry of a wall.

"Hello," he called. "Are you safe, Dangerfield? This is the police!"

The men could hear the sound of frantic blows on the opposite side of the door.

"Thank God! Quick, get me out of here. Smash in the door. It's a foot thick. Get something to batter it down with!"

The words were faint, muffled. The blows which sounded upon the other side of the door gave evidence of the thickness and strength of the portal.

Captain Harder turned to one of the men.

"How about keys?"

"I've got 'em, Captain, but where do we put 'em?"

The officer stepped back to look at the door.

There was not a sign of a lock or keyhole in it. There was a massive knob, but nothing else to show that the door differed from the side of the wall, save the hairline which marked its borders.

"Smash it in! All together!"

They flung themselves against the door.

Their efforts were utterly unavailing.

"Hurry, hurry!" yelled the voice on the other side of the door. "He's going to . . . No, no! Don't. Oh! Go away! Don't touch that door. Oh . . . Oh . . . Not that!"

The voice rose to a piercing wail of terror, and then was silent. The squad pounded on the door, received no answer.

Captain Harder whirled to examine the loft.

"There's a bar over there. Let's get this door down."

He raised the whistle to his lips, blew a shrill blast. The two men who had been guarding the stairs came up on the run.

"Get this door down!" snapped the police captain. "And let's make it snappy."

They held a block of wood so that it formed a fulcrum for the bar, inserted the curved end, started to pry. The door was as solid as though it had been an integral part of the wall. Slowly, however, the men managed to get the bar inserted to a point where the leverage started to spring the bolts.

Yet it was a matter of minutes, during which time there was no sound whatever from that mysterious inner room.

At length the door swayed, creaked, pried unevenly, sprung

closed as the men shifted their grips on the bar to get a fresh purchase.

"Now, then, boys!" said Captain Harder, perspiration streaming down from his forehead and into his eyes. "Let's go!"

They flung themselves into the work. The door tottered, creaked, slowly pried loose, and then banged open.

The squad stared at a room built without windows. There was ventilation which came through a grating in the roof. This grating was barred with inch-thick iron bars. The air sucked out through one section, came blowing through another. The air seemed fresh enough, yet there was an odor in that room which was a stale stench of death. It was the peculiar, sickeningly sweet odor which hangs about a house which has been touched by death.

There was a table, a reclining chair, a carpet, a tray of food, a bed. The room gave evidence of having been lived in.

But it was vacant, so far as any living thing was concerned.

On the floor, near the door which had been forced, was a pile of clothing. The clothing was sprawled out as though it had covered the form of a man who had toppled backward to the door, stretched his full length upon the floor, and then been withdrawn from his garments.

Captain Harder bent to an examination of the garments. There was a watch in the pocket which had stopped. The stopping of the watch was exactly five minutes before, at about the time the officers had begun pounding at the door.

There was a suit of silk underwear inside of the outer garments. The tie was neatly knotted about the empty collar. The sleeves of the shirt were down inside the sleeves of the coat. There were socks which nested down inside the shoes, as though thrust there by some invisible foot.

There was no word spoken.

Those officers, reporters, detectives, hardened by years of

experience to behold the gruesome, stared speechlessly at that vacant bundle of clothing.

Charles Ealy was the one who broke the silence.

"Good heavens! There's been a man in these clothes and he's been sucked out, like a bit of dirt being sucked up into a vacuum cleaner!"

Captain Harder regained control of himself with an effort. His skin was still damp with perspiration, but that perspiration had cooled until it presented an oily slime which accentuated the glistening pallor of his skin.

"It's a trap, boys. It's a damned clever trap, but it's just a trap. There couldn't have been . . ."

He didn't finish, for Ruby Orman, speaking in a hushed voice, pointed to one of the shoes.

"Try," she said, "just try fitting a sock into the toe of that shoe the way this one is fitted, and try doing it while the shoe's laced, or do it and then lace the shoe afterward, and see where you get."

"Humph," said Ealy, "as far as that's concerned, try getting a necktie around the collar of a shirt and then fitting a coat and vest around the shirt."

Captain Harder cleared his throat and addressed them all.

"Now listen, you guys, you're actin' like a bunch of kids. Even supposing there was some one in this room, where could he have gone? There ain't any opening. He couldn't have slid through those bars in the ventilator."

Some of the detectives nodded sagely, but it remained for Rodney to ask the question which left them baffled.

"How," he asked, "was it possible to get the foot out of that laced shoe?"

Captain Harder turned away.

"Let's not get stampeded," he said.

He started to look around him.

"Cooked food's been brought in here at regular intervals . . . the man that was here was Dangerfield, all right. Those are his clothes. There's the mark of the tailor, and there's his gold-scrolled fountain pen. His watch has his initials on, even his check book is in the pocket.

"I tell you, boys, we're on the right track. This is the place Dangerfield's been kept, and it's that inventor who's at the bottom of the whole thing. We'll go knock his place over, and we'll probably find where Dangerfield is right now. He was spirited away from here, somehow.

"Those clothes were left here for a blind. Don't get stampeded. Here, feel the inside of the cloth. It's plumb cold, awfully cold. If anybody'd been inside those clothes within five minutes, the clothes'd be warm."

One of the officers nodded. His face gave an exhibition of sudden relief which was almost ludicrous. He grinned shamefacedly.

"By George, Captain, that's so! Do you know, for a minute, this thing had me goofy. But you can see how cool the clothes are, and this watch is like a chunk of ice. It'd be warm if anybody had been inside those clothes."

"Who," asked Sid Rodney, "was it that was calling to us through the door?"

Captain Harder stepped to the door, dragged in the bar.

"I don't know. It may have been a trick of ventriloquism, or it may have been a sound that was projected through the ventilating system. But, anyhow, I'm going to find out. If there's a secret entrance to this room, I'm going to find it if I have to rip off every board of the walls one at a time."

He started with the bar, biting it into the tongue and groove which walled the sides of the room. Almost instantly the ripping bar disclosed the unique construction of that room.

It consisted of tongue and groove, back of which was a layer of thick insulation that looked like asbestos. Back of that was a layer of thick steel, and the steel seemed to be backed with concrete, so solid was it.

By examining the outside of the room, they were able to

judge the depth of the walls. They seemed to be at least three feet thick. The room was a veritable sound-proof chamber.

Evidently the door was operated by some electro-magnetic control. There were thick bars which went from the interior of the door down into sockets built in the floor, steel faced, bedded in concrete.

Captain Harder whistled.

"Looks like there was no secret exit there. It must have been some sort of ventriloquism."

Sid Rodney grunted.

"Well, it wasn't ventriloquism that made the jars on that door. It was some one pounding and kicking on the other side. And, if you'll notice the toes of those shoes, you'll see where there are fragments of wood splinters, little flakes of paint, adhering to the soles right where they point out into the uppers.

"Now, then, if you'll take the trouble to look at the door, you'll find little marks in the wood which correspond to the marks on the toes of the shoes. In other words, whether those shoes were occupied or not, they were hammering against that door a few minutes ago."

Captain Harder shook his head impatiently.

"The trouble with all that reasoning is that it leads into impossibilities."

Sid Rodney stooped to the vest pocket, looked once more at the gold embossed fountain pen.

"Has any one tried this to see if it writes?" he asked.

"What difference would that make?" asked the police captain.

"He might have left us a message," said Sid.

He abstracted the pen, removed the cap, tried the end of the pen upon his thumb nail. Then he took a sheet of paper from his notebook, tried the pen again.

Captain Harder grunted.

"Listen, you guys, all this stuff isn't getting us anywhere. The facts are that Dangerfield was here. He ain't here now.

Albert Crome has this place rented. He has a grudge against Dangerfield. It's an odds-on bet that we're going to get the whole fiendish scheme out of him—if we get there soon enough."

There was a mutter of affirmation from the officers, even men who were more accustomed to rely upon direct action and swift accusation than upon the slower method of deduction.

"Wait a minute," said Sid Rodney. His eyes were flaming with the fire of an inner excitement. He unscrewed the portion of the pen which contained the tip, from the barrel, drew out the long rubber tube which held the ink.

Captain Harder regarded him with interest, but with impatience.

"Just like any ordinary self-filling pen the world over," said the police captain.

Sid Rodney made no comment. He took a knife from his pocket, slit open the rubber sac. A few sluggish drops of black liquid trickled slowly down his thumb, then he pulled out a jet-black rod of solid material.

He was breathing rapidly now, and the men, attracted by the fierce earnestness of his manner, crowded about him.

"What is it?" asked one.

Rodney did not answer the question directly. He broke the thing in half, peered at the ends.

These ends glistened like some polished, black jewel which had been broken open. The light reflected from little tiny points, giving an odd appearance of sheen and luster.

Slowly a black stain spread along the palm of the detective's hand.

Sid Rodney set the long rod of black, broken into two pieces, down upon the tray of food.

"Is that ink?" demanded Harder.

"Yes."

"What makes it look so funny?"

"It's frozen."

"Frozen!"

"Yes."

"But how could ink be frozen in a room of this sort? The room isn't cold.

Sid Rodney shrugged his shoulders.

"I'm not advancing any theories—yet. I'm simply remarking that it's frozen ink. You'll notice that the rubber covering and the air which was in the barrel of the pen acted as something of a thermal insulation. Therefore, it was slower to thaw out than some things."

Captain Harder stared at Rodney with a puckered forehead and puzzled eyes.

"What things do you mean?"

"The watch, for instance. You notice that it's started to run again."

"By George, it has!" said Charles Ealy. "It's started ticking right along just as though nothing had happened, but it's about six and a half or seven minutes slow."

Sid nodded silent affirmation.

Captain Harder snorted.

"You birds can run all the clues that you want to. I'm going to get a confession out of the bird that's responsible for this.

"Two of you stay here and see that no one comes in or goes out. Guard this place. Shoot to kill any one who disobeys your orders. This thing is serious, and there's murder at the bottom of it, or I miss my guess."

He whirled and stamped from the room, walking with that aggressive swing of the shoulders, that forward thrust of his sturdy legs which betokened no good for the crack-brained scientist.

CHAPTER 4

A Madman's Laboratory

They hammered on the door.

After a matter of minutes there was an answer, a thin, cracked voice which echoed through the thick partitions of a door which seemed every bit as substantial as the door which Captain Harder had forced in order to enter that curious room where an empty suit of clothes had mocked him.

"Who it is?"

Captain Harder tried a subterfuge.

"Captain Harder, come to see about the purchase of an invention. I'm representing the War Department."

The man on the other side of that door crackled into a cackling chuckle. "It's about time. Let's have a look at you."

Captain Harder nodded to the squad of grim-visaged men who were grouped just back of him.

"All ready, boys," he said.

They lowered their shoulders, ready to rush the door as soon as it should be opened.

But, to their surprise, there was a slight scraping noise, and a man's face peered malevolently at them from a rectangular slit in the door.

Captain Harder jerked back.

The face was only partially visible through the narrow peep-hole. But there was a section of wrinkled forehead, shaggy, unkempt eyebrows, the bridge of a bony nose, and two eyes.

The eyes compelled interest.

They were red rimmed. They seemed to be perpetually irritated, until the irritation had seeped into the brain itself. And they glittered with a feverish light of unwholesome cunning.

"Psh! The police!" said the voice, sounding startlingly clear through the opening of the door.

"Open in the name of the law!" snapped Captain Harder.

"Psh!" said the man again.

There was the faintest flicker of motion from behind the little peephole in the door, and a sudden coughing explosion. A little cloud of white smoke mushroomed slowly out from the corner of the opening.

The panel slid into place with the smooth efficiency of a well oiled piece of machinery.

Captain Harder jerked out his service revolver.

"All together, boys. Take that door down!"

He gathered himself, then coughed, flung up his hand to his eyes.

"Gas!" he yelled. "Look out!"

The warning came too late for most of the squad of officers who were grouped about that door. The tear gas, a new and deadly kind which seemed so volatile as to make it mix instantly with the atmosphere, spread through the corridor. Men were blinded, staggering about, groping their way, crashing into one another.

The panel in the door slid back again. The leering, malevolent features twisted into a hoarse laugh.

Captain Harder flung up his revolver and fired at the sound of that demoniac laughter.

The bullet thudded into the door.

The panel slid shut.

Sid Rodney had flung his arm about the waist of Ruby Orman at the first faint suggestion of mushrooming fumes.

"Back! It may be deadly!"

She fought against him.

"Let me go! I've got to cover this!"

But he swept her from her feet, flung her to his shoulder, sprinted down the hallways of the house. A servant gazed at them from a lower floor, scowling. Men were running, shouting questions at each other, stamping up and down stairs. The entire atmosphere of the house took on a peculiarly acrid odor.

* * *

Sid Rodney got the girl to an upper window on the windward side of the house. Fresh air was blowing in in a cooling stream.

"Did it get your eyes?"

"No. I'm going back."

Sid held her.

"Don't be foolish. There's going to be something doing around here, and you and I have got to have our eyes where they can see something."

She fought against him.

"Oh, I *hate* you! You're so domineering, so cocksure of yourself."

Abruptly, he let her go.

"If you feel that way," he said, "go ahead."

She jerked back and away. She looked at him with eyes that were flaming with emotion. Sid Rodney turned back toward the window. Her eyes softened in expression, but there was a flaming spot in each cheek.

"Why *will* you persist in treating me like a child?"

He made no effort to answer the question.

She turned back toward the end of the hallway, where the scientist had maintained his secret laboratory with the door that held the sliding panel.

Men were struggling blindly about that door. Others were wapping their eyes in wet towels. Here and there a figure groped its way about the corridor, clutching at the sides of the banister at the head of the stairs, feeling the edges of the walls.

Suddenly, the entire vision swam before her eyes, grew blurred. She felt something warm trickling down her cheek. Abruptly her vision left her. Her eyes streamed moisture.

"Sid!" she called. "Oh, Sid!"

He was at her side in an instant. She felt the strong tendons of his arm, the supporting bulk of his shoulder, and then she was swung toward the window where the fresh air streamed into the house.

"I'm sorry," she said. "Now it's got me."

"It probably won't bother you very long. You didn't get much of a dose of it. Hold your eyes open if you can, and face the breeze. They'll have the house cleared of the fumes in a few minutes."

There was the sound of a siren from the outer street, the clang of a gong.

"Firemen to clear the house," said Sid.

They stood there, shoulder to shoulder, cheek to cheek, letting the fresh morning breeze fan their faces. Out in the yard were hurrying shadows. Men came running to stations of vantage, carrying sawed-off shotguns. More cars sirened their way to the curb. Spectators gathered.

Electric fans were used to clear the corridor of the gas. Men were brought up carrying bars and jimmies. They attacked the door. Captain Harder's eyes were still disabled, as were the eyes of the others who had stood before that door.

Sid Rodney touched the girl's shoulder.

"They're getting ready to smash in the door. Can you see now?"

She nodded.

"I think they've got the hallway pretty well cleared of gas. Let's go and see what happens."

She patted his arm.

"Sid, you're just like a big brother—some one to take care of me, some one to scold; but I like you a lot."

"Just as you would a brother?" he asked.

"Just exactly."

"Thanks," he said, and the disappointment of his voice was lost in the sound of splintering wood as the door swung back on its hinges.

They stared into a great laboratory and experimenting room. It was a scene of havoc. Wreckage of bottles, equipment and apparatus was strewn about the room. It looked as though some one had taken an ax and ruthlessly smashed everything.

Here, too, was another room without windows. Such light

as there was in the room was artificial. The ventilation came through grilles which were barred with heavy iron. It was a room upon which it was impossible to spy.

There was no trace of Albert Crome, the man whose malevolent face had been thrust through the aperture in the doorway.

The police crowded into the room.

Bottles of various acids had been smashed, and the pools upon the floor seethed and bubbled, gave forth acrid, throat-stinging fumes. In a cage by the door there were three white rats. These rats were scampering about, shrilling squeaky protests.

There was no other sign of life left in that room, save the hulking shoulders of the policemen who now moved about in a dazed manner.

Captain Harder's voice bellowed instructions. He was blinded, but he was receiving reports from a detective who stood at his side and giving a rapid summary of conditions in the room.

"He's escaped some way. There's a secret passage out of this room. Get the guards about the place to establish a dead-line. Let no man through unless he has a pass signed by me. Those instructions are not to be varied or changed under any circumstances . . ."

A man approached the officer.

"You're wanted on the telephone, Captain. I can plug in an extension here in the laboratory."

A servant, surly-faced, resentful, impassively placed a telephone extension in the hand of Captain Harder, plugged in the wires.

The blinded officer raised the receiver to his ear.

"Yeah," he said.

There came a rasping series of raucous notes, then the shrill cackle of metallic laughter and the click which announced the party at the other end of the line had hung up.

Captain Harder started fiddling with the hook of the receiver in a frantic effort to get central.

"Hello, hello. This is Captain Harder. There was a call just came through to me on this line. Trace it. Try and locate it . . . What's that? No call? He said he was calling from a downtown drug store . . . All right."

The captain hung up the receiver.

"Well, boys, I guess he's given us the slip. That was his voice, all right. He was calling from a downtown drug store, he said. Told me to look in the northeast corner of the room and I'd find a secret passage leading down into his garage. Said he ran right out in his car without any trouble at all. He's laughing at us."

One of the men picked his way through the wreckage of the room to the northeast corner. The others shuffled forward. Broken glass crunched under the soles of their feet as they moved.

CHAPTER 5

A Fantastic Secret

The man who was bending over the wainscoting emitted a triumphant shout.

"Here it is!"

He gave a pull, and a section of the wall slid back, disclosing an oblong opening.

Captain Harder was cursing as a detective led him toward this oblong.

"I'm blinded . . . the outer guard let him slip through! What sort of boobs are we, anyhow? I thought I had this place guarded. Who was watching the outside? Herman, wasn't it? Get me that guy. I've got things to say to him!"

Men went down the steep flight of stairs which led from that secret exit, and came to the garage. Here were several cars, neatly lined up, ready for instant use, also several vacant spaces where additional cars could be kept.

"Big enough!" grunted one of the men.

Sid Rodney had an idea.

"Look here, captain, it took time to smash up that laboratory."

Captain Harder was in no mood for theories.

"Not so much! What if it did?"

"Nothing. Only it took some little time. I don't believe a man could have looked out of the door, recognized the police, turned loose the tear gas, and then smashed up this laboratory and still have time enough to make his escape by automobile from the garage.

"I happened to be looking out of a window after that tear gas was released, and I saw your additional guards start to arrive . . ."

Captain Harder interrupted. He was bellowing like a bull.

"What a bunch of boobs we are!" he yelled at the men who had clustered around him in a circle. "He didn't get away at all. He stayed behind to smash up the laboratory! Then he sneaked out and telephoned me from some place in the house. No wonder central couldn't trace the call.

"Look around, you guys, for another exit from this laboratory. And keep those electric fans going. I don't trust this bird. He's likely to flood a lot of poison gas through that ventilating system of his . . . I'm commencing to get so I can see a little bit. Be all right in a few minutes, I hope."

The men scattered, examining the wainscoting.

"Here we are, captain!" called one of the men. "Take a look at this. Something here, right enough, but I can't just figure how it works . . . Wait a minute. That's it!"

Something clicked as the officer stepped back. A section of the wainscoting swung open, revealing a passage the height of a man crawling on all fours.

"Volunteers," said Captain Harder. "Damn these eyes! I'm going myself."

And he approached the passageway.

There was a stabbing burst of flame, the rattle of a machine gun, and a withering hail of bullets vomited from out of the passageway.

Captain Harder staggered backward, his right arm dangling at his side. The man who had been next to him dropped to the floor, and it needed no second glance to tell that the man was dead, even before he hit the floor.

The walls of the laboratory echoed to the crash of gunfire. Policemen, flinging themselves upon the floor, fired into the yawning darkness of that oblong hole in the wall. Here and there, riot guns belched their buckshot into the passageway.

There was the sound of the mocking laughter, another spurt of machine gun fire, then silence.

Captain Harder had his coat off, was groping with his left hand for the location of the two bullet holes in his right arm and shoulder.

"Reckon I'm going to be an ambulance case, boys. Don't risk anything in there. Try gas."

The captain turned, groped for the door, staggered, fell. Blood spurted from the upper wound, which had evidently severed an artery.

Men grabbed him, carried him to the head of the stairs where ambulance men met them with a stretcher. Officers continued to keep up a fire upon the passageway. A man brought in a basket containing hand grenades and tear gas bombs. The pin was pulled from a tear gas bomb. The hissing of the escaping gas sounded plainly while the men on the floor held their fire.

The man who carried the gas bomb ran along the side of the wainscoting, flung the bomb into the opening. It hit with a thud, rolled over and over.

There was no sound emanating from the passageway, save the faint hiss of the gas.

"Give him a dose of it and see how he likes it," said one of the men.

As though to answer his question, from the very vicinity of

the tear gas bomb, came a glittering succession of ruddy flashes, the rattle of a machine gun.

One of the men who was on the floor gave a convulsive leap, then quivered and was still. A hail of bullets splintered through the glass equipment which had been broken and scattered about. An officer tried to roll out of the way. The stream of bullets overtook him. He jumped, twitched, shivered, and the deadly stream passed on.

Sid Rodney grasped a hand grenade from the basket, pulled the pin, jumped to his feet.

The machine gun whirled in his direction.

"He's got a gas mask!" yelled one of the men who was crouched behind the shelter of an overturned bench.

Sid Rodney threw the grenade with all of the hurtling force of a professional baseball pitcher.

The missile hit squarely in the center of the opening, thudded against something that emitted a yell of pain.

The machine gun became silent, then stuttered into another burst of firing.

A livid sheet of orange flame seared its way out into the room. The whole side of the place seemed to lift, then settle. A deafening report ripped out the glass of windows in one side of the house. Plaster dust sprayed the air.

The oblong hole from which the machine gun had been coughing its message of death vanished into a tumbled mass of wreckage.

Men coughed from the acrid powder fumes, the irritating plaster dust.

"Believe that got him," said one of the men, rolling out from the shelter, holding a riot gun at ready as he rushed toward the tumbled mass of wreckage.

A human foot was protruding from between a couple of splintered two-by-fours. About it eddied wisps of smoke.

The officer was joined by others. Hands pulled the rafters and studs to one side. The body of a mangled man came sliding out.

From the blackness of that hole came the orange flicker of ruddy flame, the first faint cracklings of fire.

The mangled body had on what was left of a gas mask. The torso was torn by the force of the explosion. Parts of a machine gun were buried in the quivering flesh. But the features could be recognized.

Albert Crome, the crackbrained scientist, had gone to his doom.

Men rushed up with fire-fighting apparatus. The flames were swiftly extinguished. The wreckage was cleared away. Men crawled into that little cubicle where the scientist had prepared a place of refuge.

It was a little room, steel-lined, fitted with a desk, a table, and a cot. Also there was a telephone extension in the room, and an electrical transformer, wires from which ran to a box-like affair, from the interior of which came a peculiar humming sound.

"Leave it alone until the bombing squad gets here. They'll know if it's some sort of an infernal machine. In the meantime let's get out of here."

The sergeant who gave the orders started pushing the men back.

Even as he spoke, there was a glow of ruddy red light from the interior of the box-like affair into which the electric wires ran.

"Better disconnect those wires," called one of the men.

The sergeant nodded, stepped forward, located the point of contact, reached to jerk one of the wires loose.

"Look out, don't short circuit 'em!"

Sid Rodney had crawled back out of the passage. The sergeant was tugging at the wires. They came loose, touched. There was a flash from the interior of the box-like machine, a humming, and then a burst of flame that died away and left a dense white smoke trailing out in sizzling clouds.

"You've short circuited the thing. That other wire must

have been a ground and a button . . ."

But Sid Rodney was not listening.

His eyes happened to have been upon the cage of white rats as the voice called its warning. Those rats were scampering about the cage in the hysteria of panic.

Abruptly they ceased all motion, stood for a split fraction of a second as though they had been cast in porcelain. Then they shrank upon themselves.

Sid Rodney screamed a warning.

Men looked at him, followed the direction of his pointing forefingers, and saw an empty cage.

"What is it?" asked a detective.

Sid Rodney's face was white, the eyes bulging.

"The rats!"

"They got away. Somebody turned 'em loose, or the explosion knocked the cage around or blew a door open," said the officer. "Don't worry about them."

"No, no. I saw them melt and disappear. They just dissolved into the atmosphere."

The officer snickered.

"Don't bother yourself about rats," he said. "We've got work to do. Gotta find out what's going on here, and we've gotta locate Dangerfield."

He turned away.

Sid Rodney went over to the cage. He grasped the metal wires. They were so cold to his touch that the slight moisture on the tips of his fingers stuck to them.

He jerked one hand, and a bit of skin from the tips of his fingers pulled away.

He noticed a little pan of water which had been in the cage. It was filmed with ice. He touched the wires of the cage again. They were not so cold this time.

The film of ice was dissolving from the pan of water in the cage.

But there were no more white rats. They had disappeared, gone, utterly vanished.

* * *

Sid Rodney examined the cage. The door was tightly closed, held in place with a catch. There was no possible loophole of escape for those white rats. They had been caged, and the cage held them until, suddenly, they had gone into thin air.

There was a touch on his shoulder.

"What is it, Sid?"

Sid Rodney had to lick his dry lips before he dared to trust his voice.

"Look here, Ruby, did you ever hear of absolute zero?"

She looked at him with a puzzled frown, eyes that were dark with concern.

"Sid, are you sure you're all right?"

"Yes, yes! I'm talking about things scientific. Did you ever hear of absolute zero?"

She nodded.

"Yes, of course. I remember we had it in school. It's the point at which there is absolutely no temperature. Negative two hundred and seventy-three degrees centigrade, isn't it? Seems to me I had to remember a lot of stuff about it at one time. But what has it got to do with what's been going on here?"

"A lot," said Sid Rodney. "Listen to this:

"Dangerfield disappears. He's located in a room. There's no such thing as escape from that room. Yet, before our eyes— or, rather, before our ears—he vanishes. His watch is stopped. The ink in his fountain pen is frozen. His clothes remain behind.

"All right, that's an item for us to remember.

"Then next come these white rats. I'm actually looking at them when they cease to move, dwindle in size and are gone, as though they'd been simply snuffed out of existence.

"Now you can see the ice film still on the water there. You can see what the wires of the cage did to my fingers. Of course, it happened so quickly that these things didn't get so awfully cold . . . but I've an idea we've seen a demonstration of absolute zero. And if we have, thank Heavens, that dastardly criminal is dead!"

The girl looked at him, blinked her eyes, looked away, then back at him.

"Sid," she said, "you're talking nonsense. There's something wrong with you. You're upset."

"Nothing of the sort! Just because it's never been done, you think it can't be done. Suppose, twenty years ago, some one had led you into a room and showed you a modern radio. You'd have sworn it was a fake because the thing was simply impossible. As it was, your mind was prepared for the radio and what it would do. You accepted it gradually, until it became a part of your everyday life.

"Now, look at this thing scientifically.

"We know that heat is merely the result of internal molecular motion. The more heat, the more motion. Therefore, the more heat, the more volume. For instance, a piece of red-hot metal takes up more space than a piece of ice-cold metal. Heat expands. Cold contracts.

"Now, ever since these things began to be known, scientists have tried to determine what is known as *absolute zero*. It's the place at which all molecular motion would cease. Then we begin to wonder what would happen to matter at that temperature.

"It's certain that the molecules themselves are composed of atoms, the atoms of electrons, that the amount of actual solid in any given bit of matter is negligible if we could lump it all together. It's the motion of the atoms, electrons, and molecules that gives what we see as substance.

"Now, we have only to stop that motion and matter would utterly disappear, as we are accustomed to see it."

The girl was interested, but failed to grasp the full import of what Rodney was telling her.

"But when the body started to shrink it would generate a heat of its own," she objected. "Push a gas into a smaller space and it gets hotter than it was. That temperature runs up fast. I remember having a man explain artificial refrigeration. He said . . ."

"Of course," interrupted Sid impatiently. "That's elemental. And no one has ever reached an absolute zero as yet. But suppose one did? And remember this, all living matter is composed of cells.

"Now, this man hasn't made inanimate matter disappear. But he seems to have worked out some method, perhaps by a radio wave or some etheric disturbance, by which certain specially prepared bodies vanish into thin air, leaving behind very low temperatures.

"Probably there is something in the very life force itself which combines with this ray to eliminate life, temperature, substance. Think of what that means!"

She sighed and shook her head.

"I'm sorry, Sid, but I just can't follow you. They'll find Dangerfield somewhere or other. Probably there was some secret passage in that room. The fact that there were two here indicates that there must be others in that room.

"You've been working on this thing until it's got you groggy. Go home and roll in for a few hours' sleep—please."

He grimly shook his head.

"I know I'm working on a live lead."

She moved away from him.

"Be good, Sid. I've got to telephone in a story to the rewrite, and I've got to write some sob-sister articles. They will be putting out extras. I think this is all that's going to develop here."

Sid Rodney watched her move away.

He shrugged his shoulders, turned his attention to the empty cage in which the white rats had been playing about.

His jaw was thrust forward, his lips clamped in a firm, straight line.

CHAPTER 6

Still They Vanish

Captain Harder lay on the hospital bed, his grizzled face drawn and gray. The skin seemed strangely milky and the eyes were tired. But the indomitable spirit of the man kept him driving forward.

Sid Rodney sat on the foot of the bed, smoking a cigarette.

Captain Harder had a telephone receiver strapped to his left ear. The line was connected directly with headquarters. Over it, he detailed such orders as he had to his men.

Betweentimes he talked with the detective.

The receiver rattled with metallic noises. Captain Harder ceased talking to listen to the message, grunted.

He turned to Sid Rodney.

"They've literally torn the interior out of that room where we found the empty clothes," he said. "There isn't the faintest sign of a passageway. There isn't any exit, not a one. It's solid steel, lined with asbestos, backed with concrete. Evidently a room for experiments . . . Oh, Lord, that shoulder feels cold!

"Hello, here's something else."

The telephone receiver again rattled forth a message.

Captain Harder's eyes seemed to bulge from their sockets.

"What?" he yelled.

The receiver continued to rattle forth words.

"Well, don't touch a thing. Take photographs. Get the fingerprint men to work on the case. Look at the watch and see if it stopped, and, if it did, find out what time it stopped."

He sighed, turned from the mouthpiece of the telephone to stare at Sid Rodney with eyes that held something akin to panic in them.

"They've found the clothes of Arthur Soloman, the banker!"

Sid Rodney frowned.

"The clothes?"

The officer sighed, nodded, weakly.

"Yes, the clothes."

"Where?"

"They were sitting at the steering wheel of Soloman's road-ster. The car had skidded into the curb. The clothes are all filled out just as though there'd been a human occupant that had slipped out of them by melting into the thin air. The shoes are laced. One of the feet, or, rather, one of the empty shoes is on the brake pedal of the machine. The sleeves of the coat are hung over the wooden rim of the steering wheel. The collar's got a tie in it . . . . Just the same as the way we found Dangerfield's clothes.

"One of the men found the roadster and reported. The squad that handled the Dangerfield case went out there on the jump . . ."

He broke off as the receiver started to rattle again.

He listened, frowned, grunted.

"Okay, go over everything with a fine-toothed comb," he said, and turned once more to Sid Rodney.

"The watch," he said, "had stopped, and didn't start running again until the officer took it out of the pocket and gave it just a little jar in so doing. The hands pointed to exactly thirteen minutes past ten o'clock."

"That," observed Rodney, "was more than two hours after Albert Crome had died, more than two hours after the disappearance of the white rats."

Captain Harder rolled his head from side to side on the propped-up pile of pillows.

"Forget those white rats, Rodney. You're just making a spectacular something that will frighten the public to death. God knows they're going to be panicky enough as it is. I'd feel different about the thing if I thought there was anything to it."

Rodney nodded, got up from the bed.

"Well, captain, when they told me you were keeping your finger on the job, I decided to run in and tell you, so you'd know as much about it as I do. But I tell you I *saw* those white rats vanish."

The captain grinned.

"Seen 'em myself, Rodney, in a magician's show. I've seen a woman vanish, seen another one sawed in two. I've even seen pink elephants walking along the foot of the bed—but that was in the old days."

Sid Rodney matched his grin, patted the captain's foot beneath the spotless white of the hospital bedspread.

"Take care of yourself, old-timer, and don't let this thing keep you from getting some sleep. You've lost some blood and you'll need it. Where were the banker's clothes found?"

"Out on Seventy-first and Boyle Streets."

"They leaving them there?"

"For the time being. I'm going to have the car finger-printed from hood to gas tank. And I'm having the boys form a line and close off the street. We're going to go all over the things with a fine-toothed comb, looking for clues.

"If you want to run out there you'll find Selby in charge. Tell him I said you were to have any of the news, and if you find out anything more, you'll tell me, won't you?"

"Sure, cap. Sure!"

"Okay. So long."

And Captain Harder heaved a tremulous sigh.

Sid Rodney walked rapidly down the corridor of the hospital, entered his car, drove at once to Seventy-first near where it intersected Boyle.

There was a curious crowd, being kept back by uniformed officers.

Sid showed his credentials, went through the lines, found Detective Sergeant Selby, and received all of the latest news.

"We kept trying to locate Soloman at his home. He came in, all right, and his wife told him we were trying to get him. He went to the telephone, presumably to call police headquarters, and the telephone rang just as he was reaching for the receiver.

"He said 'hello,' and then said a doubtful 'yes.' His wife heard that much of the conversation. Then she went into another room. After that she heard Soloman hang up the receiver, and walk into the hall where he reached for his hat and coat.

"He didn't tell her a word about where he was going. Just walked out, got in his car, and drove away. She supposed he was coming to police headquarters."

Sid lit a cigarette.

"Find out who he called?"

"Can't seem to get a lead on it."

"Was he excited?"

"His wife thought he was mad at something. He slammed the door as he went out."

"These the clothes he was wearing?"

"Yes."

Sid Rodney nodded.

"Looks just like another of those things. Thanks, Selby. I'll be seeing you."

"Keep sober," said the police detective.

Sid Rodney drove to Arthur Soloman's residence.

Newspaper reporters, photographers, and detectives were there before him. Mrs. Soloman was staring in dazed confusion, answering questions mechanically, posing for photographers.

She was a dried-out wisp of a woman, tired-eyed, docile with that docility which comes to one whose spirit has been completely crushed by the constant inhibitions imposed by a domineering mate.

Sid Rodney asked routine questions and received routine answers. He went through the formula of investigation, but there was a gnawing uneasiness in his mind. Some message seemed to be hammering at the borderline of his consciousness, as elusive as a dream, as important as a forgotten appointment.

Sid Rodney walked slightly to one side, tried to get away from the rattle of voices, the sputter of flash lights as various photographs were made.

So far there were only a few who appreciated the full significance of those vacant clothes, propped up behind the steering wheel of the empty automobile.

The telephone rang, rang with the insistent repetition of mechanical disinterest. Some one finally answered. There was a swirl of motion, a beckoning finger.

"Rodney, it's for you."

Vaguely wondering, Rodney placed the receiver to his ear. There was something he wanted to think about, something he wanted to do, and do at once. Yet it was evading his mind. The telephone call was just another interruption which would prevent sufficient concentration to get the answer he sought.

"Hello!" he rasped, and his voice did not conceal his irritation.

It was Ruby Orman on the line, and at the first sound of her voice Sid snapped to attention.

He knew, suddenly, what was bothering him.

Ruby should have been present at the Soloman house, getting sob-sister stuff on the fatherless children, the dazed widow who was trying to carry on, hoping against hope.

"What is it, Ruby?"

Her words rattled swiftly over the wire, sounded as a barrage of machine gun fire.

"Listen, Sid; get this straight, because I think it's important. I'm not over there at Soloman's because I'm running down something that I think is a hot lead. I want you to tell me something, and it may be frightfully important. What would a powder, rubbed in the hair, have to do with the disappearance, if it was the sort of disappearance you meant?"

Sid Rodney grunted and registered irritation.

"What are you doing, Ruby—kidding me?"

"No, no. Tell me. It's a matter of life and death."

"I don't know, Ruby. Why?"

"Because I happen to know that Soloman had a little pow-der dusted on his hair. It was just a flick of the wrist that put it there. I didn't think much of it at the time. It looked like a cigarette ash, but I noticed that it seemed to irritate him, and he kept scratching at his head. Did you notice?"

"No," snapped Sid, interested. "What makes you think it had anything to do with what happened afterward?"

"Because I got to investigating about that powder, and wondering, and I casually mentioned the theory you had, and I felt a prickling in my scalp, and then I knew that some of that same powder had been put in my hair. I wonder if . . ."

Sid Rodney was at instant attention.

"Where are you now?"

"Over in my apartment. I've got an appointment. It's im-portant. You can't come over. If it's what I think it is, the mystery is going to be solved. You're right. It's absolute zero, and— My God, Sid, it's getting cold . . ."

And there was nothing further, nothing save the faint sounds of something thump-thump-thumping—the receiver, dangling from the cord, thumping against the wall.

Rodney didn't stop for his hat. He left the room on the run. A newspaper reporter saw him, called to him, ran to follow. Sid didn't stop. He vaulted into his car, and his foot was pressing the starter before he had grabbed the wheel.

He floor-boarded the throttle, and skidded at the corner with the car lurching far over against the springs, the tires shrieking a protest.

He drove like a crazy man, getting to the apartment where Ruby Orman spent the time when she was not sob-sistering for her newspaper. He knew he could beat the elevator up the three flights of stairs, and took them two at a time.

The door of the apartment was closed. Sid banged his fist upon it in a peremptory knock and then rattled the knob.

"Oh, Ruby!" he called softly.

A canary was singing in the apartment. Aside from that, there was no faintest suggestion of sound.

Sid turned the knob, pushed his shoulder against the door. It was unlocked. He walked into the apartment. The canary perked its head upon one side, chirped a welcome, then fluttered nervously to the other side of the cage.

Sid strode through the little sitting room to the dining room and kitchenette. The telephone was fastened to the wall here.

But the receiver was not dangling. It had been neatly replaced on its hook. But there was a pile of garments just below the telephone which made Sid stagger against the wall for a brief second before he dared to examine them.

He knew that skirt, that businesslike jacket, knew the sash, the shoes . . . He stepped forward.

They were Ruby's clothes, all right, lying there in a crumpled heap on the floor.

And at the sight Sid Rodney went berserk.

He flung himself from room to room, ripping open closet doors. For a wild moment he fought back his desire to smash things, tear clothes, rip doors from hinges.

Then he got a grip on himself, sank into a chair at the table, lit a cigarette with trembling hand. He must think.

Soloman had had something put in his hair, a powder which irritated . . . Ruby had seen that powder, flicked there—a casual gesture, probably, like a cigarette ash. The powder had irritated . . . Ruby had told some one person something of Rodney's theory. Powder had been applied to her hair . . . She had known of it . . . She had telephoned . . . She had an appointment . . . And it had become cold . . . Then the clothes at the foot of the telephone . . .

And the chair in which Sid Rodney had been sitting was flung back upon its shivering legs as he leaped from the table —flung back by the violence of the motion with which he had gone into action.

He gained the door in three strides, took the stairs on the run, climbed into his automobile, and drove like some mythical dust jinni scurrying forward on the crest of a March wind. He whizzed through street intersections, disregarded alike traffic laws and arterial stops, swung down a wide street given over to exclusive residences, and came to a stop before a large house constructed along the conventional lines of English architecture.

He jumped from the machine, ran rapidly up the steps, held his finger against the doorbell.

A man in livery came to the door, regarded him with grave yet passive disapproval.

"This is the residence of P. H. Dangerfield?"

"Yes."

"His secretary, Mr. Sands, is here?"

"Yes."

"I want to see him," said Sid, and started to walk into the door.

The servant's impassive face changed expression by not so much as a flicker, but he moved his broad bulk in such a manner as to stand between the detective and the stairs.

"If you'll pardon me, sir, the library to the left is the reception room. If you will give me your name and wait there I'll tell Mr. Sands that you are here. Then, if he wishes to see you, you will be notified."

There was a very perceptible emphasis upon the word "if."

Sid Rodney glanced over the man's shoulder at the stairs.

"He's upstairs, I take it?"

"Yes, sir, in the office, sir."

Sid Rodney started up.

The servant moved with swiftness, once more blocking the way.

"I beg your pardon, sir!"

His eyes were hard, his voice firm.

Sid Rodney shook his head impatiently, as a fighter shakes the perspiration out of his eyes, as a charging bull shakes aside some minor obstruction.

"To hell with that stuff! I haven't got time!"

And Sid Rodney pushed the servant to one side.

The man made a futile grab at Sid's coat.

"Not so fast . . ."

Sid didn't even look back. "Faster, then!" he said, with a cold grin.

The arm flashed around and down. The liveried servant spun, clutched at the cloth, missed, and went backward down the few steps to the landing.

Rodney was halfway up the stairs by the time the servant had scrambled over to hands and knees.

"Oh, Sands!" called Rodney.

There was no answer.

Rodney grunted, tried a door—a bedroom; another door—a bath; another door—the office.

It seemed vacant. A desk, a swivel chair, a leather-covered couch, several sectional bookcases, some luxuriously comfortable chairs, a filing case or two . . . and Sid Rodney jumped back with a startled exclamation.

A suit of clothes was spread out on the couch.

He ran toward it.

It was the checkered suit Sands had been wearing at the time of the interview at police headquarters. It was quite empty, was arranged after the manner of a suit spread out upon the couch in the same position a man would have assumed had he been resting.

Rodney bent over it.

There was no necktie around the collar of the shirt. The sleeves of the shirt were in the coat. The vest was buttoned over the shirt. The shoes were on the floor by the side of the couch, arranged as though they had been taken off by some man about to lie down.

CHAPTER 7

A Fiend Is Unmasked

Sid Rodney went through the pockets with swift fingers. He found a typewritten note upon a bit of folded paper. It bore his name and he opened and read it with staring eyes.

> Sid Rodney, Ruby Orman, and Bob Sands, each one to be visited by the mysterious agency which has removed the others. This is no demand for money. This is a sentence of death.

Sid Rodney put the paper in his own pocket, took the watch from the suit, checked the time with the time of his own watch. They were identical as far as the position of the hands was concerned.

Sid Rodney replaced the watch, started through the rest of the pockets, found a cigarette case, an automatic lighter, a knife, fountain pen and pencil, a ring of keys, a wallet.

He opened the wallet.

It was crammed with bills, bills of large denomination. There were some papers as well, a letter in feminine handwriting, evidently written by an old friend, a railroad folder, a prospectus of an Oriental tour.

There was another object, an oblong of yellow paper, printed upon, with blanks left for data and signature. It was backed with carbon compound so as to enable a duplicate impression to be made, and written upon with pencil.

Sid studied it.

It was an express receipt for the shipment of a crate of machinery from George Huntley to Samuel Grove at 6372 Milpas Street. The address of the sender was given as 753 Washington Boulevard.

Sid puckered his forehead.

No. 753 Washington Boulevard was the address of Albert Crome.

Sid opened the cigarette case. Rather a peculiar odor struck his nostrils. There was a tobacco odor, also another odor, a peculiar, nostril-puckering odor.

He broke open one of the cigarettes.

So far as he could determine, the tobacco was of the ordinary variety, although there was a peculiar smell to it.

The lighter functioned perfectly. The fountain pen gave no hint of having been out of condition. Yet the clothes were as empty as an empty meal sack.

Sid Rodney walked to the door.

He found himself staring into the black muzzle of a huge revolver.

"Stand back, sir. I'm sorry, sir, but there have been strange goings on here, sir, and you'll get your hands up, or, by the Lord, sir, I shall let you have it, right where you're thickest, sir."

It was the grim-faced servant, his eyes like steel, his mouth stretched across his face in a taut line of razor-thin determination.

Sid laughed.

"Forget it. I'm in a hurry, and . . ."

"When I count three, sir, I shall shoot . . ."

There was a leather cushion upon one of the chairs. Sid sat down upon that leather cushion, abruptly.

"Oh, come, let's be reasonable."

"Get your hands up."

"Shucks, what harm can I do. I haven't got a gun, and I only came here to see if I couldn't . . ."

"One . . . two . . ."

Rodney raised his weight, flung himself to one side, reached around, grasped the leather cushion, and flung it. He did it all in one sweeping, scrambling motion.

The gun roared for the first time as he flung himself to one side. It roared the second time as the spinning cushion hurtled through the air.

Sid was conscious of the mushrooming of the cushion, the scattering of hair, the blowing of bits of leather. The cushion smacked squarely upon the end of the gun, blocking the third shot. Before there could have been a fourth, Sid had gone forward, tackling low. The servant crashed to the floor.

It was no time for etiquette, the hunting of neutral corners, or any niceties of sportsmanship. The stomach of the servant showed for a moment, below the rim of the leather cushion, and Sid's fist was planted with nice precision and a degree of force which was sufficiently adequate, right in the middle of that stomach.

The man doubled, gasped, struggled for air.

Sid Rodney took the gun from the nerveless fingers, scaled it down the hall where it could do no harm, and made for the front door. He went out on the run.

Once in his car, he started for the address which had been given on the receipt of the express company as the destination of the parcel of machinery, Samuel Grove at 6372 Milpas Street. It was a slender clue, yet it was the only one that Sid possessed.

He made the journey at the same breakneck speed that had characterized his other trips. The car skidded to the curb in front of a rather sedate-looking house which was in a section of the city where exclusive residences had slowly given way to cleaning establishments, tailor shops, small industries, cheap boarding houses.

Sid ran up the steps, tried the bell.

There was no response. He turned the knob of the door. It was locked. He started to turn away when his ears caught the light flutter of running steps upon an upper floor.

The steps were as swiftly agile as those of a fleeing rabbit. There followed, after a brief interval, the sound of pounding feet, a smothered scream, then silence.

Sid rang the bell again.

Again there was no answer.

There was a window to one side of the door. Sid tried to raise it, and found that it was unlocked. The sash slid up, and Sid clambered over the sill, dropped to the floor of a cheaply furnished living room.

He could hear the drone of voices from the upper floor, and he walked to the door, jerked it open, started up the stairs. Some instinct made him proceed cautiously, yet the stairs creaked under the weight of his feet.

He was halfway up the stairs when the talking ceased.

Once more he heard the sounds of a brief struggle, a struggle that was terminated almost as soon as it had begun. Such a struggle might come from a cat that has caught a mouse, lets it almost get away, then swoops down upon it with arched back and needle-pointed claws.

Then there was a man's voice, and he could hear the words:

"Just a little of the powder on your hair, my sweet, and it will be almost painless . . . You know too much, you and your friend. But it'll all be over now. I knew he would be suspecting me, so I left my clothes where they'd fool him. And I came and got you.

"You washed that first powder out of your hair, didn't you, sweet? But this time you won't do it. Yes, my sweet, I knew Crome was mad. But I played on his madness to make him do the things I wanted done. And then, when he had become quite mad, I stole one of his machines.

"He killed Dangerfield for me, and that death covered up my own short accounts. I killed the banker because he was such a cold-blooded fish . . . Cold-blooded, that's good."

There was a chuckle, rasping, mirthless, the sound of scraping objects upon the floor, as though someone tried to struggle ineffectively. Then the voice again.

"I left a note in my clothes, warning of the deaths of you, of myself, and of that paragon of virtue, Sid Rodney, who gave you the idea in the first place. Later on, I'll start shaking down millionaires, but no one will suspect me. They'll think I'm dead.

"It's painless. Just the first chill, then death. Then the cells dissolve, shrink into a smaller and smaller space, and then disappear. I didn't get too much of it from Crome, just enough to know generally how it works, like radio and X-ray, and the living cells are the only ones that respond so far. When you've rubbed this powder into the hair . . ."

Sid Rodney had been slowly advancing. A slight shadow of his progress moved along the baseboard of the hall.

"What's that?" snapped the voice, losing its gloating monotone, crisply aggressive.

Sid Rodney stepped boldly up the last of the stairs, into the upper corridor.

A man was coming toward him. It was Sands.

"Hello, Sands," he said. "What's the trouble here?"

Sands was quick to take advantage of the lead offered. His right hand dropped to the concealment of his hip, but he smiled affably.

"Well, well, if it isn't my friend Sid Rodney, the detective! Tell me, Rodney, have you got anything new? If you haven't, I have. Look here. I want you to see something . . ."

And he jumped forward.

But Rodney was prepared. In place of being caught off guard and balance, he pivoted on the balls of his feet and snapped home a swift right.

The blow jarred Sands back. The revolver which he had been whipping from his pocket shot from his hand in a glittering arc and whirled to the floor.

Rodney sprang forward.

The staggering man flung up his hands, lashed out a vicious kick. Then, as he got his senses cleared from the effects of the blow, he whirled and ran down the hall, dashed into a room and closed the door.

Rodney heard the click of the bolt as the lock was turned.

"Ruby!" he called. "Ruby!"

She ran toward him, attired in flowing garments of colored silk, her hair streaming, eyes glistening.

"Quick!" she shouted. "Is there any of that powder in your hair? Do you feel an itching of the scalp?"

He shook his head.

"Tell me what's happened."

"Get him first," she said.

Sid Rodney picked up the revolver which he had knocked from the hand of the man he hunted, advanced toward the door.

"Keep clear!" yelled Sands from behind that door.

Rodney stepped forward.

"Surrender, or I'll start shooting through the door!" he threatened.

There was a mocking laugh, and something in that laugh warned Rodney; for he leaped back, just as the panels of the door splintered under a hail of lead which came crashing from the muzzle of a sawed-off shotgun.

"I'm calling the police!" shouted Ruby Orman.

Sid saw that she was at a telephone, placing a call.

Then he heard a humming noise from behind the door where Sands had barricaded himself. It was a high, buzzing note, such as is made by a high-frequency current meeting with resistance.

"Quick, Ruby! Are you all right?"

"Yes," she said, and came to him. "I've called the police."

"What is it?" he asked.

"Just what you thought—absolute zero. Crome perfected the process by which any form of cell life could be made receptive to a certain peculiar etheric current. But there had to be a certain chemical affinity first.

"He achieved this by putting a powder in the hair of his victims. The powder irritated the scalp, but it did something to the nerve ends which made them receptive to the current.

"I mentioned your theory to Sands. At the time I didn't know about the powder. But I had noticed that when the banker was talking with Captain Harder, Sands had flipped some ashes from the end of his cigarette so that they had lit on the hair on the back of Soloman's head, and that Soloman had started to rub at his head shortly afterward as though he had been irritated by an itching of the scalp.

"Then Sands made the same gesture while he was talking with me. He left. I felt an itching, and wondered. So I washed my head thoroughly. Then I thought I would leave my clothes where Sands could find them, make him think he'd eliminated me. I was not certain my suspicions were correct, but I was willing to take a chance. I called you to tell you, and then I felt a most awful chill. It started at the roots of my hair and seemed to drain the very warmth right out of my nerves.

"I guess the washing hadn't removed all of that powder, just enough to keep me from being killed. I became unconscious. When I came to, I was in Sands's car. I supposed he had dropped in to make certain his machine had done the work.

"You know the rest . . . But how did you know where to look for me?"

Rodney shook his head dubiously.

"I guess my brains must have been dead, or I'd have known long before. You see, the man who wrote the letters seemed to know everything that had taken place in Captain Harder's office when we were called in to identify that last letter from Dangerfield.

"Yet there was no dictograph found there. It might have been something connected with television, or, more likely, it might have been because some one who was there was the one who was writing those letters.

"If the story Sands had told had been true, the man who was writing the letters had listened in on what was going on in the captain's office, had written the warning note, had known just where Sands was going to be in his automobile, and had tossed it in.

"That was pretty improbable. It was much more likely that Sands had slipped out long enough to have written the letter and then brought it in with that wild story about men crowding him to the curb.

"Then, again, Sands carefully managed to sneak away when Harder raided that loft building. He really did it to notify the crazy scientist that the hiding place had been discovered.

"Even before you telephoned, I should have known Sands was in with the scientist. Afterward, it was, of course, apparent. You had seen some powder placed in Soloman's hair. That meant it must have been done when you were present. That narrowed the list of suspects to those who were also present.

"There were literally dozens of clues pointing to Sands. He was naturally sore at the banker for not coming through with the money. If they'd received it, they'd have killed Dangerfield anyhow. And Sands was to deliver that money. Simple enough for him to have pretended to drop the package into the receptacle, and simply gone on . . ."

A siren wailed.

There was a pound of surging feet on the stairs, blue-coated figures swarming over the place.

"He's behind that door, boys," Rodney said, "and he's armed."

"No use getting killed, men," said the officer in charge. "Shoot the door down."

Guns boomed into action. The lock twisted. The wood splintered and shattered. The door quivered, then slowly swung open as the wood was literally torn away from the lock.

Guns at ready, the men moved into the room.

They found a machine, very similar to the machine which

had been found in the laboratory of the scientist. It had been riddled with gunfire.

They found an empty suit of clothes.

Rodney identified them as being the clothes Sands had worn when he last saw the man. The clothes were empty, and were cold to the touch. Around the collar, where there had been a little moisture, there was a rim of frost.

There was no outlet from the room, no chance for escape.

Ruby looked at Sid Rodney, nodded.

"He's gone," she said.

Rodney took her hand.

"Anyhow, sister, I got here in time."

"Gee, Sid, let's tie a can to that brother-and-sister stuff. I thought I had to fight love to make a career, but when I heard your steps on the stairs, just when I'd given up hope . . ."

"Can you make a report on what happened?" asked the sergeant, still looking at the cold clothes on the floor.

Sid Rodney answered in muffled tones.

"Not right now," he said. "I'm busy."

MONKEY EYES

AUTHOR'S NOTE

I guess all of us writers dabble in the occult more or less. I was fooling around with it twelve or fifteen years ago, and I had a funny experience with a man who claimed to be a priest of Hanuman.

When you come right down to it what is a monkey?

The priests of Hanuman claim he's a man that got started downward in the chain of reincarnation. He was a man. Now he's something less than a man, and we call him a monkey.

Science tells us he's a creature that hasn't evolved to the same extent as a man. Or rather that man has evolved from a "missing link" up from the monkey family.

Rob them of their differentiations in terminology and there's not such a great deal of difference between the two schools of thought. It would be interesting to turn the clock back a few million years and see what the answer really is, or was.

This chap that I knew wouldn't ever admit he worshiped monkeys. Rather he felt he had devoted his life to hastening the monkey karma which would bring them back to the estate of man.

I remembered his theories, and one time when I was watching a serious-faced monkey with moist, sad eyes do clowning at the bidding of the dirty organ grinder who "owned" him I tried to put some of his theories in practice. I don't know ex-

actly what happened. Call it hypnotism or animal magnetism or anything you want, but the monkey came to me and clung to me, begged me for something. It broke up the show. I felt conspicuous and embarrassed, and got away. Thereby I probably turned away from what might have developed into something a little more significant than an adventure.

But some day when you get the eyes of a monkey, remember something of the theory of the priests of Hanuman. Will with all your deepest sympathy to help speed that monkey along the path of evolution, or of reincarnation.

And if you're really thinking of what you're trying to think about, instead of being conscious of the ego that's thinking the thoughts—well, something may happen. It's worth trying.

And I've heard stories of what goes on in the jungle—little still whispers, they are. They can't be authenticated, and they can't be repeated; but they're persistent whispers. Fictionized they make good stories. Perhaps some reader can tell us something about those whispers. Perhaps "Monkey Eyes" isn't quite as much fiction as it might appear. All I can say is it's founded, not on fact, but on whispers.

And that brings us back to where we started. What is a monkey?

—ERLE STANLEY GARDNER

CHAPTER 1

Suspicion

There were four men at the table: Arthur Forbes, who talked too much; Colonel Crayson, whose glazed eyes wandered aimlessly from face to face; Murasingh, who held his countenance studiously impassive; and Phil Nickers, who tried to draw out the others.

The other diner was a woman, Colonel Crayson's niece, Jean. She, too, was a fresh arrival. Nickers recognized her as a fellow passenger on the India-bound boat. Yet he had not known she was coming to Assam until the day before docking. And not until he met her at dinner did he know they were to be sheltered, at least temporarily, under the same roof.

Colonel Crayson made an excellent, if somewhat mechanical, host. Black servants flitted about. The food was good, the wine excellent. The dinner should have been a huge success.

But, very apparently, it was not. An atmosphere of distrust settled upon the board as a pall. In one way or another it affected all the diners, brought out different phases of their characters.

Phil Nickers wondered if some rumor of his errand had, in some manner, preceded him. The thought was absurd. He had embarked secretly, with no credentials other than a single letter of introduction to Colonel Crayson. Since his embarkation he had written no letters, and received none.

And yet the calm air of the warm, Indian night reeked with suspicion.

That was why Forbes talked too much, why Colonel Crayson let his glassy eyes wander from face to face, puzzled in his heavy, pop-eyed manner. Was it why Murasingh kept his face as woodenly impassive as a poker player? Nickers would have given much to know the answer to that question.

And Forbes rattled on in perpetual conversation. He touched on thousands of subjects, exhausted them in a brief rapid monologue, and pattered on to other subjects. With the cordials he branched into war-time aviation.

"Cleverest stunt of 'em all was the Yankee chap that piloted the 'captured' plane back over the German lines and got commissioned to fly back as a spy. What *was* that fellow's name? Always made up my mind I'd keep track of him, see what he did afterward. Nickley, Naker, no, by gad, it was Nickers! Wasn't any relation of yours, was he, Nickers? You're from the States."

Phil Nickers blew a casual smoke ring.

"The city directories in the States are full of persons named Nickers," he said.

Through the drifting smoke he saw Murasingh's face. The muscles themselves remained impassive, but the dark eyes glittered with red hatred. And Forbes was grinning, the frankly impertinent grin of one who has let a cat out of the conversational bag.

"Have some more Benedictine," proffered the colonel, heartily.

Nickers shook his head. He would have given much to throttle Forbes.

The dining room was up on a glassed-in porch. The huge windows slid back. Screens kept out insects, but let in soft, spice-scented breezes. Below the terraced lawn glowed mysterious lights. Night sounds, softened by the warm air, penetrated the room, mingled with the clink of glass and silver as well-trained servants bustled about their tasks.

And Arthur Forbes became suddenly silent.

Nickers was relieved when the girl flashed a signal to her uncle. The chairs scraped back. The torture of that first dinner was over.

Nickers sought his room, pleading fatigue from travel. Billiards did not appeal to him. The thought of cards bored him. And a sudden suspicion made him want to inspect his baggage. An Indian servant had unpacked his bags before dinner. But his brief case was locked, and he had dropped it into his heavy kit bag, and locked the bag.

Some flash of deep suspicion caused him to unlock bag and brief case. The papers had been replaced with an eye to order, but a misplaced letter told the story. The brief case had been systematically searched, the locks picked in a thoroughly workmanlike manner.

The papers had, of course, been carefully prepared. They were the papers that a Mr. Philip Nickers, of Seattle, Washington, U.S.A., touring to collect material for a book, would be likely to carry. The secret notebook contained data and instructions, carefully concealed among a lot of meaningless notes.

Phil Nickers looked up as a step sounded without. A gentle tap on the door announced a visitor.

Arthur Forbes grinned at him from the threshold. Moving with the silence of a shadow, he availed himself of an invitation which had not been given, and slipped into the room.

"Thought I talked too much at dinner, eh?"

Nickers made no comment.

"Had to be sure of my ground before I made the break," went on Forbes. "You'll be Phil Nickers, former army aviator, at present a detective, sent here to investigate the deaths of Harley Kent and his daughter, Audrey. I think Murasingh suspects it. You may have noticed his eyes contained rather a glitter once or twice. And we don't have many chaps from the States dropping in on us in such an elaborately casual manner. They're bound to attract attention and interest."

Phil Nickers measured his visitor with uncordial eyes.

"Some one's been interested enough to pick the locks on my baggage and make a search of my private papers."

If Forbes noticed the glare of hostile accusation which accompanied the words, he gave no sign.

"They would," he said with a chuckle. "That's Murasingh for you, efficient, prudent. You can't tell just how many of the servants he controls; but it's plenty."

Nickers remained uncordial.

"Just what was it caused you to associate my name with that of the aviator?"

"Bless you, dear chap, you're as obvious as a school boy— no, no! Don't take offense, Nickers. But down here we get a schooling in native indirectness. As far as I'm concerned, I remembered your pictures. A man who wishes to become a detective should never become nationally known and pose for motion picture newsreels. But I'd rather kept track of you anyway. You see, aviation's my hobby. I've never amounted to much as a pilot. Bad heart keeps me out of the game for one thing. But I keep track of the best of them. I heard you'd gone into business.

"Look here, old chap, don't get me wrong. I suspected your identity and your mission. I think Murasingh knows. This is a funny corner of the world, not at all like the States. And Harley Kent was a friend of mine. I'd have started an investigation myself if I'd had anything to go on, or been in any position to do it. Mind you, it may be all right. Kent was murdered, truly enough. How or by whom, are questions. But the girl, Audrey: well, until they find her body, I won't be at all certain. The charred corpse that was found in the ruins of the house wasn't Audrey. It was one of the native women. I'm virtually certain of that, despite the identification from rings and teeth. And there was a mysterious airplane heard that night. But, of course, your folks know all about that or they wouldn't have sent an aviator out on the case."

Phil Nickers balanced a pencil upon the table. In the silence which followed, his eyes remained riveted upon the slim, wooden cylinder.

"You're doing the talking," he said, at length. "I'm listening. You have a theory?"

Arthur Forbes jerked a bony thumb over his shoulder.

"To the north of here is forbidden territory," he said.

If Nickers knew what was meant he did not betray it. "Yes?" he asked.

"Quite so. All along here. The inner line beyond which whites can't go. It's recognized by treaty. In Darrang, toward the Bhutias, Akas and Daphlas. In Lakhimper, toward the Daphlas, Mirio, Abors, Mishmis, Khamtis, Singphos and Nagas; and in Sibsager, toward the Nagas."

Nickers had managed to get the pencil balanced.

"Just who is Murasingh?" he asked, shooting the question with explosive abruptness.

Forbes lowered his voice.

"String of native titles that'd take five minutes to tell. Aside from that, he's a sportsman and adventurer. Educated in England. That part of the education that has to do with reading and writing stuck. As for the rest it's a question—just as it is with any educated native. He plays polo, pilots a plane, does quite a bit of hunting, not much drinking, keeps fit, and is reputed, strictly *sub rosa*, to be fomenting trouble."

The pencil, moved by some faint puff of languid air, dropped to the table. Nickers gave his attention to rebalancing it.

"And, while you may not have noticed it," muttered Forbes, speaking now in a tone so low that the words could hardly be distinguished, "Jean Crayson and Audrey Kent were very much of a type. Both of them have blond hair, blue eyes, a milky skin, red lips, a full face, rounded figure."

Nickers let the pencil roll to the floor.

"Yes?" he asked, looking full at Forbes.

"Yes," said Forbes, arising after the manner of one whose work has been done. And, without so much as a word of good night, walked abruptly from the room.

CHAPTER 2

A Night Flight

The American extinguished the light, moved his chair to the window. There was much food for thought in what he had heard. In the main, it merely corroborated what he had heard before, what had previously been communicated to him as a basis upon which to work. But the similarity in the appearances of the two girls was something new to him. The thought flitted in and out of his mind, and bothered him. What had Forbes meant? What had he been trying to intimate?

And it bothered Nickers that the elaborate precautions he had taken to conceal the real object of his visit should so easily have been ripped aside.

He read for two hours, disrobed, and dropped into fitful slumber. The air was heavy, warm, oppressive. Nickers's body was bathed in a slime of perspiration. Straggling thoughts lodged in his mind long enough to breed nightmares.

The drone of an airplane became the buzzing of a giant bee, settling, about to attack. Nickers gave an exclamation, made a great effort to ward off the huge insect, and stirred his limbs from the lethargy of sleep to the weariness of unrested awaking.

The sound was plainer now; an airplane was actually dropping to earth not far away. Phil Nickers ripped the covers apart and hit the bare floor. Padding to the window he saw a late moon, pale, distant stars, a steely glow of cold light in the east. And a plane, glinting silver from its moon-tipped wings, banked sharply, settled, and made a three-point landing in a field some five hundred yards distant.

As the plane came to rest dark shadows flitted to the wings. A man climbed wearily from the cockpit, walked stiffly toward the house. The black, flitting shadows slipped a cloth hood over the motor, wheeled the plane toward a low shed. The moonlight caught the features of the man who strode toward the house.

The man was Murasingh.

Phil Nickers sighed and went back to bed. The air was cool, but still oppressive. The sheets were damp with perspiration. Phil folded himself into the sheets and tossed upon the pillow, his mind seething with unanswered questions.

At length he fell into fitful and unresting slumber. A dark-skinned servant, attired in white, aroused him with a cup of steaming coffee. Forbes followed the servant, looking as fresh as a dew-touched flower.

"Get your cold tub, and I'll have a chin-chin with you."

Nickers owned a great curiosity. His tub occupied but a few minutes. Dressed, shaved, with fresh linen, he felt better. A casual glance from the window told him the plane had been wheeled into the shed, the doors closed. But the field showed plainly what it was, a private landing field.

Forbes followed his glance.

"The colonel has it for his guests. Murasingh, for instance, is a regular visitor. He flies over whenever he takes a notion. Has several planes, that chap. Saw him this morning. He said he didn't sleep well so he got his plane out and went for a joy ride in the late moonlight. Come on down for breakfast. We'll probably be alone. Murasingh is making up for the sleep he lost last night. The colonel's had a cup of coffee and gone for a ride. Miss Jean's still in her room."

Phil ate a silent breakfast, aware of the ceaseless scrutiny of black eyes from behind. Aware, also, that Arthur Forbes had something on his mind.

"Like to take a look at the field?" asked Forbes, his eyes squinting meaningly.

Nickers nodded.

The two men strolled into the sunlight. The glare was eye-wearying.

Forbes glanced swiftly about him.

"I happen to know he took off shortly after midnight," he muttered. "Funny thing was he took off in one plane and came back in another. I was watching with the night glasses."

"But what's that got to do with"—Nickers checked himself—"with the high price of tobacco?" he concluded, irritably.

Forbes laughed.

"Maybe nothing. Perhaps a lot. Let's take a look at the plane."

The plane turned out to be a Waco 9, powered with a Curtiss OX5.

"Funny thing about Murasingh," genially remarked Forbes,

"he uses American planes entirely. He's got a cabin plane powered with a Wright J4. It's got more speed than this job. Then he's got another, a monoplane. That's what he took off with last night. He brought this job back."

The plane was deserted. A dark-skinned servant squatted in the shade some fifty feet away. From time to time he turned his turbaned head in careless appraisal. But he said no word, made no move.

Forbes leaned over the rear of the fuselage, then climbed to the wing step and peered down at the gasoline gauges. Of a sudden he cocked his head to one side, listening.

Nickers jerked a thumb toward the back of the pilot's seat.

"It's coming from in there," he said.

Both men listened, their ears attentive to the chattering noise which emanated faintly from some part of the plane.

Forbes gave a swift glance at the squatted native, then pulled the back cushion away from the frame. There appeared a small door, cunningly fashioned. Nickers used his knife blade to obtain a purchase, pulled the door away from its frame.

Instantly the chattering grew louder. Phil Nickers saw two small points of light glittering, a flash of white, a splotch of red. He drew back in surprise as there came a motion from within the compartment, and a monkey thrust his chattering countenance out into the light.

The eyes were wide, round, moist. The lips were stretched back from glistening teeth. The red mouth showed as a frame for the clicking tongue that chattered with a shrill, metallic note.

Phil noticed that the compartment had been fitted as a little room with a mattress, a cup of water, a little food. He saw also, a collar about the monkey's neck, a gold collar, studded with rubies.

And then the animal was out, sitting on the back of the pilot's seat, his tail curled around the edge of the cowl. The chattering arose in volume until it became a shrill patter of protest.

Phil Nickers glanced to one side. What he saw surprised him. The native watchman had become a dynamo of action. He was running swiftly toward them. In his right hand the sun caught the glint of cold steel.

From the other side came the pound of swift steps, and Murasingh shot around the corner of the shed, saw the two men, and came to an abrupt stop.

His face was cold with rage. His eyes were as two pools of red, uncontrolled fire. His lips drew back from white teeth that were as menacing as the fangs of a beast.

For a moment he stood so, apparently meditating attack, then he took a deep breath, regained control of his manner and features. But his eyes still glowed with red rage.

"Really, *gentlemen*, this is rather unusual."

The native with the knife slipped beneath the wing.

Murasingh sharply clapped his hands, rattled out a few swift words of a tongue Phil Nickers did not understand. The man instantly became motionless, waiting. But there was a tense menace about his pose.

Nickers squirmed. After all, his invasion of Murasingh's property had been unwarranted. He felt suddenly ill at ease, not sure of himself.

Forbes took charge of the situation.

"Heard a devil of a commotion in here, old man, and thought something had gone wrong. Sorry. Pet or something? You don't object?"

The eyes lost their reddish glare, became as expressionless as twin chunks of polished ebony. Murasingh was once more charmingly suave, politely hostile.

"Yes, he's a pet. Take him for a ride with me sometimes. But I didn't know he was in there this trip."

He held out his arms to the monkey.

As though steel springs had exploded inside the animal, he

went into such swift action that the eye could see only a blur of black fur. The monkey shot from the cockpit to Nickers's shoulder, from Nickers to Forbes, and fetched up in Murasingh's arms, his tail wrapped firmly about a forearm, his hairy arms clasped about the swarthy neck, his face flattened against the white lapel of the coat, eyes turning to survey the two white men.

Elaborately casual, Forbes took his leave. Nickers followed, keenly aware of the eyes that burned behind, following their every motion.

Forbes lowered his voice, making his words inaudible to any save his companion, and spoke without turning his head.

"Easy. Don't look back. Act as though we hadn't seen a thing out of the ordinary. But keep walking. *Keep moving.*"

"Why all the fuss over a monkey?" asked Phil.

"Easy, old chap, easy. We'll have a chance to talk later. Just act as though you were interested in the scenery now."

And Phil stopped, extended a pointing forefinger as though indicating some interesting bit of scenery.

It was not until they were safely ensconced in Phil's room that Forbes let down the bars, showed himself as he was, keenly excited, thoughtful.

"I'd suspected something of the sort all along," the Englishman said. "And, even now, I'm not sure of it. But did you see the collar on that monkey? It was solid gold, hand-carved, set with rubies of the finest pigeon blood. And Murasingh didn't know the brute was in there. You see he'd changed planes somewhere last night."

"But, surely, a man has a right to a pet monkey," expostulated Phil Nickers. "I've even seen 'em in the States. And here, where they're plentiful—"

Forbes, who had been pacing the room as a penned tiger might pace his cage, whirled upon Nickers.

"You've got photographs of Audrey Kent!"

Phil was the cautious detective again, reluctant to admit

definitely the confidential mission which had taken him to this strange land.

"Well, supposing I had, what then?"

"Did you notice the eyes? They were more round than the average eyes. You'll notice that Jean Crayson has the same sort of eyes."

"Well?"

"Monkey eyes, old chap, monkey eyes! Not very pronounced, but different from the ordinary run of eyes. Did you notice how Jean's eyes glisten? They're moist, shiny, and deep. You see them once in a while, eyes like that. I tried to think what it was they reminded me of. Now I know. They're monkey eyes."

Nickers lit a cigarette. "Personally, I think you're just a bit off," he said, coldly, suddenly regretting that he had allowed this man to discuss his confidential mission with him.

Forbes shook his head, without rancor.

"You just don't know the country," he said, good-naturedly.

Nickers remained coldly formal as the Englishman proceeded:

"And the collar had Sanskrit words on it! Lord, I'd have given a good deal to have had that confounded monkey hold off his jabbering for just thirty seconds. If I could have stolen that collar!"

"You'd have stolen the collar?"

"Sure!"

"Might I ask why you're so confoundedly interested?"

Arthur Forbes turned a face, suddenly gray with pain, upon his questioner.

"I was engaged to Audrey Kent," he said.

Nickers started. "Why, in that event—I was instructed to get in touch with you. You were the one who wrote to—"

Forbes nodded.

"Precisely. But I didn't want to disclose my identity until after I was sure. That was why I gave another name in the letter. Then when you showed up last night, and I had Mura-

singh at the table at the same time—it was too good an opportunity to overlook. I just kept gabbing, leading the conversation around to where I wanted it. I wanted to see if
Murasingh was suspicious. He was."

Nickers drummed on the table. "Look here, Forbes. I don't
want to go off half cocked on this thing, but I wonder if you
couldn't scare up a plane, a fast two-seater. It might come in
handy."

Forbes nodded.

"Now you're talking. There's a big cabin job I might be
able to get. It's got a Pratt & Whitney Wasp, and will fly circles around anything hereabouts."

Nickers nodded slowly.

"I can't help thinking that that monkey—well, that the
monkey will go back to where he came from. If you think
the monkey's connected with the case in any way, it might be
worth while to tag along."

Forbes interrupted.

"Look here, old chap. I'm not making any foolish statements. That monkey may not have a blamed thing to do with
what we're working on. But I've been watching Murasingh
ever since—ever since Audrey disappeared. And I'll swear
Murasingh has a finger in the pie somewhere."

"All right," Nickers nodded. "Anything that connects up
with Murasingh is our meat. Right now the monkey seems
to be a big factor in the situation as far as he's concerned.
Therefore, I'm willing to do anything we can to get the straight
of it. But I still don't see why a man can't have a pet monkey."

Forbes sat down, extended a long, bony forefinger. His
features twitched with enthusiasm and anxiety. His eyes
glowed with a fire of inner emotion.

"Look here, Nickers, this is India. Don't ever forget that
fact. Now let me tell you something: One of the sacred legends of this country is the *Ramayana*, a long, rambling ac-

count of the early doings of the Gods and Goddesses. And Hanuman is one of the main figures in the *Ramayana*. He's supposed to be the child of a nymph, by the God of the Wind—and he's a monkey god. The god Rama, who is an incarnation of Vishnu, had his wife kidnaped by a demon. The woman was taken to the demon's cave in Ceylon. Rama would have been powerless had it not been for his ally, the monkey god, Hanuman. Hanuman started a horde of monkeys bringing bowlders clean from the slopes of the Himalayas. They fetched the bowlders by the millions, over a vast expanse of country, and they threw them into the sea, bridging over to Ceylon.

"Now, all that sounds to your Western ears like any ordinary bit of folklore, an old myth that's something a bit more personal than a fairy tale. But this is India. Don't forget it. Right now there exists a powerful caste that considers itself bound to the god Hanuman as priests. And they worship the monkeys as being symbolic of their god. It's all rather a complicated mess, but it simmers down to the fact that the priests of Hanuman either worship the monkeys or else consider that they owe a service to the monkeys to get them started on a higher spiral of evolution.

"It's mixed up with reincarnation theories, and no end of secret stuff, and no white man knows the whole inside of the thing. But you can take it from me that there are temples devoted to monkey worship in the midst of the jungles. And that gold collar with the Sanskrit words on it, studded with rubies, carved cunningly by hand—well, that collar isn't found on any ordinary pet monkey, and it isn't found on any ordinary jungle monkey."

Forbes got up, flung himself into a regular stride of rhythmic pacing. Nickers shook himself after the manner of one shaking off the effects of a deep sleep, troubled with dreams. He stared at the pacing figure intently, studiously.

Certainly there was nothing about Arthur Forbes to suggest mental unbalance. He had talked too much at dinner, to be sure, but he had explained that. In the light of his explanation, his conduct seemed highly rational.

He was tall, spare, big-boned. His joints were large, made his hands and wrists awkward. His cheek bones were high and prominent; his eyes gray, framed in a network of wrinkles. A small mustache set off the square chin, the prominent nose. Tropical living had left him untouched by that flabby softness which so frequently comes to the white man.

Phil Nickers reached a sudden decision.

"Let's start after that plane."

Forbes shook his head.

"Not now. Get all the sleep you can today. The monkey will go back tonight, after the moon gets up."

And so it was settled.

CHAPTER 3

Into the Himalayas

The late moon slipped over the eastern hills. Like a piece of pitted orange peel it glowed redly, giving a certain hazy, indefinite light.

Arthur Forbes stood concealed in the long shadow of a hedge. Night glasses were glued to his eyes.

"There he goes," he said.

Through the still air sounded the throb of an engine, swelling in volume until it became a muffled roar. A silvery shadow glided smoothly along the field, quivered, hung poised, then zoomed upward.

Forbes snapped the glasses back into a case, looked at Nickers. Nickers was already stepping toward the pilot's seat of the powerful plane.

"Not much of a place for a field, but we got in, and we can get out," he said.

The motor throbbed to life. With blocks under the wheels,

Nickers opened and closed the throttle, warming up the engine. He tested his gauges, manipulated the controls, glanced at Forbes, and nodded.

The motor slowed as Forbes jerked out the blocks, climbed into the inclosed cabin, adjusted safety belt, and once more adjusted the night glasses. His finger pointed northeast. Nickers nodded, opened the throttle. The plane glided swiftly. Jolts ran up from the landing wheels, jolts that became momentarily shorter, sharper. A hedge loomed ahead as an indistinct blotch of regular shadow. Phil pulled back the stick, gave her all she had.

Like a startled teal, the plane shot up into the air, banked, circled, and stretched out to the northeast. Phil throttled her down to moderate flying speed. The inclosed cabin shut out enough of the motor noise to make loud conversation audible.

Below them the ground, broken and hilly, slipped swiftly by. Roads showed in the moonlight, winding and twisting, following the contours of hills that were almost invisible from the plane. Houses on hilltops, native settlements, fields, the glint of water. The moon rose higher. The shadows shortened. The sky seemed a dreamy, silver haze.

Forbes kept his glasses at his eyes, gave Phil flying directions. But the plane ahead winged steadily to the northeast as a homing pigeon in flight. Once or twice when they seemed to be getting too close, Phil swung his plane in a circle rather than take elevation. They wanted to keep their quarry above them, so he would be outlined against the glow of the sky.

And then, after nearly an hour, Arthur Forbes tapped Phil on the knee.

"He's changing his course. Perhaps he's arrived," he said.

But Phil frowned and banked. There had been no need for the observer's remark. The plane ahead was plainly visible, and there was something in the way that course had been changed which suggested a return rather than one banking for a spiral to the landing field.

Phil dropped, seeking to make himself invisible against the

ground below. They were now flying over an elevated plateau, cut with shadowed cañons, timbered with a thick growth of trees. Ahead loomed a massive mountain wall.

Too late Phil realized the real significance of the maneuver of the other plane. By dropping close to the ground he had hoped to make himself invisible. But the moon was high enough to throw a shadow, and he came close enough to send a black shadow from his plane scudding over the tree tops. The air above him screamed into life. A twisting, diving apparition roared from the heavens; and, above the roar, punctuating it at intervals with steady regularity, sounded a *rat-a-tat-tat-tat*.

"A machine gun!" yelled Forbes. "He installed a machine gun on the job and trapped us."

And so it seemed. They were flying low over a wilderness, far from the treaty lines. Below was only a forest, cañons, tumbling streams. There was no place where a plane could land without crashing. And Murasingh was above them, mercilessly holding to their tail, raining machine gun bullets.

But Phil had superior speed. He jerked the throttle open, zoomed, banked, twisted, seemed to be sideslipping into the jagged tops of moonlit trees, swung, scudded along over the tree tops like a frightened fowl, then zoomed again.

Murasingh was outmaneuvered, left behind by the superior power and speed of the faster plane. The machine gun spat a spiteful farewell, and then Phil found himself holding his course without pursuit.

Forbes pointed to several holes in the fabric of the plane, a spattered series of zigzag cracks in the shatterproof glass of the cabin.

Nickers grinned, nodded, and held the course of the plane, climbing steadily, gaining altitude. Forbes swept the ground below with his night glasses, finally picked out the other plane, saw that it was turning back. Had they, then, been led on a wild-goose chase? Or was Murasingh seeking to cut off their escape, getting ready to swoop down upon them for a final burst of gunfire. It was a miracle they had not been shot down. But the giant plane continued to purr through the night.

Higher and higher they went. The moon slid up into the heavens, and a faint tinge of brassy light glittered over the eastern rim of the universe. But the ground below remained unchanged, a high plateau, covered with trees, interspersed with cañons, rimmed by steep, rocky mountains that finally swept up into a sky-piercing tumble of jagged pinnacles.

It grew lighter rapidly. Phil knew that his only salvation lay in guarding against a surprise attack, and he chose to gain such an altitude the other could not hope to sit in the sky above him, waiting to make up for the deficient speed in a power dive.

It grew colder and lighter as they climbed. At eighteen thousand feet the ground below was but a blur of tumbled terrain. The tree tops blended together to give the impression of a level meadow.

Phil glanced at the gasoline gauge of the starboard tank, saw that the black half circle had swung so that it almost covered the top of the gauge. He pointed to it, shouted to Forbes.

"About half the gasoline supply is gone!"

Forbes nodded, sweeping the country below with his glasses. The sun came up, gilding them with cold radiance, but not, as yet, touching the country below, which still slumbered in the gray light of early dawn.

Phil sighed, swung the plane back. With half of their gasoline supply exhausted, prudence demanded that they swing back. To be caught in this country without gas would be fatal. He swung the cock to the port gasoline tank and settled back for a long period of steady flying. To his surprise, the motor coughed, missed, sputtered.

His frantic eyes swept the gauge on the port side, and then his fingers leaped to the cock, switching back to the depleted tank on the starboard side.

Neither man spoke. They had no need. Their eyes met in a single swift glance, then abruptly looked away. The port tank, carefully filled before their departure, showed an ominous black circle in the gauge. One of the bullets from the machine gun had punctured it.

Now, at an altitude of nearly nineteen thousand feet, the plane had enough gasoline left for only a few minutes of flight. Behind them the ground was known. It offered no opportunity for a forced landing. Ahead lay their only chance. The motor would work more efficiently at a lower elevation, but their height gave them a greater gliding radius.

The plane roared ahead. The sun swept a long finger of golden light across the ground below. Both men scanned the country ahead eagerly. Within a few minutes they would be either safe upon that ground or else mangled in death.

In the meantime the plane roared with as steady a throb of reassuring power as though its flight was not bounded by minutes.

A ridge lay ahead. Beyond it there seemed to be a little bare ground bordering a stream. Beyond that another stretch of plateau was lost in the morning mists.

The motor coughed, sputtered, throbbed into life again, and then abruptly died. The sudden silence, broken only by the whine of air through the struts, made the high spaces seem an aching void.

Phil nosed the plane into as flat a glide as was safe. He wanted to inspect the ground along that stream from as high an elevation as was possible. Then, if it should prove impossible to land, he would have a chance to keep going. Otherwise he could spiral down.

As they glided Arthur Forbes studied the ground below through his glasses. Untroubled by the vibration of the motor, he was now able to make things out clearly.

The ridge drifted closer. The ground beyond it opened out, showed where the forest came to a stop, the level land bordering the creek caught the glint of sunlight.

Forbes puckered his brow, snapped out a handkerchief, and wiped the lenses of the powerful glasses, then resumed a survey of the ground. At length he slowly shook his head. Steady gray eyes met eyes of steel. Neither faltered.

"Rocks and brush. A side stream runs through, and there's a bog or marsh below that. We can't make it."

"Better than the trees? We might pancake in."

"Just about a toss-up. Better keep going and see what's below those mists. We can see through 'em when we get directly overhead."

The two men could hear each other plainly now, get the little tone variations which bespoke emotion. Both were under a strain, flipping dice with death, and death had the odds. But both voices were steady, cool.

The ridge with the open ground by the stream slipped astern. The ground below showed in a dim circle through the mists, walled on all sides by a blanket of chalky white where the mists thickened. Only from directly above could the ground be distinguished.

And it was trees, nothing but forest, a vast unbroken procession of nodding tree tops that appeared as a smooth meadow until the glasses were trained upon them.

On and on went the plane, gliding at its greatest gliding angle. Down below, the trees marched in endless succession through the little circle of clear vision. Lower and lower dropped the plane, gliding like a sailing hawk.

The tree tops became plainly visible to the naked eye. They stretched their waving branches closer and closer, reaching for the plane with a grasp that must inevitably clutch the landing wheels. Then the vast machine would pitch forward, nose-dive into a crash against heavy branches. Too late now to turn and try the open ground about the creek. They had gone past, and their only hope lay in keeping on. The trees reached up. One tall fellow almost touched the wheels, sending high branches reaching up out of the mist. To the men in the plane it seemed the tree had almost jumped at them.

It was the end.

Forbes sighed—a long-drawn sigh. And then Nickers uttered a swift exclamation. He slammed the stick forward. The plane shot down, gathered speed. Then Phil pulled back on the joy stick, sent the tail skidding down. Level, cleared ground was directly below.

The landing wheels reached cautiously down. The plane touched ground, bounced once or twice, then rolled heavily. A rock caught under the left wheel. The plane, without power to drag it evenly, started to swing, wobbled slightly, and skidded to a stop.

Phil flung open the cabin door, heaved a great sigh of relief, and stepped to the ground. His steel eyes caught the gray eyes of Arthur Forbes, and the two men smiled silently. The mists were thicker here, but to the rear could be seen the towering forest, coming to such an abrupt termination that it seemed the work of man must be responsible for the clearing.

To the left appeared regular blotches of bulk, indistinct in the mist. Ahead the ground swept on until it vanished in the thin steam from the forest. Overhead the sky shone a pale blue, globules of moisture drifting slowly across the field of vision.

"We're here," said Nickers.

"And getting here may not be so good. Those are buildings over there—and we're 'way on the wrong side of the treaty line. The whites are trying to educate 'em to regard that line as obsolete. But the natives regard their rights as sacred."

He broke off, glanced at the forest.

"Perhaps we'd better slip into the trees. Not that it's much good, but it's prolonging things a bit."

Phil's hand touched his shoulder.

"Too late," he said.

Forbes followed the direction of the pointing finger.

CHAPTER 4

"Time to Be Tried!"

Gray shapes were striding solemnly out of the mists. In the lead appeared a wizened old man, garbed in gray, his hands folded upon his chest. Behind him strode natives, marching solemnly, their hands folded upon their chests.

And then Phil's eyes seemed to jerk themselves to the extreme limit of their sockets. He could hardly believe that which he saw. For, behind the natives, marching every bit as solemnly, although awkward in their strides, appeared the black outlines of monkeys, formed in file, marching gravely, tails curled and encircling the necks of the following monkeys. And each of the monkeys had his hands folded upon his chest in solemn mimicry of the men who strode ahead.

Phil heard Arthur Forbes's low voice in his ear.

"And, unless I'm mistaken, this is the place we were due to make an inspection of. I think you'll find this is where Murasingh keeps his plane!"

The procession marched with grim silence.

The leader came abreast of the plane, swung slightly to the left, circled it. The trail of monkeys marching with folded arms, encircling tails, stretched so far into the mist that by the time the wizened old man had completed a circle of the plane the end of the monkeys' line had not yet entirely appeared.

The man made a sharp noise, seemingly by pursing his puckered lips. It was a shrill, penetrating sound, a single keen squeak.

As though by magic, the entire line halted.

In silence the watchers and the watched appraised each other.

The old man was stooped by great age. His dark skin had thickened and wrinkled until it resembled the skin of an old potato. The eyes were glittering, yet expressionless. The wasted neck seemed hardly able to support the withered head. The bony shoulders protruded upward in two knobs from beneath the gray robe. The feet were bare, dust-covered.

The natives behind were swarthy, powerful men. On their faces appeared a certain uniformity of expression. They were lean, yet powerfully built. Their features showed a grim asceticism, and in their eyes was a certain something, a burning flame of devouring fanaticism.

The old man's puckered lips parted. Harsh speech husked from his withered throat. At the first words Nickers knew that he could not understand. But a swift glance told him that his companion was following the conversation.

The old man ceased talking.

Nickers glanced at Forbes. Forbes broke into speech, the same speech that the man had used. He seemed to be explaining something. His hands made an inclusive, sweeping gesture toward the airplane. Then he bowed courteously, spread out his palms in a circling, courteous motion.

As he ceased his talk the old man nodded his withered head slowly, solemnly, impressively.

"Believe I've made a sale," muttered Forbes in an undertone.

But again there came grave, husky speech.

Again Forbes made answer, and this time Nickers was able to detect an undertone of anxiety in his answer. Again the hands gestured.

And then the old man took a tottering step toward the plane, glanced back at those behind him, unfolded his arms, and started a clumsy dance. It was as though a spavined truck horse had tried to cavort as a colt. There was a hideous suggestion of a game in what the man was doing. But it was

a game of youth played with the decadence of withered age.
First on one foot, then on the other, he hopped until he
was at the plane itself. Then he extended a wrinkled claw,
attached to a forearm that was unbelievably skinny. The
brown talons ripped a small bit of fabric from the wings.

Nickers uttered an exclamation, made a move as though
to stop him. But Forbes held his hand in a viselike grip upon
Nicker's arm.

"Hold everything. Steady, old chap, steady!"

With the sound of ripping fabric the old man hopped to
the other side of the plane, waving the bit of cloth as though
it had been a trophy of skill won at some friendly game.

Behind him the natives unfolded their arms, skipped toward
the plane, tore bits of cloth, and waved them with high glee.
Their eyes remained deadly serious, tinged with the reddish
glow of dangerous fanaticism. But their lips were drawn back
from white teeth in the semblance of a happy grin.

There remained the line of monkeys, moist round eyes
watching intently the antics of the humans. Then face turned
to face. The monkeys chattered some shrill command and
came trooping forward.

"Monkey see, monkey do," muttered Forbes, the first to
catch the significance of the action.

Like brown projectiles cannonballed from a gun, the monkeys trooped across the dust-covered bare ground, leaped to
the plane, and began ripping the fabric.

Phil Nickers groaned.

From out of the mists came monkeys, droves of monkeys,
troops of monkeys. Shrilling their chatterings to the high heavens, they leaped upon the plane, grabbed a bit of cloth, a
fragment of wood, and scampered away.

And other monkeys came from the trees about where they
had been watching, concealed by the heavy foliage.

"Millions of monkeys," groaned Phil. "The plane's gone."

Forbes nodded.

"The game is to take things easy and prolong the end as long as possible. There may be a chance yet, but it's a slim one."

The monkeys scuttled up and over the plane, and beneath their vandal touch it melted like a lump of ice over which boiling water is poured. In a startlingly short space of time there remained nothing of the graceful plane except the heavier things which were anchored with nuts and bolts, were welded to the frame, or were too heavy to move.

The old man shrilled some command. The monkeys took to the trees or fell in behind the natives. Each monkey carried some bit of the wrecked plane.

The puckered lips husked out a dry command.

"He says 'walk,'" muttered Forbes.

And so they walked in a strange procession. The old man led the way, stalking like some grim corpse, partially mummified. Back of him came the two white men. Behind them the file of natives, and, behind the natives, the file of serious monkeys, aping the solemnity of their leaders, marching with a gravity as outwardly profound as that of a supreme court marching to affirm a sentence of death.

The buildings loomed larger through the mist as the men approached. There was the glitter of gold, the solid gray of old masonry.

Forbes, keeping his eyes ahead, his face upturned, muttered comments from the side of his lips.

"Notice the old pile. And that's real gold you see on the stone. Sanskrit letters, made of pure gold. They carved the rock and then pounded the gold into the stones, just like a dentist would make a filling. Good God! Look at that ruby over the door. In the form of an eye. See it? Evidently this is the headquarters of priests of Hanuman. But it's some isolated sect that no white man knows anything about. They're fanatics. Be careful, and, whatever you do, don't offend the monkeys. Treat them as though they were sacred.

"There are other people in the house. Get the flicker of

motion from that window on the second floor? Seems to be real glass in the windows. Bet these places could tell a story if the stones had the power of speech.

"Hangar over there on the left. Seems to be empty. But there must be a place around here somewhere where Murasingh keeps his planes. Remember he switched planes last night. That is where he picked up the monkey—forgot it was in the plane, or else didn't search. The monkey probably climbed in for a joy-ride. I say, looks as if they were going to throw us in a dungeon. See the bars on the windows?"

Nickers marched stolidly on, seeing everything, yet keeping silent. He realized now the desperate situation they were in. Their captors were fanatics, and they would stop at nothing.

A door opened before them. As the sunlight was breaking up the rolling clouds of light mist, the men were thrust into a dungeon. A door clanged, and they were left to themselves. Nickers chuckled.

"Takes an airplane to get a change of environment."

Forbes grinned.

"Righto. But this is India."

"What's the next move?"

"Lord knows. These natives claim to be within their rights in killing white men who get into this section of the country. That's only half the story. They'll try their damnedest to keep any news of this place from leaking out to the outside world. This gold didn't come over a million miles to get here. There must be a regular ledge of it around here somewhere. Then there's the religious end. These priests of Hanuman take their stuff pretty seriously. Hello, somebody's coming."

Outside of the door sounded a strange shuffle, slip, slap, shuffle, slop, slop, shuffle. The noise sounded along the mud floor. A bolt shot back from the massive door, and it swung noiselessly back.

Two natives flanked the doorway, and they were armed with

glittering knives whose blades fairly radiated a razor keen-ness.

Between the natives was a woman. And if ever woman observed the name of witch this woman did. In age she approximated the age of the withered native who had led the procession to the plane. But there was about her a look of malevolent hardness, a glittering-eyed cunning, a hard-jawed selfishness. Her nose hooked down to her chin. Her round chin protruded outward, seemed almost to touch the beak of that huge nose. As she opened her mouth, pink, toothless gums showed back of the wrinkled lips. Her head shook and wagged in perpetual palsy.

Upon her shoulder sat a gorgeous green parrot, tail feathers sweeping in a blaze of brilliance. The beady, twinkling eyes of the parrot, hard as twin diamonds, glittered about the dungeon.

"Time to be tried! Time to be tried!" crooned the old hag.

The parrot on her shoulder took up the refrain, speaking in the toneless falsetto which comes from the roof of a hard mouth.

"Time to be tried!"

Nickers could not repress a start of surprise.

"But she's English!" he exclaimed. There could be no mistaking the modulations of tone. And her skin was white, a leathery whiteness to be sure, but white, nevertheless.

"This is India," whispered Forbes.

The woman nodded her shaking head. "This is India, and it's time to be tried."

"Time to be tried," came the echoing squawk.

"I've come to prepare you for the ordeal, come to tell you what you must do, how you must act."

"Goofy as a bedbug!" muttered Nickers, but Forbes kicked him warningly.

"This is a monkey world," went on the hag, speaking her well-modulated English, the words seeming to come from the tip of her sharp tongue, each as hissing as the swish of a knife.

"The monkeys rule. We guide the monkeys, but they do the ruling. It's well that you should know something of the priests of Hanuman. Most people will tell you we worship the monkeys. They're wrong. We serve the monkeys. They're men the same as you two, and they've slipped in the wheel of incarnation, down, down, down."

She paused and the parrot took up the refrain.

"Down, down, *ark! ark! awarrruk!*"

"And we're raising 'em up," chanted the woman. "Up, up, up! And our work can't be interfered with. You two: what are you? Just two insignificant lives in the Wheel of Life. But what are we? What's our work? We're dealing with millions of souls, restoring them to free will and understanding.

"It will take time. Oh, yes. It'll take time, all right! We've been at it a couple of thousand years, and we'll be at it a couple of thousand years more. But we've got two souls! Hear that! Two of our monkeys have developed above the group soul of animals into the individual souls of men. You don't know, you two. You'll say they're just well-trained monkeys. But we know. We can see the soul gleaming through their eyes. Before the work of saving those two souls, bringing up the whole band into light of understanding, your lives aren't worth that!"

She tried to snap her fingers, but the claws gave only a rasping sound of skin rubbing against skin.

"The Grandharaus are servants of Agni, the god of light; bodyguard of Soma, right-hand assistants to Varuna the divine judge. There are twenty-seven in all. Three groups of nine, and each of the nines is split into three groups. Three of the Grandharaus are from the subjects of Hanuman. And we've brought to light two of those suppressed Grandharaus of the monkey men! They've been weighted down by thousands of lives of sin. Their destinies, their karma has slipped until they've almost been blotted out in a single group soul. But we've got their souls back. One of the two is the judge. You'll be taken to his court. The other one you can't see. He's preparing for his wedding. Yes, a wedding. We've got to have an Apsaras for the Grandharaus. And we've found her, a woman with monkey eyes!"

The parrot chanted.

"Monkey eyes, *arawk*! The woman with monkey eyes."

Forbes shot a meaning gaze at Nickers. Phil felt a cold sweat bursting from the pores of his skin. The crone went on:

"Who can tell, maybe a million years ago, maybe two million years there came the dividing line. One branch of the souls went down. The other branch was held chained to the Wheel of Life, through hundreds of thousands of incarnations. Life after life, death after death. And one soul slipped down, and one went up. But the things that are to be will be. And always there remains the carry-over of karma. And the humans that left the monkey karma have a look in their eyes. One can always tell. And we're bringing them back together. The two paths are coming together again. That's our work. That's the work of the priests of Hanuman. I've told you so you'll know what the trial is about. And you'll know why we can't allow a pair of human lives to interfere with that work now it's so near completion. You'd be willing to die rather than to plunge the whole monkey tribe back a million years in the cosmic scheme of things, wouldn't you?"

And the parrot, teetering back and forth on the palsied shoulder, joined in a toneless chorus.

"Wouldn't you? Wouldn't you? *Arawwwwk!*"

"Good God, they're not kidnaping a white girl to mate with a monkey?" hissed Nickers, and then was sorry he spoke, for the skin upon Arthur Forbes's face was as white as parchment. The veins stood knotted upon his forehead, and the taut skin gleamed with slimy perspiration.

"Come and be tried. Come and be tried!" chanted the old witch.

"Come and be tried," squawked the parrot.

And the two natives, whirling deftly, presented the points

of their keen knives just below their left shoulder blades. Under the prick of those knives they followed the woman as she turned and slippety-slopped, shufflety-slapped her lethargic feet along the clay-bricked floor.

"Come and be tried, come and be tried!" chanted the woman, her feet shuffling through the dust, sending little clouds of powdery white eddying up around her legs.

Nickers gave a longing look at the open ground, at the cool shadows of the forest. For a moment he felt the urge to jump wildly forward and sprint for the cover of those trees. But what he saw in the shadows stopped him.

Monkeys were gathered upon the limbs, watching in silent conclave. They were so still, so motionless that he had some difficulty in seeing them at all. But, after he once saw them, he realized something of the numbers of the monkey colony. They were by the thousands, the ten thousands, and they seemed to have some peculiar psychic alignment with those priests of Hanuman, those red-eyed fanatics who had started with a theory of a division in the life-stream, back in the dim antiquity of a million or more years ago.

"Come and be tried! Come and be tried!"

A door, studded with gold letters, swung noiselessly open and the two prisoners were ushered into something that served as an assembly room and a court of justice.

Instead of chairs running in a circle around the floor, against the walls, there was a long rail, and back of this rail were elevated perches, strung in tiers up to the ceiling. Upon these perches, sitting noiselessly, necks craned forward, moist eyes swimming with interest and curiosity, were the monkey people.

A raised platform, made of dark, polished wood, was in the center of the railed-off space. Upon this platform were several chairs. Back of one of the chairs was a dark curtain of black tapestry, embroidered with gold.

The chairs were occupied by the native fanatics. In one of

the center chairs sat the withered old man who had led the procession to the plane.

The prisoners were placed before the platform. The old witch circled thrice around the dais.

"Come and be tried! Come and be tried!" she chanted.

And then there was silence, a tense silence, a waiting, quivering silence of suspense. All were waiting for something to happen. All eyes were turned upon the vacant chair back of which was the black curtain.

The curtain bellied, shook, parted. A robed body came through the parted cloth. And, in the brief glimpse that Nickers had of the robed figure, before it came into the light, he could have sworn that a pair of human hands pushed the body out through the curtains.

But when the curtains fell back into place, leaving the robed judge well within the room, there was no further hesitation. The figure walked awkwardly around the chair and took a seat. A dark hand plucked off the hood that had shielded the features.

Nickers gave an audible gasp.

He had expected a monkey, some larger ape than the average of his species. He had even been prepared for some evidences of trained intelligence. But he was totally unprepared for that which his eyes actually encountered.

The face had simian features, but those features had, somehow, taken on the caricature of a human face. The long upper lip, the short nose, the glittering eyes, round and swimming with a moist film, were startlingly human. And the face was almost white, nearly hairless. Perhaps it was a dye, perhaps it was some freak of breeding, but the fact remained that the beast was a gross caricature of a man.

"Steady, old chap," muttered Forbes, but his voice showed that he, too, despite his assumption of ease, was shocked and surprised.

The ape, almost as large as a man, seemed to have some of the intelligence of humankind, coupled with the cunning of a beast. He surveyed the gathering with round, moist eyes. Then his paw banged upon the arm of the chair, and every one in the room stood up. Again the arm banged. The audience resumed their seats.

The old man arose, pointed to Forbes, then to Nickers.

The old man sat down.

The ape turned his head aimlessly from side to side as though wondering what was expected of him next. The old hag again circled the platform.

"He that was a man and now is a man is about to judge," she intoned.

"*Awwwwwk!*" squawked the parrot.

The roving eyes of the ape caught those of Phil Nickers. Instantly their gaze locked.

In the depths of those swimming brown eyes Phil saw something that interested him. For one wild moment he seemed to get the viewpoint of these people about him. Back of the surface, into the very depths of the monkey soul he looked. And what he saw was an individuality struggling for expression.

Phil wondered if there could be any real basis for the statements these of the monkey-clan made. Had this been a man who had drifted back to beast in the scheme of evolution, who would again return to man's estate?

A great sympathy welled within his mind, and it was as though the ape sensed that sympathy. The eyes softened, glowed with an affectionate regard. The ape flung up a hairy arm.

"They will live! They will live!" shrieked the woman. "They understand!"

And the squawk of the parrot punctuated the last exclamation.

It needed but that wordless intonation of the talking bird to snap Phil Nickers back to the world of reality. He suddenly felt his sympathy leaving him. The ape was a beast.

The parrot was but a bird, trained to mimic sounds, to echo words. The people about him were fanatics. And something in the very idea of men devoting their lives to beasts, almost worshiping a great, white-faced ape, aroused a sense of revulsion within him.

His eyes were still locked with those of the ape. The hairy arm with open palm was still upraised.

And a sudden transformation came in those brown eyes. The kind sympathy, the soft affection that had welled within those round orbs vanished; they became instead flinty hard.

Dimly Phil realized his position, strove mightily to stimulate kindness and sympathetic understanding. It was in vain. The mood had left him.

The hard eyes of the ape became almost human in their antagonism. The palm that had been raised and opened, closed into a fist. The hairy arm swept downward in a crashing circle. The fist banged against the arm of the chair.

And it did not need the hoarse croaking of the old crone to tell Phil what that descending arm meant.

"They die! They die!" shrieked the hag.

"They die!" echoed the parrot.

"They die!" roared the natives.

And the old man sucked in his puckered lips and nodded sagely.

The natives with knives instantly pricked the prisoners to their feet, marched them from the hall, out into the sunlight. Surrounding them came other natives, and, from the trees, trooped monkeys. The monkeys who had been in the hall remained, perhaps ready to participate in some additional ceremony of judging.

"Man, you almost got away with it!" whispered Forbes. "Ten seconds more and they'd have accepted us." There was no regret in his tone, nothing but praise. "I know something of monkey psychology," he went on, still in a whisper. "It's hard to move 'em. But you sure had that ape eating out of your hand for a minute or two."

"And when I lost my grip, I signed our death warrants," replied Phil. "It was that damned parrot that spilled the beans."

It was apparent that the guards were taking them across the yard to another building.

"Probably immediate execution," commented Forbes casually.

But his guess was wrong. It seemed the monkey tribe was awaiting some other development, for a door opened, the prisoners were escorted into a dark and gloomy corridor, and then taken down a short flight of steps. Dank, damp air assailed their nostrils. A bare room walled with massive square stones opened before them. A barred window grilled the blue sky.

The natives ran swift hands over their clothes, took from them knives, keys, even pencils and pens. Every object which might have furnished a tool of escape or a weapon of attack was stripped from them. A heavy door clanged shut, and the two men were left to stare at each other.

"Bum place. Not even a seat," commented Forbes.

And Phil Nickers noticed that there were no bed, no blankets. Apparently it was intended to keep the prisoners only for a short time.

CHAPTER 5

"Monkey See, Monkey Do"

Forbes seemed to read his thoughts.

"Evidently they figure we won't have any use for a bed," he said. "Looks like the end of the trail, old chap. Sorry I got you into it."

"We're not dead yet," muttered Phil, fastening his eyes upon the barred window.

He tried the bars, found that they were embedded in solid masonry. No slightest chance to work loose a bar. He banged the stone wall with his shoe, trying to ascertain from the sound how thick it was.

"Must be like a fort; sounds as if it were three or four feet through," he muttered.

"They build 'em strong," agreed Forbes, and laughed. "Wish the beggars hadn't taken all our matches and cigarettes. It'd help to blow a few smoke rings."

Phil walked to the window, surveyed the scenery visible.

There was no glass over the opening. The bars were sufficiently close to keep one from getting even a shoulder out into the air.

Through the window appeared a section of the landing field, a distant view of a corner of the other buildings, and a stretch of tree fronds where the heavy timber crept up to the clearing.

"This place has been here for some time," announced Forbes, who had been inspecting the walls. "Notice how the mortar has crumbled. See, you can even pick it out in pieces. Chance to work out quite a bit of it. They've had other prisoners before who had the idea. See where some one worked all the way around the stone on this inner wall. He worked out all the mortar he could with his finger, and then had to stop. Just back an inch or two, and the rock's probably a foot thick. But the mortar's badly shot."

Phil turned with a smile.

"That's why they took away our knives and keys. They know the mortar could be picked out. But we're just as helpless as the other poor chap that wore out his finger getting the mortar worked loose. Say, I guess we're going to have a visitor. Unless that's Murasingh coming down in a plane, I'm a poor judge of aviation."

Forbes joined him at the window.

Together they watched the speck in the sky grow to a

great man-bird, side-slip, circle, straighten and land.

Several of the natives ran eagerly to the plane. Murasingh arose from the cockpit, loosed his helmet, swept back goggles, and engaged in rapid conversation with the natives.

"Bet they've a lot of chatter to hand each other," chuckled Nickers.

The monkeys came trooping in from the trees, gathered about the plane in an attentive circle. For some ten minutes the little group remained unchanged. Murasingh talking with the natives, the monkeys sitting in attentive silence.

Then one of the natives moved forward. Murasingh stooped, picked up a shapeless bundle from the bottom of the cockpit, heaved the bundle gently over the side. The eager hands of reaching natives stretched up.

And, at that moment, the bundle assumed shape, straightened so that the men who watched from the prison dungeon could see what it was.

"Good Heavens, a girl!" exclaimed Phil.

"Jean Crayson—in her night-clothes," agreed Forbes, his lips white. "He drugged her, hid her in the plane. Remember what I said about her having eyes like Audrey Kent's? They're rounder than most eyes."

Each stared at the white, drawn face of the other. Nickers gasped.

"To think of a white girl—bride of an ape-man—here!"

Suddenly a great bitterness filled Phil's soul. He might face death himself as merely a part of the game, but this kidnaping of attractive women, the hideous fate that was in store for them, the menace of the whole organization of the priests of Hanuman, caused his very soul to revolt.

"Look here, Forbes," he said, turning a white, strained face away from the light, regarding the four walls of the gloomy dungeon. "I'm not going to stand for this. I'm going to get out of here, put a stop to the whole thing."

Forbes extended a cold, white hand.

"I'm with you, old chap. But how we're going to do it is another thing."

"If I get my hands on that smooth, polished, educated devil of a Murasingh I'll leave a vacancy in the world," promised Phil.

And, as though his words had been heard, the door of the cell swung back and Murasingh grinned from the threshold.

"Gentlemen, good morning! You arrived a little sooner than I did. I trust you've been made comfortable."

His eyes glowed with dancing mockery.

"I thought you were just taking a casual joy-ride in a plane, and tried to warn you back. You know it's not healthy for whites to disregard their treaty promises and invade certain sections of India."

Phil crouched, moved slowly toward him.

Murasingh whipped an ugly automatic from his pocket, covered the men. His eyes were as hard as black flints.

"Don't try it, boys. I'd hate to have to kill you, but I can. And if you so much as threatened me, your death wouldn't be pleasant. As it is, I think I can promise you a reasonably swift death. But there are other ways that might not be so pleasant. There was one poor devil that went through it. You might be able to imagine what happened. He was tied hand and foot. One of the men ran to him, pinched off a bit of flesh and ran away laughing, as though it was some new game. Another and another did the same thing. The monkeys were watching from the trees. The new game appealed to them. After all, you know, they're little men, actuated by all the cruelties of a savage, yet containing all of the possibilities of development of a man himself.

"I know how you boys feel. But you've cut in on this game. No one asked you to do a damn thing except mind your own business. But you had to come prying and snooping. There's a work going on here that's bigger than you and bigger than me, and bigger than all of us put together. Don't think for a moment you can interfere with that work. You must have some conception of it. They tell me one of you almost convinced the judge. In that case, you'd have been allowed to come in as one of the priests—after you'd gone through a sufficient course of training.

"I dropped in to tell you chaps good-by. You'll be here until midnight. The wedding takes place at one o'clock. You won't be here for the wedding—a double wedding with the rising of the old moon. Good-by."

The door clanged. There was the rasp of a lock shooting bars into the solid wall of squared rock.

"And that's that," muttered Phil, his hands slimed with cold perspiration.

"That's that," agreed Forbes, and tried to grin.

"We couldn't have rushed the automatic, and we've got until midnight."

Phil broke off to stare meditatively at Forbes.

"He must have drugged her, sneaked into her room, loaded her into the plane, tied her down. That's why we didn't see anything of her when the planes were doing their stuff. Of course he's a fanatic, like all the rest. Sincerely believes in all this stuff. As far as he's concerned we're just fellows who butted in and asked for what we got."

There descended a silence. Each man was wrapped in his own thoughts.

Phil Nickers fell to pacing the floor.

"There's a way. There must be a way. Somehow, somewhere. Good Lord! A situation like this can't exist—"

He stopped, mid-stride, to stare at the window.

A monkey sat in the window, propped between the bars, regarding him gravely. A shadow moved across the ground, and another monkey thrust an eager, curious face over the other's shoulder.

"Think of how they train 'em," muttered Forbes. "Of

course, it's natural for the monkeys to imitate people. They work on that. How awful it must have been to teach them that tearing a human being to pieces was a game. Their fingers are as strong as steel nippers."

The monkeys regarded him in moist-eyed gravity.

Phil suddenly dropped to all fours, scampered around the floor, chattering like a monkey, running, cavorting, crawling, leaping.

Forbes regarded him with startled, wide eyes. "Steady, old chap, steady. Death comes to us all. Take it easy. Don't let the damn beasts get on your nerves."

But Phil continued to run around.

"Start chasing me," he hissed. "Get started after me. Run."

"What in thunder?"

"Don't argue. Get down while we've got their attention. Start running. Chase me around."

Forbes dropped doubtfully to hands and knees, crawled clumsily.

Phil chattered shrilly.

The monkeys became excited, stirred uneasily, chattered to themselves. Other shadows came across the yard, blotted light from the window. Monkey after monkey came to see the cause of the excitement.

Phil ran on hands and feet, avoided Forbes's reaching hand, stopped before the joint between two of the square stones on an inner wall, picked out a bit of mortar, threw it at Forbes.

Then the Englishman got the idea.

"Great stuff, old chap! It may work!"

And he, chattering shrilly, ran to the same place, picked out a bit of mortar, hurled it.

Back and forth the two men went, cavorting like huge dogs, running, jumping, and every few minutes pausing to pick a bit of mortar from the same place between the rocks and hurl the soft, crumbing white pebble at the other.

The monkeys in the window chattered shrill glee.

Suddenly one of them dropped, swung from his tail that

was looped around the bars, then leaped lightly to the floor. In a mad scamper he went to the exact point in the wall where Phil had been getting mortar, picked out a bit with his wire-strong fingers, and hurled it at one of the monkeys in the window.

Almost on the instant there came a furry flood of dark animals pouring through the window. In a mad kaleidoscope of action they chased each other, stopping to grab mortar from the chink and fling it at each other.

More monkeys came. The men withdrew from the race, leaned back against the wall, panting for air, watching the scampering monkeys.

Phil's palms were bleeding, his knees raw, but a slow smile of content swept his face.

The monkeys had pulled out all of the mortar that could have been reached by human fingers. Now they were plunging their slender, sinewy arms in between the rocks, picking out little chunks of mortar, flinging them wildly, chattering, scrambling, scampering. And they enjoyed the game.

A monkey snatched a bit of mortar from a different place, getting it where it was more accessible. Phil made a swift kick at the animal. The monkey avoided the kick, stopped to chatter his rage and surprise. But the others continued the game.

Then the chase slowed. The monkeys became interested in prying into the wall. Minutes lengthened into an hour, and still the monkeys worked, exploring, chattering, pulling out mortar. Bit by bit they loosened the mortar all the way around the stone. The mortar became harder as it went deeper into the wall, but the tough little fingers made short work of pinching out bits, dragging it to the floor.

Finally they wearied of the game. One of the monkeys jumped for the window, paused, hesitated a bit, saw the green tops of waving trees, and scampered for the cool forest. Another joined him, and soon the cell was deserted save for the human occupants.

*   *   *

Phil stooped to the floor, began picking up the fine chunks of mortar.

"This comes first," he said. "We can't let the guards get suspicious."

For more than an hour they labored frantically, getting the mortar picked up, throwing it through the bars. At length they had the cell well cleaned, and Phil was able to turn his attention to the stone which had been partially loosened.

He placed his hands against the face of the stone, heaved, grunted, twisted, withdrew his hands and shook his head. There were two red blobs upon the rock where his bleeding palms had strained.

"Still solid. Can't loosen it a bit, but there's a lot of mortar gone. I'll keep tugging, first one direction, then the other. Then you can try it for a while."

He inserted fingers in the crack in the wall, tugged at the stone, then placed palms against it again and pushed. Alternately he tugged and pushed, pushed and tugged. When he was exhausted Forbes tried it for a while.

"No use, old chap," remarked Forbes, after a bit of last, straining effort, during which they had crowded their grimed, perspiring faces together to both pull and tug at the stone in unison. "It's too heavy and it's still anchored too well. The thing must be two feet square, and no knowing how far back it goes. The mortar gets stronger as it gets back where it's protected from the air. I have a hunch we're on a wrong tack."

The men slipped to the floor, sat slumped against the wall, surveying each other dispiritedly. It had been their one chance and they seemed to have lost.

The sun swung away from the window. The heat became more pronounced. Flies droned lazily. Phil noticed that Forbes was nodding, dozing. His own eyes felt leaden. The lids closed, opened, blinked, and fluttered closed again.

Phil Nickers slept, a fitful sleep of dreams, of irritated slaps at crawling flies that clung to his greasy skin. His eyes opened at length, sleep swollen and bloodshot. His temples throbbed and pounded.

But his first, automatic concern was for that which had awakened him. A single glance told him all he needed to know. A monkey, holding some glittering object in its paw, was racing around the cell. Behind him came half a dozen other monkeys in mad pursuit. The animals paid no attention to the motionless forms of the sleepers. It was the brushing of a furry body against his shoulder that had awakened Phil.

The monkey who held the coveted prize wheeled and dodged, but Phil's hand, snapping out, caught the animal by the tail.

With a shrill squeak of rage, he turned, and flashed glittering teeth. But that which he had been holding dropped from his paw.

Phil made a grab for it, not realizing what it was, hardly knowing why he had interfered in the chase. He let go the monkey's tail as he grasped the glittering object. The monkey jumped for the bars, stood in the window, jabbering monkey-curses. The other animals followed him, remained grouped just without the bars.

Phil gasped as he saw what he had secured. It was a diamond ring, set after the fashion of an engagement ring, and it was engraved with Sanskrit characters on the inner circle.

The size of the stone alone was enough to command attention. It was a crystal-clear diamond of the finest water, and light radiated in snapping scintillations from its facets. It was larger than any diamond Phil had ever seen, and more brilliant.

He glanced at the monkeys, wondering where the ring had come from, sensing that it had been pilfered from one of the principals who were to take part in the wedding ceremony.

And then, as he saw the round, inquisitive eyes watching him greedily, Phil conceived a brilliant idea. He took the diamond between thumb and finger, made a quick pass, and thrust his fingers into the chink the monkeys had made in the stone side of their cell.

Apparently the diamond was in his fingers when he thrust his hand to the wall. Actually the diamond had been slipped to his other hand. Therefore, when he slowly withdrew his empty fingers from the dark chink, the gesture was convincing.

Then Phil gazed solemnly at his snoring partner, and smiled, with his face turned toward the window. Then he, too, crawled back against the wall and pretended to sleep.

The monkeys looked at each other.

Such things they could understand. The strange man-creature had stolen the gem from the monkeys, and had now hidden it in that strange dark crack in the wall. Then the man had gone to sleep.

The leading monkey cautiously dropped along the wall, his powerful, furry tail looped about the bars of the window. For several seconds he hung swinging back and forth, while Phil anxiously surveyed him from half-closed eyes.

Then the monkey dropped to the flag floor, and scampered across to the wall. He plunged his hand gropingly within, pulled forth his arm, and inspected that which he held in his grasp. It was nothing but a round piece of dead white mortar. He made a grimace, dropped the bit of mortar to the floor, screwed his forehead into washboard wrinkles and reached again.

The other monkeys trooped into the room.

Phil remained motionless, his eyes closed to mere slits, watching with tense anxiety, praying that Forbes would not awaken and frighten the little workers.

The afternoon sun slanted to the west. The cell became darker. Both men leaned against the wall, breathing regularly, rhythmically. The monkeys worked feverishly. They had apparently seen the gem go in that crack, they had not seen it come out. And they had become fond of the diamond, wanted to survey its glittering surfaces. There was nothing to fear from these two sleepers, and so they pulled out bit after bit of mortar, each monkey thinking he had secured possession of the gem until that which his fingers had closed upon was brought to light.

It was not until dusk approached and Arthur Forbes terminated a snore in a snort, moved, rubbed his eyes, that the monkeys took alarm, scampered off into the gathering shadows.

Phil made a swift leap for the stone.

At the bottom of the wall was a considerable pile of mortar fragments. The monkeys had worked their way well around the stone, searching for their plaything. And each monkey had dug for himself. As a result a dark band showed about the entire outline of the stone.

Phil tugged at the rock, pushed, tugged again. A very faint, crunching sound transmitted itself through the stone.

"I believe it's working loose. Lend a hand," hissed Phil.

The two men strained, twisted, pulled, pushed. At length the rock budged slightly on one end. The other was firmly anchored.

"If we keep it up long enough there's a chance," agreed Forbes.

There followed hours of sweating labor. The obstinate rock seemed malevolently intelligent in its resistance. The men nipped their fingers, tore nails loose, groped, pushed, pulled, sought for a finger hold. And, at length the rock slid back. They pushed it out, heard the thud with which it fell to the floor.

Phil was first through the opening, worming and twisting, aided by such pressure as Forbes could apply. Then Arthur Forbes, tired, almost exhausted, slipped his feet through the opening, felt Phil's fingers clutching his ankles.

The mortar on the inside of the wall had set until it was like cement. The hard particles scraped their flesh as they wormed through the hole, accounted for the hours of final effort.

"Seems to be a blind room without a single window," remarked Phil, keeping his voice in a whisper.

"Wish we had matches," agreed Forbes, his tone worried. "We haven't the faintest idea of whether it's a dungeon, or a snake pit, and we've got to hurry—there's the wedding."

"There's the wedding," agreed Phil. "We can't be particular about the room. And no matter what's here it can't be any worse than what we've left. Let's go."

"Easy, old chap. This is India, you know, and that whole room with its crumbling mortar and all may be nothing but a trap. These fellows like to get prisoners to kill themselves trying to escape. Let's make sure. It's just a little queer, you know, that that diamond ring should have turned up so opportunely. Let's keep our arms interlaced, and then feel cautiously. There may be a pit in the center of the floor for all we know."

"Good idea," agreed Phil. "But we've got to work fast. They'll be coming in to look us over any minute now. And that stone from the wall is as good as written directions telling them where to go to look for us. They know the place, and we don't."

With arms interlocked, feeling with outstretched fingers, shrouded in pitch darkness, the men groped their way about the room.

Of a sudden Phil felt his companion stumble, draw back.

"Just as I suspected. There's a pit in the center of the floor here. Watch out. I nearly fell, would have if it hadn't been for your arm. Let's see how far it goes, what it's like."

Phil came forward, cautiously, finger tips scraping the floor. Abruptly his arms swept off into black space. He continued to grope about the edge.

"Circular," he said at length. "Let's keep working around it. I'll tear off a bit of cloth from my shirt and leave it here so we'll know when we get back to the starting point."

There was the sound of tearing cloth, and then the noise of garments rasping along stone as the two men explored the pit. It was Phil whose exploring fingers found the stairs. They were stone stairs, rounded by years of use. Moving in the darkness, not knowing what was below, their ears attuned for the scraping rustle which would mean the presence of a deadly snake, the two men descended.

CHAPTER 6

The Halls of Hanuman

For some thirty feet they went down. The stairs circled the pit, swinging in a spiral. At the bottom began the game once more of finger-tip exploration. This time it took them but a matter of seconds to become oriented. They were at the entrance of a walled passageway, arched at the top, some eight feet wide, leading on a gradual slope. Water had oozed through the stones until a green slime had formed over the rocks. There was a damp, dank, stagnant smell, and the darkness teemed with the suggestion of living things.

But only once did they hear the scraping of a scaled body moving over the stones, and that noise grew less, terminated in a long-drawn hiss. The men pressed on, knowing that death lay behind, not knowing what was ahead.

A regular throbbing of the atmosphere seemed to pulse in their blood before their ears became directly conscious of it as sound.

"Tom-toms," remarked Forbes. "You never hear 'em but what you know you've been listening to 'em long before you first heard 'em."

"Where are they?" asked Phil, turning his head in the darkness, this way and then that, after the manner of a bird listening to a whistle.

"Have to keep going to tell. It's the hardest sound in the world to locate."

As they progressed, the sound of the tom-toms grew louder, seemed to come from above them. Phil touched his hand to the side of the passage, and noticed that the walls were now dry and free from the green slime.

"We've been underground for a while. Now we've climbed back up," he announced.

"And we must have covered at least half a mile," said Forbes. "You know I'm wondering—" He broke off and lapsed into silence.

They went for some hundred feet farther, and then a current of air, striking Phil's left cheek, caused him to stop and investigate.

A door led from the stone passageway. That door had been left slightly ajar, and through the crack came a current of drier air.

Phil thrust his hand into the opening, pulled. Slowly the heavy door creaked back. Ahead was a flight of stairs, and from the top came the first faint light the men had seen since they entered upon the passageway. As they started up, walking cautiously, a sound from above caused them to stop abruptly.

The faint slithering of rhythmic sound could come only from feet descending the stairway. The men exchanged glances in consternation. Perhaps their escape from their cell had been discovered. In that event the searchers might have decided to cover both ends of the passage. Or, on the other hand, the approaching feet might merely belong to some of the priests of Hanuman, who were using the passage as a means of communication with other parts of the temple buildings.

The stairs offered no place where they could conceal themselves, unless they trusted to chance that the others would walk past them in the darkness. And the same was true of the passageway.

Now they could see the feet approaching, faint shadows outlined against the dim light from above. No word was spoken; by faint pressures of the hand alone Nickers conveyed to his companion the idea that but two approached, that they would take their chances on a hand-to-hand encounter in the darkness. It was better to surprise them and attack them than to play fugitive and run into a trap.

They crouched, bracing themselves. The feet of the figures who descended the stairs were now more plainly visible. And Phil's eyes detected the hairy legs as soon as Arthur Forbes's hissed warning penetrated the darkness.

One of those who descended was an ape!

Of necessity that changed the plans of the two who crouched in the darkness. They would be no match for the ape. They dropped back, cautiously, a step at a time, feeling their way, trusting to luck that they should make no noise.

As they regained the passage, the darkness above them was split by the beam of an electric flashlight which cut through the darkness, illuminated the arched passageway, the stairs, the dancing shadows.

The men braced themselves for an uneven conflict. In close quarters the great strength of the giant ape would make their own efforts puny by comparison.

And then a voice purred and rippled through a guttural dialect which was strange to the listeners. But they recognized the sound of the voice. It was Murasingh, talking to the ape-man as one would chat with an intimate friend.

Was it pose or could the ape-man understand the language? The men glanced at each other, and then stiffened. For the light flickered its beam at their very feet. The sound of shuffling feet was upon them, and the strange pair literally brushed past.

It was the ape-man who saw them. Perhaps it was that his eyes were more accustomed to darkness, perhaps some keen sense of smell enabled him to detect the presence of others.

He uttered a shrill sound sequence which seemed to be like words, sounded startlingly like the dialect in which Murasingh had been talking.

The men who crouched in the darkness of the passageway could not understand the words, but there could be no mistaking the sudden shrill tone in which they were uttered.

Phil Nickers raised his foot, swung it as swift and true as a football player punting the ball down a muddy field. He aimed his toe for a point above the flashlight, and connected with the wrist of Murasingh.

The light snapped out, clattered against the stones of the passageway. And all became struggle, noise, confusion. The ape-man gave short, shrill screams of rage, perhaps mingled with terror. Murasingh, not knowing the numbers nor identity of those who opposed him, fought wildly in the darkness.

Phil swung his fist chin high, in a long, pivoting swing, had the satisfaction of feeling a tingle of pain run up his forearm as the blow connected.

There was the sound of a falling body, and then a hairy arm shot out through the darkness, grazed his own body. Fingers that were as steel gripped the shoulder of his coat.

Phil flung himself forward and down, swung a futile blow with his left. The mighty arm did not so much as quiver when Phil's weight hurled against it. But the cloth gave way and Nickers sprawled free on the floor of the passageway.

But he sensed that other great arm was busy, not concerning itself with him, but reaching for his companion. There was the swish of rapid motion above, the sound of feet dragging over the flags. Something slid over Phil's sprawling figure. He flung up his hands and encountered the shod feet of Arthur Forbes. The man was being dragged as though he was a sack of meal, the feet trailing behind.

Phil rolled to hands and knees, braced himself for a tackle, and then his hands closed upon something cool and metallic. In an instant he realized that he had the flashlight he had kicked from Murasingh's hand. Would it work?

He grasped it, pressed the button. A reassuring beam of light stabbed the darkness. And Phil thrust that stabbing beam directly into the face of the ape.

Man or animal, enough of the animal remained in the ape to give him a fear of that sudden light. Phil had a picture stamped indelibly upon his memory of a hairy ape, the face almost devoid of hair, pale and thin of skin, lips twisted back from glittering fangs, nostrils that were merely two dark, quivering holes, eyes that were wide, dark-pupilled, moist with fright.

And in that swift stab of light he saw also Arthur Forbes's white face, drained of color, lifeless, with that hairy hand reaching at his throat, ready to tear out the flesh.

The light made the ape recoil, jump back. His hairy arms flashed up, using his hands as shields to keep the blinding light from his eyes. And Arthur Forbes, released from the grasp of the man-beast, thudded to the stone flags.

As the ape-man recoiled, Phil pushed the light ahead, taking every inch he could gain, keeping his advantage pressed home. A huddled something on the stones moved, tripped Phil, sent him sprawling. Hands clutched at his arm, pulled the flashlight down.

Phil had a brief glimpse of Murasingh, lying upon the stones, his face white with pain but grim with determination. Then there was the flash of a steel blade, and a knife bit through the cloth of his coat, razored the skin apart, sent a warm trickle of blood flowing down his arm.

Phil felt himself tottering forward, and doubled his left fist, sent it crashing down ahead of him, a stiff-armed jolt with all the impetus of his falling body behind it.

The fist grazed the countenance of the man below. The flashlight was torn from Phil's grasp, and the two locked on the floor in a hand-to-hand struggle. The ape-man, terrified by the cold fire that had been plunged in his face, was running awkwardly back, down the passage, toward the room from which Phil and his companion had escaped.

Forbes was still unconscious. The struggle was hand to knife, finger to throat, between the fanatic and Phil Nickers. Murasingh seemed intent upon plunging the knife to a vital spot. But he was underneath, fighting against the crushing weight of the man above. And Phil pressed that advantage to the limit, keeping on top, groping for the hand with the knife, smashing home vicious short-arm jabs with his fist.

At length his questing fingers caught the lean wrist that was wielding the knife. Phil's fingers tightened, gave a twist, and the knife slithered along the dark stone.

Murasingh sought his throat. Phil's fingers were first to their goal. He tightened his grip. The struggles of the man below grew less violent, suddenly subsided. Fearing a trap, Phil continued the pressure for a moment or two more, then released his grip. Murasingh lay still.

Phil turned to Forbes, found that there was a pulse, and pulled his companion to a semi-upright position against the side of the passageway. Then he returned to Murasingh, a recollection of the automatic with which the fanatic had been armed, sending his fingers questing through the man's clothing.

And he found it, gripped the precious metal in his damp hand with a strange sense of power. He groped about until his hands once more closed upon the flashlight. Now he was willing to meet the foe in any numbers, under any conditions.

A rustle of motion apprised him of Forbes's motions. He swung the flashlight, encountered dazed eyes.

"It's all right, old man. How d'you feel?"

"Like a chunk of meat that's been through the sausage grinder. I'm groggy, but guess I'm all right aside from that. What happened?"

"I frightened the ape with the flashlight. He wasn't the one that acted as judge, but another. Guess he's the one that was to be the bridegroom. He's gone for help. Murasingh is out, but he gave us a flashlight and automatic before he went. Feel up to walking? We've got to stop that wedding, you know."

For answer, Forbes staggered to his feet.

"I'm just shaken up a bit. We're going to *stop* that wedding, even if we have to walk in and fight the outfit."

They ascended the stairs, trapped between two flanking dangers. Up the passage lay the menace of being trapped within cramped quarters. Down the passage lay the menace of the hideous ape-man. From up the stairs came the booming of the great drums. As they pounded, the rhythmic chant of throbbing sound which entered the pulsations of the blood, seemed to stir the very soul with monotonous repetition of sound.

The light grew stronger as they ascended. From a corridor ahead came a mellow glow. There seemed to be no particular light source. It was merely that there was light. The hallway glowed with a soft radiance that was almost phosphorescence. So might the interior of a rotting log seem to a tiny grub.

Phil stopped, surprised at the lighting effect. And, as he stood there—dimly conscious of the weird surroundings, the boom of drums, and the shuffle of many feet upon stone floors —the scream of a woman knifed the night.

There was a wild terror in that scream, a blood-curdling horror that stabbed the eardrums. Forbes straightened, turned toward the source of that sound. Phil gripped the automatic, and there sounded the flutter of filmy draperies. A woman rushed out from a side corridor, saw the men, paused in terror, and turned wide eyes back over her shoulder.

From behind her came the sound of a low laugh, demoniacal, triumphant. The woman turned again and her terror-darkened eyes surveyed the two men.

Of a sudden, wild incredulity flooded her countenance.

Phil heard a choking gasp at his side.

"Audrey!" muttered Forbes, and the word was as a prayer.

"Arthur!" she cried.

He went to her in a swift flash of motion that took no heed of threatening dangers. "Arthur," she said once more, as his arms folded about her, and the tone was a caress.

"Come back and be married. Come back and be married!" chanted the dry voice of the old hag.

"Come and be married! *Awwwrk!*"

There was the slippety-slop of feet on the stone.

The girl's eyes darkened once more with terror. Phil could see her blue lips whispering rapid words to Arthur Forbes, saw him stiffen. And then there was the pad-pad of swift feet, and the hairy arm of a man-ape reached out.

A body followed the arm, a grimacing face. Phil recognized the ape as being the one he had encountered in the passageway below. By some secret side-exit he had returned to the rooms above.

But now there was no fear upon the bestial countenance, merely a savage leer of animal triumph. At the sight of Arthur Forbes, his lips curled back from glittering fangs. For a moment he stood so.

Phil raised the automatic.

A bounding ball of swift motion cut across the sights. With a gasp of surprise Phil realized what had happened. Arthur Forbes had moved to the attack.

His left and right flashed squarely into the face of the snarling beast, staggered it. But those long, hairy arms, so heavily muscled that they seemed as the legs of a lion, swept up, encircled the man in a hideous embrace. The snarling face of the enraged beast was thrust close. The bared fangs snapped for the throat.

Forbes jerked his head back and to one side, dodged the menace of that first spring. The girl screamed again. Pattering feet ran down the corridor.

Forbes struggled valiantly, sought to free one of his arms, to press back against the crushing pressure that enfolded him. As well have sought to struggle with a steam hammer. With a gloating snarl of cruel bloodlust upon its countenance, the ape freed one hairy arm, reached upward with talon fingers, and cruelly sought to pluck out his adversary's eyes, one at a time.

But that motion gave Phil the chance he sought. The line of the sights ceased to show a blur of bodies struggling for life, and showed instead merely a furry body with white face twisted into an expression of fiendish rage.

He squeezed the trigger.

The hall reverberated to the roar of the explosion. The hairy body staggered, then stood erect. One of the arms clutched at the side of the head.

Arthur Forbes wormed free. The ape staggered forward. Forbes braced himself, swung a terrific right, catching the beast full upon the chin. It wobbled backward, and Forbes sprang to the side of the girl.

"This way," called Phil, sprinting to their side, pointing down a side passageway.

Over their shoulder he could see a confused throng. There was the old man with the wizened countenance, his rheumy eyes expressionless, glittering darkly, the old woman with the parrot perched perpetually upon her shoulder; and the swarming natives, robed as for some strange ceremony. Behind them were the drummers, and behind them, in a room that radiated soft light, a horde of monkeys, sitting upon perches, tails twisting and twining.

The couple ran down the corridor. Phil remained behind, the automatic menacing those who followed. A native lowered a deadly knife, charged, chanting some weird song.

Phil's finger squeezed the trigger. The native stumbled back, clutching his shoulder, stumbled, fell sprawling. The others swarmed over him, steady, relentless. The corridors reëchoed the force of the explosion, sending it back multiplied a hundredfold.

The old man was the leader, and the natives seemed to look to his leadership, suiting their pace to his. After that one wild rush by the native, the throng advanced in a steady manner, as remorseless as the welling of an incoming tide. The old man was making such time as his withered limbs permitted. The others suited their pace to his.

"It's a blind corridor, that's why they're taking their time, old chap," said Forbes, looking ahead.

Phil's grip tightened. He knew there were only a few more shells in the gun. Before that revengeful horde, seeking his death in such a remorseless, deliberate fashion, he would be torn to pieces. Anything was better than that. And there was the thought of the girl.

"The last shots are for the three of us," she pleaded softly. "You don't know the cruelty of them. Please."

But a line in the masonry caught Phil's eye. He acted upon a hunch, placed his shoulder against it and pushed. The wall seemed to yield, and than a door swung back upon well-oiled hinges.

"This way," he called, and pushed the others within.

Two of the natives, barefooted, dark, the light rippling along powerful muscles, dashed forward, knives flashing back.

One of the knives glittered through the air, thudded against the rock wall and tinkled to the pavement. The other was never thrown. Once more Phil's finger squeezed the trigger, and the man with upraised knife faltered, stumbled, and slumped forward.

CHAPTER 7

Flight

It was a low exclamation from the girl that attracted Phil's attention as the door swung back into place and a bar clicked into the masonry.

Audrey Kent was bending over a bed; and on the bed, a gold and stone affair, studded with gems, covered with gold tapestry, lay the slumbering form of Jean Crayson.

The men exchanged swift glances. The impediment of that unconscious figure would greatly lessen their chances of escape. The three might escape. The three, burdened with a

sleeping, drugged girl, would be almost certain to face re-
capture.

But that single glance sufficed for each to know the mind
of the other.

Phil tossed the automatic to Forbes.

"You and Miss Kent try to make it. I'll follow."

And he stooped to the bed, slipped strong arms under the
sleeper, throwing the gold tapestry about her.

"We stick together," grumbled Forbes in a low voice. "If
it's death we take it standing up and smiling."

It was then that Audrey Kent seemed to recover from the
sheer panic that had gripped her. She laughed, a low, rippling
laugh.

"Don't be silly, Mr. Whoever-you-are."

There was a window in the wall, open, unbarred. Soft night
breezes flicked the delicate curtains which filmed the opening.
Forbes thrust his head out.

"Can do," he said. "It's not over six feet. I'll hand the girls
down."

He vaulted lightly. The thud of his landing feet could be
heard in the room. Audrey Kent followed, dropped into his
waiting arms. Phil lowered the sleeping form, and jumped.
From the temple came the sound of a long wail, a cry of sheer
animal anguish.

They ran across the bare ground, not knowing where they
were going or for what purpose, surrendering themselves to
blind flight, trying to leave behind them the memory of that
nightmare, escape the crowd of fanatical pursuers.

A door swung open, a long streamer of light oblonged a
golden path across the field. Phil, looking up from his labored
running, saw the glint of reflected light from some silvery
object.

"The cabin plane," he yelled. "Quick. It's our only chance!"

They altered their course. From the door came a pell-mell
of figures that sent dancing shadows across the oblong of
golden light. At their lead was a terrific spectacle, the ape-

man who had sat in judgment, his mighty chest thrust forward, head up, jaw set, lips curled back from bare fangs.

He ran, not as a man, but as an ape, assisting himself in the running by touching the ground with the bare knuckles of his hands, swinging along by the aid of those mighty arms. And he made two feet to every one that the crowd behind him covered.

Forbes reached the plane, slammed open the door, bundled in the girl, jumped for the starter. There sounded the mechanism of whirring springs. The motor throbbed into life.

It was then that Phil Nickers noticed the ropes running from wing tips to stakes, saw the blocks under the landing wheels. There was no time to communicate his discovery, no time to waste in first getting the drugged girl into the cabin.

He laid her along a wing, dived underneath, pulling blocks out, ripping rope from driven stakes. Their only chance was that Forbes could send the plane in a ground run to the other end of the field, leaving the pursuers behind, then turn and take off. As for Phil, he felt that he could only fight as long as possible, delay matters for a few seconds.

Phil emerged from under the far wing tip, pointed to the unconscious figure on the wing, waved his hands to urge the plane on, knowing that Forbes could stop at the other end of the field to get the sleeping girl in the cabin.

And then he turned toward his pursuers.

He expected to hear the song of the motor gather in volume. Forbes could taxi the plane sufficiently to finish warming up the motor. And with the engine he could dodge the pursuers. But there was no increase in the steady roar of the motor. Forbes was waiting. That would be the girl's order.

Phil dashed for the door of the cabin.

The great ape-man was before him. A mighty arm plucked him from the step as a man might pluck an orange from a tree. Phil was hurled back, spinning. Before him loomed the solid front of advancing foe. The ape reached out great arms, scooped from the wing the figure that was rolled in golden tapestries.

And Phil, recovering his balance, unarmed, charged in a low tackle, straight for the ape. Forbes flung open the door of the cabin, thrust out the barrel of the automatic, pulled the trigger.

There was no report. The firing pin clicked with a metallic noise of hollow futility.

The ape staggered at Phil's impact, then regained his balance. One arm encircled the golden tapestry. The other dropped, caught Phil's neck in a crushing embrace. And then the ape turned toward those who were almost upon them.

His face twisted up in the agony of that superhuman grip which was literally crushing the muscles of his neck to jelly, ripping apart the vertebrae, Phil saw the white face of the ape-man. It was illuminated from the open doorway. Each change of facial expression was indelibly stamped upon Phil's memory.

The ape looked at the old man, the natives, then at the slumbering features of the drugged girl, at the white, horror-frozen features of those in the plane, so near and yet so far from liberty.

Of a sudden the eyes lost their brute ferocity. The face was flooded with an expression such as comes to a human being in a moment of great renunciation. The ape-man shot out a hairy paw, literally flung Nickers into the plane. Then he extended the drugged figure, gently thrust her within.

And then they were upon him, a frenzied throng of shouting madmen. But the ape-man held them back, his great chest flung outward. The motor roared into increased speed, and the plane moved slowly and majestically out upon the field, out of the ribbon of light that came from the open door, out into the darkness of the calm night.

The ape-man turned, and Phil was able to see that there

were tears in his eyes. But the expression of self-sacrifice still stamped his features with a something that was not only human, but more than human.

Then the throng swept past him, clutching hands tried for the tail assembly. One man, more swift than the others, reached for one of the wing tips. But the prop had swirled up a vortex of seething air, thick with dust. The dust-cloud swept into the eyes of the pursuers. The current of wind held them back even as the plane gathered speed.

And, just before the dust-cloud swirled about the lone form of the giant ape, he swung up one arm, in a gesture of farewell.

The plane swept down the field. Phil had grasped the throttles, his strained neck muscles aching with pain, his eyes seeming to protrude from their sockets. But his trained fingers guided the plane with a great sweep, into a huge circle.

He had no time to get the direction of what wind there might be. He needed to warm up the motor a few more degrees. And he must guard against crashing into the trees which lined the field. How far did he dare go? Would the foe chase after him on the inside of a circle and head him off? He could only take a chance.

He cut the plane in a series of ground antics like the zigzag of a huge bumblebee with one wing gone. Droning, snarling, ripping through the night, the plane skidded and twisted. The engine temperature rose. Phil pulled back on the stick. The wheels left the ground. Directly below appeared a light, a sea of upturned faces, clutching hands. Somehow the field had been flooded with light, disclosing the plane, the enemy. And the plane had got off just in time, for the clutching fingers barely missed the tips of the wings. One or two caught the bar of the landing wheels, but the terrific speed tore it from their grasp. Had those fingers caught a wing tip, however, the story might have been different.

The plane wobbled as it was, then zoomed upward. A row of black tree tops appeared ahead, swept toward them. But the plane leaped upward like a bird, the tree tops were below, and the motor sang a song of roaring power.

Phil took his direction from the stars, headed back upon a blind course. He was flying through the night as a fish might swim in a dark sea. Overhead were the glittering points of stars. Below was a great blotch of darkness, broken only by a fast-disappearing square of golden light. That light was filled with dancing shadows, bounded by the sides of great buildings, gold letters wrought in the solid stone, forming some Sanskrit sentence.

And in the center of that lighted pandemonium stood a solemn figure, apart from the rest, head bowed upon mighty chest in sorrow. It was the ape who was not a man, nor yet an ape. The animal that had surrendered victory for something that was higher and better.

The blob of light became a small circle, no larger than a dime, then slipped behind, faded, reappeared, and vanished forever. The plane roared on. The lights illuminated the instrument board, showed the various gauges and speed indicators. By reflection it showed the ovals of blurred, strained faces, peering into the night.

Phil caught Forbes's eye, gave a forced, strained smile, and received a wan smile in return.

"I wish we could have taken that ape!" shouted Forbes.

Phil nodded. His mind was filled with the events of the past twenty-four hours. And he knew that the sudden flood of lights on that landing field omened danger. Murasingh had another plane, a lighter, faster plane, armed. Perhaps he had several planes there.

But the darkness gave them their hope of salvation. If it would only mist up with a fog he could sit back relieved. From time to time he glanced toward the east, anxiously.

The motor roared on. The east glowed with a soft light. The horn of the old moon slipped up over the horizon. Ahead showed fleecy clouds, seemingly like balls of soft cotton, drifting slowly between the plane and the ground. The glare of the moon tinged them with gold and black shadows.

And then it came. The other plane had evidently been following a compass course, watching, waiting. The rising moon had betrayed its quarry. A sudden snapping sound marked the indication of a hole in the cabin. The glass rippled into a series of radiating cracks. Another snapping sound marked another hole.

Phil snapped the plane over on one wing, sideslipped, twisted, rolled, and zoomed. The other plane was in sight now, a huge shadow of the night, swooping as an owl might swoop upon a mouse. From its bow came a spitting series of ruddy flashes.

Phil swung the plane, gave an anxious glance toward the clouds, then sent the plane sideslipping for the nearest.

The other plane followed, ripping machine gun bullets into the night. The cloud sent up welcoming streamers. Then the moonlight and stars vanished, swallowed in a sea of moisture. Phil kicked the rudder, swung the stick, glanced at the instruments, seeking to read the turn and bank indicator, get back to an even keel.

The plane righted, wobbled drunkenly, shot through the cloud and dived for the earth. Phil straightened her out, looked for another cloud. One loomed ahead and lower. From the white mist behind them shot the other plane, straight on their tail.

They flung into the second cloud, and Phil resorted to a desperate maneuver. He flung the stick over, kicked the rudder, banked, turned, whipped back the stick, and zoomed. For a moment he held himself braced. They had flipped about in a complete turn almost in a vertical bank. They stood a big chance of crashing into the pursuing plane.

But the danger passed. They shot out into the night, climbed back up into the first cloud, and then Phil turned at right angles. The cloud was thicker in this direction. They flew for more than a minute before they again debouched into the weak moonlight. The pursuing plane was nowhere in sight.

Minute after minute passed while they roared on this new course and then Phil swung sharply, back to the south. The tachometer showed the motor was performing at its best, hitting like a top. The air was bumpy along the clouds, but the plane rode through the bumps, handling splendidly. Phil knew that nothing vital had been touched by those deadly bullets.

Below appeared a cluster of twinkling lights. Farther ahead showed another blob of golden illumination. They were approaching settlements.

A mountain, jagging the glowing sky with distinctive turrets, gave Phil a landmark. Forbes pointed out a gray sweep of landscape and Phil nodded. The song of the motor died from a deep-throated roar to a monotone of droning power as the nose dipped and the ship settled toward the ground.

Below could be seen the terraced grounds of Crayson's house. Farther on appeared the sweep of the field, somewhat to the west of where Phil had expected to find it. But the distinctive landmark of the towering mountain had served as an unfailing guide.

The plane settled, turned in a spiral, circled the field, and then came on in for an easy landing. A tawny native ran out to grasp the wing tip.

As he saw the occupants of the plane emerge into the moonlight, his features underwent a spasm of surprise. Then they settled into emotionless impassivity. He made no comment in answer to Phil's question in English, or to Arthur Forbes's sharp comment in the native tongue.

They lifted the still slumbering figure, carried her to the dark house. Through a back entrance they slipped and encountered a pacing figure, haggard of eye, blue of lip, pale of skin.

Arthur Forbes explained.

Colonel Crayson heard him in utter silence, then turned to Audrey Kent.

"Can you tell how you happened to arrive at that place?"

She shook her head, slowly, thoughtfully.

"I guess it's just the same story of being drugged and kidnaped."

"Humph!" snorted the colonel. "We'll take it up with the authorities."

"The thing that can't help but impress you," went on the girl, "is their utter sincerity. The old woman I'm not so sure about. She's just a cracked old witch. But the rest are devoting their lives to a cause. Aside from the living exile of it, they treated me as a queen. Of course, they were grooming me, trying to get me to understand their life work, their ambitions, and there was the wedding that was to come—"

She broke off and shuddered.

"I think, Colonel," she went on, "it'd be better not to let Jean know anything. Just let her sleep it off and ask no questions."

The colonel fell to pacing the floor again, but it seemed that years had fallen from his shoulders. His lips were colored again, his eyes more clear.

"This is India," he said at length.

"And those people are sincere," muttered the girl. "After all, who can say there's not something in their work?"

And the thoughts of all three turned to that last sight they had had of the man-ape, standing with head bowed in sorrow, while about him raged the boiling turmoil of maddened priests.

The rays of morning light shrouded the room on a soft, gray cloak. From without came the long-drawn drone of a high flying motor.

"Murasingh!" muttered Phil.

Colonel Crayson went to his desk, buckled on a heavy service revolver.

"We'll meet him," he said simply, but his eyes were pools of glassy menace.

They stepped out into the freshness of the dawn.

"Do you suppose there's any possibility he thinks we're shot down?" asked Forbes.

But Phil with puckered brows was watching the golden ribbons of streaming dawn, and the little man speck that was circling high overhead.

The plane circled, swung, hung poised.

The rim of golden sun that slipped over the eastern hills sent soft rays bathing the circling plane.

"I wonder—" began the girl, but broke off as the plane dipped forward, slowly circled down in a spiral that became tighter and tighter.

Phil knew, tried to pull the girl away. But she remained, calm, steady, watching the plane spinning down.

It crashed half a mile away. Murasingh was a gentleman in that. He did not bring the shock of his tragic death home too closely to the Crayson house.

They persuaded the girl to go back. The men went to the plane. That which had been Murasingh was a huddled bundle of shapeless flesh. But the paper which he had pasted to the instrument board had survived the crash. Upon it appeared a brief message:

For the good of the cause.

Murasingh, high priest of the secret cult of Hanuman, leader in the two-thousand-year long experiment to return an ape to human status, had offered his life in payment of his crimes against the British law, a mute plea not to let his acts bring disaster on the great experiment he held higher than life itself.

Phil turned back to the house, his soul sickened, face pale. The words of the girl came to him. "They're so utterly sincere."

At the entrance he met Jean Crayson, with sleep-dilated eyes.

"Something crashed? I was asleep and I felt the earth jar. It shook the house. In some manner I seem to have had a horrible nightmare, and—oh, who left me this?"

She looked with uncomprehending eyes at the golden tapestry that shrouded her limbs, then sank into a chair.

"A funny dream," she said, and slipped off to sleep.

Phil gazed down at her face, noticed the peculiar contour of the eyes. After all, there was a something about them that reminded him faintly of the round eyes of the man-ape.

He reached in his pocket, pulled out the diamond ring with the strange characters engraved in its golden circlet.

Moved by some strange impulse, he stooped and pressed the ring upon the sleep-limpened fingers of the girl's left hand.

Then he tiptoed from the room.

NEW WORLDS

CHAPTER 1

Flood!

Phil Bregg was a stranger in the city, and felt the fact to the very utmost. He was heart-heavy and homesick, and he was sick of the rain. It had started the night before. On the Western cattle ranges he had seen occasional cloudbursts; never such a rain, however, as was sheeting down in the city. Being a stranger, he failed to realize that the rain was a phenomenal downpour. He took it much for granted, even when he had found the street curb-full.

Now, swaying in the subway as the train lurched over the rails, he studied those opposite him—the steaming garments, the soggy feet. It was early, too early for the rush hour. He shuddered.

Life in the big city was all right for those who wanted it, not for him. He idly noticed the headlines of a newspaper in the hands of a reader opposite him. "Unprecedented Flood Conditions Sweep Country."

Phil Bregg yawned. Then his eye caught a subheadline. "Arizona Drenched!"

An involuntary exclamation came from Phil's lips. The man who held the newspaper looked up, caught Phil's eye on the sheet, and fastened him with a look of cold disapproval. He was the type of man, Phil noticed, who was particularly good at eying people with disapproval. Phil, with the ready friendliness of the open spaces, sought to explain matters.

"Arizona's my state," he said. "I seen it was raining there, and that's sure some news."

In his own state the remark would have brought forth a smile, a greeting, perhaps a handshake. On the New York subway it merely caused people to stare at him with cold, impersonal curiosity. The man who held the paper folded it so Phil couldn't see the headlines. No one said anything.

Phil felt a red flush mounting under the bronzed skin. His big hands felt awkward and ill at ease. He seemed all hands and feet, felt ashamed, yet realized bitterly that it was these others who should feel ashamed.

A hand touched his sleeve. He looked down and to one side. A girl was smiling up at him.

"I spent a winter in Arizona," she said, "and I know just how you must feel. It's funny it's raining there. Why, down in Tucson—"

Nothing in his life had ever felt quite so good to Phil as the touch of that hand, the sound of the words, the friendliness in her eyes. And yet he realized she was violating the customs of the city simply to make him feel a little less hurt, that she had realized and understood.

"Tucson, ma'am! You know the place? Why—"

And the car suddenly, abruptly lurched to a dead stop.

Phil looked at the black walls of the subway and forgot the words that were on his tongue. He felt very much buried alive. His wet garments were clammy. There was the dank drip of death in the air.

"Ugh!" he said.

The girl's form was tense, she was staring at the windows.

There was a red light ahead, between the rails. Now a man came running forward. The motorman lowered a glass. There was a jumble of words. Out of the darkness ahead came the tail end of another subway train, backing up.

Their own car lurched into motion, started backing.

The girl gave an exclamation.

"Trouble ahead. I'll be late at the office!"

But the car continued its reverse, gathering speed. And the train ahead was also reversing.

"What's the trouble?" yelled a man in the back of the car, but the question was unanswered.

An air whistle screamed a warning signal at intermittent intervals. There came a burst of light, and the car stopped.

A guard bellowed orders.

"Everybody'll have to get off here and go to the surface. Take surface transportation to your destination. There's trouble ahead in the subway!"

There was a muttered chorus of protest. Some man was demanding the return of his fare. Others were clamoring for explanations.

"Hurry!" bawled the guard. "There's water in the subway!"

Phil Bregg didn't know cities, but he knew men, and he knew emergencies. He recognized an undertone of something that was akin to panic in the tones of the guard's voice.

"Hurry," he said. "It sounds serious." And he gripped the arm of the young lady who had been in Tucson.

She let him make a way for her through the crowd, swirled up the stairs in the midst of a confused boiling mass of jabbering people.

They emerged into a drab, wet daylight, and were greeted by water. The street was filled from curb to curb. Taxicabs were grinding forward slowly. Here and there cars were stalled. People were standing open-mouthed, up to their ankles in water, watching the street. Here and there one more determined than the rest was wading knee deep across from curb to curb.

The rain was sheeting down from a leaden sky without interruption or cessation.

Phil grinned.

"I've seen cloudbursts in Arizona," he said, "and a fellow's saddle can get awfully wet at times, but I don't think I've ever been wetter in my life."

The girl's face was puckered with concern.

"This is serious," she said, "and the water seems to be rising. There's quite a current you can feel."

Phil pointed to some of the towering skyscrapers that stretched upward until their towers were lost in the moisture.

"Well there seems to be lots of room to climb!"

She nodded.

"Let's get inside. I want to telephone the office. But I guess this is one day I can be late without any one calling me on the carpet about it. I'm due there at a little before eight."

They climbed marble stairs, pushing their way through a crowd of people who were taking refuge there from the water, people who were staring, silent, wet, looking very much like sheep huddled on a small island in the midst of a rising river.

There was a narrow lane left for occupants of the building to push their way up through the huddled figures, and Phil Bregg's broad shoulders pushed a way for the girl through this lane.

They entered a foyer which looked very normal and workaday. A cigar stand was in one corner. A uniformed elevator starter was starting the elevators. A long board of colored lights marked the progress of the cages as they shot up and down.

"Sorry," said a voice; "no loitering in the foyer. If you've got business, go on up."

"I want a telephone," said the girl.

The man in uniform made a motion with a gloved hand.

"Sorry, but there's an emergency. No loitering in the foyer. Those are orders."

He turned away to speak to a frightened-faced woman who was holding a whimpering child in her arms.

"Sorry, but you can't stay here . . ."

And the words were lost in the noise that was made by two dozen people storming into the entrance at once. For the water, in place of streaming silently past the building in a rising sheet, had suddenly reared the crest of a miniature wave, and rose a good eighteen inches at once.

Phil pushed the girl toward an elevator.

"You can get a telephone in an office upstairs," he said. "There's going to be a riot here."

The girl allowed herself to be pushed into the elevator. The door clanged, and the cage shot upward.

"There must be a broken dam somewhere," explained the girl. "There couldn't be this much water collected from the rain. And the drains are probably clogged. Heavens, I hate to think of the people that must be crowded in the subway! I hope the water doesn't get any higher!"

The elevator was whisking upward.

"Express to the thirtieth floor," said the operator.

"Thirtieth," said the girl.

The cage swung to a sickening stop, a door opened, and, abruptly, the lights went out. The elevator operator worked the handle of the door, swung the elevator control from side to side.

"Lucky you called," he grinned. "Power's off."

Phil Bregg instinctively took the arm of the girl with the manner of a protector. "Let's get to a telephone," he said. "Maybe your office won't keep open, after all."

The girl looked around her at the marble corridor, lined with doors.

"Here's an insurance office," she said in a tone that strove to be cheerful and matter of fact. "They'll have a telephone."

She tried the door, it was locked. . . .

They walked down the corridor, trying doors. Here and there a man ran past them. From the street below sounded a vague rumbling, rushing noise. It was so like the roar of traffic that neither one paid any attention to it for a while.

They finally found an open office. The place was deserted.

The girl went to the telephone, tried it, muttered an exclamation.

"The line's dead," she explained.

Through the windows the sound of the roar became louder. There was a shrill note underlying it, a wailing ululation of sound that was like a composite scream.

"Let's look out," she said. "It sounds like traffic has resumed. I can get a cab."

She walked to one of the front windows of the deserted office, peered out, gave a little scream and jumped back, hand to her throat.

"What is it? You're not hurt?" said Phil Bregg.

She motioned toward the window.

"Look!"

He pressed his face to the glass, looked down.

The buildings formed a concrete cañon, irregular in its skyline, broken here and there by much lower buildings. Phil, unaccustomed to these cañons of steel and concrete, could see nothing wrong for a second or two until his eyes focused through the dampened surface of the window upon the street below, a threadlike thoroughfare along which black objects were moving.

At first he thought traffic had started again. Then he saw it was sweeping in one direction, and in one direction alone. Next he observed that traffic wasn't moving of its own accord. A sullen, roaring stream of water was rushing in a black torrent through the street, sweeping automobiles along, sending black specks which were people swirling and spinning, sweeping them onward.

Here and there a man was swimming, trying vainly to stem the tide. A man clutched at an open window in one of the buildings as he was swept by, tried to crawl in. He was painfully slow and deliberate about it. He seemed to be hardly moving. Phil wanted to shout at him to wake up.

Then he saw that it was the power of the current which was pulling the man back into the stream. The muscles fought against the grip of the torrent, and the man dragged himself in the window.

Another man caught the side of the same window, tried to pull himself in. The water dragged him back, broke loose his handhold, sucked him into the current once more and whisked him off.

Phil located the source of the roaring sound. The water was rushing against the corners of the buildings, piling up in frothy masses of tumbled foam, just as water rushes over a submerged rock in a mountain torrent.

Phil turned back to the girl, grinned.

"Well," he said, "it's a long ways below us. Let's walk up to the top floor and look over the city. Maybe we can see where the water's coming from."

"It's fifteen stories up," said the girl.

Phil grinned.

"It'll be good exercise. Let's try it."

She nodded, white-faced, tense. They started climbing. Somewhere, in the big office building, a girl was having hysterics, and the sound of her screams echoed from the mahogany doors and the marble facings of the hall. Every once in a while some one would run down a corridor shouting.

They stopped twice to rest, then dragged themselves up to the last floor.

"There's a tower," said the girl. "Let's see if it's open."

They found a winding staircase, continued to climb, came to a door that was open. Rain was whipping through the oblong of the opening, and water was trickling down the stairs, forming in little pools.

"Looks like somebody's left the door open," grinned Phil. "Raised in a barn, maybe."

He took her elbow, and they fought their way through the doorway. As they did so, the big skyscraper shivered a little, as though a restless tremor had run through the steel framework. The tower seemed to swing slightly, oscillate.

"Must be moving in the wind," said Phil.

They pushed against the wind to the edge of the building.

The rain stung their faces, then, as the wind let up for a moment, ceased to beat against them.

They looked down.

The water was hissing along the street now. There were no more automobiles being swept along on the crest of the tide. Phil had an idea the stream was now too deep for automobiles.

But there were innumerable black dots that were being swirled past, and those black dots were screaming, shouting, twisting, turning, vanishing from sight. The street corner was a vast whirlpool into the vortex of which men were being drawn like straws.

The rain ceased abruptly.

Drifting cloud scud overhead broke for an instant, and there was just a glimpse of sunshine.

"It's clearing up!" called Phil.

And the rain seemed to have ceased over some considerable area. The patch of blue sky widened. The warm rays of the sun shone reassuringly.

A man came rushing from a little penthouse on the top of the building. In his hand he carried an instrument that looked like a ship captain's sextant. He stood at the side of the building, raised the instrument to his eyes.

For a moment he stood so, the sunshine gilding him, a morsel of a man standing outlined against the rim of the lofty building. Then he lowered the instrument, took the magnifying glass on the reading arm to his eye, whipped a watch from his pocket, and apparently saw Phil and the girl standing there for the first time.

He stared at them with eyes that were wide, seemed a little glassy.

"Over five degrees out of the proper position in the plane of the ecliptic!" he shouted. "Do you hear me? Over five degrees!"

Phil Bregg glanced at the woman, then stepped forward, interposing his bulk between her and the man.

"That's all right, brother," he said in a soothing tone.

"There's been a dam broke somewhere, and the water's coming up, but it'll go down in a little while."

The man made an impatient gesture.

"Fools!" he said. "Don't you see what's happening? The water won't go down. It'll come up and up. It's the destruction of a race!"

And he turned on his heel, strode rapidly toward the penthouse.

"I've seen 'em get the same way when there's been a stampede," said Phil, smiling reassuringly at the girl. "It's clearing up now. The water'll be going down in a few minutes. These busted dams make the water come up fast, but it goes down just as fast."

Yet there was a vague disquiet in his soul which manifested itself in his voice.

The girl nodded bravely, but there was a pallor about her lips.

"Let's go talk to that bird," said Phil, suddenly. "I'm wondering what he was staring at the sun for with that sextant. I was on a hunting trip with a chap once that could look at the sun every noon and point out right where we were on the map, and he'd never been anywheres near the country we were hunting in before."

"Yes," said the girl. "Sea captains use those instruments to check there . . . Oh, oh, look! Look! *Look!*"

CHAPTER 2

Beginning of the End

Far down the street the towers of one of the great skyscrapers loomed, topped by a central dominant tower, the whole structure dotted with windows which showed as regular black oblongs, small and dark, contrasting with the white of the building.

That tower which dominated the very sky itself was leaning over at a sharp angle. As the girl pointed the tower tilted again, checked itself, swayed, and then started to fall.

It was slow, majestic in its fall, like the descent of a mighty giant of the forest under the ax of the woodsman. The building swung over, moving faster and faster, yet seeming to take an eternity in its collapse.

When it had reached an angle where the central tower seemed to be almost at forty-five degrees, the top of the structure buckled. Masonry broke loose and crashed out as an independent shower of debris.

That was the beginning of a sudden disintegration of the skyscraper. The frame seemed to buckle in a dozen places. The speed of descent increased. The building vanished amongst the smaller edifices which surrounded it.

For an instant there was silence. The skyscraper had simply vanished. Then came a terrific cloud of fine rock dust, a great spray of water, and, after a second or two, a shivering roar that shook the consciousness, tore at the ear drums, seemed to reverberate alike through ground and air.

And, as though that roar had been a signal, the clouds swallowed up the sun again, and the sheeted rain whipped down in torrents.

The man came running out from the penthouse.

"What was it?" he asked, impatiently.

The girl's white lips moved, but made no sound.

"One of the buildings fell," said Phil, and his own voice was high-pitched with excitement, as well as a recognition of their own danger.

The man nodded.

"Foundations undermined by the rush of water, ground giving way," he said. "There'll be earthquakes, too."

His own voice had lost its excitement, seemed calm and controlled now.

"Look here," yelled Phil, "we're in danger here. Let's get out of this building. It's swaying right now!"

And the building swayed, jarred, shivered, as though touched by an invisible giant hand.

"Danger!" the man said; "there is no danger. Our fate is assured. I had hoped this might be a spot of high ground when the compensated stresses of balance should get to work, but apparently they are retarded, or else my calculations were in error."

"What do you mean?" asked Phil.

The man shrugged his shoulders.

"It's the end. Look here. I've got my complete observatory up there on the tower. I've been able to predict this for years. Not as to the time—except within a few years. The newspapers gave me a lot of publicity three years ago, then every one forgot about me. I wasn't even a joke any more.

"And now it's happening, just as I said it would. Astronomically it's been inevitable. Historically it's authenticated. Yet man would never listen."

"What," asked Phil, "are you talking about?"

"The flood," said the man. "Every savage tribe has an old legend of a great flood that swept over the earth. It rained and the waters rose. Everywhere we find geological evidences of such a flood. Yet the thing, as described, is obviously impossible. It couldn't rain enough to raise the waters of the earth to the point described in the legends of the flood.

"But there's another factor. The earth has changed its poles. There's abundant evidence that our north pole, so-called, was once the abode of tropical life, and that the climate changed overnight.

"There are mastodons frozen into the solid ice. They've been there for thousands of years. Their stomachs are filled with bulbs and foliage which were tropical in character. Yet their flesh is sufficiently well preserved so that it can be cooked and eaten.

"What does that mean? It means that in the morning they were roaming about, eating their meal of tropical fruits. It means that by night they were dead and frozen stiff and have been frozen for thousands of years.

"The earth changed its poles. That changed the tides, caused old continents to fall, new ones to arise, and water came rushing in from the ocean. It's only logical that such a phenomenon was accompanied by terrific rains as the warmer air became condensed in the colder climates which were created. That led to the belief that the flood was caused by rain. It wasn't. The rain was merely a factor.

"The so-called flood was caused by a changing of the poles of the earth. The Biblical account, in the main, is entirely correct. Except that man, trusting to his limited powers of observation and the inadequate knowledge of the time, attributed the rise of water to the rain.

"Its the same form of reasoning that made you seek to ascribe this beginning of the rise of waters to the breaking of a dam."

The man ceased speaking, looked from face to face.

"But," said the girl, "is this another flood? I thought there wouldn't be any more . . ."

The scientist laughed.

"This isn't a flood. It is merely a changing of the earth's poles. You might as well be philosophic about it. Nature always progresses. She does that by a series of wave motions. She builds, she sustains, and she destroys, and she rebuilds upon the ruins of destruction. That is the law of progress."

The building gave another shiver.

Phil took the girl's arm.

"At least," he said, "we can fight for our lives. We'll go down to the level of the flood. Then when the building starts to fall we can jump into the water."

The scientist laughed.

"And when you're in the water, what then?"

Phil Bregg clamped his bronzed jaw.

"We'll keep on fighting," he said. "If Nature wants to destroy me she's probably strong enough to win out in a fight, but nobody can ever say I was a quitter."

He became aware that the scientist was contemplating him with dreamy eyes, eyes that were filmed with thought.

"Every time there's been a destruction on a grand scale," he said, "Nature has saved a few of the species. That's the attitude that's in harmony with evolution, young man, and I think I'll just tag along with you, as long as I have the power to function on this plane of consciousness; it'll be interesting to see just what Nature does to you.

"Wait just a minute until I get an emergency package I've had prepared for just such a contingency."

And he jog-trotted into the penthouse.

The girl shuddered.

Phil Bregg looked at the girl, and grinned.

"It seems too cruel . . . too awful. Think of it, a whole city!"

Phil shook his head, solemnly.

"Not a whole city," he said, "a whole world!"

Whatever else he might have said was checked by the arrival of the man, carrying a canvas sack, slung over his shoulder with a rope.

Phil Bregg looked at the man's slight figure, at the bulging sack, and grinned.

"Pard," he said, "you may be a shark on this scientific stuff but there's a lot about packing things that you don't know. Here, let me show you how we pack a bedroll on a shoulder pack when we're out deer hunting, and have to leave the broncs and pack into a country where there ain't any water."

He took it from the man's shoulder, made a few swift motions, slung the ropes into a sort of harness, slipped the sack to his own broad back.

"There you are," he said. "See how she rides? Right close to the back. That keeps you from fighting balance all the time—"

His words were swallowed in a terrific roar. The air seemed

filled with noise, and the skyscraper upon whose summit they stood swayed drunkenly, like a reed in a breeze.

They fought to keep their balance.

"Another skyscraper down," said Phil grimly.

The scientist pointed.

"The skyline," he said, "is changing!"

And it was obviously true. From where they stood they could see the older towers of the lofty buildings of the downtown section, and they were falling like trees before a giant gale. Here and there were buildings cocked over at a dangerous angle, yet apparently motionless. But even as they looked, their eyes beheld two buildings toppling over simultaneously.

"The ones down on the lower ground are going first. The ocean's sweeping away the foundations," said the scientist. "It is all as I predicted. And do you know, they actually held me under observation in the psychopathic ward because I had the temerity to make such a prediction.

"In the face of the unmistakable evidences that such a thing had happened in the past, the absolute assurance that it was bound to happen in the future, the indisputable evidence that Nature destroys the old before she starts to build the new, mere men, serene in their fancied security, contemplated imprisoning me because I dared to see the truth. They'd have done it, too, if they hadn't finally decided I was 'harmless,' something to be laughed at.

"Laughed at! And because I dared to read aright the printed page of the book of nature that was spread out where all might see it!

"I talked to them of the procession of the equinoxes. I spoke to them of the gradual shifting of the poles, of the variation of Polaris. I spoke to them of changing stresses, of unstable equilibriums, and they laughed. Damn them, let them laugh now!"

Phil tapped him on the shoulder.

The man shook his shoulder free of Phil's hand.

"I know what's going to happen. I'll stay here and die contented, at least being privileged to watch a part of the destruction I predicted!"

The girl spoke then.

"No, we can't leave you here, and my friend has all your emergency equipment. You'd better follow."

That clinched the argument. He came at their heels without further comment.

CHAPTER 3

Into the Water

Phil Bregg led the way, setting a pace down the winding stairways that taxed them to keep up. From time to time, as they plunged downward, the building gave little premonitory shivers of a fate that could not long be delayed.

"The beginning of earthquakes," said the man in the rear. "As the new stresses and gravitational pulls start in, there will be increased disturbances. And it's going to be interesting to see whether the orbit of the moon is going to be affected. If it isn't, there'll be cross tidal influences which'll twist the very structure of the earth. In fact, there's a law of tidal limits within which tides destroy the substance. Take, for instance, the question of the asteroids. There's a very good chance that some tidal. . . ."

The words were drowned out as the whole building swayed drunkenly upon its foundations, then swung gradually, but definitely out of the perpendicular, shivered, and remained stationary again.

"Hurry!" screamed the girl.

Phil Bregg, accustomed to dangers, having the ability to adjust himself rapidly to new emergencies, turned to grin at her reassuringly.

"That's all right. Going down's faster than coming up. We're making pretty fair progress right now. It won't be long until we reach the water level."

It was hard to make any progress now. The stairways were smooth marble, and they were inclined at an angle. But the trio fought their way down, making the best speed they could, waiting momentarily for the building to come crashing down about them.

Only once did they encounter any other people. That was a man who was running down one of the corridors. He cried out some unintelligible comment to them, but they could not understand, nor did they dare to wait.

They had long since lost track of floors. Their knees ached with the effort of descending, keeping their balance on the slanting steps. They had no idea whether there were two floors or twenty below them, whether the water was rising or falling.

And, abruptly, as they rounded a corner in the sloping stairway, emerged upon a slanting corridor, they came to the water level.

Windows at the end of the hall were smashed in by the force of the water and the drifting debris which dotted the current. The water was muddy, turbulent, a sea of dancing objects. Here and there people drifted by, clinging to floating objects, or fighting their way in frantic strokes toward some building which seemed to offer a place of refuge.

"What floor is it?" asked the man.

"The eighth, I think," said the girl.

Suddenly Phil checked himself with an exclamation of astonishment.

"Look!" he said.

There was a door sagging open. The glass which composed the upper half had been broken. A big plate glass window in one side had cracked, and a big piece had dropped out of the center, which held a sign.

That sign read:

ALCO MOTORBOAT CORPORATION

And back of the plate glass, held in position on wooden supports, looking neatly trim and seaworthy, was a big motor cruiser with a cabin and a flight of mahogany stairs leading up from the floor to the hull.

"Let's get in there!" said Phil.

The girl shook her head.

"We could never get it out."

"It weighs a terrific amount," said the scientist, "but, wait a minute. There's a chance! Look here!"

The building was leaning drunkenly. The water was rising steadily, and a part of the inclined floor was already slopping with little wavelets that were seeping in through the cracked partitions.

"If we had that partition out of the way, and . . ."

As he spoke, the building shivered again. The floor rocked. The cruiser slipped from its wooden supports. The mahogany stairway crashed into splinters. The cruiser careened over on its side, then began to slip down the wet floor.

"Out of the way!" yelled Phil.

They fought to one side.

The cruiser skidded down the slope of the wet floor, hit the frosted glass and mahogany partition marked in gilt letters with the words:

OFFICES OF THE PRESIDENT
PRIVATE

Those partitions suddenly dissolved in a mass of splinters and a shower of broken glass. The sliding cruiser, moving majestically down the wet incline into deeper water, as though she were being launched down greased skids, came to rest against the far wall of the building, floating calmly upon a level keel, in water which was some six or eight feet deep.

"Regular launching," said Phil. "Personally, I consider

that an omen. That's the outer wall. If we could only get her through there she's ready for sea."

"Wait," said the scientist. "There's just a chance! If we could tow her over to that other end, and then had the partitions out between those two big windows, she'd just about go through. There's some dynamite in that sack of emergency equipment. Here, let me have it. I may bring the building down about us, but I'll make a hole right enough."

He tore at the sack with eager fingers.

Once his feet slipped on the wet floor, and he fell, but he scrambled up, dragged an oiled silk container out of the sack, opened it.

"Dynamite," he said, "and there's a bit of a more powerful explosive, something that's the last word in scientific achievement. Here, let me get over there."

He fought his way toward the side of the building, busied himself there for a few moments, then gave an exclamation of disappointment.

"Matches!" he said. "Of course I had to forget them. Those in my pocket are wet."

Phil laughed.

"Well, that's a habit of the cow country that's hard to get away from. I've got a waterproof match box in my pocket. Here they are, catch!"

He tossed over the match box. The little man caught it with eager hands. There was the scrape of a match, and then the sputter of flame and a hissing steam of thin blue smoke.

He was scrambling toward them.

"Quick!" he said. "Out of the way!"

They got out into the outer corridor. The explosion came almost at once, a lightning quick smash of dry sound that was like the explosion of smokeless powder in a modern cannon.

They were impatient, eager in their desire to see what had happened. Of a sudden that cruiser, floating so serenely upon the water, seemed a thing of refuge, something of permanent stability in this world which had suddenly swung over on a slope, where skyscrapers careened drunkenly and crashed into showers of rock dust and twisted steel girders.

They found that the explosive had done its work. There was a great jagged hole in the building, against which the water lapped with gurgling noises.

"Now to get her out," said Phil. "We'll have to have power of some sort!"

But he had reckoned without the force of the current. Already an eddy had been created in the water, and the cruiser had swung broadside, the keel at the bow scraping along the tile floor of that which had been a display room.

"The first thing is to get aboard, anyway," he said.

He took the girl's arm, piloted her down the inclined floor to the side of the boat, found that the side of the deck was too far above water for him to reach.

"I'm giving you a boost!" he said. And he shifted his grip to her knees, gave her a heave, and sent her up to where she could scramble to the deck. "Now see if there's a rope," he called to her.

"One here," she said.

"Okay, fasten one end and throw over the other end."

She knotted the rope, flung it over.

"You and the emergency stuff next," said Phil to the scientist, and he grasped him, swung him out into the water, sent him up the rope, flung up the sack, grasped the end of the rope himself, pulled himself to the deck.

"Well, well, here's a boat hook, all lashed into place, and there's a little boat with some oars, all the comforts of home!" he laughed. "I took a cruise once, down the coast of Mexico. Some of the other fellows got seasick, but I didn't. It was a small yacht, and the motion was just like riding a bucking bronco. I was used to it."

And he untied the boat hook, an affair of mahogany and polished brass. "All spiffy," he said. "Well, folks, here we go out to sea!"

And he caught the boat hook about one of the jagged

girders of twisted steel, and leaned his weight against it. Slowly, the boat swung from the eddy which was circling in the half-submerged room, and slid its bow out to the opening.

Almost at once the current caught them, whipped the bow of the boat around. The stern smashed against the side of the building with a terrific jar. The impact knocked Phil from his feet.

He rolled over, grasped at a handhold, gave an exclamation of dismay. He felt sure the shell of the craft would be crushed.

But she was strongly built, the pride of the corporation that had kept her on display, and her hull withstood the strain. She lurched over at an angle, and the water rushed up the hull, then she won free, and they found themselves out in the center of the stream of water, rushing forward, buildings slipping astern.

"We've got to find some way of steering her," yelled Phil. "If the current throws us against one of those buildings we'll be smashed to splinters. Can we start the motor?"

The scientist made no reply. He was too busy taking observations.

It was the girl, standing in the bow, who screamed the warning. The boat was swinging in toward the ruins of a collapsed structure. Just ahead of it a new building was in the course of construction, and the steel girders, thrust up through the black waters, were like teeth of disaster, thrust up to receive the boat.

In the office where it had been on display the boat seemed a massive thing. Out here in the swirling waters it seemed like a toy.

Phil Bregg ran forward.

"How much rope is there?" he asked.

"A whole coil of the light rope. Then there's a shorter length of the heavy rope."

Phil nodded.

"I'll show you how we handle charging steers in the cattle

country when we get a loop on 'em." he said.

His bronzed hands flashed swiftly through the making of knots. He swung the rope around his head, let the coil gain momentum, and swung the loop out, straight and true.

It settled over the top of one of the girders. Phil swung a few swift dally turns around the bitts in the bow, shouted to the girl to get the heavier rope ready.

Then the rope tautened, the craft shifted, swung broadside, and the rope became as taut as a bowstring.

Phil eased the strain by letting the rope slip slightly over the bitts, then, when he had lessened the shock, made a reversed loop, holding the line firm.

The current boiled past the bow. The line hummed with the strain.

"Maybe we can hold it here, for a while, anyway. The heavy rope will serve when we can get a chance to drop it over. There's a winch here, and I can probably run the boat in closer."

He turned to look behind him, and grinned, the sort of a grin that an outdoor man gives when he realizes he is facing grave danger.

"Looks like we've got to stay right here. If we break loose we're gone!"

And he pointed to a place where a building had collapsed, forming an obstruction in the current. The water fell over this like a dam, sucked in great whirlpools which gave forth an ever increasing roar.

A small boat, sucked into those whirlpools, would be capsized or crushed against the obstruction, and those who were thrown into the current would be hurtled downward.

It was at that moment that the scientist came toward them.

"The forces of stress equalization are at work now," he observed. "You doubtless notice the peculiar agitation of the water, the waving of the buildings . . . Ah, there goes our skyscraper! An earthquake of increasing violence is rocking the soil."

The skyscraper in which they had taken refuge came down with a roar, and then it seemed as though the boat was shaken as a rat is shaken by a terrier. It quivered, rocked, creaked. And the skyline flattened as by magic. Buildings came down with an accompaniment of sound which ceased to be a separate, distinguishable sound, but was a vast cadence of destruction, a sullen roar of terrific forces reducing the works of man to dust.

Where one had seen the more or less ruined skyline of a city, there was now only a turbulent, quake-shaken sea of heaving water and plunging debris.

And on the horizon loomed a vast wave, a great sea with sloping sides, a mighty wall of water that came surging toward them.

"Quick," yelled Phil, "down in the cabin and close everything. It's our only chance."

And he pushed at the girl and the scientist, got them down the little companionway into the snug cabin. He followed, closed the doors, shutting out a part of the undertone of sound which filled the air.

The interior was littered with advertising matter relating to the seaworthy qualities of the little craft, the completeness of the equipment which was furnished with it.

A sign, scrolled in fancy lettering, carried the slogan of the company: "Craft that are ready to cruise."

"Maybe there's some gasoline in the—"

Phil had no chance to finish. The boat swung. There was a jar as the mooring line parted, and then they were thrust upward, and upward. The boat veered, rolled, and went over and over like a chip of wood in a mill race. Everything that was loose in the cabin was plunged about. There was no keeping one's feet.

Phil felt his head bang against the cooking stove, struggled to right himself, and his feet went out from under him. His head slammed against the floor. The craft rolled over and over, and Phil lost consciousness.

CHAPTER 4

Rushing—Where?

He was aware of a slight nausea, of a splitting headache. He could hear voices that impinged upon his consciousness without carrying meaning. Slowly, bit by bit, he began to remember where he was. He remembered the disaster, the earthquake, that last wild rush of the tidal wave.

The words ceased to be mere sounds, and carried intelligence to his brain.

". . . must be a fire."

It was the girl who spoke.

"I should say it was a volcano, well away from us. There will probably be others," came from the scientist.

Phil sat up, and became conscious of a more or less violent rocking. The interior of the boat was almost dark. It was visible in a peculiar red half-light that showed objects in a vague, unnatural manner.

"Hello," said Phil, conscious of the throbbing in his head.

They came toward him, looks of concern on their faces.

"Are you all right?"

"Right as a rivet," said Phil. "What happened?"

"We went over and over. We all got pretty badly shaken. You got a blow on the head and have been unconscious for several hours. The sky's overcast, both with clouds and some sort of a dust. There's an illumination that makes everything seem reddish, that Professor Parker thinks is from a volcano."

Phil nodded.

"So you're Professor Parker. I'm Phil Bregg of Fairbanks."

He glanced at the girl.

"I'm Stella Ranson," she said "and I was employed as a secretary. I guess that's all over now. Ugh!" and she shuddered.

Phil found that they had placed him on one of the little berths in the cabin. He swung his feet over.

"Well, we seem to be on an even keel now. What can I do to help—anything?"

The man who had been introduced as Professor Parker shook his head.

"The sea's comparatively calm. We have reason to believe there are earthquakes going on, probably quakes of considerable magnitude. We have found there is some gasoline in the fuel tanks, and a little kerosene in the stove and storage tanks. But we have no reason to waste any of it by starting the motor. So we're waiting. There is some motion, but it's not at all violent, and there's no wind to speak of. The rain's keeping up. You can hear it on the deck."

And Phil became conscious of an undertone of steady drumming which now impressed his senses as the beat of rain.

"Well," Phil grinned, "things could have been worse. When do we eat, if at all?"

"There's some cold concentrated rations in the emergency kit," said Parker. "We were just discussing trying a fire in the kerosene cook stove and warming up some of the concentrated soup. We'll have to go pretty light on rations for a while, until we—er—experience a change."

"Drinking water?"

"The boat seems to have been fairly well supplied," said Parker. "Evidently they used her as a sort of a closing room where they could get a customer, cook a demonstration meal, and close the order."

"Then there must be some canned goods or something stored in her."

"We haven't found any as yet. There are cooking utensils, however."

Phil grinned at them.

"Find me a little flour, bacon and some baking powder, and I can give you some real chow," he said.

There was a heartiness about his voice, an enthusiasm in his manner which radiated to his listeners. Despite the blow he had suffered, Phil was a well built, husky man of the outdoors, and he was accustomed to roughing it.

Parker grinned; the girl smiled.

"Well," she said, "eat, drink and be merry, because tomorrow . . ."

And her voice trailed off into silence as she realized the deadly aptness of the familiar saying.

Professor Parker made a remark to fill in the sudden silence.

"I don't want you folks to get a mistaken impression about me. My title of 'professor' is merely a courtesy title. In fact, it has been applied in recent years more in a spirit of derision."

He was a small wisp of a man, pathetically earnest, with eyes that were intelligent, yet washed out in expression. Phil noticed that he appealed to the motherly impulses of Stella Ranson, those maternal instincts with which every woman is endowed, be she an infant or a grandmother.

"Well, I don't know why anyone should laugh at you!" exclaimed Stella, jumping to his defense. "You've been right, and it was horrid of the newspapers to give you the razz that way!"

Phil nodded his assent. "Now you are talkin', ma'am. And, if you'll get out that soup powder, professor, I'll get the fire going, and then I'll be having a look around. There are lots of trick storage spaces on these yachts, and I may run onto a bit of flour yet."

And he turned to the stove, primed it, pumped up the pressure tank, and had a fire going within a short time. Then he started an exploring expedition and, to his delight, he found that the couple had entirely overlooked a storage space in a closet back of the little sink.

This closet had a label on the inner side of the door:

"Balaced Ration for a Six Weeks' Cruise—Suggested Supplies."

Phil grinned at them.

"Probably their idea of a six weeks' cruise when they were showing the ample storage space in the boat didn't agree with a healthy cowpuncher's idea of food; but it'll last for a while."

And he set about the preparation of a camp meal.

The girl watched him with wistful eyes.

"It must be great to live in the open! Lord, how I hate office buildings and apartments! I'd like to live for a while right out in the open."

Phil grinned, "Why don't you?"

"I'm chained to an office job, and . . ."

And with an abrupt little gasp, she realized that the office and the apartment were no more; that she was having her wish for a life in the open.

For a second there was the hint of panic in her eyes, and then she laughed, a throaty little laugh.

"To-morrow," she said, "I'll take charge of the cooking. I've done quite a bit of it. But I did want to see some of your camp cooking tonight."

Phil Bregg chuckled.

"Maybe one meal of my cooking'll do what the flood didn't do, and put you under!"

And he rolled up his sleeves, looked around him.

"Thunder!" he said. "Here I am wondering about fresh water for washing, and it's raining cloudbursts outside. Let's set some buckets and see that the tanks are filled up. There must be quite a water storage system here if they advertise the capacity of the boat for a six weeks' cruise!"

"Here," she said, "you take the buckets and fill the tanks. I'll do this and you can give us a camp meal some other time."

And she stepped to the stove, took over the duties of chef, while Bregg and Parker fought their way out into the rain, set buckets where they would catch rain water, used some canvas coverings they found to act as funnels, and gradually filled the tanks.

The girl called them to a steaming, savory repast, and Phil, accustomed to camp fare, served any old way by a masculine cook of rough and ready attainments, felt suddenly intimate and homelike as he saw the table, spread with a clean cloth, and Stella Ranson's eyes smiling at him. But he had a healthy appetite, and he made a sufficient dent in the food to make him realize that the supply he had discovered in the cupboard would last far short of six weeks unless he curbed his hunger.

They resumed their water carrying after the meal. Phil, working on the outside, became soaked to the skin. But the water tanks were filling, and the boat seemed as dry as a chip, a seaworthy little craft.

There was very little wave motion, and Phil called the attention of the professor to that fact.

"Yes," said Professor Parker, "this is not the sea proper. As nearly as I can determine, we are being swept in by the inrush of a body of water. Our direction is northwesterly, or it would have been northwesterly under our old compass. I don't know what is happening now. The compass keeps veering, and I'm satisfied it is due to a magnetic disturbance rather than a change in our course.

"A continuation of our progress will take us to higher land, if the land is undisturbed. But we must remember that terrific tides and currents are being set up. It is possible we are 'drifting' on a tide that is traveling at a rate of speed which would be incredible were not the earth toppling on its axis."

"You think it is?" asked Phil.

The light of fanaticism came into the washed-out eyes of the little man. "I know it is!" he said. "I knew it would happen, I predicted it, and I was ridiculed. They laughed at me simply because their scientific ideas, which were all founded upon terrestrial stability, didn't coincide with mine."

Phil nodded. "What do we do now, keep a watch?"

Professor Parker shrugged his shoulders.

"It won't do any good. But I want to make some calculations and check over certain data I've gathered. There's no reason why you two shouldn't sleep. Then I'll wake you up if anything happens."

Phil regarded his wet clothes.

"That's okay," he said. "There's a stateroom forward. Miss Ranson can take that. I'll bunk down here in the main cabin and give these clothes a chance to dry."

The girl nodded, crossed to Professor Parker. "You'll call me if anything happens?"

He nodded.

"And promise you won't work too hard?"

He smiled up at her.

"Yes, I will. If you'll promise to sleep."

"I'll try," she said.

Phil wished her good night, caught the wistful light in her eyes, saw her lips smile.

"As for you," she said, her lips smiling, "you certainly made quite a pick-up in the subway! I'm afraid I just wished myself off on you as a nuisance."

Phil gasped. "If you only knew . . ."

But she gently closed the door of the cabin.

"Don't try to tell me," she called. "Go to sleep."

Phil Bregg removed his soggy garments.

"A wonderful girl!" he said to Professor Parker.

But the scientist didn't hear him. He was bent over the table, illuminated by the electric light which was running from the yacht's storage battery, and his fingers were dashing off figures on a sheet of paper, while his eyes had lost their washed-out appearance and sparkled with excitement.

Phil felt instant drowsiness gripping him as he lay back on the berth and pulled one of the blankets over him. Outside, the rain pelted down on the roof of their little craft, and the hypnotic effect lulled him into almost instantaneous slumber.

He felt, during the night, that he was riding a bronco in a rodeo, that the horse was taking great leaps that took him entirely over the grandstand on the first jump. That the second jump went over a range of mountains, and the higher atmosphere roared past them with a sound as of thunder.

There followed third and fourth leaps, and then a steady rhythm of roaring noise that filled the air.

Gradually the roaring subsided, and he felt the strange steed he rode coming down to earth. He breathed a sigh of relief, but there was a vague wonder in his mind as to whether he hadn't "pulled leather" on one of those long first leaps.

But he was too drowsy to worry, and he went off to sleep again.

He awoke to find his shoulder being shaken, and his eyes opened to find daylight and the face of the professor.

Phil sat upright instantly.

"You were going to call me," he said, "and let me stand watch!"

Professor Parker's eyes were reddened slightly, and his face showed lines of strain, but he seemed filled with enthusiasm and strength.

"There was nothing you could have done," he said. "And the phenomena wouldn't have interested you. On the other hand I wouldn't have missed them for anything.

"During the night a series of terrific tidal waves swept us on our course with a speed that I don't even dare to contemplate. The ocean seems to be rushing somewhere with a force and velocity which is absolutely unprecedented.

"What I am afraid of is that we may get into some huge vortex and be sucked down. I want to be able to steer clear of it if possible, and there's a little wind. Do you suppose we could set a sail?"

"It isn't a sailboat. It's a motor cruiser," said Phil, "but we might be able to get something on her that'd give us a chance to steer a bit, not to go any place, but to keep her pointed. Where's Miss Ranson?"

"Asleep. She came out about midnight, or what would have been midnight, and said she hadn't slept much. But she went back, and I think she's asleep. It's only four o'clock in the morning now, but the sun's up."

Phil looked out of the porthole.

"Why, it's quit raining!"

"Yes. It's been clear for three hours. I've been trying to check our progress by the stars, but they've changed position so rapidly I came to the conclusion the earth was still spinning.

"However, about half an hour ago it steadied down, and the course of the sun seems quite normal, around a plane which would indicate we are in the southern hemisphere, and, I should say, not a great distance from the new temperate zone. We may find the climate quite delightful."

Phil Bregg reached for his clothes, kicked off the blanket.

"Maybe we'll find a new continent or something."

The tone of the scientist was dry.

"Yes," he said, "maybe!"

In that moment Phil realized how utterly hopeless the man considered their plight. He was not expecting to live long, this strange man who had been predicting the catastrophe for years, but he was putting in every minute taking astronomical observations, checking data.

Phil grinned.

"How about breakfast?" he asked. Professor Parker frowned.

"I am afraid," he said, "that we will have to regulate the rapidity with which we consume our somewhat meager stock of rations. Now it is obvious that—"

The door of the little stateroom opened, and Stella Ranson stood on the threshold, smiling at them. She looked fresh as some morning flower glinting dew encrusted petals in the sunlight.

"Good morning, everybody; when do we eat?"

"Come on in and act as reinforcements," grinned Phil. "The professor doesn't need much food, and he's getting the idea that we should go on a diet or something. Now let's get this thing organized, professor. You act as chief navigator and collector of data. Miss Ranson can take charge of the interior, and I'll handle all the rough work and keep the crowd in grub. What do you say?"

"How can you keep us supplied with food when there is no food to be had?" asked the professor. "The world is devoid of life. There isn't so much as a duck within sight, and, if there were, we are without means to reduce it to food."

Phil grinned.

"You don't know me. I've never gone hungry for very long yet, and I've been in some mighty tough country. Once down in Death Valley the boys thought they had me stumped, but I fooled 'em by feeding 'em coyote meat and telling 'em it was jackrabbit meat I'd cut off the bone."

Professor Parker shook his head, unsmilingly.

"Oh, well," grinned Phil, "I'm going to rig a sail. You can argue with Miss Stella. I think she'll do more to convince you."

And Phil went up on deck to survey the mast, figure on a sail. The sunlight felt mellow and warm, and he stretched his arms, took a deep inhalation of the pure air, and then, as his eyes swept the horizon, suddenly blinked, rubbed his hand over his eyes, and shouted down the companionway.

"Hey, there. Here's land!"

CHAPTER 5

A Tree-Top Landing

No storm-tossed mariners, lost in an uncharted sea, ever greeted the cry with more enthusiasm. They might have been at sea for weeks instead of hours, the way they came swarming up the stairs. Even Professor Parker's face was lit with joy, and with a vast relief.

The upthrust mountain which reared above the ocean was close enough to show the fronds of foliage, the long leaves of palms that were like banana palms.

"Thought you said we were in the temperate zone," said Phil. "This looks like what my geography said the South Sea Islands looked like."

The scientist nodded.

"Quite right. I said we were in the new temperate zone. I didn't say anything about what zone it had been."

"But," protested the girl, "how could we have left New York yesterday and been swept down into the tropics?"

The professor grinned.

"That's the point. We weren't. The tropics were swept up to us. Take a bowl of water, put a match in it, turn the bowl. The match doesn't turn. That's because the water doesn't turn in the bowl. There isn't enough friction between the glass and the water to turn the bowl and its contents as a unit.

"To a more limited extent that's true of the earth, although I've had trouble getting my scientific friends to believe it. Simply because the water hasn't lagged behind in the daily rotation of the globe is no sign that it wouldn't lag if the motion were changed.

"The earth has been rotating in one way for millions of years, and the water has fallen into step, so to speak. Now look at that island. See how rapidly it's going past. Looks like we're moving at a terrific speed, but the earth is evidently swinging true on its new orbit.

"However, I look for the motion of the water to cease shortly. There should be a backwash which will do much to stem the force of the rushing water . . . Unless I'm mistaken, here it comes. Look there to the south. Isn't that a wall of water? Sure it is, a massive ground swell. It's moving rapidly. We must be in a very deep section of the ocean, or it would be breaking on top.

"Let's get down and close everything tightly."

"Judas Priest!" groaned Phil. "Have I got to ride some more bucking broncos?"

"Quite probably," was the dry retort, "you'll have worse experiences than riding high tidal waves, my young, impatient, and impetuous friend!"

They tumbled back down the companionway again, battened everything down. The wave struck them before they were aware of it. They were swung up, up, up, and then down, then up again on a long swell, then down.

Then there was a roar and a smaller wave, the crest curling with foam, came at them. The roar sounded like a cataract.

"We'll go over sure," said Phil, but he spoke with a grin. Fate had handed him so many buffets of late that he was beginning to take it all as a joke.

The wave hit them, but the little craft, angling up the foaming crest, kept on its keel, and the top of the wave went boiling by, leaving them rocking in a backwash.

"Now," said Professor Parker, "that should mark the beginning of some turbulent water, with, perhaps, a storm. Let's see where our land is."

And he thrust a cautious head through the companionway, suddenly ducked down.

"It's right on us!" he yelled.

Phil jumped up, and was thrown from his feet by a jar that shivered the boat throughout its length. Then there was a scraping sound, and the crash of splintering wood.

The boat listed over at a sharp angle, held for a moment, then dropped abruptly to the tune of more splintering noises. Phil's feet skidded out from under him. He flung up an arm to protect his head, and came to a stop on the berth where he had spent the night. A moment later Stella Ranson catapulted into him, breaking the force of her fall by his arms, which caught her in a steady firm grip.

"Easy all," said Phil. "Where's the professor? This looks

like the end of the boat. All that splintering must have meant
the timbers are crushed to smithereens!"

He scrambled to his feet, bracing himself, holding the girl
against the sharp incline of the deck.

"Great heavens, we're up a tree," he said.

The voice of the scientist came from one side of the cabin
where his watery eyes were plastered up against a porthole,
surveying the countryside.

"We are not only up a tree," he said, "but we seem to be
pretty well lodged there. We rode in on the crest of a wave
which deposited us in the branches of this tree. I do not know
the species, but it seems to be something like a mahogany
tree. Undoubtedly, it is a tropical tree.

"We have sustained injuries to our boat, and the wave is
quite likely to be succeeded by other waves. There's higher
ground up the slope of this mountain, and I suggest we make
for it without delay."

Phil grinned at the girl.

"Translated," he said, "that means we've got the only tree-
climbing boat in the world, and that we'd better beat it while
the beating's good. Let's get that rope and put some knots in
it. Then we can lower down our blankets and provisions. Personally, I'm a great believer in having all the comforts."

They fought their way to the outer deck of the boat, found
that a jagged branch was stuck through the hull, that the
boat would not float without extensive repairs first being
made. There followed a period of activity, during which they
knotted a rope, lowered down bundles of blankets and provisions.

Finally, they were safe on the ground, the boat marooned
high in the tree, more than twenty feet above the ground.
The waters had receded and roared a sullen, although diminu-
tive surf, some twenty yards away from the roots of the tree.

"Well," said Phil, "I always hated to carry camp stuff on
my back, but we can't go hungry, so here's where I start. This

is entirely in my department. I'll make a couple of trips with the heavier stuff and then we'll be established in camp."

The other two protested, but Phil adhered to his statement, refusing to allow them to participate in the work of carrying the camp equipment up the slope. He divided it into two huge bundles, so heavy that neither the scientist nor the woman could lift them from the ground. Yet Phil swung one of the big rolls to his shoulder, and led the way up the slope.

They found a trail which Phil pronounced to be a game trail, although there was no sign of game. They followed this trail through a tangle of thick foliage to a ridge, up the ridge to a little shelf where a tree and an overhanging rock furnished shelter.

Here they made camp, some three hundred feet above the level of the ocean. Phil suggested they go higher, but the scientist, taking observations by holding his small sextant on the sun, insisted that the world had finished its weird toppling. He was inclined to think the poles had changed positions by a long swing of the globe, and that a new equilibrium had been established.

While he could make no accurate calculations in advance of knowledge of where the island was upon which they had effected a landing, he was inclined to think that the site of the new north pole was somewhere in the vicinity of England.

But all was mere conjecture, and Phil Bregg was more interested in matters at hand than in abstract scientific problems.

He made a trip back to the boat, brought up the second bundle of provisions, blankets, tools which he had taken from the yacht, and started making a camp with a dexterity which brought forth little exclamations of admiration from the girl, and approving nods from the scientist.

"Now," said Phil, "what we need is a little more knowledge of what sort of a place we're in, and maybe some fresh meat. That means weapons. I've got a hand-ax, and I can sharpen up a sort of Indian spear and harden the point in the fire. That might net us a hog, or maybe a rabbit, if they have rabbits.

"But I saw some hog tracks on that trail, and while the up-heaval may have washed some of them away, and may have frightened the balance of them into cover, I'll see what can be done."

He built a fire, cut down a hardwood sapling, trimmed it into a pointed spear, hardened the point in the fire, Indian fashion, and grinned at his audience.

"Here's where the hunting instinct comes in, and where the knowledge of reading trail I've picked up is going to help. You folks just promise me you'll stay here. I'll scout around. It's pretty hard to go out in a strange country where there's a heavy growth of brush and timber, and find your way back, unless you're accustomed to it. So don't leave the place.

"I'll be back inside of a couple of hours, and I may have game."

The girl promised to wait in camp. The scientist showed no disposition to leave. He was propped with his back against a stone, a pencil and notebook in his hands, jotting down im-pressions.

"And only put dry wood on that fire," warned Phil.

"Why?" asked the girl.

"Wet wood makes a smoke."

"But don't we want to make a smoke? Shouldn't we signal?"

Professor Parker favored her with a peculiar glance.

"To whom," he asked, "did you contemplate sending a signal?"

And, as realization of their predicament thrust itself once more upon the girl's consciousness, Phil softened the blow for her with a grin and a joking remark.

"I want to save the smoke to cure a ham I'm going to bring in," and he swung the spear into position, and started up the slope, climbing steadily, yet stealthily.

* * *

He reached the summit of the peak within a matter of fifteen minutes, and was able to confirm his original impression
that they were on an island. It was not over two miles broad,
but seemed to stretch for eight or ten miles in a general
easterly direction. It was a tumbled mass of jagged crests and
Phil strongly suspected that what he was seeing as an island
was merely the top of a high mountain range which had been
entirely above water before the world had swung over in its
change of poles.

He followed a game trail, saw fresh pig tracks, heard a
rustle in the brush. A little darting streak of color rushed
across the trail, and Phil flung his spear and missed.

He chuckled.

"Better have used a rope," he said to himself, and went
after his spear.

He had not yet reached it when he heard a deep-throated
grunt behind him, the swift patter of hoofed feet on the trail.
He sent a swift glance over his shoulder, and saw a wild boar,
little eyes red with fury, curved tusks champing wickedly,
charging at him. The boar was very high of shoulder, very
heavy of neck, long of head and tusk. And it was savage beyond description.

Phil made one wild leap for his spear, caught it up, tried
to whirl.

The boar was on him before he had a chance to swing the
spear around so the sharpened end faced the charging animal.
But he did manage to make a swift, vicious thrust with the
butt end. The wood caught the animal flush on the tender
end of the nose, deflected him in his charge, sent him rushing
past, knocking the spear from Phil's hand, throwing Phil, himself, off balance.

But Phil recovered, grabbed at the spear again, waited for
the animal to turn.

The boar, however, seemed to have had enough. He swung
from the path into the thick foliage and vanished from sight,

although the branches continued to sway and crack for some seconds after Phil had lost sight of him.

Phil gripped the handle of his spear, surveyed a skinned knuckle, and grinned.

"Well," he said to himself, "that's the first lesson. Hang on to your weapons. That was a nice ham that went away, although he might have been a bit tough, at that."

He was commencing to enjoy himself. Being out in the open, with nothing but his hands and a sharpened spear of hardwood with a fire hardened point, called for his knowledge of woodcraft, made him feel the thrill of the hunter.

He took careful marks so that he would have no difficulty in returning to the proper peak when he was ready to come back. Those landmarks were the significant ones which would have been overlooked by an amateur woodsman, yet which would be always visible from any direction.

Phil found himself surveying his clothes, wondering if the girl knew how to sew. It began to look as though they would be forced to make clothes of skins, fashion a shelter, cache away food.

He saw that there were some species of fruits on the trees, and suddenly remembered that he was hungry. The fruit looked edible, and Phil picked a tree which was not so large but what he could climb it, leaned his spear against the bole, and started up.

He reached the top, pulled off some of the fruit that was soft enough to eat, sliced away a thick, green skin, and found that the interior was pink, slightly acid, rather sweetish. There were seeds in the interior as in a cantaloupe, and Phil scraped out the seeds, cut away slices of the thick fruit, and devoured them eagerly.

But his stomach craved meat, and he realized that it was the part of wisdom to conserve his reserve rations. Therefore, the situation called for a kill of some sort. So he started to slide down the tree.

He had reached a point in the lower branches some ten feet from the trail, and directly above it, when a very slight motion in the shadows attracted his attention.

He froze into instant immobility.

No one but a woodsman would have seen that flicker of moving shadow within shadow, but Phil had trained his senses until they were as alert as those of a wild animal, and he not only saw the motion, but he sensed the menace of it with some subtle sixth sense which placed him on his stomach along the overhanging limb.

A moment later the motion became substance. A dark-skinned man, naked save for a breech cloth which was wrapped about his hips and middle, emerged into the sunlight which patched the trail.

CHAPTER 6

Jungle Death

Phil saw the woolly head, the wide nostrils through which a piece of white bone had been thrust. He saw, also, that the man's eyes were on the ground, that he was following trail, and realized, with a sudden thrill, that the trail he was following was Phil's own shoeprints in the loamy soil.

The man carried a bow in his hand, an arrow ready on the string. There was a quiver over his shoulder, and in this quiver were some dozen arrows, their feathered tips showing as bits of gaudy color against the darkness of the foliage covered mountainside.

There could be no mistaking the menace of the man's approach. It was the approach of a killer stalking his kill, of a hunter crawling up on his prey.

The bare feet of the savage made no sound upon the trail. His advance was like the advance of a dark cloud sliding across the blue sky, ominous, silent, deadly.

Phil realized the danger to the girl and the scientist. Unversed in woodcraft, they would fall easy prey to such prowling savages. It became imperative for Phil to ascertain whether the man was alone or whether he was but the outpost of a large force, scouting up the slope.

And the quick eyes of the savage would soon see the telltale tracks leading to the tree, the rough spear which was thrust against the bole. Phil had no doubt the arrows in the quiver were tipped with a deadly poison. The man had but to fling up his bow, send an arrow winging to its mark, and Phil Bregg would be killed as swiftly and mercilessly as one shoots a puma down from a tree.

There was but one thing to do—to steal a page from the hunting tactics of the puma himself, and Phil flattened himself on the limb, tensed his muscles.

The native came to the point where the tracks turned. He grunted his surprise, started to look up.

Phil dropped from the limb.

But the man-made shoes with which civilized peoples clothe themselves are far inferior to the sharp claws of a mountain lion, when it comes to jumping down from branches which overhang trails, and Phil's feet, slipping from the smooth bark of the limb, threw him off balance, and made him bungle the noiseless efficiency of his spring.

He came through the air, arms and legs outspread, trying to imitate the lion, but resembling some huge bat. The native, moving with that swift coordination which characterizes those who have lived their lives in the wild, whether beast or man, jumped back and flung up his bow.

But Phil didn't miss entirely. His clutching hand caught a tip of the bow as he went down, and jerked it from the hand of the naked savage. And Phil, remembering several occasions when he had been pitched from his saddle by the fall of a horse, managed to get his legs in under him by a convulsive motion of the stomach muscles.

He lit heavily, the bow flying to one side, the arrow flipping from the string.

The savage uttered a yell, and gave a leap forward.

Phil was still off balance.

He felt the impact of the brown flesh, the sudden tenseness of the iron-hard muscles as the man threw himself upon him, reaching for his throat.

Then Phil managed to get his shoulder under the savage's stomach, got his heel dug into the loamy soil of the trail, and straightened, sending the savage up and off balance.

The man slipped to one side, recovered himself with cat-like quickness, and leapt forward. His teeth had been filed to points, and now, as he leapt, his mouth was open, snarling like an animal. The lips were curled back, and the white of the filed teeth showed as a twin row of menace.

Phil Bregg knew something of the science of boxing, knew the deadly effect of a blow that is not delivered helter skelter, but is well timed.

Phil Bregg snapped his right for the jaw.

The gripping hands were almost at his throat when his blow, slipping under the naked, outstretched arm, crashed home on the button of the jaw.

As the blow struck, Phil lowered his shoulder, gave a follow-through which sent the savage's head rocking back, lifted him from the heels of his feet, hurtled him through the air, smashed him down upon the dark soil of the tropical forest with a jar that shook the leaves of the trees, dislodged Phil's spear, and sent it slithering down the side of the tree.

Phil jumped on the savage, wrested the quiver of arrows from his back. As he had expected, he found that the steel tips of the arrows were discolored by some dark substance which was undoubtedly a poisonous preparation.

The savage was unconscious, and seemed likely to remain unconscious for some time. Phil picked up the bow, tested the twang of the string between his thumb and forefinger. The bow was a powerful one, and the taut string gave forth a resonant note like the string of a violin.

Phil dragged the native away from the trail, covered the inert form over with some heavy leaves he cut from a low shrub with his pocket knife, possessed himself once more of his spear, and slung the quiver of poisoned arrows over his shoulder. Then he strung an arrow on the bow, ambushed himself back to a tree, and waited.

If there were more natives coming, Phil wanted to be in a position to attack upon terms which would give him something of a chance, even if it was a slender one. This, he realized, was no sporting event in which he should make of the conflict something of the nature of a game. This was a life and death struggle in which he must meet cunning with cunning, ferocity with ferocity, and win, not only for the sake of his own safety, but for the safety of the girl as well.

However, there seemed to be no more savages treading the trail. Phil heaved a sigh of relief. That meant this single native, probably on a hunting expedition, had come across the tracks of Phil's boots in the soil, and had followed them, intent upon gathering a head for his collection, and without bothering to back-track to find out where the man had come from.

Phil stepped out from cover, uncertain as to whether to proceed with his explorations or to return to the camp and make certain that the others were safe.

He finally decided that the savage, upon regaining consciousness, would seek to follow his trail, and knew that if he left a plain trail back to the camp he would simply be bringing danger upon those whom he wished to protect.

So he started along the trail, running lightly upon the balls of his feet, the quiver thumping his back, the arrows rattling against the sides of the container. He wanted to find a stream of running water. If he could do that, he felt reasonably certain of his ability to shake off the man who would undoubtedly try to follow.

He found the stream in a little cañon between two of the headlands. He turned, as though he were going downstream, and was careful to leave a track on the bank, showing the direction in which he had plunged into the water.

As soon as he was in the stream, however, he reversed his direction and waded up it until he found a rocky ledge upon which he could emerge without leaving any imprint.

He followed this ledge for several hundred yards, then found an overhanging tree from the branches of which there hung a green creeper. By taking hold of this creeper he managed to swing far out into the tangled mass of vegetation before he dropped.

He was satisfied that a single man, trying to follow his trail, would be baffled. A party of eight or ten, by dividing on either side of the stream, might be successful, but the lone savage, stalking him unaided, would be at a loss.

Phil fought his way through the dense tangle of vegetation, searching for a game trail by which he might make a more silent progress.

A slow sound, throbbing the air, keeping tempo with the pulse of his blood, suddenly impinged upon his consciousness. He became aware then that he had been hearing this sound for some time without taking conscious thought of it.

It was a sound which had started at so low a note that it had insinuated itself upon his senses with a gradual insidious approach that had made it seem a natural part of the physical environment, rather than something new and startling.

Once aware of it, he paused to listen. It was the throbbing of a drum. From the sound, it must be a distant drum, massive, resonant. The sound came from no particular place, seemed no louder in one quarter of the compass than in the others. Yet when he stopped to listen to it, when he took conscious note of its existence, the sound was sufficient in volume to dominate the whole island.

It was, he gathered, some master drum which was used to transmit signals. He had heard of such drums, had heard of messages which were transmitted by savage tribes with the speed of telegraphed news.

He tried to take note of the pulsations.

To his ear they seemed to be entirely alike, a monotone of rhythm that came and went, ebbed and flowed, swelled and died.

The drum rose louder and louder in its tone, then began to die away. The notes seemed to possess less volume. Then the beating became so low that it was hard for the senses to tell whether the impulses they detected came from the pound of the heart or the throbbing of the drum.

When Phil had about convinced himself that the sound had ceased entirely, the wind swung a little, and, for a moment, he could hear it again distinctly. Then the breeze ceased to rustle the leaves, and there was no more sound.

He was about to start forward when he heard another drum. This sound could be located. It was away off to the left. While it was deep in its tone, nevertheless there was not the heavy resonance about it that characterized the beating of that master drum.

More, he sensed at once that this drum was sending some message. There was a rapidity about the strokes, a variation in the periods of pulsation, which was at once apparent.

He tried to line up the sound accurately, and fancied that he had it pretty well located, when it ceased abruptly. There was none of the gradual tapering off into silence which had characterized the other sounds from the big drum. It was simply that the drum was beating with steady resonant volume at one moment, and at the next it had ceased.

Phil listened.

The silence of the tropical jungle hemmed him in.

Then he heard something else, a rapid pound, pound, pound, that seemed to jar the earth. He crouched down in the shadows, and waited. The pounding grew louder, kept the same rhythm. A dark shape, moving through the trees, became visible.

Phil saw it was a savage, naked except for the loin cloth, and that the man was running down some established trail. The sound of his bare feet thudding on the ground was the noise that Phil had heard, some little time before he glimpsed the runner, and that thudding of the feet continued some little time after the naked savage had vanished in the jungle growth.

Phil waited, aware now that he must move with caution. He was on an island that was peopled with a savage and war-like tribe. He had no weapons worthy of the name, no means of escape. And he had the responsibility of caring for two people, both of whom were utterly helpless as far as any actual ability to care for themselves against any such obstacles.

Phil decided that he would work his way back to the camp, taking care not to leave a trail that could be followed, warning the two that they must take no chances of showing themselves, getting them, perhaps, in a better place of concealment.

He started through the brush, realizing that the trail which the native had followed was but a short distance below him. Evidently that trail had crossed downstream, then zigzagged up on the side of the stream he had crossed.

He had not taken more than a single step when he heard the smaller drum again, volleying forth a message, and almost at once the big master drum started its deep-throated booming.

Phil, standing there, perspiring, alarmed, every sense alert, could not be certain, but he felt that the big drum was relaying the same message that had been received by the smaller drum, sending it booming forth to every part of the island.

For there could be no question now but what the big drum was conveying a message. The change in tempo of the throbbing sounds could be readily perceived.

Suddenly the noise of a rifle shot cracked out, and it was followed almost at once by two more shots.

The noise of the reports drowned out the sound of the drums as they echoed from crag to crag.

Then, after the noise of the shots had died away, there sounded the noise of the big drum again, booming forth a series of repeated signals. There were three rapid beats, a delayed moment, then two slow beats, a pause, and then one single booming beat of noise. Following that was silence, a silence which lasted for several seconds. Then the big drum repeated the signal.

Phil listened to the repetition of that signal for several minutes, and came to the conclusion, without having any evidence to base it on, other than the fact that the smaller drum was silenced, that the big drum was booming forth something in the nature of a call signal, waiting for a reply from the smaller drum.

Phil decided that the girl and Professor Parker could hear the signal of the master drum, which was booming in increased volume with every repetition. Indeed, it seemed that the signal must carry to every part of the island.

And Phil felt certain that the warning conveyed by that drummed signal would be sufficient to apprise the girl of the presence of hostile savages, and that she would use every precaution to insure against discovery.

The savage he had found had been armed only with bow and arrow. The sound of the rifle shot indicated the presence of a more civilized man, and it was very possible that some other white man, better armed, had been caught by the same tidal currents which followed the shifting of the poles of the earth, and that those currents had deposited him upon the same island.

Phil changed his plans, determined to make his way toward the place from which he had heard those rifle shots, particularly as they had seemed to be almost in the same locality as the source of the drum beats from the smaller drum.

Phil had an idea speed meant everything. He cast caution

to the winds, broke from his concealment, found the trail the running savage had been following, and set out along it with swinging strides that devoured distance.

But Phil was taking care lest he should run into an ambush, and his trail-wise eyes took in every detail of his surroundings.

The trail was beaten hard by naked feet. It wound like a black ribbon through the dense growth of tree and shrub, vine and creeper, following the contours of the upper levels with a slope that showed some considerable engineering efficiency in its construction, an efficiency which is the result of laborious study in civilized schools, yet which comes instinctively to game animals and savages.

Phil dropped down a gully, following the trail, saw where a branch trail turned into the shrub on a shoulder of the next ridge, and decided to follow that branch trail. He was, he realized, getting close to the place from which that shot had sounded. Had he been trailing a deer hunter, he would have started to look for a dead deer along in here.

He slowed his pace, moved with every sense alert, his eyes taking in every bit of the slope, penetrating the shadows of the jungle.

It was the sight of a brown foot protruding into a patch of sunlight which sent him jumping into the shrubbery beside the trail, the bow raised, arrow on the string.

But the foot remained motionless, the toes pointing upward.

Phil stepped forward, silently, cautiously.

The foot was motionless. As he walked, a leg came into view above the foot, then another foot and leg, the latter twisted into a grotesque position.

Then, rounding a tree trunk, he saw the man.

CHAPTER 7

The Murderer

He knew, then, the target that had received those rifle bullets. The man had been struck in the back, a little to one side of the right shoulder blade. The bullet had ranged through the chest, emerging from the left side. Death had been instantaneous, and the heavy drum stick, padded with a ball of animal hide which the fingers of the right hand still held, told the story.

There was a huge drum suspended from the branches of the tree by a twisted grass rope. The drum was made from a section of a hollowed tree trunk, and the hide which stretched across it was apparently exceedingly heavy. Phil found himself wondering if it could be a strip of elephant hide.

The drummer was dressed as the others had been dressed, simply in a loin cloth. But there was no ivory ornament thrust through his nose, although the skin of the chest showed a species of tattooing.

Phil stepped around the body, mindful of the presence of the man with the rifle, mindful, also, of the fact that the savage had been shot down without warning, and in the back.

The possibility that the man who had fired that rifle shot would be a friend and ally became more remote as Phil reconstructed the scene of the shooting.

The drummer had been standing before the drum, in the very act of beating the resonant hide. Then had come the shot, and the force of the bullet had hurled him to one side, sprawled him in the position in which he now lay.

But how about the other shots?

Obviously this man had been taken completely by surprise. That meant that he had not received any warning of the presence of his slayer until the bullet had crashed him down into death.

He must, then, have been killed with the first shot.

Phil looked around, and suddenly recoiled with horror.

He had found the mark of those other bullets!

She was a slip of a girl, hardly more than nineteen or twenty, slim formed, delicate of limb, shapely of body. She, too, was attired in nothing save a loin cloth, and even in death the beauty of her figure was apparent. Sprawled as she was upon the leaves of the forest, her body disfigured by two bullet holes, she remained beautiful with that grace which is the property of youth alone.

She had been running, Phil decided, when the shots had brought her down. The first shot had dropped her, the second had finished the gruesome task.

Evidently she had been standing beside the man when he had been beating the drum. The first shot had killed the man, sent her into headlong flight. And Phil, reconstructing the scene, remembered the short interval between the first shot and the following shots, realized that she had covered quite a bit of space in that brief interval.

She had evidently flashed into flight with the speed and grace of a deer, only to be brought down as ruthlessly as though she had, in fact, been a fleeing denizen of the forest.

A sudden rage possessed Phil Bregg. Whether these people were hostile or not, the man who had fired those shots, be he native, American or European, was a coward and a murderer.

By picking the angles of the bullets from the positions of the bodies, Phil was able to determine almost exactly the spot from which the shots must have been fired.

It was a little ridge, some fifty yards away, to which there was a cleared path in the jungle. It was obvious that the man who did the shooting must have been on this ridge, equally obvious that he was not there any longer, or, if there, that he was making no display of hostility, since Phil had been in plain sight of the point when he had walked up to the body of the drummer.

Phil concluded the man had moved away, and he walked boldly along the cleared space, straight to the ridge. He found that he had been correct in his surmise. There was no one in sight when he arrived at the ridge, although there remained ample evidence that a man had been there.

There was a burned match, the glittering gleam of three empty rifle shells, lying where the ejector of the repeating rifle had thrown them. There was, on a closer inspection, a little pile of dark ash which smelled strongly of stale tobacco. The man evidently smoked a pipe, and had scraped out the bowl of its dead residue before refilling it with fresh tobacco.

Phil consulted the trail, and found the track of feet that were covered with shoes, made after the fashion of civilized footwear. He got to hands and knees and surveyed the ground. He found a few grains of fresh brown tobacco, still pleasantly fragrant and moist.

The man had evidently refilled his pipe after the shooting, and the burned match indicated that he had lit his pipe. Phil was armed only with a bow and arrow, a rude, home-made spear. He sensed that this man would be hostile, that he was a cold-blooded murderer. The deaths of the savages had shown his utter ruthlessness, the fact that he had filled and lit his pipe indicated some of the callousness of his nature.

But Phil knew that the island swarmed with savages, and he realized that he could expect short shrift should he fall into the hands of these savages. Undoubtedly the ruthless slaying of the man at the drum, and the young girl who had been with him, would stir the savages to a rage against all intruders upon their island, even had they been friendly in the first place. And Phil, reflecting upon the attitude of the man he had seen stalking him with such deadly ferocity, knew that there had been no opportunity for friendly relations.

There remained, then, his predicament, between the devil and the deep sea. There was a man somewhere ahead who was a murderer. But, at least, he might be prevailed upon to give shelter to his own kind, and he evidently possessed but little fear as to his own safety.

He had killed the natives and then moved away, doing the whole thing as casually as a hunter might shoot a rabbit.

Phil took up the trail, moving cautiously.

The ground was too hard to leave him any footprints other than an occasional heel mark. Apparently the man he sought had walked calmly and serenely straight down the trail.

Phil sniffed the air.

He thought he detected the odor of tobacco smoke, and pushed forward more rapidly. If his man was smoking it would be easy to tell when he was within some distance of Phil.

The odor of burning tobacco became stronger, held the unmistakable tang of a pipe about it. The trail Phil followed grew broader, another trail intersected it, and Phil became conscious of a blue cloud of smoke drifting through the branches of some trees a hundred yards away.

He moved cautiously, convinced himself the smoke came from pipe tobacco, burning fragrantly. Its very volume caused Phil some misgivings. But, he reflected, the man might well be smoking some gourd pipe which held an enormous quantity of tobacco.

He worked his way cautiously toward the eddies of smoke which filtered through the trees.

He left the trail, moved through the forest like a wild animal, keeping to the open spaces so as to avoid rustling branches or breaking twigs. He had learned the art of stalking from Indians, and had learned his lessons well. His progress through the forest was as that of a drifting shadow.

He pushed through a light tangle of bush, paused behind the trunk of a tree, saw that the poisoned arrow was on the string of the bow, and then slipped out into the open.

He noticed the eddying blue of the tobacco smoke, and knew at once that he had been trapped.

For the smoke eddied from no pipe held in the lips of a man, but came instead from a rock where a little pile of tobacco had been stacked so that the burning base sent wisps of smoke from the grains of tobacco that had been piled on top of the red-hot grains underneath.

The man he hunted had, then, cunningly arranged this trap, so that any one trailing would come sneaking up on the smoke. Phil knew the answer at once, even before a cracked laugh grated on his ears.

He looked up, in the direction of that laugh.

He saw gleaming eyes, loose lips, teeth that were stained, a face that was covered with stubble, the shoulders and left sleeve of a coat that had once been white, and the black muzzle of a rifle, the latter trained directly upon his heart.

"Well, well," cackled the man, "look what walked into my little trap!"

Phil stepped forward, boldly.

"I hoped I'd find you. You seem to have means of taking care of yourself, and I seem to be on a hostile island."

He determined that he would say nothing whatever about the presence of his companions. He felt that it would be far better if this man knew nothing of the fact that a young, attractive white woman was on the island.

The rifle covered him.

"I wouldn't come no farther, and I think I'd drop that bow!" said the man.

Phil relaxed his grip, let the bow drop to the ground, shook the quiver from his shoulder, let it clatter to the ground, and then gave the man with the beady eyes his best grin.

"Captured it from a native," said Phil, trying to speak easily, frankly, as though he had no question of the ultimate friendship between himself and this man. "The chap was stalking me, so I dropped down on his shoulders and took his weapons."

The man with the rifle laughed.

"That tobacco sure smells good," went on Phil, "got any more of it?"

And he took a step forward, making it a point to walk

casually, as though he expected to be invited to sit down and join the other in a social pipe.

"That's far enough," rasped the voice. "Get back there! Get back there, damn you, or I'll shoot you just as I would a native!"

The eyes glittered, the loose lips lost their grin, and the face became a mask of menace. Phil realized the fact that the man's trigger finger was about to tighten, and he jumped back.

For a second or two there was a stark hatred, the desire to murder, a red blood lust in the eyes of the man. Then the face slowly relaxed.

"Come alone to the island?" asked the man.

Phil nodded casually.

"Yeah," he said, "I got shipwrecked."

He was trying to place the man's nationality, decided that for all his ready use of the language, he was not an American, nor was he English. He was, perhaps, a racial mixture.

The man laughed again.

"Don't lie," he said. "I know everything that goes on here on the island. There's three in your party, and one of 'em's a damned pretty woman. I want that woman."

Phil felt the red blood of rage mounting his forehead. He forgot discretion, forgot the fact that the other held him covered.

"Well, you're frank about it," he said. "That's about the way I had you figured, at that. Now try and find her, you cowardly murderer!"

But the words seemed to have no effect other than to arouse a certain amusement in the man who held the rifle.

He chuckled, and the chuckle was rasping, as unclean as his face and the sleeve of the garment that had once been white.

"Heh, heh, heh," he chuckled, "gettin' independent, ain't you? Well now, my friend, let me tell you something. I can control these natives because they fear me. I've held the whip hand over 'em all the time, and I'm ruthless.

"I've got a house around the corner of the trail that's a regular castle. I built it before the natives got hostile. Afterwards they got independent, and I had to kill off a couple. That brought about a showdown. They tried to attack me.

"When I got finished with 'em they were good dogs. I've kept other white men off this island, and there isn't a firearm on it except what I've got. I've got plenty.

"That's the way I keep the natives in line. They can't reach me, but I can kill them off whenever I want to, and I give 'em orders, rule 'em with an iron hand. That's the only way to rule if you're goin' to rule.

"I told 'em not to beat that drum down there. It disturbs my sleep when I'm taking a nap. They laid off for a while, but today they violated my orders, so I went down there and put a little of the fear of God into 'em.

"And I figured some of them might come trailing me, so I set a little trap for 'em. I hadn't figured you'd walk into it. That's the way to deal with these natives, kill off a couple of 'em every so often, then they get all worked up and start after me, I set a little trap and kill off a couple more. Then I go and live in my castle for a while until they come to their senses."

Phil held his face expressionless.

"Well," he said, "how about us, what are you going to do with us, give us shelter?"

The man laughed.

"I'll give you shelter, in a savage's belly! I'm the one that encouraged 'em in cannibalism. They did it on the sly until I came here. I got 'em in the belief that it was a good thing, to come right out in the open and do it. They never bother in here, the government, although they've got the place listed on the map.

"But I keep out the traders. It's a good system. That leaves me king of the island. I should kill you right now, but I'd rather leave you to wander around and play hide and seek

with the natives. That'll keep their mind off of me for a
while, and they need something like that to divert their attention from the little disciplining I gave them.

"Well, I'll be moving on. Don't let 'em capture you alive
if you know what's good for you. They've got pleasant little
methods of torture. They say the flesh tastes better when it's
about half cooked while a man's still alive. I don't know.
I'm virtuous. I ain't never tried it. But I hear their screams
every once in a while on a still night. The natives have a
ceremonial feast every time after there's a battle with any of
'em on the other island.

"Put up the best fight you can. They'll get you in the long
run, but while you're running around in the bush playing
hide and seek they won't be after me, and I can get in some
sleep.

"They'll get you finally. They always do get 'em. There
was a ship came ashore here a couple of months ago. Funny
weather. Funny the last couple of days, too. The damned
island settled a bit, or the ocean raised, I don't know which
it was, big tidal waves and everything. Guess that was what
brought you in.

"Must have been a hole in the sea down here to the south
somewhere. The ocean boiled past at ninety miles an hour,
judging from the roar of it. Oh, well, it's a high island, and
it's been here for a while, and it'll be here for a while again.

"The natives'll turn over the woman to me. I've got 'em sold
on the idea it's bad medicine to eat a white woman—clever,
eh?"

And the man got to his feet, disclosing a giant figure, unkempt, dirty, yet radiating ruthless power and brute strength.

"You stay right here for five minutes. You move up on this
ridge before then, and I'll save the savages a job. After that
five minutes is up you can go anywhere you damned please.

"Watch out for their arrows. They're tipped with a funny
kind o' poison. It'll numb the nerves and paralyze you for a

while, but it won't kill you. You'll come to after a hour or two
—ready to be cooked on the hoof. They say it makes the
meat taste a lot different.

"They've got a big bed o' coals, and they truss you up and
broil you a bit at a time over the slow fire. Don't know where
so many men get the idea cannibals boil 'em in a kettle. They
don't. They broil 'em. That's the only way human meat is any
good.

"So long!"

And the man abruptly stepped down from back of the ridge.

CHAPTER 8

Captives

Phil failed to heed the warning about remaining where he
was, but he knew better than to charge up the ridge. Instead,
he tried to estimate the probable direction in which the man
was traveling, and struck off into the forest, making a wide
semicircle.

He fought his way through thick growth, came to a more
open ridge, and streaked up it with the best speed he could
command. He gasped for breath, but he knew he must hurry
if he stood any chance.

In the end he missed out by a matter of a few seconds.

He felt that the tall man would turn frequently to watch his
back trail, that this would slow down his progress, and that
there was a chance to ambush him by leaping from the bush
on the side of the trail.

But he saw the shadow of the other's long-limbed progress
slipping by up the ridge while he was still ten feet away, and
he knew that it would be sheer suicide to charge through
the tangled shrubbery. The man could snap the rifle into position before Phil would have a chance.

So he remained motionless, watched the other stride by on the trail above. Then Phil slipped up to the trail.

The man was covering the ground with great strides, moving at a rate of speed which was faster than a smaller man could have traveled at less than a jog trot.

Phil watched him travel; saw, almost at once, his destination. It was a castle which had been built on a ridge of rock, a castle which was impregnable to anything except an attack by artillery.

The construction was of a cobbled concrete that made the structure gleam white in the sunlight. It was built on the top of the ridge, at the very apex of a massive outcropping of native rock.

There was but one place by which the castle could be reached and that place had a barred gate with a huge lock which stood out even at the distance from which Phil was observing it.

A wall ran around the castle, a wall that was surmounted with jagged coral and broken glass. The rock dropped away on all sides in a sheer slope that was smoothed over by the aid of concrete so that its sides were as glass. The trail ran up the winding zigzag, passed under the barred gate, and came to another gate, a mere opening in the wall.

Gunpowder might have reduced the fortress, but as far as the simple savages were concerned, armed as they were only with crude weapons, it represented an absolutely impregnable retreat in which one man could live unmolested.

Now that Phil knew the truth about the people who inhabited the island, he realized the gravity of the position in which he had left his companions, knew that it was vitally necessary that they be warned, given the real facts of the situation without delay.

He slid down the slope of the ridge, picked up the landmarks which gave him the location of the shelf of rock where he had left Stella Ranson and Professor Parker, and plunged into the dense shrubbery.

He was afraid to follow any man-made trails, and the forest growth was too thick to penetrate without losing too much time in forcing his way through the tangled mass of creepers and vines, to say nothing of the noise that would be made by such a means of progress.

But the place was cut up with trails made by hogs, trails which led in zigzags or ran directly through tangles of brush. Phil dropped to all fours and followed those trails, trusting to his sense of direction to carry him to his ultimate goal.

Twice he disturbed bands of hogs that were resting in the thickets, and they tore away with great gruntings, startled squeals, their short legs rattling and clumping over rock and down timber.

Aside from those, he encountered no sign of life, either man or beast, and finally arrived at the bottom of the ridge where he had left his party. He gave a low whistle.

There was no answer.

Fearing the worst, he started the laborious ascent, up the rock slope which led to the shelf where he had established camp.

He slipped around the screen of a bush, and came upon that which he had feared to find. The camp was in a state of confused disorder, blankets torn and scattered, the canned goods either cut open or rolling about on the rock floor. There was no sign, either of the professor or the girl, save a torn bit of cloth which had come from the girl's skirt.

Phil knew much of woodcraft, and he had trailed packhorses over long and difficult stretches of country. Now he set himself the task of trailing the raiding party which had captured his companions.

And the task was absurdly easy. The trail led up the slope and around a shoulder, where a broad, well-used trail led along a ledge of rock below which flashed the blue of the ocean.

Looking along this rocky ledge, down toward the ocean, Phil could see what appeared to be a gigantic serpent, writhing along the rocky trail. It was, in fact, a long line of men, naked, excited, walking in single file along the narrow trail, and in the center of this writhing line of brown backs and black heads appeared the light colors of the garments worn by Professor Parker and Stella Ranson.

Phil left the trail and kept to the ridge, keeping just below the skyline. He worked his way along until he could see the party below him enter a dense clump of trees. They did not emerge.

Closer inspection showed Phil the tops of thatched houses showing dimly through the trees. He knew that something had to be done, and done fast, but he was alone and virtually unarmed.

Then he thought of the strange hermit, of the gun which the hermit had held, of the big automatic which was strapped to the cartridge belt which circled the hermit's waist.

Phil had to possess himself of those weapons. How?

And, as he stood there thinking, the natives themselves furnished him with the idea which he needed. They started throbbing out a message on the big master drum.

Phil could make out the drum now, and the drummer. The drum was made of wood, and a huge savage swung a mallet as one would swing a sledge. The resonant wood boomed out its deep note, a series of signal calls.

Phil crawled on his stomach, slipping over the skyline of the ridge, like a deer slipping through a pass on the approach of hunters. Once he had passed the skyline he got to his feet, slipped down the slope until he came to the trail he had followed earlier in the day, and raced along at top speed.

His heart was pounding and his lungs laboring by the time he came to the forks in the trail. There was no time for caution, so he flung himself blindly forward, half expecting to see some hostile native arise in front of him.

But things were as he had left them when he had started to trail the killer. The two natives were sprawled out, stark in death. The big drum still hung from the tree.

Phil inspected that drum closely.

It was suspended by a long rope, and there was a sufficient surplus of rope to answer Phil's purpose.

He picked up the drumstick, swung it in a powerful blow, squarely upon the head of the drum. The booming note resounded over the island. Phil, trying to remember the sound sequence of the drumming he had previously heard, repeated the blows, imitating the first signals which had been given by the savage as nearly as possible.

He swung the drumstick for a full five minutes. Then he picked up a native spear which lay near the dead warrior, planted it in the ground, fastened a springy branch to it, tied the drumstick to the branch, and raced up the trail to a place from which he could see the castle.

He found that his ruse was working.

The owner of the place, armed to the teeth, probably seething with indignation, was coming down the steep trail from the castle with long strides, his rifle thrust forward.

Phil timed his approach, then ran back to the drum, gave a few more beats, and started twisting the ropes which held the drum. When he had them twisted tightly, he adjusted the spear at just the proper angle, affixed the drumstick and springy bow in place, and let the drum go.

The untwisting ropes swung the drum in a half circle, brought the head against the drumstick. There came a low, abortive, yet plainly audible sound from the drum, which was arrested in its progress. Then the spring of the limb slowly let the drum head slide past the stick, and the drum made another revolution, again hitting the drumstick.

It was a makeshift device, good only for a matter of a few revolutions, but it served Phil's purpose.

He ran back up the trail, plunged into the brush by the side of the divide just in time. He could see the long legs of his man coming on the run.

The drum continued at intervals to send forth low noises far different from the deep booming that had come from it when it had been struck a smart blow with the padded striker, yet noises which were of a sufficient volume to be plainly audible.

And, over all, there sounded the deep booming of the master drum.

But the long-legged giant, striding up with murder in his mind, was not a simple, trusting soul to be caught in a trap unaware. Evidently natives had tried to ambush him before, and he slowed his progress to peer cautiously into the brush when he entered the region where the undergrowth was thick enough to furnish cover.

Phil knew that it would only be a matter of seconds before the drum would cease to give forth sound, due to the relaxing of tension on the rope.

He tensed his muscles, finally determined on a rush. The man was peering cautiously and intently into the shadows. A rush seemed suicide, yet Phil could think of no other way.

He worked his feet firmly in under him, and the drum gave forth a low moaning sound, due to the rubbing of the hide-covered head of the striker, rubbing against the drum head, just as he was preparing to rush. That peculiar sound aroused the curiosity of the long-legged ruler of the island sufficiently to overcome his prudence. He started forward.

Phil charged.

The man was unbelievably quick. Yet Phil had anticipated that quickness. It was impossible that the man could have lived so long on the island, going out occasionally for food and to inflict his discipline upon the natives, without having been enough of a woodsman to protect himself against ambushes.

He jumped to one side, flung the rifle around and fired all with one motion.

The bullet missed. Phil felt the fan of its breath against his cheek.

He flung himself forward, head down, like a runner sliding head first into a base.

The gravel scratched his hands and chin. There was a cloud of loamy soil, twigs and decayed foliage thrown up. And the maneuver surprised the man with the rifle, for the second shot missed.

Then Phil's hands gripped the ankles, he flung himself up and around. The man swung the clubbed rifle. The blow caught Phil upon the shoulder, numbing him with sickening pain, but he hung on.

His adversary dropped the gun with an oath, and Phil knew that he was reaching for the automatic at his belt. Phil flung up his right hand, hooked the fingers in the belt, yanked as hard as he could, striving to get to his feet.

The tension on the belt had an unexpected result. The buckle gave way, and belt and gun thudded to the earth. The big man swung his right foot back for a kick at Phil's face, and Phil, pushing forward while the man was standing on one leg, threw him off balance.

That gave Phil a chance to get to his feet.

They faced each other, two men, each unarmed save for nature's weapons, and neither having the slightest doubt as to the sort of struggle upon which he was embarking. It was a fight to the death.

The long-armed man swung over a terrific blow. Phil ducked it and planted a swift right smash to the stomach, and had the satisfaction of hearing the tall man give a grunt of pain.

He pressed his advantage, swinging a left, right, left.

Then the long arms closed on him. But Phil knew something of wrestling, and sensed that the other was punch groggy. He broke the hold, flung him away, and set for the delivery of the final smashing blow that would end the conflict.

The tall man swung wildly, awkwardly. Phil stepped forward, easily assured of victory now. He needed but to walk inside of the swing, slam home his right, and . . .

His foot slipped on a round pebble. He lurched, back, off balance, directly in the path of that vicious swing.

He tried to dodge, made a frantic but futile effort to block the blow with his elbow. But he was falling, the fist crashed into the side of his jaw, and he saw a great flash of light, then streaking ribbons of black, then felt himself falling into black oblivion.

Something crashed the back of his head after he felt that he had been falling for hours, and he realized that it was the ground which had hit him, the back of his head thudding into the soil of the trail.

He fought with himself to keep his senses, to get his eyes open and his vision cleared.

He managed to open his eyes, but all he could see was a confused blur of dancing tree-tops against the blue of the sky. Then he saw something else, a weird figure which swung about between him and the tree-tops. Gradually that figure took form and substance. It was the long-legged man, once more in possession of the rifle, although still punch drunk, swinging the clubbed weapon in a blow that would undoubtedly brain the prostrate cowpuncher.

Phil saw the rifle swinging down, gave every ounce of will power he possessed into a last desperate attempt at rolling to one side.

He rolled, flung out his hand. He could hear the whooshing whistle of the rifle butt as it just grazed his head. Then his hand, outflung, touched a hard object.

His senses were clearing rapidly. He knew at once that his hand rested on the automatic which had been jerked from the waist of the long-legged ruler of the island.

Phil rolled over and over, clutching the belt, holster and gun in his hand.

He knew the other would fire, was raising the gun.

He jerked the weapon from its holster.

The rifle roared.

Phil scrambled to his hands and knees, his face stung by the flying particles of dirt, thrown up by that rifle shot.

"Drop it!" he yelled.

The man tried for another shot.

But he was dealing with a man who had learned the use of a short gun out in the open spaces where one must be able to shoot the head off of a coiled rattlesnake without taking time to line up the sights along the barrel.

Phil fired twice, and the bullets, plowing their way along the side of the gun stock, slammed into the right hand of the man who held it, ripping away the trigger finger, smashing bones.

With a howl of pain, he dropped the gun.

"Turn around," said Phil.

The man hesitated, then turned.

"Put your hands back of you."

The command was obeyed.

CHAPTER 9

The New World

Phil pulled the man's coat off, ripped it into shreds, bound the arms, then gave attention to the wound. The right hand was badly smashed, bleeding freely. Phil stopped the bleeding by making a rough tourniquet.

"Now," he said, "you're going to march straight to that native village, and instruct the chief to turn over the captives he's taken into your charge. You'll keep out of sight when you make the command, and I'll have the guns trained right on your back. If anything goes wrong you'll be the first to go."

The tall man was white of face, and his eyes were filled with sullen hatred.

"I can't walk. That bullet's smashed my hand all to pieces, made me sick all over."

Phil prodded him menacingly with the gun.

"You asked for it," he said. "You've done a lot of killing in your time, and I imagine you've had very little mercy for the ones that were on the receiving end of your guns. Now you're going to be a good dog and get started, or I'm going to put you out of the way right here. It's either your life or the life of two who are worth a hundred of you, and if you think I'll hesitate about shooting, you're just a bad judge of character."

The man who had been master of the island until a few moments previous, sighed, started to walk.

"Untie my hands so I can keep my balance," he said.

Phil jabbed him in the back with the business end of the rifle he had confiscated.

"Don't talk, walk," he ordered.

The man immediately lengthened his stride.

"Any treachery, and you get shot. If they're killed before we arrive, you get shot. So remember that you're going to be the one who determines your fate!" snapped Phil.

The man ahead of him said nothing, but strode on, purposefully, grimly silent.

They swung into a trail which ran to the right, dropped down a steep slope. The trail widened, and other trails came feeding into it. The sound of the drum grew louder.

A watcher jumped out into the trail, snapped his bow up. The tall man with the bound arms called out something to him in a guttural tongue and the native dropped the bow, turned, and ran at top speed.

The tall man lengthened his stride.

The sound of the big drum ceased. There sounded the rattle of voices clamoring a chorus of sudden panic. Phil gathered that the watchman had warned them of the approach of the man who carried thundering death with him.

"Stop here," said Phil's captive.

Phil held the gun ready, cocked.

"Remember," he said, "the first sign of treachery, and you get your backbone blown to splinters."

"Hell," snorted the tall one, "I ain't a fool."

He raised his voice in a sharp call.

Instantly the chattering sound of the many voices which came from beyond the screen of trees subsided.

The tall man called a few sharp commands in the strange tongue. He was answered by someone from beyond the screen of foliage, and then raised his voice again, this time giving harsh rasping orders which thundered down the leafy aisles.

There was a period of silence.

"It's a damn fool thing, coming into the village," he muttered to Phil. "They ain't found the dead drummer yet. If they had, they'd be mad enough to rush me. As it is, I've run a bluff, and told 'em I'd kill their king if they didn't send out two men with the man and the woman they've captured. I left orders for all the rest of 'em to get down on the ground and lie on their faces.

"But they'll make trouble before we get away. They've been wanting me for a long while. They're frightened now, but they'll try to cut off our escape when we start back . . ."

There was a bit of motion ahead, then Phil saw two natives, so frightened their knees wobbled, bringing the two captives along the trail.

"Tell the natives to go back," said Phil.

And his captive obediently rattled forth another order.

Then Phil raised his own voice, called to the girl.

"It's okay," he said. "Come on the run!"

She gave a glad cry, started to run. Professor Parker joined her, his face wreathed with smiles.

"Well done," he said; "that was a masterly—"

The tall captive rasped forth an oath.

"Never mind that stuff. Get back quick. They'll be trying to ambush us! Save your breath for running. Let's go."

And, despite the bound arms which interfered with his balance, he turned and started at a long jog trot up the trail.

"Can you keep up?" Phil asked the girl.

"I think so," she said, "but, tell me, how—"

"Later. We've got work ahead of us, and I've got to watch this spindle-shanked hombre in front. He's about as trustworthy as a rattlesnake."

They ran on in silence, their feet beating the trail in rhythm. Behind them all was silence.

The moist air of the jungle growth seemed heavy and oppressive. The trail was steep, and the man in front stumbled twice, finally stopped.

"I've got to have my hands free," he panted.

Phil stepped forward. "I'll just get the keys to your castle," he said. "Then you won't feel so anxious to run off and leave us."

The lips twisted back in a snarl, as a rattling volley of oaths showed that Phil had discovered the man's intentions and checkmated him.

Phil searched the pockets, found the keys, unbound the man's hands.

"Keep well ahead and in the trail," he warned.

The man laughed grimly, pointed back around the shoulder of rock.

"Look at 'em," he said. "Trying to get ahead of us and ambush us."

Phil looked.

There, winding up the face of the cliff, was a swarming horde of naked men, armed with bow and arrow and spear, climbing in swift silence, some six hundred yards away.

They were making an almost miraculous speed up the sheer slope of the rock.

Phil flung up the rifle, fired.

The bullet hit the rock directly in front of the leader, flinging up a cloud of dust and stinging splinters of rock.

Phil slammed the lever of the gun, fired again and again. The savages flung themselves down behind whatever meager shelter they could secure. Phil waited until one raised a cautious torso, got to his feet, started to climb again, and then fired. The bullet slammed from the rock, making a little geyser of stone dust. The savage hurled himself back and down behind his shelter.

"Man," said Phil's captive, "that's shooting, and I don't mean maybe!"

Phil motioned.

"Get started," he said.

The tall man shook his head.

"Look at 'em, over on the other side. They'll head us off!"

So natural was he, so genuine did his consternation appear, that Phil swung about, half raised the rifle.

He heard a warning shout from the girl, the swift rustle of menacing motion, and the big man came down on him like a swooping hawk.

The spring had been well timed. Phil was downhill from his assailant, and the force of the rush brought him down to his knees. The man's wounded hand seemed to check him not at all. His hands clasped about the rifle.

Phil felt the impetus of the other's charge wresting the rifle from his grip. He suddenly loosed his grip on it, dropped to his knees, shook off the other man.

That individual, possessed of the rifle, let forth a roar of rage and swung the muzzle, only to find Phil, still on his knees, the butt of the automatic in his hand, eyes glittering, tense, and ready. The cowpuncher, trained in a quick and sure draw, had snaked the smaller weapon from its holster with a speed that was almost incredible.

"Drop it!" he yelled.

The tall man hesitated, and in that instant of hesitation there sounded the sharp *twang* of a bowstring. Something flashed through the air in a whispering path of hissing menace, struck the man square between the shoulders. With a thudding sound the arrow arrested its progress, quivered there in the man's back.

Phil snapped his automatic around, fired into the jungle growth in the general direction from which the arrow had come. The report of the weapon rang out on the hot air, subsided with a volley of echoes.

There came the sound of running steps, a crashing of brush, and silence.

The tall man dropped the rifle, swayed. His eyes were already glazing. The snarl came to his lips. He tried to curse, and his voice failed him. He wobbled, tottered, crashed to the earth.

Phil grabbed the gun. "No time for sentiment, folks. Let's go while we may."

It was well that his forest training had enabled him to mark each turn of the path, each intersection which marked the branches of the trail. Now he ran with swift certainty of direction.

From the high divide, with the castle well within reach, and a downhill trail to follow, he called a halt, looked back.

The savage band had once more gone into motion. Here and there, through breaks in the foliage, could be seen the moving flash of dark skin as some runner pressed ahead of his mates up the trail.

Then came a wild shout from the place where the tall man had fallen. The shout was taken up, became words, was hurled back down the trail from screaming throat to screaming throat, a wailing cry of savage exultation.

Then the big drum began to boom forth some code message.

Phil nodded.

"They've found him. He was the one they wanted. I imagine we won't be bothered now if we move fast."

And move fast they did.

It was only after Phil had fitted the keys to the iron gate, heard the welcome click of the lock, that he felt safe. He ushered the others into the gate, closed and locked it, went through the smaller gate, and surveyed the domain to which he had taken title by right of conquest.

There was a massive patio to the rear, a plateau which ran out over the outcropping of rock, surrounded by the smooth sides of the wall. On this plateau were trees and vines. There was a very commodious house, furnished with hand-carpentered furniture. The whole thing was an impregnable fortress, well equipped with guns and ammunition.

Phil climbed to the roof, looked out over the ocean.

Suddenly he let out a yell. Around a jutting promontory of the island appeared the white bow of a huge boat, cutting through the water at cautious half speed.

Phil's shout attracted the others.

They crowded to him. Watched in silence as the length of the boat came into view.

She was a large passenger steamer, and she had been battered by mountainous seas, yet had won through. Her lifeboats were either carried away or were stove in by the high seas. She had a tangle of wreckage on her boat deck, and more wreckage on the bow of the main deck, but she was cutting through the water slowly, majestically.

Professor Parker nodded.

"We could have expected it," he said. "Most of the larger boats that were afloat when the world swung over were undoubtedly turned topsy turvy by the terrific waves. You will remember that our own craft rolled over and over. But it righted itself because it was small and buoyant. Big boats, once over, would never right themselves, but would go down.

"But somewhere there were undoubtedly boats that won through.

"While the catastrophe was world-wide, it is certain that some sections were spared, just as this island was spared. And the terrific current swept most of the north sea shipping down to this vicinity. It is almost exactly what I expected to find, this boat, and—"

But Phil was not listening to explanations. There was a flag in a flag locker on the top of the castle. Grabbing it out, he tied one corner to the halyard, raised it and lowered it along the stumpy, homemade flagpole.

There came a cloud of steam from the whistle of the boat. The steam stopped. Another cloud followed, then another. As the third cloud of steam was emerging, the sound of the first whistle came to their ears.

"Three whistles!" said Phil. "A salute! They see us!"

Professor Parker nodded his satisfaction.

"Now," he said, "we can get some authentic news. If there are any unsubmerged continents that have survived the period of stress equalization and tidal inundations, they doubtless have sent out radio broadcasts. And you will notice that the boat retains its radio equipment."

Phil turned to the girl.

"Suppose," he said in a low voice, "there are no more continents, and we have to begin life anew. Would you—er— I mean, is there anybody, such as a husband, that you left behind?"

She laughed at him, extended her left hand.

"Not even engaged," she said.

Phil grinned.

"In that case," he observed, "you ought to be ready to take things as they come, Miss Ranson."

She looked at him with that frankness of appraisal which characterizes the modern girl.

"Yes," she said; "it's a new world, and I'm ready for it, regardless of what it is. I'm not afraid of the future . . . and you'd better begin calling me Stella, Phil."

And Phil Bregg, his face lighted with a zest for life, grinned at her.

"Bring on the new world," he said. "I like the people in it!"

RAIN MAGIC

Is "Rain Magic" fact or fiction? I wish I knew.

Some of it is fiction, I know, because I invented connecting incidents and wove them into the yarn. It's the rest of it that haunts me. At the time I thought it was just a wild lie of an old desert rat. And then I came to believe it was true.

Anyhow, here are the facts, and the reader can judge for himself.

About six months ago I went stale on Western stories. My characters became fuzzy in my mind; my descriptions lacked that intangible something that makes a story pack a punch. I knew I had to get out and gather new material.

So I got a camp wagon. It's a truck containing a complete living outfit—bed, bath, hot and cold water, radio, writing desk, closet, stove, et cetera. I struck out into the trackless desert, following old, abandoned roads, sometimes making my own roads. I was writing as I went, meeting old prospectors, putting them on paper, getting steeped in the desert environment.

February 13 found me at a little spring in the middle of barren desert. As far as I knew there wasn't a soul within miles.

Then I heard steps, the sound of a voice. I got up from my

typewriter, went to the door. There was an old prospector get-
ting water at the spring. But he wasn't the typical desert rat. I
am always interested in character classification, and the man
puzzled me. I came to the conclusion he'd been a sailor.

So I got out, shook hands, and passed the time of day. He
was interested in my camp wagon, and I took him in, sat him
down, and smoked for a spell. Then I asked him if he hadn't
been a sailor.

I can still see the queer pucker that came into his eyes as
he nodded.

Now sailors are pretty much inclined to stay with the water.
One doesn't often find a typical sailor in the desert. So I asked
him why he'd come into the desert.

He explained that he had to get away from rain. When it
rained he got the sleeping sickness.

That sounded like a story, so I made it a point to draw
him out. It came, a bit at a time, starting with the Sahara dust
that painted the rigging of the ship after the storm, and
winding up with the sleeping sickness that came back when-
ever he smelled the damp of rain-soaked vegetation.

I thought it was one gosh-awful lie, but it was a gripping,
entertaining lie, and I thought I could use it. I put it up to him
as a business proposition, and within a few minutes held in
my possession a document which read in part as follows:

> *For value received, I hereby sell to Erle Stanley Gard-*
> *ner the story rights covering my adventures in Africa,*
> *including the monkey-man, the unwritten language, the*
> *ants who watched the gold ledge, the bread that made*
> *me ill, the sleeping sickness which comes back every*
> *spring and leaves me with memories of my lost sweet-*
> *heart, et cetera, et cetera.*

After that I set about taking complete notes of his story. I
still thought it was a lie, an awful lie.

Like all stories of real life in the raw it lacked certain con-

necting incidents. *There was no balance to it. It seemed disconnected in places.*

Because I intended to make a pure fiction story out of it, I didn't hesitate to fill in these connections. I tried to give it a sweep of unified action, and I took some liberties with the facts as he had given them to me. Yet, in the main, I kept his highlights, and I was faithful to the backgrounds as he had described them.

Because he had just recovered from a recurrence of the sleeping sickness, I started the story as it would have been told to a man who had stumbled onto the sleeping form in the desert. It was a story that "wrote itself." The words just poured from my fingertips to the typewriter. But I was writing it as fiction, and I considered it as such.

Not all of what he told me went into the story. There was some that dealt with intimate matters one doesn't print. There was some that dealt with tribal customs, markings of different tribes, et cetera, et cetera. In fact, I rather avoided some of these definite facts. Because I felt the whole thing was fiction, I was rather careful to keep from setting down definite data, using only such as seemed necessary.

Then, after the story had been written and mailed, after I had returned to headquarters, I chanced to get some books dealing with the locality covered in the story, telling of tribal characteristics, racial markings, et cetera.

To my surprise, I found that every fact given me by the old prospector was true. I became convinced that his story was, at least, founded on fact.

And so I consider "Rain Magic" the most remarkable story I ever had anything to do with. I'm sorry I colored it up with fiction of my own invention. I wish I'd left it as it was, regardless of lack of connective incident and consistent motivation.

Somewhere in the shifting sands of the California desert is an old prospector, hiding from the rain, digging for gold, cherishing lost memories. His sun-puckered eyes have seen

*sights that few men have seen. His life has been a tragedy so
weird, so bizarre that it challenges credulity. Yet of him it can
be said, "He has lived."*

—ERLE STANLEY GARDNER

CHAPTER 1

Through the Breakers

No, no—no more coffee. Thanks. Been asleep, eh? Well,
don't look so worried about it. Mighty nice of you to wake
me up. What day is it?

Thursday, eh? I've been asleep two days then—oh, it is?
Then it's been nine days. That's more like it. It was the rain,
you see. I tried to get back to my tent, but the storm came up
too fast. It's the smell of the damp green things in a rain. The
doctors tell me it's auto-hypnosis. They're wrong. M'Gamba
told me I'd always be that way when I smelled the jungle
smell. It's the sleeping sickness in my veins. That's why I came
to the desert. It doesn't rain out here more than once or twice
a year.

When it does rain the jungle smells come back and the
sleeping sickness gets me. Funny how my memory comes back
after those long sleeps. It was the drugged bread, *king-kee*
they called it; but the language ain't never been written down.
Sort of a graduated monkey talk it was.

It's hot here, come over in the shadow of this Joshuay palm.
That's better.

Ever been to sea? No? Then you won't understand.

It was down off the coast of Africa. Anything can happen
off the coast of Africa. After the storms, the Sahara dust
comes and paints the rigging white. Yes, sir, three hundred
miles out to sea I've seen it. And for a hundred miles you

can get the smell of the jungles. When the wind's right.

It was an awful gale. You don't see 'em like it very often.
We tried to let go the deckload of lumber, but the chains
jammed. The Dutchmen took to the riggin' jabberin' prayers.
They were a weak-kneed lot. It was the Irishman that stayed
with it. He was a cursin' devil.

He got busy with an ax. The load had listed and we was
heeled over to port. The Dutchmen in the riggin' prayin', an'
the Irishman down on the lumber cursin'. A wave took him
over and then another wave washed him back again. I see it
with my own eyes. He didn't give up. He just cursed harder
than ever. And he got the chains loose, too. The deckload slid
off and she righted.

But it was heavy weather and it got worse. The sky was just
a mass of whirlin' wind and the water came over until she
didn't get rid of one wave before the next bunch of green
water was on top of her.

The rudder carried away. I thought everything was gone,
but she lived through it. We got blown in, almost on top of
the shore. When the gale died we could see it. There was a
species of palm stickin' up against the sky, tall trees they were,
and below 'em was a solid mass of green stuff, and it stunk.
The whole thing was decayin' an' steamin' just like the inside
of a rotten, damp log.

The old man was a bad one. It was a hell ship an' no mistake. I'd been shanghaied, an' I wanted back. Thirty pound
I had in my pocket when I felt the drink rockin' my head. I
knew then, but it was too late. The last I remembered was the
grinnin' face of the tout smilin' at me through a blue haze.

The grub was rotten. The old man was a devil when he was
sober, an' worse when he was drunk. The Irish mate cursed
all the time, cursed and worked. Between 'em they drove the
men, drove us like sheep.

The moon was half full. After the storm the waves were
rollin' in on a good sea breeze. There wasn't any whitecaps.
The wind just piled the water up until the breakers stood

fourteen feet high before they curled an' raced up the beach.

But the breakers didn't look so bad from the deck of the ship. Not in the light of the half moon they didn't. We'd been at work on the rudder an' there was a raft over the side. I was on watch, an' the old man was drunk, awful drunk. I don't know when the idea came to me, but it seemed to have always been there. It just popped out in front when it got a chance.

I was halfway down the rope before I really knew what I was doin'. My bare feet hit the raft an' my sailor knife was workin' on the rope before I had a chance to even think things over.

But I had a chance on the road in, riding the breakers. I had a chance even as soon as the rope was cut. The old man came and stood on the rail, lookin' at the weather, too drunk to know what he was looking at, but cockin' his bleary eye at the sky outa habit.

He'd have seen me, drunk as he was, if he'd looked down, but he didn't. If he'd caught me then I'd have been flayed alive. He'd have sobered up just special for the occasion.

I drifted away from him. The moon was on the other side of the hull, leavin' it just a big, black blotch o' shadow, ripplin' on the water, heavin' up into the sky. Then I drifted out of the shadow and into golden water. The moon showed over the top of the boat, an' the sharks got busy.

I'd heard they never struck at a man while he was strugglin'. Maybe it's true. I kept movin', hands and feet goin'. The raft was only an inch or two outa water, an' it was narrow. The sharks cut through the water like hissin' shadows. I was afraid one of 'em would grab a hand or a foot an' drag me down, but they didn't. I could keep the rest of me outa the water, but not my hands an' feet. I had to paddle with 'em to get into shore before the wind and tide changed. I sure didn't want to be left floatin' around there with no sail, nor food; nothin' but sharks.

From the ship the breakers looked easy an' lazylike. When I got in closer I saw they were monsters. They'd rise up an' blot out all the land, even the tops of the high trees. Just before they'd break they'd send streamers of spray, high up in the heavens. Then they'd come down with a crash.

But I couldn't turn back. The sharks and the wind and the tide were all against me, and the old man would have killed me.

I rode in on a couple of breakers, and then the third one broke behind me. The raft an' me, maybe the sharks all got mixed up together. My feet struck the sand, but they wouldn't stay there.

The strong undertow was cuttin' the sand out from under me. I could feel it racin' along over my toes, an' then I started back an' down.

The undertow sucked me under another wave, somethin' alive brushed against my back, an' then tons o' water came down over me. That time I was on the bottom an' I rolled along with sand an' water bein' pumped into my innards. I thought it was the end, but there was a lull in the big ones, an' a couple o' little ones came an' rolled me up on the beach.

I was more dead than alive. The water had made me groggy, an' I was sore from the pummelin' I'd got. I staggered up the strip of sand an' into the jungle.

A little ways back was a cave, an' into the cave I flopped. The water oozed out of my insides like from a soaked sponge. My lungs an' stomach an' ears were all full. I tried to get over a log an' let 'er drain out, but I was too weak. I felt everything turnin' black to me.

The next thing I knew it was gettin' dawn an' shadowy shapes were flittin' around. I thought they was black angels an' they were goin' to smother me. They stunk with a musty smell, an' they settled all over me.

Then I could feel the blood runnin' over my skin. It got a little lighter, an' I could see. I was in a bat cave an' the bats were comin' back. They'd found me an' were settin' on me in clouds, suckin' blood.

I tried to fight 'em off, but it was like fightin' a fog. Sometimes I'd hit 'em, but they'd just sail through the air, an' I couldn't hurt 'em. All the time, they was flutterin' their wings an' lookin' for a chance to get more blood.

I'd got the weight of 'em off, though, an' I staggered out of the cave. They followed me for a ways; but when I got out to where it was gettin' light they went back in the cave. It gets light quick down there in the tropics, an' the light hurt their eyes.

I rolled into the sand an' went to sleep.

When I woke up I heard marchin' feet. It sounded like an army. They was comin' regular like, slow, unhurried, deliberate. It made the chills come up my spine just to hear the *boom, boom, boom* of those feet.

I crawled deeper into the sand under the shadows of the overhangin' green stuff. Naked men an' women filed out onto the beach.

I watched 'em.

Chocolate-colored they were, an' they talked a funny, squeaky talk. I found afterward some of the words was Fanti and some was a graduated monkey talk. Fanti ain't never been written down.

It's one of the Tshi languages. The Ashantis an' the Fantis an' one or two other tribes speak branches o' the same lingo. But these people spoke part Fanti an' part graduated monkey talk.

An' among 'em was a monkey-man. He was a funny guy. There was coarse hair all over him, an' he had a stub of a tail. His big toes weren't set like mine, but they was twisted like a foot thumb.

No, I didn't notice the toes at the time. I found that out later, while he was sittin' on a limb gettin' ready to shoot a poisoned arrow at me. I thought every minute was my last, an' then was when I noticed the way his foot thumbs wrapped around the limb. Funny how a man will notice little things when he's near death.

Anyway, this tribe came down an' marched into the water, men, women, an' children. They washed themselves up to the hips, sort of formal, like it was a ceremony. The rest of them they didn't get water on at all. They came out an' rubbed sort of an oil on their arms, chests, an' faces.

CHAPTER 2

Life or Death

Finally they all went away, all except a woman an' a little kid. The woman was lookin' for somethin' in the water—fish, maybe. The kid was on a rock about eight feet away, a little shaver he was, an' he had a funny pot-belly. I looked at him an' I looked at her.

I was sick an' I was hungry, an' I was bleedin' from the bats. The smell of the jungle was in my lungs, so I couldn't tell whether the air was full of jungle or whether I was breathin' in jungle stuff with just a little air. It's a queer sensation. Unless you've been through it you wouldn't understand.

Well, I felt it was everything or nothin'. The woman couldn't kill me, an' the kid couldn't. An' I had to make myself known an' get somethin' to eat.

I straightened out of the sand.

"Hello," said I.

The kid was squattin' on his haunches. He didn't seem to jump. He just flew through the air an' he sailed right onto his mother's back. His hands clung to her shoulders an' his head pressed tight against her skin, the eyes rollin' at me, but the head never movin'.

The mother made three jumps right up the sand, an' then she sailed into the air an' caught the branch of a tree. The green stuff was so thick that I lost sight of 'em both right there. I could hear a lot of jabberin' monkey talk in the trees, an' then I heard the squeaky voice of the woman talkin' back to the monkeys. I could tell the way she was goin' by the jabber of monkey talk.

No, I can't remember words of monkey talk. I never got so I could talk to the monkeys. But the people did. I am goin' to tell you about that. I'm explainin' about the sleepin' sickness, an' about how the memories come back to me after I've been asleep.

Maybe they're dreams, but maybe they ain't. If they're dreams, how comes it that when I got to Cape Coast Castle I couldn't remember where I'd been? They brought me in there on stretchers, an' nobody knows how far they'd brought me. They left me in the dead o' night. But the next mornin' there were the tracks, an' they were tracks like nobody there had ever seen before.

There's strange things in Africa, an' this was when I was a young blood, remember that. I was an upstandin' youngster, too. I'd tackle anything, even the west coast of Africa on a raft, an' the Fanti warriors; but I'm comin' to that directly.

Well, the woman ran away, an' the monkeys came. They stuck around on the trees an' jabbered monkey talk at me. I wished I'd been like the woman an' could have talked to 'em. But the monkeys ain't got so many words. There's a lot of it that's just tone stuff. It was the ants that could speak, but they rubbed feelers together.

Oh, yes, there was ants, great, woolly ants two inches long, ants that built houses out of sticks. They built 'em thirty feet high, an' some of the sticks was half an inch round an' six or eight inches long. They had the ants guardin' the gold ledge, an' nobody except Kk-Kk, the feeder, an' the goldsmith could come near there.

The goldsmith was nothin' but a slave, anyway. They'd captured him from a slaver that went ashore. The others died of the fever, but the natives gave the goldsmith some medicine that cured him. After that he couldn't get sick. They could have done the same by me, too, but the monkey-man was my enemy. He wanted Kk-Kk for himself.

Finally I heard the tramp of feet again, an' the warriors of the tribe came out. They had spears an' little bows with long arrows. The arrows were as thin as a pencil. They didn't look like they'd hurt anything, but there was a funny color on the points, a sort of shimmering something.

I found out afterward that was where they'd coated 'em with poison an' baked the poison into the wood. One scratch with an arrow like that an' a man or beast would die. But it didn't hurt the flesh none for eatin'. Either of man or beast it didn't. They ate 'em both.

I saw it was up to me to make a speech. The men all looked serious an' dignified. That is, they all did except the monkey-man. He capered around on the outside. His balance didn't seem good on his two feet, so he'd stoop over an' use the backs of his knuckles to steady himself. He could hitch along over the ground like the wind. His arms were long, long an' hairy, an' the inside of his palms was all wrinkled, thick an' black.

Anyhow, I made a speech.

I told 'em that I was awful tough, an' that I was thin, an' maybe the bat bites had poisoned me, so I wouldn't advise 'em to cook me. I told 'em I was a friend an' I didn't come to bother 'em, but to get away from the big ship that was layin' offshore.

I thought they understood me, because some of 'em was lookin' at the ship. But I found out afterward they didn't. They'd seen the ship, an' they'd seen me, an' they saw the dried salt water on my clothes, an' they figgered it out for themselves.

I finished with my speech. I didn't expect 'em to clap their hands, because they had spears an' bows, but I thought maybe they'd smile. They was a funny bunch, all gathered around there in a circle, grave an' naked like. An' they all had three scars on each side of their cheek bones. It made 'em look tough.

Then the monkey-man gave a sort of a leap an' lit in the trees, an' the monkeys came around and jabbered, an' he jabbered, an' somehow I thought he was tellin' the monkeys about me. Maybe he was. I never got to know the monkey talk.

An' then from the jungle behind me I heard a girl's voice, an' it was speakin' good English.

"Be silent and I shall speak to my father," she said.

You can imagine how I felt hearin' an English voice from the jungle that way, an' knowin' it was a girl's voice. But I knew she wasn't a white woman. I could tell that by the sound of the voice, sort of the way the tongue didn't click against the roof of the mouth, but the lips made the speech soft like.

An' then there was a lot of squeaky talk from the jungles back of me.

There was silence after that talk, an' then I heard the girl's voice again.

"They've gone for the goldsmith. He'll talk to you."

I didn't see who had gone, an' I didn't know who the goldsmith was. I turned around an' tried to see into the jungle, but all I could see was leaves, trunks, an' vine stems. There was a wispy blue vapor that settled all around an' overhead the air was white way way up, white with Sahara dust. But down low the jungle odor hung around the ground. Around me the circle stood naked an' silent. Not a man moved.

Who was the goldsmith?—I wondered. Who was the girl?

Then I heard steps behind me an' the jungle parted. I smelled somethin' burnin'. It wasn't tobacco, not the kind we have, but it was a sort of a tobacco flavor.

A man came out into the circle, smokin' a pipe.

"How are yuh?" he says, an' sticks forward a hand.

* * *

He was a white man, part white anyway, an' he had on some funny clothes. They were made of skins, but they were cut like a tailor would cut 'em. He even had a skin hat with a stiff brim. He'd made the stiff brim out of green skin with the hair rubbed off.

He was smokin' a clay pipe, an' there was a vacant look in his eyes, a blank somethin' like a man who didn't have feelin's any more, but was just a man-machine.

I shook hands with him.

"Are they goin' to eat me?" I asks.

He smoked awhile before he spoke, an' then he takes the pipe out of his mouth an' nods his head.

"Sure," he says.

It wasn't encouragin'.

"Have hope," came the voice from the jungle, the voice of the girl. She seemed to be standin' close, close an' keepin' in one place, but I couldn't see her.

I talked to the man with the pipe. I made him a speech. He turned around and talked to the circle of men, an' they didn't say anything.

Finally an old man grunted, an' like the grunt was an order they all squatted down on their haunches, all of 'em facin' me.

Then the girl in the jungle made squeaky noises. The old man seemed to be listenin' to her. The others didn't listen to anything. They were just starin' at me, an' the expression on all of the faces was the same. It was sort of a curiosity, but it wasn't a curiosity to see what I looked like. I felt it was a curiosity to see what I'd taste like.

Then the goldsmith rubbed some more brown leaf into the pipe, right on top of the coals of the other pipeful.

"The girl is claimin' you as a slave," he says.

"Who is the girl?" I asked him.

"Kk-Kk," he says, an' I didn't know whether he was givin' me a name or warnin' me to keep quiet.

Well, I figured I'd rather be a slave than a meal, so I kept quiet.

Then the monkey-man in the tree began to jabber.

They didn't look up at him, but I could see they were listenin'. When he got done the girl squeaked some more words.

Then the monkey-man made some more talk, and the girl talked. The fellow with the pipe smoked an' blew the smoke out of his nose. His eyes were weary an' puckered. He was an odd fellow.

Finally the old man that had grunted an' made 'em squat, gave another grunt. They all stood up.

This is the show-down, I says to myself. It's either bein' a white slave or bein' a meat loaf.

The old man looked at me an' blinked. Then he sucked his lips into his mouth until his face was all puckered into wrinkles. He blinked his lidless eyes some more an' then grunted twice. Then all the men marched off. I could hear their feet boomin' along the hard ground in the jungle, on a path that had been beaten down hard by millions of bare feet. I found out afterward that same path had been used for over a hundred years, an' the king made a law it had to be traveled every day. That was the only way they could keep the ground hard.

I guess I'm a meal, I thought to myself. I figgered the goldsmith would have told me if I had been goin' to be a slave. But he'd moved off with the rest, an' he hadn't said a word.

The monkey-man kept talkin' to the bunch. He didn't walk along the path, but he moved through the trees, keepin' up in the branches, right over the heads of the others, an' talkin' all the time, an' his words didn't seem happy words. I sort of felt he was scoldin' like a monkey that's watchin' yuh eat a coconut.

But the old man grunted at him, an' he shut up like a clam. He was mad, though. I could tell that because he set off through the trees, tearin' after a couple of monkeys. An' he pretty nearly caught 'em. They sounded like a whirlwind, tearin' through the branches. Then the sounds got fainter, an' finally everything was still.

I looked around. There was nobody in sight. I was there, on the fringe of beach, right near the edge of the jungle, and everything was still an' silent.

Then there came a rustlin' of the jungle stuff an' she came out.

She had on a skirt of grass stuff, an' her eyes were funny. You know how a monkey's eyes are? They're round. They don't squint up any at the corners. An' they're sort of moist an' glistening on the surface. It's a kind of a liquid expression.

Her eyes were like that.

For the rest she was like the others. Her skin was dusky, but not black, an' it was smooth. It was like a piece of chocolate silk.

"I'm Kk-Kk, the daughter of Yik-Yik, and the keeper of the gold ledge," she said. "I have learned to speak the language of the goldsmith. You, too, speak the same language. You are my slave."

"Thank God I ain't a meal," I said. That was before the doctor guys discovered these here calories in food; but right then I didn't feel like a half a good-sized calorie, much less a fit meal for a native warrior.

"You will be my slave," she said, "but if you pay skins to my father you can buy your freedom, and then you will be a warrior."

"I ain't never been a slave to a woman," I told her, me bein' one of the kind that had always kept from being led to the altar, "but I'd rather be a slave to you than to that old man on the boat out yonder."

There was something half shy about her, and yet something proud and dignified.

"I have promised my father my share of the next hunt in order to purchase you from the tribe," she went on.

"Thanks," I told her, knowin' it was up to me to say somethin', but sort of wonderin' whether a free, white man should thank a woman who had made a slave outa him.

"Come," she said, an' turned away.

I had more of a chance to study her back. She was lithe, graceful, and she was a well-turned lass. There was a set to her head, a funny little twist of her shoulders when she walked that showed she was royalty and knowed it. Funny how people get that little touch of class no matter where they are or what stock. Just as soon as they get royal blood in 'em they get it. I've seen 'em everywhere.

I followed her into the jungle, down under the branches where there wasn't sunlight any more; but the day was just filled with green light.

Finally we came through the jungle an' into a big clearin'. There were huts around the clearin' an' a big fire. The people of the tribe were here, goin' about their business in knots of two an' three just like nothin' had happened. I was a member of the tribe now, the slave of Kk-Kk.

Most of the women stared, an' the kids scampered away when they seen me look toward 'em; but that was all. The men took me for granted.

CHAPTER 3

Guardians of Gold

The girl took me to a hut. In one corner was a frame of wood with animal skins stretched over it. There were all kinds of skins. Some of 'em I knew, more of 'em I didn't.

She squeaked out some words an' then there was some more jabberin' in a quaverin' voice, an' an old woman came an' brought me fruits.

I squatted down on my heels the way the natives did, an' tried to eat the fruit. My stomach was still pretty full of salt water an' sand, but the fruit tasted good. Then they gave me a half a coconut shell filled with some sort of creamy liquid that had bubbles comin' up in it. It tasted sort of sour, but it had a lot of authority. Ten minutes after I drank it I felt my neck snap back. It was the delayed kick, an' it was like the hind leg of a mule.

"Come," says the jane, an' led the way again out into the openin'.

I followed her, across the openin' into the jungle, along a path, past the shore of a lagoon, and up into a little cañon. Here the trees were thicker than ever except on the walls of the cañon itself. There'd been a few dirt slides in that cañon, an' in one or two places the rock had been stripped bare. After a ways it was all rock.

An' then we came to somethin' that made my eyes stick out. There was a ledge o' rock an' a vein o' quartz in it. The vein was just shot with gold, an' in the center it was almost pure gold. The quartz was crumbly, an' there were pieces of it scattered around on the ground. The foliage had been cleared away, an' the ground was hard. There was a fire goin' near the ledge an' some clay crucibles were there. Then there was a great bellows affair made out of thick, oiled leather. It was a big thing, but all the air came out of a little piece of hollow wood in the front.

I picked up one of the pieces of quartz. The rock could be crumbled between the fingers, an' it left the gold in my hand. The gold was just like it showed in the rock, spreadin' out to form sort of a tree. There must have been fifty dollars' worth in the piece o' rock that I crumbled up in my fingers.

I moved my hands around fast an' managed to slip the gold in my torn shirt. The girl was watchin' me with those funny, liquid eyes of hers, but she didn't say a word.

There was a great big pile of small sticks between me an' the ledge of gold. I figured it was kindlin' wood that they kept for the fire. But finally my eyes got loose from the ledge of gold an' what should I see but the sticks movin'. I looked again, an' then I saw somethin' else.

It was a big ant heap made outa sticks an' sawdust. Some of those sticks were eight or ten inches long and half an inch around. And the whole place was swarming with ants. They had their heads stickin' out of the little holes between the sticks.

They must be big ants, I thought; but I was interested in that gold ledge. There must have been millions of dollars in it. I took a couple of steps toward it, an' then the ant heap just swarmed with life.

They were big ants covered with sort of a white wool and they came out of there like somebody had given 'em an order.

The girl shrieked somethin' in a high-pitched voice, but I didn't know whether it was at me or the ants.

The ants swarmed into two columns of maybe eight or ten abreast in each column, an' they started for me, swingin' out in a big circle as though one was goin' to come on one side, an' one on the other.

An' then they stopped. The girl ran forward an' put her arms on my shoulders an' started caressin' me, pattin' my hair, cooin' soft noises in my ears.

I thought maybe she'd gone cuckoo, an' I looked into her eyes, but they weren't lookin' at me, they were lookin' at the ants, an' they were wide with fear.

An' the ants were lookin' at her. I could see their big eyes gazin' steadylike at her. Then somethin' else must have been said to 'em, although I did not hear anything. But all at once, just like an army presentin' arms in response to an order, they threw up their long feelers an' waved 'em gently back an' forth. Then the girl took me by the arm an' moved me away.

"I should have told you," she said, "never to go past the line of that path. The ants guard the yellow metal, and when one comes nearer than that they attack. There is no escape from those ants. I took you to them so you could help me with the feed. Now we will feed them."

That all sounded sorta cuckoo to me, but the whole business was cuckoo anyway.

"Look here," I tells this jane. "I'm willin' to be the slave of a chief's daughter—for a while. But I ain't goin' to be slave to no ant hill."

"That is not expected," she said. "It is an honor to assist in feeding the ants, a sacred right. You only assist me. Never again must you come so near to the ants."

I did a lot of thinkin'. I wasn't hankerin' to come into an argument with those ants, but I was figurin' to take a closer slant at that gold ledge.

She took me away into the jungle where there was a pile of fruit dryin' in the sun. It was a funny sort of fruit, an' smelled sweet, like orange blossoms, only there was more of a honey smell to it.

"Take your arms full," she said.

Well, it was my first experience bein' a slave, but I couldn't see as it was much different from bein' a sailor, only the work was easier.

I scooped up both arms full of the stuff. The smell made me a little dizzy at first, but I soon got used to it. The girl picked up some, too, an' she led the way back to the ant pile.

She had me put my load down an' showed me how to arrange it in a long semicircle. I could see the ants watchin' from out of the holes in the ant pile, but they did not do anything except watch.

Finally the girl made a queer clicking sound with her tongue an' teeth an' the ants commenced to boil out again. This time they made for the fruit, an' they went in order, just like a bunch of swell passengers on one of the big ocean liners. Some of 'em seemed to hold first meal ticket while the others remained on guard. Then there must have been some signal from the ants, because the girl didn't say a word, but all of the first bunch of ants fell back an' stood guard, an' the second bunch of ants moved forward.

They repeated that a couple of times. I watched 'em, too fascinated to say a word.

After a while I heard steps, an' the old goldsmith came along, puffin' his pipe regular, a puff for every two steps. He reminded me of a freight engine, boilin' along on a down grade, hittin' her up regular.

He didn't say a word to me, nor to the ants, but the ants heard him comin' an' they all formed into two lanes with their feelers wavin' an' the goldsmith walked down between those lanes an' up to the gold ledge. There he stuck some more wood on the fire, raked away some ashes, an' pawed out a bed of coals.

Then I saw he had a hammer an' a piece of metal that looked like a reddish iron. He pulled a skin away an' I saw lots of lumps an' stringers of pure gold. It was a yellow, frosty-lookin' sort of gold, and it was so pure it glistened.

He picked up some of the pieces an' commenced to hammer 'em into ornaments.

"What do yuh do with that stuff?" I asked the girl, wavin' my hand careless like so she wouldn't think I was much interested.

"We trade it to the Fanti tribes," she said. "It is of no use, too soft to make weapons, too heavy for arrow points; but they use it to wear around their fingers and ankles. They give us many skins for it, and sometimes they try to capture our territory and take the entire ledge. If I had my way we would stop making the ornaments. Our people do not like the metal, and never use it. Having it here just makes trouble for us, and the Fantis are fierce people. They are killing off our entire tribe."

I nodded as wise as a dozen owls on a limb.

"Yeah," I told her, "the stuff always makes trouble. Seems to me it'd be better to get rid of it."

The old goldsmith raised his head, twisted his pipe in his

mouth and screwed his rheumy eyes at me. For a minute or two he acted like he was goin' to say somethin', an' then he went back to his work.

It was a close call. Right then I knew I'd been goin' too fast. But I had my eye on that ledge o' gold.

I guess it was a Fanti that saved my life; if it hadn't been for seein' him, the ants would have got me sure. Those ants looked pretty fierce when I saw 'em boilin' out in military formation, but by the time it came dark they didn't seem so much.

I got to thinkin' things over. Bein' a slave wasn't near so bad as it might be, an' one of these days I was goin' to get away in the jungle an' work down to a port. All I needed was to have about ninety pounds o' pure gold on my back when I went out an' I wouldn't be workin' as a sailor no more.

Sittin' there in the warm night, while the other folks had all rolled into their huts, I got to thinkin' things over. As a slave, I wasn't given a hut. I could sleep out. If the animals got bad I could either build up the fire or climb a tree. But there was fifty or sixty other slaves, mostly captured warriors of other tribes, an' it wasn't so bad.

There was a place in the jungle where the hills formed a bottleneck, an' there the tribe kept sentries so the Fantis couldn't get in, an' so the slaves couldn't get out. Gettin' through the jungle where there wasn't a trail was plain impossible.

I picked up a lot of this from the girl, an' a lot from usin' my eyes.

Night time the ants didn't see so much, an' the gold seemed a lot more. I wondered how I could work it, an' then a scheme hit me. I'd go out an' make a quick run for the ledge, chop off a few chunks o' quartz, an' then beat it back quick. I'd be in an' out before the ants could come boilin' out of their thirty-foot ant hill. It seemed a cinch.

I sneaked away an' managed to find my way down the trail

to the gold ledge. It was dark in the jungle. The stars were all misty, an' a squall was workin' somewheres out to sea. I could hear the thunder of the surf an' smell the smells of the jungle. There wasn't any noise outside of the poundin' surf.

I'd taken my shoes off when I dropped onto the raft, an' they'd got lost while I was rollin' around in the water, so I was barefoot. The ground had been beaten hard by millions of bare feet, an' so I made no noise. The hard part was tellin' just when I got to the gold ledge, because I didn't want to steer a wrong course an' fetch up against the ant heap.

I needn't have worried. I smelled the faint smell o' smoke, an' then a pile o' coals gleamed red against the black of the jungle night. It was the coals of the goldsmith's fire. I chuckled to myself. What a simple bunch o' people this tribe was!

An' then, all of a sudden, I knew someone else was there in the jungle. It was that funny feelin' that a man can't describe. It wasn't a sound, because there wasn't any sound. It wasn't anything I could see, because it was as dark as the inside of a pocket. But it was somethin' that just made my hair bristle.

I slipped back from the path and into the dark of the jungle. Six feet from the trail an' I was hidden as well as though I'd been buried.

I got my eye up against a crack in the leaves an' watched the coals of the camp fire, tryin' to see if anything moved.

All of a sudden those coals just blotted out. I thought maybe a leaf or a vine had got in front of my eyes, but there wasn't. It was just somethin' movin' between me an' the fire. An' then it stepped to one side, an' I saw it, a black man, naked, rushin' into the cliff of gold. He worked fast, that boy. The light from the coals showed me just a blur of black motion as he chipped rocks from the ledge.

Then he turned and sprinted out.

I chuckled to myself. The boy had got my system. It was a cinch, nothin' to it.

An' then there came a yell of pain. The black man began to do a devil's dance, wavin' his hands and legs. He'd got right in front of me, within ten feet he was, an' I could just make him out when he moved.

From the ground there came a faint whisperin' noise, an' then I could sense things crawlin'. I felt my blood turn to lukewarm water as I thought of the danger I was in. If those ants found me there—

I was afraid to move, an' I was afraid to stand still.

But the black boy solved the problem for me. He made for a tree, climbin' up a creeper like a monkey. Up in the tree, I could hear his hands goin' as he tried to brush the ants off. And he kept up a low, moanin' noise, sort of a chatter of agony.

I couldn't tell whether the ants were leavin' him alone or whether they were watchin' the bottom of the tree, waitin' for him.

But the creeper that he'd climbed up stretched against the starlit sky almost in front of my nose. I could see it faintly outlined against the stars. And then I noticed that it was ripplin' and swayin'. For a minute I couldn't make it out. Then I saw that those ants were swarmin' up the tree.

That was the end. The moanin' became a yellin', an' then things began to thud to the ground. That must be the gold rock the fellow had packed away with him, probably in a skin bag slung over his shoulder.

Then the sounds quit. Everything was silent. But I sensed the jungle was full of activity, a horrid activity that made me want to vomit. I could smell somethin' that must have been blood, an' there was a drip-drip from the tree branches.

Then the coals flickered up an' I could see a little more. The ground was black, swarmin'. The ants were goin' back and forth, up an' down the creepers, up into the tree.

Finally somethin' fell to the ground. It couldn't have been a man, because it was too small, hardly bigger than a hunk o' deer meat; but the firelight flickered on it, an' I could see that the heap was all of a quiver. An' it kept gettin' smaller an' smaller. Then I knew. The ants were finishin' their work.

I held my hands to my eyes, but I couldn't shut out the sight. If I'd moved I was afraid the ants would turn to me. I hadn't been across the deadline, but would the ants know it? I shuddered and turned sick.

After a while I looked out again. The ground was bare. All of the ants were back in their pile of sticks. The last of the firelight flickered on a bunch o' white bones. Near by was the gleam of yellow metal—gold from the rocks the Fanti had stolen.

Sick, I went back along the trail, back to the camp, not tellin' anybody where I'd been or what I'd seen. I still wanted that gold, but I didn't want it the way I'd figured I did.

I didn't sleep much. They gave me a tanned skin for a bed and that was all. It was up to me to make myself comfortable on the ground. The ground was hard, but my bunk on the ship had been hard. It was the memory of that little black heap that kept gettin' smaller an' smaller that tortured my mind.

I lived through the night, an' I lived through the days that followed; but I saw a lot that a white man shouldn't see. After all, I guess we think too much of life. Life didn't mean so much to those people, an' they didn't feel it was so blamed precious.

And I worked out a cinch scheme for the gold ledge. As the slave of Kk-Kk I had to assist her in feedin' the ants. Every night I had to bring up some of the fruit. Kk-Kk wouldn't let me feed it to 'em. It was the custom of the tribe that only the daughter of the chief could feed the ants. But I got close enough to find out a lot.

Those ants were trained. Kk-Kk could walk among 'em an' they took no notice of her. She was the one who fed 'em. The old goldsmith could walk through 'em whenever he wanted to, an' they didn't pay any attention to him. They'd been trained that way. But nobody else could cross the deadline. Let any one else come closer than that an' they'd swarm out an' get started with their sickenin' business. Once they'd started there was no gettin' away.

I saw 'em at work a couple of times in the next week. They always managed to get behind the man at the gold ledge. Then they closed in on him. No matter how fast he ran they'd swarm up his legs as he went through 'em. Enough would get on him so he couldn't go far, an' there was always a solid formation of two-inch ants swarmin' behind, ready to finish the work.

But they fed 'em only one meal a day, in the afternoon. I got to figgerin' what would happen if there should be two feeders. They couldn't tell which was the official feeder, an' they'd been trained to let the official feeder go to the gold ledge.

I knew where they kept the pile of dried fruits that the ants liked so well. An' I started goin' out to the ant pile just before daybreak an' givin' 'em a breakfast. I'd take out a little of the fruit so there wouldn't be any crumbs left by the time the goldsmith came to work.

At first I could see the ants were suspicious, but they ate the fruit. There was one long, woolly fellow that seemed to be the big boss, an' he reported to a glossy-backed ant that was a king or queen or somethin'. I got to be good friends with the boss. He'd come an' eat outa my hand. Then he'd go back an' wave his feelers at the king or queen, whichever it was, an' finally, the old boy, or old girl, got so it was all right. There was nothin' to it. I was jake a million, one of the regular guys. I could tell by a hundred little things, the way they waved their feelers, the way they came for the food. Oh, I got to know 'em pretty well.

All of this time Kk-Kk was teachin' me things about the life an' customs of the tribe. I could see she was friendly. She'd had to learn the language of the goldsmith, so that if anything should happen to him she could educate another one as soon as the tribe captured him.

For the tribe I didn't have no particular love. You should have seen 'em in some of their devil-devil dances, or seen 'em in the full moon when they gave a banquet to their cousins, the monkeys. Nope, I figured that anything I could do to the tribe was somethin' well done. But for Kk-Kk I had different feelin's, an' I could see that she had different feelin's for me.

An' all this time the monkey-man was jealous. He was in love with Kk-Kk, an' he wanted to buy her. In that country the woman didn't have anything to say about who she married, or whether she was wife No. 1 or No. 50. A man got his wives by buyin' 'em, and he could have as many as he could buy an' keep.

After a coupla weeks I commenced taking the gold. At first I just got closer an' closer to the deadline. I can yet feel the cold sweat there was on me the first time I crossed it. But the ants figgered I was a regular guy, part of the gang. They never said a word. Finally, I walked right up to the ledge, watchin' the ground behind me like a hawk. Then I scooped out some o' the crumbly quartz and worked the gold out of it. After that it was easy.

I didn't take much at any one time, because I didn't want the goldsmith to miss anything. I wasn't any hog. Ninety pounds I wanted, an' ninety pounds was all I was goin' to take, but I wasn't a fool. I was goin' to take it a little at a time.

CHAPTER 4

A Fanti Raid

Then came the night of the big fight.

I was asleep, wrapped up in my skin robes, not because of the cold, because the nights are warm an' steamy down there, but to keep out as much of the damp as I could, an' to shut out the night insects that liked my soft, white skin.

There came a yell from a sentry up the pass, an' then a lot o' whoopin' an' then all hell broke loose.

There was a little moon, an' by the light o' that moon I could see things happenin'.

Our warriors came boilin' outa their huts. One thing, they didn't have to dress. All a guy had to do was grab a spear an' shield, or climb up a tree with a bow an' arrow, an' that was all there was to it. He was dressed an' ready for business.

They evidently had the thing all rehearsed, 'cause some of 'em guarded the trail with spears, an' used thick shields to ward off the poisoned arrows, an' others swarmed up in the trees an' shot little poisoned arrows into the thick of the mass of men that were runnin' down the trail.

It was a funny fight. There wasn't any bangin' of firearms, but there was a lot o' yellin', an' in between yells could be heard the whispers of the arrows as they flitted through the night.

After a while I could see that our men were gettin' the worst of it. I was just a slave, an' when a fight started the women watched the slaves to see they didn't make a break for liberty, or start attackin' our boys from the rear.

Maybe I'd like to escape plenty, but I wanted to do it my own way, an' stickin' a spear in the back o' one of our boys didn't seem the way to do it. Then again, I wouldn't be any better off after I had escaped. My white skin would make trouble for me with the others. I wasn't the same as the other slaves, most of whom were Fantis anyway. They could make a break an' be among friends. If I made a hop I'd be outa the fryin' pan an' in the fire.

But I wasn't used to bein' a spectator on the side lines when there was fight goin' on. So I took a look at the situation.

When the alarm came in, the fire watchers had piled a lot of fagots on the big blaze, an' all the fight was goin' on by what light came from the fire. The fagots had burned off in the center an' there was a lot of flaming ends, fire on one side, stick on the other.

I whispers a few words to Kk-Kk, an' then we charged the fire, pickin' out the sticks, whirlin' 'em an' throwin' 'em into the mass o' savages that was borin' into our men.

She'd said somethin' to the slaves, an' they was all lined up, throwin' sticks too. They wasn't throwin' as wholeheartedly as Kk-Kk an' me was; but they was throwin' em, an' together we managed to keep the air full of brands.

It was a weird sight, those burnin' embers whirlin' an' spiralin' through the air, over the heads of our boys, an' plumb into the middle o' the Fanti outfit.

I seen that I'd missed a bet at that, though, because we was really tearin' the fire to pieces, an' it was goin' to get dark in a few minutes with the blaze all bein' thrown into the air that way.

One of our warriors had collected himself a poisoned arrow, an' he was sprawled out, shield an' spear lyin' aside of him. The arrows were whisperin' around pretty lively, an' I seen a couple of our slave fellows crumple up in a heap. That shield looked good to me, an' while I was reachin' for it, I got to wonderin' why not take the spear too. There wasn't anybody to tell me not to, so I grabbed 'em both, an' then I charged into the mêlée.

Them savages fought more or less silent after the first rush. There was plenty of yells, but they were individual, isolated yells, not no steady war cries. I'd picked a good time to strut my stuff, because there was more or less of a lull when I started my charge.

My clothes had been torn off my back. What few rags remained I'd thrown away, wantin' to get like the natives as fast as possible. My skin was still white, although it had tanned up a bit, but there wasn't any mistakin' me.

Our boys had got accustomed to the idea of a white man bein' a slave, an' they hadn't run into the white men like the

Fanti outfit had. Those Fantis had probably had a little white meat on their bill o' fare for a change o' diet; an' some expedition or other had come along an' mopped up on 'em. Anyhow, the idea of a white man as a fightin' machine had registered good an' strong with 'em.

There's somethin' funny about a native. They can say all they want to, but his fears are the big part of him, no matter how brave he gets. Those whirlin' brands o' fire wasn't makin' 'em feel any too good, an' then when I come chargin' down on 'em hell bent for election it was too much.

They wavered for a second, then gave a lot of yells on their own an' started pell-mell down the trail, each one tryin' to walk all over the heels of the boy in front.

Funny thing about a bunch of men once turnin' tail to a fight. When they do it they get into a panic. It ain't fear like one man or two men would feel fear. It's a panic, a blind somethin' that keeps 'em from thinkin' or feelin'. All they want to do is to run. There ain't any fight left in 'em.

It was awful what our crowd done to those boys. As soon as they started to run, the laddies with the spears started making corpses. An' I was right in the lead o' our bunch. Don't ask me how I got them. I don't know. I only know I was yellin' an' chargin', when the whole Fanti outfit turned tail, an' there I was, playin' pig-stickin' with the backs of a lot o' runnin' Fanti warriors for targets.

We gave up the chase after a while. We'd done enough damage, an' there was a chance o' trouble runnin' too far into the jungle. The crowd ahead might organize an' turn on us, an' we'd got pretty well strung out along the jungle trail.

I herded the boys back, an' there was a regular road o' Fanti dead between us an' where the main part o' the battle had taken place.

Well, they called a big powwow around the camp fire after that. I seen Kk-Kk talkin' to her old man, Yik-Yik, an' I guess she was pretty proud of her slave. Anyhow, Yik-Yik sucked his lips into his mouth like he did when he was thinkin', an' then he called to me.

He got me in a ring o' warriors before the fire, an' he made a great speech. Then he handed me a bloody spear and shield, an' daubed my chest with some sort of paint, an' painted a coupla rings around my eyes, an' put three stripes o' paint on my cheeks.

Then all the warriors started jumpin' around the fire, stampin' their feet, wailin' some sort of a weird chant. Every few steps they'd all slam their feet down on the hard ground in unison, an' the leaves on the trees rattled with their stamping. It was a wild night.

Kk-Kk was interpreter. She told me they were givin' me my liberty an' adoptin' me into the tribe as a great warrior. It was not right that such a mighty fighter should be the slave of a woman, she told me.

Well, there's somethin' funny about women the world over. They all talk peace an' cooin' dove stuff, but they all like to see a son-of-a-gun of a good scrap. Kk-Kk's eyes were soft an' glowin' with pride, an' I could see she was as proud of me as though she'd been my mother or sweetheart or somethin'.

An' seein' that look in her eyes did somethin' to me. I'd been gettin' sorta sweet on Kk-Kk without knowin' it. She was a pretty enough lass for all her chocolate color. An' she was a square shooter. She'd stuck up for me from the first, an' if it hadn't been for her I'd have been a meal instead of a slave. It was only natural that I should get to like her more an' more. Then, when I'd got used to the native ideas an' all that, she got to lookin' pretty good to me.

Anyhow, there I was in love with her—yes, an' I'm still in love with her. Maybe I did go native. What of it? There's worse things, an' Kk-Kk was a square shooter. I don't care what color her skin was. An' remember that she was the daughter of a king. There was royal blood in her veins, an' that makes a difference, race, or color or what not.

Anyhow, like it or not, I was in love with her, an' I still am.

Oh, I know I'm an old man now. Kk-Kk is awful old now if she's livin', because those natives get old quickly, an' I ain't no spring chicken myself. But I love her just the same.

Well, a white man is funny about his women. He ain't got no patience. When he falls in love he falls strong, an' he wants his girl. I didn't have patience like the monkey-man had. I couldn't wait around. I went to Kk-Kk the next day an' told her about it.

It was at the ant meal time when we was packin' fruit to 'em. I was still helpin' her even if I wasn't a slave any more. I did it because I wanted to.

Well, I told her; her eyes got all shiny, an' she dropped the dried fruit in a heap an' threw her arms around my neck, an' she cried a bit, an' made soft noises in the graduated monkey talk that is the real language of the tribe. Bein' all excited that way, she forgot the language of the goldsmith an' went back to the talk of her folks.

The ants came an' got the fruit, an' they crawled all over our feet eatin' it. If she hadn't been so happy, an' if I hadn't been so much in love we'd both have realized what it meant, the ants crawlin' over us that way an' not offerin' to bite me, or actin' hostile at all. It showed that I'd been makin' friends with 'em on the side.

Well, after a while she broke away, an' then she did some more cryin' an' explained that she was the daughter of the chief. The man that married her would be the chief of the tribe some day. That is, he'd be the husband of the tribe's queen.

Now in that tribe the men bought their wives. The man who married Kk-Kk was the man who'd buy her hand from her old man. But, bein' as she was the daughter of the chief, an' the future queen of the tribe, it'd take more wealth to buy her hand than any single man in the tribe could muster.

She told me how many skins an' how many hogs an' how much dried meat an' how many bows an' arrows an' spears, an' how many pounds of the native tobacco an' all that would be required.

I didn't pay much attention to the long list of stuff she rattled off. I had over sixty pounds of pure gold cached then, an' I felt like a millionaire.

After all, what was all this native stuff compared with what I had? I was a rich man for a common, ordinary sailor boy. I could take that gold right then an' walk into any of the world's market places an' buy what I wanted. Yes, an' there's even been cases of women of the higher muck-a-mucks sellin' themselves or their daughters in marriage for less than sixty pounds of pure gold.

Well, I laughed at Kk-Kk an' told her not to worry. I'd buy her hand from the old man. I didn't worry about the price. I was a sailor lad, an' I had the hot blood of youth in my veins, an' I was in love with Kk-Kk, an' she was standin' there with her eyes all limpid an' misty an' her arms around my neck, an' I had sixty pounds of pure gold. What more could a man want?

An' then I heard a noise an' looked up.

There was the monkey-man, squattin' on the branch of a tree an' lookin' at us, and his lips were workin' back an' forth from his teeth. He wasn't sayin' a word, but his lips worked up an' down, an' every time they'd work, his teeth showed through.

I stiffened a bit, although it wasn't that I was afraid. Right then I felt that I could lick all the monkey-men in the world, either one at a time or all together.

Kk-Kk was frightened. I could feel the shivers runnin' up an' down her arms, an' she made little scared noises with her lips.

But the monkey-man didn't say anything. When he saw that we knew he was watchin', he reached up his great arms, caught the branch of a tree above him, swung off into space, caught another limb with his great feet, an' swirled off into the

forest. All that was left was the twilight an' the chatterin'
of a bunch of monkeys, an' the whimperin' noises Kk-Kk was
makin'.

I patted the girl on the shoulder. Let the monkey-man
storm around through the treetops. A lot of good that would
do him. He wasn't in a position to buy the hand of Kk-Kk,
an' he wasn't likely to be in the position. I had a big chunk
of pure gold stored up. I didn't think it'd be any trick at all
to complete the purchase.

By next day, though, I knew I was up against a funny problem. I had all the gold I could carry, but gold wasn't any
good. I had enough of it to purchase a whole tannery full of
choice skins, but I couldn't trade the gold for skins. The tribe
I was with didn't care anything for the gold except as somethin' to trade to the Fanti boys. An' all the tradin' was done
by the chief. The tribal custom prohibited the others from
doin' any tradin', even from havin' any of the gold.

I commenced to see it wasn't as simple as I'd thought it
was goin' to be.

An' all the while I got more an' more in love with Kk-Kk.
She was just the sort of a woman a real adventurin' man
wants. She'd keep her head in any emergency. She was strong
an' tender. There wasn't an ache nor a pain in her system.
When she moved she walked like it wasn't any effort at all. If
the trees looked easier than the trail she'd swing up in them an'
go from branch to branch, light as a feather driftin' down wind.

I'm tellin' you she was strong as an ox an' as graceful
as a panther. A woman like that'd go with a man anywhere.
An' she was sweet an' tender. When she thought I was blue
for the white race an' home an' all that, she'd draw my head
down against her breast an' croon to me as soft an' low as
the wind sighin' through the tops of the jungle trees.

I wanted to take her away with me. Any one could see the
tribe was doomed. The very gold that gave them their tradin'
power was their curse. The Fantis desired that gold. They

might get beat in one battle, might get beat in a thousand, but as long as the ledge was there, there'd be invaders fightin' to get possession of it.

It'd be only a question of time until the tribe was wiped out, defeated, captured, an' the women turned into slaves. They couldn't stand the climate in the interior. Four or five miles back from the ocean was their limit. The Fantis wanted that gold ledge. Every so often there'd be a battle, an' when it was over there'd be dead an' wounded. There was always plenty more of the enemy, but there was a few less of our boys after every fight.

If I could get away an' take Kk-Kk with me, an' a pack load of gold, what I could carry an' what Kk-Kk could carry, we'd be fixed for life. We could go out into the cities an' hold up our heads with any of 'em.

But I knew I was goin' to have trouble gettin' Kk-Kk to see things that way. I might get her to leave with me, but she'd been brought up with the idea that her obligation to the tribe was sacred. She wouldn't take any of the gold. You see she hadn't ever had to deal with money, an' she did what she thought was right, not what she thought would make the most money for her.

While I was thinkin' things over, the monkey-man comes swingin' into the council an' tells 'em he's goin' to buy the hand of Kk-Kk at the next full moon. That was all he said. He wouldn't tell 'em where he was goin' to get the stuff or anything.

But it was enough to get me worried. An' it bothered Kk-Kk.

There was lots o' wild rumors goin' along in those days. There was a report that the Ashantis an' the Fantis were gettin' together for a joint attack. They was determined to get that gold ledge.

I tried to get Kk-Kk to advise the tribe to leave the thing.

Without that gold they'd be safe from attack, an' the gold didn't mean so much to 'em anyhow.

But they were just like the rest of the nations, if a man could compare a savage tribe with a nation. They wanted their gold, even when it wasn't doin' the rank an' file of 'em any good. They were goin' to fight for it, lay down their lives for it if they had to, an' all the time only the ruler had any right to use the gold to trade with.

They knew they could have peace by goin' away. They must have seen they couldn't last long stayin' there. Every battle left 'em a little weaker. But no, they must stay an' die for their ledge of gold, an' they didn't even know the value of it. It's funny about gold that way.

There was another rumor goin' around that made me do a lot of thinkin', an' that was of a white man that was camped a couple of days' march away. He had a big outfit with him, an' he was shootin' big game an' prospectin' around in general.

A wild idea got into my head that if I could sneak away an' get to him with fifty or sixty pounds of gold I could trade it for mirrors, guns, blankets an' what not that would look like a million dollars to the old chief. Then I could buy Kk-Kk an' maybe I could talk her into goin' away with me.

I really had enough gold, but I was gettin' a little hoggish. I wanted more. The love of a woman like Kk-Kk had ought to make a man richer than the richest king in the world, but I was a white man, an' I'd been taught to worship gold along with God.

In fact, I'd only had that God worship idea taught me on Sundays when I was a kid. On week days the god was gold. My folks had been rated as bein' pretty religious as common folks go. But even they hadn't tried to carry religion past Sunday. Gold was the god six days of the week, an' I'd been brought up with the white man's idea.

So I had to get me a little more gold. I wanted it so I could go to the white man's camp with all the gold I could carry an' still have as much left behind, hidden in the ground, waitin' for me to come back.

The next mornin' I decided to take a chance an' scoop out a big lot o' quartz. I got out with the food for the ants all right; I hadn't even thought about trouble with them for a long while. They'd quit bein' one of my worries. I walked over to the ledge and dug into the quartz.

An' then somethin' funny struck me. It was a feelin' like somethin' was borin' into my back. I whirled around an' there was the monkey-man sittin' on a limb, watchin' me.

He was up in a tree, squatted on the limb, his hands holdin' a bow with one of them poison arrows on the string an' it was then I noticed the way his toes came around the under side of the limb an' held him firm. Funny how a fellow'll notice things like that when he's figurin' he has an appointment in eternity right away.

CHAPTER 5

The Monkey-Man

I stared into the monkey-man's eyes, an' he stared back. I'd read somewhere that a white man always has the advantage over the other races because there's some kind of a racial inferiority that the other fellows develop in a pinch.

Maybe it's true, an' maybe it ain't. I only know I stared at the monkey-man, an' he fidgeted his fingers around on the bow string.

I was caught red-handed. One of those poison arrows would almost drop me in my tracks. I wouldn't have a chance to get outside of the deadline.

It looked like curtains for me. Then a funny thing happened. I thought at the time it was because of my starin' eyes an' the racial inferiority an' what not. Now I know the real reason. But the monkey-man lowered the bow, blinked his eyes a couple of times, just like a monkey puzzlin' over a new idea, an' then he reached up one of those long paws, grabbed a branch overhead, swung up into the higher trees, an' was off.

It looked like he'd gone to get some witnesses, an' it was up to me to bury my gold an' be snappy about it. I could see the ants were finishin' up the last of the feed I'd given 'em, an' I wouldn't have to be afraid of some of that bein' left.

I took the gold an' sprinted for the place where I kept it hid. I buried the new batch with the other, an' then strolled back to the clearin', tryin' to look innocent.

I felt a big weight on my chest. Somehow I felt the monkey-man was goin' to get me. If he could make his charges stick I was sure due to be a meal before night.

But the funny part of it was he didn't make any charges. He wasn't even there at all. Funny. I walked around an' passed the few words of the language I'd picked up with some of the warriors, an' then I saw Kk-Kk.

It was sort of a lazy life, livin' there that way. The tradin' power of the gold ornaments gave the tribe the bulge on things. They didn't have to work so awful hard. Funny, too, they didn't savvy rightly about the gold. They thought it wasn't the metal, but the way the goldsmith worked it up into rings an' bracelets an' such like, that made it valuable. Gold as such they couldn't understand.

Anyhow, the warriors didn't have anything to do except a little huntin' once in a while. The women did all of the real work, an' there wasn't much of that.

Kk-Kk an' me walked down to the beach an' I watched the green surf thunderin' in. Her arm was nestled around me an' her head was up against my shoulder. I felt a possessory sort of feelin' like I owned the whole world. I patted her head an' told her there wasn't anything to be afraid of, that I was goin' to make good on buyin' her an' that I'd boost any price the monkey-man was able to raise.

She felt curious, but when she seen I didn't want to answer questions she let things go without talkin'. She was a wonderful girl, the kind that any man could be proud of, particularly a rough, seafarin' man that had sailed all the seas of the world an' knocked about in all sorts of weather.

I broke away from her when the sun was well up. I knew she'd go down to the ocean with the tribe for her bath.

That was my chance. I raced into the jungle to the place where I'd left my gold.

All that a man could pack away was gone. There wasn't over twenty pounds left. The ground had been dug up an' the gold rooted up. It was there in the sun, glistenin' soft an' yellow against the green of the jungle an' the rich brown of the earth.

For a minute my heart made a flip-flop, an' then I knew. The monkey-man hadn't given the alarm at all. He'd come to know somethin' of the power of the gold, an' when he saw me feedin' the ants an' helpin' myself at the gold ledge he realized I must have a bunch of it cached away. That had been why he hadn't shot me with a poisoned arrow. He'd swung up out of sight in the high tree an' waited for me to lead him to the place where I'd buried the gold. With his trainin' in slippin' through the branches of the trees there hadn't been anything to it. He followed me as easy as a bird could flit through the branches.

Now he'd taken all the gold he could carry. He'd been in a hurry. He hadn't stopped to bury the rest some place else, even, or to cover it over with earth. Why? There was only one answer. He'd made a bluff about buyin' Kk-Kk from her old man, an' he wanted to make good. He'd heard about the white man an' his camp, an' he'd got the same idea I'd had, an' he'd got a head start on me.

I had a skin pouch with a couple of straps goin' over the shoulders. I loaded the gold that was left in it an' made my start. I knew there'd be trouble gettin' past the sentries at the bottleneck, but I couldn't wait for night. The monkey-man could slip through in the trees. I'd have to rely on bluff and nerve.

It wasn't gettin' past 'em that was the hard part. It was carryin' the gold out. As a warrior, I was entitled to go out in the jungle to hunt, to come an' go as I pleased. It was what was in that skin pouch that would make the trouble.

Then I got another idea. There'd been a kill the day before of some little sort of an antelope that ran around the jungle. I knew where some of the meat was. The gold didn't amount to much in size, an' I raced over an' stuffed some animal meat on the top of it. It was sink or swim, an' I couldn't wait to fix up any fancy plan.

I grabbed a spear an' a shield an' started down the path. The sentries flashed their white teeth at me an' blinked their round eyes. Then one of 'em noticed the pack on my back an' he flopped his spear down while he came over to investigate.

I didn't act like I was the least bit frightened. I even opened the sack myself, an' I made a lot of motions. I pointed to the sun, an' I swung my hand up an' down four times tellin' 'em that I'd be away four days. Then I pointed to the meat an' to my mouth, explainin' that it was for food.

I threw in a little comic stuff an' had 'em laughin'. They laughed easy, those jungle men who were so blamed ignorant they didn't know the power of gold.

It was a cinch. I was on my way, headin' into hostile territory, knowin' that the Fantis were in the country an' that I'd be a fine meal for 'em. It's a funny sensation, figgerin' that you're only valuable for the meat you can be made into, estimatin' your calory value on the hoof.

Anyhow, the thing had been started an' I had to see it through. After I got into the country where the white men went, the color of my skin would protect me from the tribes. The white man gets respect from the blacks. He kills a lot of blacks to do it, but he gets results.

It was the first few miles that had me worried. I had to go through the Eso country an' into the Nitchwa country, an' I was in a hurry. I couldn't go slow an' cautious like, an' I couldn't take to the trees like the monkey-man could.

The first day I almost got caught. A bunch of Fanti warriors came down the trail. I swung off to one side, workin' my way into the thickest of the jungle, an' hidin' in the shadows. I thought sure I was caught, because those boys have eyes that can see in the dark. But I got by.

The second day I didn't see a soul. I was gettin' in a more open, rollin' country, an' I only had a general idea where I was goin'. There was a hill that stood up pretty well over the rest of the country, an' I got up on that an' climbed a tree.

Just at dusk I see 'em, hundreds of fires twinklin' through the dusk like little stars. I figgered that'd be the camp of the white man.

It ain't healthy to go through the jungle at night. There are too many animals who have picked up the habits of man an' figger that turn-about is fair play. They relish the flesh of a man, more particularly a white man, as a delicacy.

We don't think nothin' o' stalkin' a nice buck an' having our mouth water an' think how tasty he's goin' to be broiled over a bed o' coals. But if the buck turns around an' starts stalkin' us an' lickin' his chops over how nice we're goin' to taste it's a different affair altogether.

I know, because for two hours I worked through the country with eyes glarin' out of the jungle all around, an' soft steps fallin' into the trail behind me. They were animals, stalkin' along behind, a little afraid of the white man smell, hesitatin' a bit about closin' the gap an' makin' a supper outa me, but feelin' their mouths water at the thought.

Yes, sir, I know how it feels to be hunted by somethin' that's just figgerin' how nice you're goin' to taste after he's got his paws on you.

Well, finally I came to the camp of the white man. I could see him sittin' there, all bearded an' tanned. He was wearin' white clothes an' sittin' before a fire with a lot o' native servants waitin' around with food an' drink an' what not.

I walked up to him, pretty well all in, an' motioned to my mouth. I'd been so used to talkin' to the natives that way that for a moment I forgot that this man talked my language.

Then I told him. "I come to trade," I says, an' dumped out the gold on the ground.

He went up outa the canvas chair like he'd been shot.

"Another one!" he yelled. "An' this one's white!"

Then he clapped his hands, an' black men came runnin' up an' grabbed me.

"Where did yuh get it? Where is it? Is there any more? How long will it take to get there?" he yells at me, his face all purple, with the veins standin' out an' the eyes bulgin'.

I'd forgotten how excited white men got at the sight of gold.

"Gold! Gold!" he goes on. "The country must be lousy with gold! There was a big ape hanging around camp this morning. He seemed a higher species of ape, almost human. I stalked him and shot him for a specimen. Can you imagine my surprise when I found that he was carrying a skin filled with gold?

"And this is the same gold. I'd recognize it anywhere. Come, my good man, come and tell me if you have ever seen a similar creature to this great ape. I have preserved him in alcohol and intend to carry him intact to the British Museum."

I could feel myself turnin' sorta sick at the idea, but there was nothin' for it. He was draggin' me along to a big vat. There was the monkey-man, a bullet hole in his back—in his back, mind you. He hadn't even shot him from the front, but had sneaked around to the rear. The "specimen" was floatin' around in the alcohol.

I turned away.

"Tell me, tell me," pleads the guy, "do you know him? Your gold comes from the same source. Perhaps you have seen others of the same species.

"After I shot him I was overcome with remorse because he might have showed me the way to the gold deposit if I had merely captured him. But I shot before I knew of the gold."

I did some rapid thinkin'. If this bird thought I knew where the gold came from he'd force me to show him, or perhaps he'd kill me an' stick me in alcohol. So I looked sad.

"No, I don't know," I tells him. "I saw this man-monkey carryin' a skin full of somethin' heavy. I followed along until he set down the sack an' went to sleep. Then I sneaked up, seen it was gold, an' figgered a monkey-man didn't have no use for gold."

He nods his head. "Quite right, my friend. Quite right. A monkey can have no use for gold. And how about yourself? You possibly have no use for it. At any rate you admit it was part of the gold that belonged to the monkey, so you should restore it to the original pile, and I will take charge of it."

I seen this bird was one of the kind that want everything for nothin' an' insist that a guy mustn't hold out on 'em.

I told him that I'm only too glad to oblige, but I want some calicos an' some mirrors an' blankets an' a gun an' some ammunition, an' some huntin' knives an' beads. After that he can have the gold.

We dickered for a while, an' finally I dusted out, takin' two porters with me, frightened to death but loaded down with junk. I was carryin' the rifle, an' I was watchin' my back trail. The old boy might figure I was a specimen.

I got back all right. We had one brush with the Fanti outfit, but the roar of the gun made 'em take to the tall timber. I had the porters lay the junk down about two miles from the place where our tribe was camped, an' I sneaked it up to the bottleneck myself, carryin' three loads of it. Then I came on up to the sentries, shook hands, walked past an' got a couple of warriors to help me with the plunder.

Kk-Kk was there, all dolled up in all her finery, paradin' around the village. That's a custom they got from the Fantis. When a girl's offered for sale in marriage she decks herself out with everything the family's got an' parades around the village. That's a notice to bidders.

I knew Kk-Kk was doin' it for me. She had to comply with the customs of the tribe, but she figgered I was the only bird that could make the grade an' she trusted to my resourcefulness to bring home the bacon.

CHAPTER 6

African Justice

My stuff was a riot. When I had the fellows spread it out on the ground the boys' eyes stuck out until their foreheads bulged. Most of 'em had never seen the trade goods of the white man. They'd been kept pretty well isolated with the hostile Fanti outfit hemmin' 'em in by land an' the open ocean thunderin' on the beach.

The knives made the hit. The warriors were hunters enough to appreciate a keen-edged bit of shiny steel. The blankets didn't take very well, neither did the calico, but the knives, the mirrors, an' the beads were drawin' cards that couldn't be beat.

Old Yik-Yik screwed up his eyes an' sucked in his mouth, the way he had when he was thinkin', an' then he jabbers out a bunch of graduated monkey talk. The goldsmith was there an' he blinks his rheumy eyes an' sticks out his hand.

"The old bird says you've bought the girl," he tells me.

I could feel my heart do a flip-flop. It was all matter-of-fact to them, the buyin' of a wife, even if she did happen to be the future queen of the tribe. But to me there was only one Kk-Kk in the world, an' now she was to be mine. The only man that knew my secret was the monkey-man, an' he was floatin' around in a vat of alcohol. I could settle down in the tribe an' be happy the rest of my life.

But, in spite of it all, I was feelin' off color. My head felt light. When I'd turn it quick it seemed to keep right on goin' for a couple of revolutions. An' my feet felt funny, as though they wasn't settin' firm on the ground.

But what of it? Wasn't I goin' to marry Kk-Kk? What was a little biliousness more or less?

An' then there was a bunch o' yellin'. I looked up an' seen a couple of the sentries bringin' in a captive. Another meal, I thought to myself, wonderin' if maybe he'd be in time to furnish the spread at the weddin' feast.

I looked again, an' then my mouth got all dry an' fuzzy.

It was one of the porters that had carried out my stuff. Probably he had sneaked back to try an' find the gold, or else some of the hunters had caught him. In either event my hash was cooked. When he told 'em what I'd traded to the white man—

I strained my ears. Some of our crowd talked Fanti, an' maybe the porter talked it. He did. I heard 'em jabberin' away, an' the porter pointed at me an' at the stuff on the ground.

I stole a look at Yik-Yik. His eyes was as hard as a couple of glass beads, an' his lips was all sucked in until his mouth was just a network of puckered wrinkles.

He spits out some words an' a circle forms around me. The goldsmith was still there an' he kept right on actin' as interpreter, but I didn't need to follow half what he said.

An' then, all of a sudden, I stiffened up to real attention. It seemed the old man was accusin' Kk-Kk o' betrayin' the tribe.

For a minute or two I thought he'd gone clean cuckoo, an'

then I seen just how it looked to him. Kk-Kk was in love with me. The monkey-man, who she didn't like, had threatened to buy her. There was a white man in the country. What was more likely than that she'd slipped me out a bunch of gold?

I tried to tell 'em, but they would not listen. Kk-Kk looked all white around the gills for a minute, an' then she walked over to my side.

"We shall meet death together," she said, dignified as a queen had ought to be. But I wasn't goin' to stand for it. I tried to tell 'em about how I had the ants trained. I volunteered to show 'em. I tried to get 'em to feed me to the ants. But they wouldn't listen to me. Kk-Kk was the only one they'd listen to, an' she wouldn't say a word. She wanted to die with me.

Then was when I knew I was sick. The whole ground started reelin' around, an' I felt so drowsy I could hardly hold my eyes open. My head was burnin' an' throbbin' an' it seemed as though the damp odors of the jungle was soaked all through my blood an' was smotherin' me under a blanket of jungle mist.

Their voices sounded farther an' farther away.

I heard the goldsmith tellin' me the sentence the chief was pronouncin'. He had to lean up against my ear an' shout to make me understand.

It seemed they had a funny bread made out of some berries an' roots. When a fellow ate it he lost his memory.

The old king had decided not to kill us, but to feed us this bread an' banish us from the tribe.

Since we'd committed the crime against the tribe because we wanted to marry, it seemed like proper justice for the old boy to feed us *king-kee*, the bread of forgetfulness, so we wouldn't ever remember about the other.

It was a horrible punishment. If I hadn't been comin' down sick I'd have made a break an' forced 'em to kill me, or turned loose with the rifle an' seen if I couldn't have escaped with Kk-Kk.

But I was a sick man. I felt 'em stuffin' somethin' in my mouth, an' I swallowed mechanically an' cried for water.

Then I remember seein' Kk-Kk's eyes, all misty an' floatin' with tears, bendin' over me. Then I sank into a sleep or stupor. Everything snuffed out like a candle goin' out.

Lord knows how much later I began to come to. I was in Cape Coast Castle. They told me some natives had brought me on a stretcher, sat me down before the door of the buildin' where they kept the medicines, an' gone away. It had been done at night. They found me there the next mornin' sick with the sleepin' sickness.

When I woke up I couldn't tell 'em who I was, where I'd been, or how I got there. I only knew I wanted somethin' an' couldn't tell what it was.

A boat came in, an' they shipped me on her. The surgeon aboard got interested in my case. Every time it rained I'd sleep. There was somethin' in the smell of dampness in the air.

He treated me like I'd been a king, an' took me to Boston. There was some German doctor there that had specialized on tropical fevers. They had me there for six months studyin' my case.

The doctor told me I was victim of what he called auto-hypnosis. He said I went to sleep when it rained because I thought of sleep when it rained.

I told him it was the fever in my blood comin' out when it got damp, but he just shook his head an' said auto-hypnosis, whatever that might mean.

He tried for six months to get me over it, an' then he gave it up as a bad job.

He said for me to come to California or Arizona an' get out in the desert, where it only rained once or twice a year, an' to always be in my tent when it rained.

I followed his advice. For fifty years now I've been livin' out here in the desert.

Every time it rains an' I smell the damp air, it acts on me like the jungle smells when I had the sleepin' sickness, an' I go to sleep. Sometimes I fall asleep and don't waken for two weeks at a stretch.

But it's funny about me. Now that I'm gettin' old, my memory's comin' back to me. Particularly after I wake up, I can recall everything like I've just told it to you.

Of course I'm an old man now, nothin' but a bum of a desert rat, out here scratchin' around in the sand an' sagebrush for a few colors of gold. I got me a placer staked out over there at the base of that hill.

Ain't it funny that I have to spend my life lookin' for gold, when it was grabbin' the gold in big chunks that made all my troubles? Oh, well, it's all in a lifetime.

Of course I'm too old to be thinkin' of such things now. But I get awful lonesome for Kk-Kk. I can see her round, liquid eyes shinin' at me whenever I wake up from one of these long sleeps. I wonder if she's got her memory comin' back, now that she's gettin' old—an' I wonder if she ever thinks of me—

Yes, sir. Thankee, sir. Another cup of that coffee will go kinda good. When a man's been asleep for eight or nine days he wakes up sorta slow. I'll drink this coffee an' then I'll be headin' over toward my placer claim.

I'm sorry I bothered you folks, but that rain came up mighty sudden, an' the first thing I knew I was soakin' wet an' sleepy, smellin' the damp smell of the earth an' the desert stuff. I crawled in this bunch of Joshuay palms, an' that's the last I remember until you came along an' poured the hot coffee down me.

No, thanks, I don't believe I'll stay any longer.

My tent's fixed up mighty comfortable over there, an' when I wake up this way it seems like I've been with Kk-Kk in a dream world. I like to think about my lost sweetheart.

So long, boys. Thanks for the coffee.

A YEAR IN A DAY

CHAPTER 1

The Invisible Death

Of the five men who sat in that palatial room, Carl Ramsay had the gift of dramatic expression. He thought in blurbs, talked in motion picture subtitles.

The hour of midnight chimed from the expensive clock on the mantelpiece. Somewhere a cuckoo clock sounded.

"A new day," said Carl Ramsay.

Tolliver Hemingway, multimillionaire, stirred uneasily.

"The day I am to die," he said, and forced a laugh.

Nick Searle of the *Star* scraped a match along the sole of his shoe and grunted.

"One chance in a thousand."

Inspector Hunter glowered about him, and his eyes were a challenge.

"One chance in ten thousand. One chance in a million," he said.

No one contradicted him, but Carl Ramsay of the *Clarion* uttered another subtitle.

"The Death Day Dawns," he murmured.

Arthur Swift surveyed the men in the room with curious eyes. It was his first experience with men of this type. Inspector Harrison Hunter, forceful, driving, alert; Tolliver Hemingway, multimillionaire, suave, polished, dignified, yet somewhat nervous beneath the external polish; Nick Searle, veteran reporter of the *Star*; Carl Ramsay, of the *Clarion*, who had been aptly described as "the man with the tabloid mind"; and, himself, a young teacher of physics in the state university. It had been Searle who had called him in, to cover the case for the *Star* from a scientific angle.

Yet Swift could see nothing to cover.

The room was locked, guarded. The five men were to keep a constant vigil for twenty-four hours within that locked room. Every bit of food they were to eat during that time had been hermetically sealed in cans. It would be consumed immediately after the cans were opened. Every bit of liquid they were to drink was contained in bottles that had been sealed and certified.

The room was on a third story. The windows opened out upon magnificent grounds, landscaped, cared for, and guarded. The side of the house was perfectly blank, devoid of any projection up which a man might climb. Searchlights played about the grounds. Floodlights illuminated the side of the building. A hundred armed deputies patrolled the place.

Such precautions seemed so elaborate as to be absurd. Under ordinary circumstances they would have been. But these were not ordinary.

Six of the richest men in the city had received letters on a single day. Those letters had been uniform in their terms. The men were to signify their willingness to pay a certain sum of money, which sum varied in each instance, or they were to die.

None of the men paid the slightest attention to those letters, save to turn them over to the police.

Then I. W. Steen, the millionaire head of a publishing company which included several magazines and two newspapers, one of which was the sensational *Clarion*, received a second letter.

That letter announced the day and the hour of his death

in the event he did not comply with the request. Steen turned that letter over to the police and took precautions against attack.

The precautions were in vain.

Seated in his private office, in conference with the heads of his various publications, a sickening sweet odor became noticeable in the room. Ten seconds later Steen was dead. No other occupant of the room suffered the slightest inconvenience, the slightest sensation of discomfort, although all of them noticed the peculiar odor.

Two days later C. G. Haymes received a summons through the mail. It was in the nature of an ultimatum. He was to signify his willingness to comply with the terms of the man who signed himself "Zin Zandor," or he, too, was to die.

The hour of his death was not given. But the day of the death was announced.

C. G. Haymes had been frankly worried. He had placed himself in the hands of the police. They had isolated him in his home, surrounded the place with guards. He, too, had become good "copy," and the newspaper reporters who enjoyed the confidence of the administration had been permitted to cover the case. They had done it with an air of boredom. Steen's death had been due to fright, they felt; the autopsy disclosed no organic lesion. There was no chance that coincidence would repeat itself.

Yet, while the reporters were lounging about at ease, while the police cordon surrounded the place, while even the servants had been excluded, C. G. Haymes died, and the manner of his death was as the other's. A sickening sweet odor that had been noticed by the other occupants of the room, yet had not seemed to affect them in the least, a cry of anguish from the millionaire, a sudden spasm, and death.

Three of the remaining millionaires had capitulated.

They had followed the routine indicated in the letter for showing their willingness to pay. And they were paying, transmitting the money to the dreaded Zin Zandor by means which they refused to divulge. For Zin Zandor had made it apparent that any information given to the police would result in death.

Tolliver Hemingway alone of the remaining men who had been threatened refused to be cowed. He hurled forth his defiance, and the mail had brought him the information that he would meet his death on the twenty-fourth day of June.

Now midnight had struck on the twenty-third of June, and the clocks clacked off the seconds of the fatal twenty-fourth.

"Well, we might as well have a drink," said Inspector Hunter, pouring himself a stiff jolt from some of the prewar whisky the millionaire's cellars had furnished.

"None for me," said Hemingway. "I think I'll go easy on the drink. One can't tell . . ."

The inspector snorted.

"Don't be foolish. You're absolutely safe here. Every bit of food and drink in this room has been checked by two police chemists. I wouldn't even waste the time to sit here with you, only the public are in a panic over this Zandor fellow, and we've got to show them how powerless he is in the face of adequate precautions. In the meantime our paper and handwriting experts are at work on those letters. They were all written on a Remington typewriter, and all on the same machine. The stationery has been traced to a job lot that went to one of the big stationery firms. It's a cinch."

He drained the whisky.

Carl Ramsay scribbled a sentence in a notebook, and, as he wrote, read aloud the words he jotted down for future reference.

"The Man Who Dares Not Eat," he intoned. "We'll run a picture over that."

Nick Searle snorted.

"You've got a cinch with that yellow journal of yours, Ramsay. Wish I had things as easy."

Arthur Swift stirred in his chair uneasily.

"You both have a snap compared to me. What am I supposed to do?"

Searle laughed.

"Look wise and feel foolish. Along about nine o'clock we'll cook up a column or two for you to write about the scientific angle of the thing. I'll dope out what I want, you can stick in a couple of high-sounding scientific terms, something about metabolism and the oxidation of tissue. We'll run your picture at the head of the column. There'll be a catchy headline, 'Noted Professor Explains Hysteria,' or something of the sort. The idea will be that there was something akin to hypnotic suggestion in the minds of the men who died."

Carl Ramsay lit a cigarette.

"Better headline than that," he said: " 'Scientist Pits Skill Against Death.' "

Searle stretched, yawned.

"You ought to have the city editor I've got to go up against," he said gloomily.

And Arthur Swift, watching Ramsay, suddenly saw a peculiar thing. The right hand of the reporter seemed to vanish. He rubbed his eyes. The hand was back in place.

But, for a split fraction of a second, the right hand of the tabloid reporter had simply vanished. It had not only dissolved into space, but the right arm, almost to the shoulder, had ceased to exist.

It could hardly have been a mere freak of the imagination. Neither could it have been an optical illusion. For Arthur Swift had been able to see everything else within that room clearly and with normal vision.

Tolliver Hemingway, the millionaire, was taking a cigarette from a gold case. Searle was biting the end from a cigar. Ramsay was smoking. His left hand was conveying the cigarette from his lips. Inspector Hunter was finishing the last of the generous drink he had poured.

Everything was entirely normal, save and except for that sudden disappearance of Carl Ramsay's right hand. It had happened that Arthur Swift was watching that right hand. He had seen it suddenly become nothing. He had blinked his eyes, and the hand was back, reaching for a notebook. It could not have been more than a tenth of a second that the hand was gone, perhaps not half that long. Yet it most certainly had disappeared.

"Look here," said Swift, "did you fellows notice anything just then?"

They looked at him, and as their eyes saw the expression on his face, they snapped to rigid attention.

"What?" asked Searle.

"Shoot," said Inspector Hunter.

"Your hand," said Swift, addressing himself to Ramsay, "it seemed sort of—er—well, sort of funny."

And then a strange thing happened.

Ramsay opened his lips to make some reply, and the sounds that came forth were not words. They seemed a peculiar rattle of gurgling noise that beat with consonant harshness upon the eardrums, rattled against the intelligence with such terrific rapidity that they were like static on a radio receiver.

"What?" asked Swift.

Ramsay drawled slightly, in his normal irritating tone of voice, as he reached for the pencil and scrawled a line across the notebook.

"Guard Goes Goofy," he scribbled, and said: "That'd look fine under your picture. It shows what hysteria will do. Sort of fits in with a general theory. Get a man to believe that a sickening sweet odor will produce death upon him alone, and then fill the room with such an odor, and the man who believed it would be fatal would kick off. Good thought that. I'll write it up with a by-line by Professor Somebody-or-other: Scientist Suggests Solution."

Inspector Hunter snorted. "Foolish to have amateurs in a place like this."

Searle frowned. "One of the first things you've got to learn, Swift, in a situation of this kind, is to see things and see them accurately. Don't go letting your imagination run away with you. Now all the *Star* wants is the use of your name and some scientific terminology. Maybe you'd better curl up and take a nap."

But Tolliver Hemingway, accustomed to appraise character with unerring accuracy, leaned forward.

"Tell us what you saw?" he said.

Arthur Swift turned red. Under the rebuke of the reporter who had employed him, he realized how absolutely foolish it would sound for him to mention that the right hand and arm of a man had disappeared—had become simply as nothing.

"Why—I guess—."

The steady, keen eyes of the multimillionaire bored into the young man's face.

"Yes. Go on. Nothing's too absurd to be given careful attention."

"Well," blurted Swift, "if you've got to know; it sounds sort of goofy, but—"

He broke off as a cry of alarm burst from the lips of Carl Ramsay.

"The odor!" he cried.

And there could be no doubt of it. The room was filling with a peculiar odor, a something that was like orange blossoms, yet was not like orange blossoms. It was too sickeningly sweet to be pleasant, yet so cloyingly rich that it was not unpleasant.

Tolliver Hemingway was on his feet, his gray eyes snapping.

"All right, boys; don't think I'm afraid, and don't think any hysteria is going to get me. Inspector, I've one request. If anything *should* happen, search every man in this room, from his skin out. I have an idea this—"

He paused. A look of surprise came over his features. He clutched at his throat.

"I . . . am . . . not . . . afraid," he said, thickly, speaking slowly as though paralysis gripped the muscles of his throat.

"It . . . is . . ."

And he swayed on his feet, lurched forward, flung out a groping hand. The hand clutched the rich cloth which adorned the table on which Inspector Hunter had set his empty glass, and on which the whisky bottle reposed. The cloth came off. The glass crashed to the floor. The bottle rolled across the room.

Tolliver Hemingway crashed to the floor.

He was dead by the time they managed to open his collar and take his limp wrist in their fingers.

Inspector Hunter rushed to the window.

Outside, the searchlights played silently across the darkness of the grounds, their beams interlacing, bringing trees and shrubs into white brilliance, casting shadows which were, in turn, dispersed by the rays of other cross-lights, flickering and flitting. The whole side of the building was covered by floodlights, and the inspector had no sooner thrust his head from the window than a voice from below called up.

"All right, inspector?"

"Anybody come near here?"

"No, sir. Of course not, sir. Our orders were to shoot on sight."

"Who's there with you?"

"Laughlin, O'Rourke, Maloney, and Green."

"One of you sound the alarm. The others wait there. Shoot any stranger on sight."

Inspector Hunter whipped a service revolver from his belted holster, and fired two shots from the open window, signal to the various guards. Almost immediately a siren screamed forth the agreed signal of death.

Inspector Hunter turned back to the room, then, suddenly snapped his revolver to the level.

"Get your hands up, Searle!"

The surprised reporter, in the act of shooting the bolt on the door, regarded the inspector with a puzzled frown.

"I've got to get to the paper. I can handle this so much better on the ground than I can over the wire. We'll get out an extra—"

There was no mistaking the cold calm of Hunter's voice.

"Get away from that door or I'll shoot you like a dog. You know what this means. It's the beginning of a reign of terror. This is once that the news comes second. You men will remain here. The murder will be kept absolutely secret until we've exhausted every possible clew.

"And every man in this room is going to be searched from the skin out. Everything in this room, including the very air, is going to be analyzed. Damn it, I'm going to get at the bottom of this!"

And Nick Searle, white-faced in his rage, slowly turned back from the door.

"The *Star* will break you for this," he said, in a low tone, vibrant with anger. "You can't pull a stunt like this and get away with it."

"The hell I can't," said Inspector Hunter, his cold eyes glittering over the barrel of his service revolver. "Get back in the corner, and take your clothes off. Every damned one of you take your clothes off."

He turned to the window.

"Green, send up some doctors, and two of the chemists. Let no one else come in to the grounds or the house. Let no one leave. Keep your mouth shut. Have two men come up here and knock on the door. Let them have their revolvers in their hands. Let them shoot to kill at the first sign of disobedience to my orders."

And then Inspector Hunter slammed down the window.

The sickening sweet odor was still in the air, but it was not as noticeable as before.

"Boys, take off your clothes and stand over there in the

corner, naked as the day you were born."

Ramsay sneered. "Inefficient Inspector Insults Interviewer."

Searle added another thrust: "Police Inspector Drinking at Time of Tragedy."

Hunter whirled on him.

"You'd use that? After my pulling the wires to get you in here so you'd have an exclusive?"

"I'd use anything," said Searle, his face still white. "The news comes first. You can't hush this thing up, and you can't stall it. The *Star* will get scooped by every paper on the street."

Inspector Hunter shook his head, slowly.

"It won't get out."

"Aw, hell. It's getting out right now. There were reporters watching the house, watching the grounds. Think they heard those shots and the alarm siren without putting two and two together? They'll have extras on the streets within an hour announcing the death, and they'll make a pretty shrewd guess at what's happened afterward."

Hunter lowered the gun slightly.

"The department will issue flat denials. We'll deny the death. We can't let this get out. It would rock the city. It would start a reign of terror. This means the police are powerless."

"You can't hush it up. Your denials will only get you in bad at the start, and give the other papers that much more prestige when you finally have to admit the truth."

Hunter shook his head.

"This is an emergency the like of which has never faced the city before."

He jerked up his revolver as one in whom the last vestige of indecision has vanished.

"Get over there and get your clothes off."

"Hunter Has Hysterics!" rasped Ramsay. "Intoxicated Inspector Incarnate Inefficiency!"

"Get your clothes off!" yelled Hunter.

There was a double knock at the door.

His eyes squinting over the barrel of his revolver, Hunter threw open the door. Two uniformed policemen with drawn guns stood gaping on the threshold.

"Boys, see that these men strip!"

Nick Searle moved slowly, reluctantly.

"You'll strip, too, damn you," he said, "or I'll write an article accusing you of the murder."

"Examiner Evades Equal Examination," sneered Ramsay, moving, however, toward the corner indicated by Hunter.

"No. I'll join you. That's fair. That's what I wanted these boys up here for," said Hunter, throwing down his gun, and taking off his collar and tie as he moved to the corner.

The police chemists found four naked men and a corpse in the room. They made a minute examination of every article in the room. They analyzed every single thing that they fancied might have played a part in the tragedy. They examined even the tobacco in the cigarettes, the paper with which they were tipped. They found nothing.

Dawn found the men working frantically.

It also found extras on the streets, intimating that there had been a tragedy despite the vigilance of the police. It found a crowd surging about the streets which bordered the spacious grounds of the millionaire's mansion.

Noon found Hunter throwing up his hands in helpless despair.

Three o'clock found him pleading with the reporters to be reasonable and give him a break. But Searle and Ramsay, insisting upon the right of the press to print the news, were obdurate.

They were released from custody at three fifteen.

Searle took Swift to the *Star* offices. There they wrote frantically. Swift was given a rewrite man. He gave a few scientific terms covering possible causes of death, made some comment upon atmospheric poisons, and then read the proof on an article that was more wildly speculative than any thoughts he had dared to formulate or utter.

"Celebrated Physicist Hints at Atmospheric Poisoning," he read, then, lower down, in smaller type: "Mysterious Ray Penetrates Walls and Locked Doors. Possibility that Radio May Act as Transmitting Medium. Scientist Confirms Report that Intoxicated Inspector Delayed Transmission of News to Eager Public."

The cashier handed Swift a check that was three times the amount of a month's pay at the state college.

"We'll want a follow-up to-morrow. You'll get the same rates," he said.

"In the meantime?"

"Do anything you want. Keep in touch with the office."

Swift bowed, reached for his hat.

At that moment the telephone shrilled sharply. One of the men barked excitedly as he listened to the sounds that rasped through the receiver.

Another reporter came in, breathless.

"Here's a photo of the letter," he said, and rushed to the dark room.

"Better stick around, Swift," said Searle. "Hell's to pay."

CHAPTER 2

Trailing an Evil Genius

Events of the next two hours were crowded.

Six new letters had been mailed. Five had been to wealthy men. The sixth had been to none other than the President of the United States of America. Five of the letters contained a demand for money. The sixth letter demanded that the nation accept Zin Zandor as dictator.

The penalty in each case for refusal was death.

The millionaires were to begin paying tribute immediately. The government was given thirty days within which to comply with the demand. At the end of thirty days the President was to die, first of a series of martyrdoms only to be ended by surrender.

But sheer luck had given the law a break.

Post office employees had been instructed to note anything unusual in the mail, particularly anything unusual in the mail addressed to wealthy or prominent people.

One Steve Roscin, a mail carrier, driving to a mail box to pick up the mail, had noticed rather a striking figure striding away from the box.

It was a man well over six feet tall, thin, slightly stooped. The figure was muffled in an overcoat, despite the fact that the day had been oppressively warm. There was a long black beard which concealed the lower part of the face, dark glasses over the eyes, and a crush hat, pulled well down.

But the postman had caught a good look at the right hand. It was a peculiar ring on the third finger that had caught his eye. He described the ring as being carved in some grotesque fashion in the shape of interlaced triangles of white against a background of red.

The postman insisted that the ring was fully as large as a twenty-five cent piece, perhaps larger where it bulged out into a circle of mingled gem and design.

At the time he had paid no great attention to the man, noting only the overcoat, the beard, and the unusual ring. But when he had opened the green box, his eye had alighted upon six letters at the top of the pile of mail.

The uppermost letter had been addressed to the President of the United States of America. The other five letters were addressed to people of prominence in financial circles.

The postman had acted quickly. He had slammed the mail box shut, jumped into his car and whirled about in pursuit of the strange figure.

At the corner he was in time to see the man climb into a red roadster of speedy design, whose make the postman had been unable to determine. In the gathering dusk, the roadster had shot away from the curb and easily outdistanced the lighter car which the postman was driving.

He had abandoned the futile pursuit, and had telephoned to headquarters at once. Experts had appeared, examined the letters for finger-prints, opened them, found their terms, and had immediately started a search for the tall man in the red roadster who wore a peculiar ring and who wrote his letters on a Remington typewriter.

The police predicted an arrest within twenty-four hours, stating they would make a house-to-house canvass of the city if necessary.

Arthur Swift, caught in the excitement of the investigation, remained at the *Star* offices until nearly midnight.

By that time the telephones were ringing constantly, giving new clews, cases of arrest of suspects. Garages were combed for red roadsters, people were asked to report any tall figure with beard and overcoat that had been seen at or about the time.

The police adopted the theory that the beard was a disguise, that the overcoat was merely to prevent recognition, and that the man probably did not live anywhere near the place where the mail box was located, but had written the letters, then driven to some isolated section to mail them.

By midnight there were no fewer than fifty tall suspects incarcerated at police headquarters, awaiting a complete check of their activities for the day.

Arthur Swift caught Nick Searle for a short conference.

"Look here, Searle, there's one thing about this business that's strange."

"Meaning?"

"The time those letters were mailed."

"What of it?"

"They must have been already written, held ready for mailing, but the mailing was to be at a certain definite time."

"The time?" asked Searle, smiling, rather patronizingly.

"The time was when the person who did the writing was certain the death of Tolliver Hemingway had taken place."

Searle continued to smile, the smile of calm superiority.

"Wrong, Swift. The time was when the writer knew that the people had been advised of the death of Hemingway."

Swift shook his head.

"No. You see it would have taken the letters twenty-four hours to be delivered at the very least. Therefore, had the writer been absolutely certain of Hemingway's death, he would have mailed the letters, knowing the press would have the facts long before those letters were read by his victims."

The smile melted from Searle's features.

"By George, there's a thought there! Then you mean the person who committed those murders wasn't absolutely certain the murders had been committed. He only released certain agencies of destruction, knowing that they *should* work, but those agencies were not sufficiently certain to make him positive of their success."

Swift, knowing that he now held Searle's attention, nodded.

"That," he said, "is one possible explanation. The other is harder to comprehend, but yet, in some respects, more logical."

"Shoot," said Searle.

"That the person who ordered the mailing of those letters was one of the persons who were in the room with Hemingway, and was, therefore, unable to communicate with his accomplices until after Inspector Hunter had released him."

Searle dropped into a chair, as though his knees had suddenly weakened.

"Not that, Swift. That would make four of us suspects— and you, being of scientific training, would be the first they'd go after. They'd slam us in cells and start giving us third degrees that would make us wish we'd never been born. Why, we've been panning the inspector, calling him intoxicated and all that. Lord, how he'd delight in having some legitimate excuse to get us thrown in the jug and work us over."

Swift nodded.

"I hadn't thought of it from exactly that angle, but I was wondering about Ramsay."

"What about him?"

"You remember I mentioned seeing something just before Hemingway's death?"

"That's right, you did."

"Well, I'm going to tell you what that something was. It sounds incredible, but for a split fraction of a second, Ramsay's hand vanished. The hand and the biggest part of the arm just melted into space."

Searle knitted his brows.

"Listen, son, you haven't batted around the way I have, and you don't realize what tricks nervous strains will play on a man. They sometimes kick about the reporters being so hardboiled and calloused, but a man ain't worth a damn as a reporter until he does get calloused. You were all worked up, and your eyes just started playing tricks on you. Even if they didn't, how could anybody have managed to bring about the death of Hemingway without leaving any clew at all?"

Swift was stubborn.

"Somebody did. And it must have been done by unusual methods. Therefore, anything unusual—"

Searle surrendered the point. "All right. Let's drop around and see Ramsay. We'll ask him what he knows about it. That'll convince you. Ramsay's on the square."

They got hats and coats, went out into the velvety midnight. They found Ramsay's room, knocked on the door, got no answer, walked in.

Searle turned on the light.

Swift stood by the door.

The click of the switch showed a scene of confusion. Drawers were pulled from the dresser. The mattress had been slit in a dozen places, and the stuffing pulled out, strewn over the floor. The bedclothes were wadded into a knot. A suitcase had been cut open. The clothes closet showed a pile of garments, the pockets pulled wrong side out.

A letter file had been dumped in a chair, and the wind from the open window had sifted various letters about the room. All over the floor, even on the walls were drops of blood, and those blood-drops were scarcely dry.

Searle made a wry face.

"Another victim," he said.

Arthur Swift made a hurried examination of the various letters and papers while Searle was telephoning the police. Among some of the more recent letters he found a bit of paper which contained a single word: "Tonight."

That bit of paper was undated and unsigned, but, in the lower right hand corner was the imprint of a seal, an affair of interlaced triangles, the impression of which was visible only when the paper was held at an angle to the light.

Swift laid the letter or note back in the pile of papers.

"Know anything about rings?" he asked Searle.

That individual impatiently shook his head.

"To thunder with all that hooey. The thing that we've got to find out is the method of death. Then we can guard against it. And we've got to trace each individual victim. Imagine what it means when some individual can inflict death at will upon any certain man he may select, regardless of the precautions with which that individual is surrounded! Then he writes a letter demanding certain things of the government, threatening to take the life of the President.

"And he can do it, too. Make no mistake about that, Swift. I've seen 'em come, and I've seen 'em go. I know the work of the fanatic and of the bluffer. But this man is different. He works too efficiently, too damned efficiently. Imagine picking a time right after midnight to bump off Hemingway! He picked the very time when everybody was the most alert. He did it to show how little he cared for us or our precautions."

"Maybe," responded Swift. "But you've got to admit that ordinary measures get us nowhere in this case. Now there were rings made along in the fifteenth century that were known as poison rings. They were large, made especially to hold a quantity of poison, and I have a hunch such a ring figures in this case. I'm going to find out."

"How did the murderer get the ring in contact with Hemingway?" asked Searle.

"Perhaps he poisoned him with a slow moving poison that was implanted in his system days before."

Searle grinned. "Wrong again. He gave Hemingway the option of avoiding death at any time by simply paying out money."

Swift made for the door.

"Anyway, I'm going to beat it before the police arrive. After the way you've being panning Inspector Hunter it'll be only a question of hours until he figures out a scheme for getting you on the inside. I don't want to be around."

And he walked out, went to a nearby hotel, registered under an assumed name, took off his clothes and sank into deep slumber.

By morning he was ready to run down his theory. He called on certain antique ring dealers and made known his wants, a poison ring of large capacity, answering a general description.

There were five prominent dealers in such jewelry. Three of them gave him blanks. But the fourth scratched his head, consulted his books.

"It is possible we might get you such a ring. We sold one a little over sixty days ago to a man who makes a hobby of rings. He buys, holds for a while, then sells or trades."

Swift whipped out a pencil.

"Give me his address. I'll pay you a commission if I make a deal."

"Marvin is the name," said the dealer. "I'll give you the address in a letter of introduction."

Marvin was at home, genial, cordial. He was a little man with puckery eyes and perpetually smiling lips. He was hardly the type one would have picked as a murderer.

Swift broached the subject of rings, gradually leading the way around to various poison rings.

"I had a magnificent specimen a couple of months ago," said the collector. "But my physician took a fancy to it and I gave it to him."

Art Swift nodded, as though the information were of but casual interest, talked for half an hour, purchased a small antique ring, and finally announced an obscure physical ailment which had been bothering him for some time.

Marvin suggested a good physician.

"Don't know any," remarked Swift.

"Try mine. Dr. Cassius Zean."

Swift yawned.

"Thanks, I may look him up. Well, I've got to be going. It's been a pleasure to chat with you. Good morning."

Dr. Zean! The name filled him with curiosity. The man whose name was Zean might well have adopted a name such as Zin Zandor.

He called a cab, went at once to the doctor's office.

An office girl was busy at a typewriter. Swift moved over so that he could see the make of the machine. It was an Underwood. A white-uniformed surgical nurse bustled in and out of the outer office. She had Swift fill out a card with his name, address and occupation.

The doctor, it seemed, was in, but would see no one that day. It would be necessary to make an appointment. Art Swift made an appointment for the latter part of the week, but insisted upon an immediate interview. The nurse withdrew to take the message to the inner office. She was gone for some time. Swift felt the uncomfortable feeling which he experienced at times when he felt people were talking about him.

While he was sitting there, twisting his fingers, his brain racing with thoughts and conjectures, he heard the telephone on the desk at his elbow give a series of clicks.

The desk, he saw, was one where the surgical nurse held forth when not busy elsewhere. He wondered if the telephone was merely an extension of the telephone in the private office and if the clicking of the bell clapper denoted a conversation starting by the removal of the other receiver.

Casually, he half turned in his chair. The girl at the desk was clacking out letters on the typewriter. Her eyes seemed to be entirely occupied. Stretching forth an arm, moving with the air of one who is bored and restless, Swift inserted his hand under the receiver, cupped the palm and gently lifted the receiver so that the spring tension on the hook caused a contact.

Instantly he heard the metallic raspings from the receiver which showed a conversation was being carried on over the line. Swift was sitting in a chair which brought his ear not very far from the level of the desk. He managed to work a book under the receiver, holding it up a half inch or more from the hook. Then he slumped down until his ear was but an inch or two from the edge of the desk.

The conversation became faintly audible.

"Send a messenger after it right away. We need some . . ."

"Can't let you have it for half an hour."

"All right. They're raising hell, making a house-to-house search of the city. Better be careful about mentioning that ring. Somebody may ask you about it."

"No chance of that. Send a messenger directly to room 920, knock once, then pause and knock twice. Will I know this messenger?"

"No, this will be a new one."

"All right. G'by."

"G'by."

There was a series of clicks from the wire. Swift slipped the book out from under the receiver. The girl at the other desk continued tapping the keys of the typewriter.

The surgical nurse appeared, frowning, to communicate the doctor's refusal to see any one except by appointment. Swift acknowledged defeat and left the office.

His mind fairly reeled with the information he had received. The telephone conversation doubtless referred to the search that was being made for the tall man with the odd ring. It was very possible that Dr. Cassius Zean was none other than the mysterious and sinister Zin Zandor.

Swift debated whether to call up Searle, finally decided to do so. He went to a public telephone, called the newspaper office, and found that Searle was out. He left a message for him.

"Tell him I've got something hot. I'll call again in half an hour. If he comes in, have him wait."

CHAPTER 3

Unchained Lightning

As he hung up the telephone, a daring thought possessed Swift.

Why not stroll up to room 920, knock once, pause, and then knock twice? The voice over the telephone had said the doctor wouldn't know the messenger!

The thought had no sooner entered Swift's mind than it crystallized into action. He sprinted for the elevator, was whisked to the ninth floor and walked the corridor upon nervously impatient feet.

At 920 he paused, contemplated the plain door for several seconds, was painfully conscious of the throbbing of his pulse, and knocked. He paused, knocked twice.

There was a vague shadow flitting over the ground glass square. Then the shadow took bulk and sharpness of outline. Swift had visions of a tall, sinister figure with a cold eye, and was absolutely unprepared for the short, stumpy man with fleshy jowls who glared at him.

"Well?"

"Messenger. Told to get somethin' here," said Swift, slurring his words together to disguise his nervousness.

The doctor glowered at him from eyes that were as twin chunks of polished ebony.

"Come in," he said. "You're early."

"Am I?" asked Swift, striving to appear casually unconcerned. "I was told to come in half an hour. I walked around for a while, didn't have my watch."

The doctor grunted.

Swift noticed that he was slow and lagging in his movements, that his lips were a sickly blue, that the flesh sagged down in flabby pouches. There were pouches beneath the eyes, pouches below the cheek bones, a pouch below the chin, and a sagging pouch at the belt. The doctor was wheezing from the effort of walking toward the door.

He went to the door on his right, which Swift surmised must lead to the reception room, and locked it. Then he turned toward a door enameled a pure white.

"Just making a final test," he said.

Art Swift got a glimpse of a long, well-lighted room. There were white tables, chairs, a long sink, a battery of test tubes, bottles, retorts, microscopes, and a cage full of canaries. These canaries sang in nervous, chirping voices, fluttering restlessly from perch to perch.

Dr. Zean left the door open as he entered the room.

"Sit down," he wheezed over his right shoulder. "You must be the man that's detailed to cover Washington."

Swift resolved on a bold stroke.

"I am," he said. "The chief sent me down here to get my stuff and get started."

"Know how to use it?"

"Only generally. I understood you were to give me instructions."

The doctor turned, frowned. His ebony black eyes bored into Swift's features. The blued, flabby lips quivered.

"All damn foolishness trying to— Oh, well, you aren't to blame."

He reached in the cage. The birds fluttered their protests at the invading hand, flung themselves against the gilded bars. At length the fat fingers closed about a slim, yellow body. The bird gave a shrill cry of alarm, then was pulled from the cage, wings fluttering and flapping, occasional feathers drifting to the floor.

Dr. Zean raised a hypodermic, jabbed the needle into the fluttering bird. Almost instantly there came a rapid change. The fluttering wings began to move more rapidly. They gave forth a low humming sound.

"Watch," said the doctor and liberated the bird.

The wings were moving so fast now that it was impossible to see them. They were like the wings of a humming bird, giving forth a low, droning sound. The canary hung for a split fraction of a second, poised in the air, then zipped into flight. Such a flight it was!

The bird seemed like a yellow streak, moving with incredible speed. Swift turned his head to follow the flight, turned it back again. Try as he would, he could not keep the bird in sight. Neither could he lose sight of it. The canary was merely a flash of yellow.

So rapidly did it move that the eye could see it only as a swift flicker of motion. Like an electric spark, it was impossible even to tell the direction of its flight. One time the bird seemed to be going in one direction, yet almost immediately it appeared in the opposite side of the room.

No direction in which Swift could direct his eyes but what that droning yellow streak zipped across his field of vision with such rapidity that it seemed there must be half a dozen of the birds in the air at once. In fact, there were several occasions when there seemed to be three different birds flying in opposite directions at the same time.

Swift rubbed his startled eyes.

The husky voice of the doctor took up a brief explanation, a word of warning.

"Time," he said, "is an illusion of the senses. Space is an illusion. If there's anything in infinity as an established fact, then there can be no limit to either time or space. To think of something that has no limit, yet has an existence, is absurd. Our finite minds place a limit on everything. So does existence.

"Therefore, the limitation of space and of time are the limitations and fallacies of the mind. It's like a single tube radio set. It has a limited range. That doesn't mean the radio waves that it receives are limited to that field. Same way with the human mind.

"Now some organisms live much more rapidly than others. Their concept of time is so radically different that the life energy is used up in a few hours.

"Naturally, if one could determine the particular gland which controls that time element it would be possible either to speed up life or slow it down. The dog uses up his allotted life energy in seven or ten years, the horse in a longer time. And there are cell organisms that live but a few hours.

"There's no time for details. You wouldn't understand them, anyway. But the point I'm making is that the extract I am able to furnish doesn't do anything to give new energy. It simply directs the speed with which the existing energy is burned up. So you've got to be careful of the dosage. It's barely possible that one could take a sufficient dose to live up a whole lifetime in five minutes.

"The effect of this extract is to speed up everything. It wears off as quickly as it takes effect. The muscles, the nerves, the brain, the heart, all function according to the new scheme of things. And your strength is multiplied accordingly.

"We don't know what strength is. Take the elbow, for instance. It's a fulcrum for the forearm. The raised forearm is a lever of the third class. The power is applied but a few inches from the fulcrum. Yet a strong man can raise a fifty- to eighty-pound weight in his hand without difficulty.

"Take a pencil and paper, calculate the moments of force and you'll see that this calls for an utterly incredible amount of power to be applied to the forearm. In fact the bone wouldn't stand such a strain. Take the forearm of a cadaver, put such a weight in it and raise it by mechanical means and the bone snaps.

"Therefore strength has something mental about it. The mind acts on the molecular structure in some way. Gravitation is the tendency of the molecules of all matter to draw together in proportion to the mass. Because of the greater mass of the earth it attracts an object many millions of times more than the object attracts the earth."

The doctor ceased speaking and glared at Art with a look of hostility.

"Damn it, your mouth has flopped open as though the whole thing was strange to you. I've repeatedly warned those who sent you to see that this preliminary ground was covered first. I can't be running a kindergarten here!

"Now here's a box. That box contains two dozen little capsules and one big capsule. The little capsules contain enough of the extract to speed up your physical and mental processes at the rate of one hundred to one. Each capsule terminates in a hollow needle. When you are about to make use of a capsule take a deep breath, insert the needle, squeeze the capsule.

"Within the space of three deep breaths you will find your processes speeded up. You will move, think, breathe, talk one hundred times faster than normal. The small capsules last for about thirty seconds. Then the effects wear off. During that half minute you have lived fifty minutes of your normal life at a rate one hundred times as rapid as ordinary. Remember that your fast motions will be utterly invisible to ordinary eyes. If you talk, your speech will be unintelligible.

"It will be advisable to take two or three preliminary doses so you can accustom yourself to your new rate of life, and be able to gauge your motions accordingly.

"Now the big capsule is to be used only in the event of a major emergency. Every man is similarly equipped. It will speed up your life at the ratio of five hundred to one."

There was an imperative pounding at the door which led to the reception room. Dr. Cassius Zean stifled an impatient exclamation, and wheezed his way to the door.

"I'm busy," he said.

The girl's voice that drifted through the panels contained some note of alarm. Art Swift could not hear the words. The doctor shot the bolt. The surgical nurse appeared in the crack of the open doorway. Art Swift kept his back turned.

There was the hissing of a sibilant whisper.

"Very well. I'll attend to it at once," said the doctor.

The nurse turned, paused, swung back. Art Swift could feel her eyes upon him.

"Turn around!" she cried.

Art turned, and, as he turned, he took a swift step toward the pair.

The girl's eyes burned into his own. Her lips parted in a screamed warning. "He's a spy!"

Dr. Cassius Zean flung a hand toward his hip.

The girl jumped into the room and kicked the door shut. Her face was chalky white, the lips a thin line of grim determination.

"A knife!" she cried. "No noise!"

But Dr. Zean was lugging a heavy revolver from his hip pocket.

Art Swift was unarmed. The girl was coming toward him, fury blazing from her eyes. The doctor was raising the revolver.

Art made a wild leap.

The girl went through the air and tackled him with outstretched arms, a tackle that would have done credit to a football star. Despite himself, the surprise of the attack, the weight of her hurtling form, threw Swift from his feet. He staggered, tried to catch his balance and crashed to the floor.

"Crack him!" he heard the girl say.

He saw Dr. Zean's arm upraised, bringing down the weapon in a crushing blow, and flung up his knees, swung to one side.

The blow missed.

"Then shoot him, quick!" yelled the girl. "He's breaking my grip!"

Even as she screamed the words, her hands slipped from the struggling body, and Art Swift lunged out with a circling arm, caught the ankle of the pudgy doctor, and gave a jerk. The foot slipped, the ankle gave, and the huge bulk came down with a thud. The girl's hands had been busy. She was scratching at his face, biting, kicking.

Art rolled over, got to one knee, heedless of the fury of the nurse. He swung his right arm. The fist connected with the purpled jaw, but, even as he struck the blow, Swift realized that something was wrong. The flesh he hit was the color of fresh putty. The lips were blued, parted, gasping. The tongue protruded. Dr. Zean's heart had given out, the excitement proving too much.

There remained the girl.

Swift flung his arms about her, held her helpless. He grabbed a roll of bandage that had become tangled in his feet and whipped it about her hands. She tried to scream then, but he stifled the sound, thrust the roll into the parted teeth. There followed a subdued gurgle. He tied the gag in place, endured the white-hot fury of her eyes, finished binding the wrists and ankles.

There was a closet opening from the room. He pushed her in there, gave a final inspection to the knots, closed and locked the door.

Then he turned to the doctor. He was dead, this pudgy physician who had isolated the extract that governed the tempo of conscious life.

As Swift started to search his pockets, there sounded a knock at the door of 920. A pause, two knocks. It was the messenger!

Art Swift grabbed the coat collar of the inert clay and dragged the pudgy form along the floor to the door of the laboratory. He pushed the man inside, closed the door, and walked toward 920. His fist was clenched. He was ready to strike the instant the man walked across the threshold.

He slipped the bolt, threw open the door.

"Come in," he said, and then gasped his astonishment.

The figure that entered the room was that of a young woman, well-formed, beautiful. She smiled at him graciously.

"You are Dr. Zean? I was to receive certain things. Doubtless there is no explanation necessary," and her lips parted in a smile.

Art Swift floundered in a confused greeting, invited her to be seated.

Should he tie and gag her? But she was so smiling, so innocent in appearance, so refined in her manner. Violence was unthinkable!

Then, as he hesitated, another thought flashed across his mind. Why not give her that which she sought, send her away, and follow? She would lead him to the rest of the gang.

He bowed deeply.

"If you'll excuse me a moment," he said, and went toward the door of the laboratory. He was careful to open it in such a manner that she could not see the corpse, and promptly closed it behind him.

He searched shelves, finally found that which he sought, a little pile of metal boxes in which were capsules similar to the ones the doctor had shown him.

He took a box of the extract, returned to the girl, and gave her as much of the doctor's talk as he could remember.

"You look as though it was all news to you!" he stormed, just as the doctor had stormed at him. "I can't run a kindergarten here. Why can't they explain these rudimentary preliminaries to you before you come? Take this box and go."

"Hadn't I better try a capsule?"

He grunted, still keeping in the part of a testy scientist, impatient at having to explain fundamentals to an ignorant woman.

"I don't care what you do!"

She flashed him a smile, opened the box, took out a capsule, took a deep breath, jabbed the needle into her arm, squeezed the capsule.

Then Art Swift realized that he, too, must test this diabolical extract of some nameless gland, or the girl would be able to vanish, moving a hundred times more rapidly than he could.

He grabbed a capsule from the box she held in her hand.

"I'll take one with you," he said, and took a deep breath.

The girl was breathing deeply. Her cheeks were flushed, her eyes were brilliant with excitement and with the stimulus of this strange substance.

Swift felt the bite of the needle, felt his blood tingle with the sting of the extract, and glanced at the clock on the wall. It was precisely two fifteen. The second hand of the mechanism was tick-tocking around its smaller circle. The minute hand pointed at the figure three, the hour hand at two.

The girl's potion took effect first.

He suddenly saw her start to get up. Then it was as though

she became a blur of motion. She walked, and her feet moved so rapidly the eye could scarcely follow. She talked, and her lips showed only as a filmy substance. The sound of her words was as the clatter of a watchman's rattle.

She made toward the door, moving so fast that she was as a streak of whizzing speed, and then something clicked in Swift's brain. Just as he was trying with leaden feet to move and intercept her, he suddenly saw her moving at normal speed, her hand on the door-knob.

"Well, I guess I'll be going," she said.

Swift wondered if the effect of the extract had worn off so quickly.

"Just a moment," he said, sparring for time.

"Yes?" she asked.

"You felt the effect of the extract?" he wanted to know, curious as to her feelings.

"Just a slight dizziness. When does it take effect? It seemed to make you almost unconscious. You must have sat motionless for nearly five minutes. I talked to you and you didn't answer. You seemed sick. I was alarmed."

A sudden explanation flashed upon Art Swift. He looked at the clock. It was three seconds past two fifteen. The second hand seemed to have stopped in its motion. But there was a low-pitched sound coming from the clock, a long-drawn rasping of some sort of slow-moving mechanism.

He listened, attentively.

"T . . . O . . . C . . . K," said the clock, and the second hand moved an infinitesimal fraction of an inch of crawling motion.

He pointed toward the clock.

"Can't you see? You're under the influence of the extract now."

She regarded him with startled eyes, then moved toward the clock.

As she walked, Art watched her clothing. It was flattened against her figure as though pressed by some invisible hand.

Then he remembered a strange, whizzing sound that had been in his ears as he had moved.

The girl modestly pulled at her skirt. It remained plastered against her limbs.

Swift laughed.

"The atmospheric pressure remains the same," he said. "You are moving just one hundred times more rapidly than normal. Naturally, your speed through the atmosphere forces your clothing against you. There's no use struggling with it. You'd have to remain still for some apparently perceptible interval to give the air currents a chance to adjust themselves."

The girl laughed, a nervous, throaty laugh.

Swift found himself keenly interested in the various physical phenomena which surrounded them.

"Do you mean to say we've speeded up our lives so we live fifty minutes while that second hand clacks through thirty seconds?"

He nodded.

"And when I'm in the room," said the girl, "and take the drug, then what do I do?"

Of a sudden, Art Swift knew exactly what she was to do.

"Simple," he said. "Train yourself to sit absolutely still. Remain motionless with your body for minutes on end. Move only your right arm. That will enable you to put the poisoned cigarette in the hand of the victim without being detected. The motion of the hand will be far too swift for ordinary senses to detect. If any one should happen to be looking directly at you he will see your right hand apparently disappear. So be careful not to make the motion until every one is looking in some other direction."

"But what if they should flash me a quick glance?"

"Quick?" He laughed. "The quickest glance they could flash you would be so slow that you would see their eyeballs move as though by slow clockwork."

"And the cigarette?"

"Will have the extreme end of it filled with the poison. The victim inhales it fully into his lungs and dies. The other occupants of the room sense only the greatly diluted odor of the poison gas as a sickening sweet smell."

"Goodness!" she exclaimed. Then, her eyes filling with some sort of emotion he could not fathom: "I must be going."

She moved toward the outer door.

"I'll see you to the elevator," said Swift, and opened the door, taking care to slip a metallic box of the capsules into his hip pocket.

The outer office looked just as it had when Swift had first seen it. The furniture, the windows, the rugs. But as he opened the door he seemed pulling against a great weight, and he noticed the sudden vacuum swirl the rugs into bulging ripples of slow motion.

He understood then what he had done. He had jerked that door open with a motion one hundred times as swift as the ordinary opening of a door. It had disturbed the atmospheric equilibrium of the room.

Alarmed, he glanced at the stenographer to see if she had noticed it, to see if she would sense anything unusual in a strange man's emerging from the private office, escorting a young woman to the door.

As he looked, she was about to glance up from her typewriter. She was striking the letters of the machine, glancing toward the door. Swift pressed the arm of the girl.

"Notice the mechanics of alarm," he said.

They watched.

Slowly, the girl's eyes swung upward. The lips sagged open in what was doubtless to be a gasp, but it was so ludicrously slow that they both laughed. The right hand pressed down on one of the keys of the typewriter. They saw the type bar slowly move upward to strike the paper.

The bar struck the paper, remained pressed against it for what seemed seconds, then slowly began to drop back. The carriage started a sluggish movement to make way for the next letter which was already being pressed, and still the girl's eyes had not fully raised to the two figures who were watching her.

"Let's move and see if she can follow us," said Swift.

He grabbed the girl's arm, darted to one side.

The typist's eyes were raised now, but they stared in wide-eyed, frozen alarm at the place where they had been and not at the place where they were.

CHAPTER 4

Outlawed from Mankind

They darted to the outer door, tugged it open, slipped into the outer corridor.

"I didn't get your name," said Swift.

"Louise Folsom."

"You're the Washington agent?"

"Er—yes, the Washington agent."

She jabbed a forefinger to the button of the elevator.

They waited for a short time in silence; then, suddenly, Swift burst out laughing.

"Foolish. You can't get an elevator."

"Why can't I?"

He pointed to the glass door through which could be seen the cables controlling the cages. The strands were crawling at such a slow rate it seemed the cable was hardly moving.

"We're speeded up too fast. You'll have to wait for what'll seem a very long time, or else take the stairs."

"Nine flights?"

"Nine flights."

"How long will it seem to me if I go down on the elevator?"

"Nearly ten minutes."

She paused, uncertain.

"I rather think I'll wait. Nine flights is a long way."

This gave Swift the opportunity he was looking for.

"All right. But be careful when you get in the cage. Move so slowly that you seem to be fairly crawling. Try to take eight or ten seconds to get into the elevator. Don't try talking with anybody until the effect of the extract wears off. You've got your box?"

She nodded.

Swift turned and left her, walking down the corridor.

He noticed a red light flash on over the elevator door, saw the bottom of one of the cages come creeping into view and slowly crawl to position before the door. This was the break for which he had been waiting, and, as the girl concentrated her attention on the elevator, Swift darted for the stairs.

He went down the nine flights with such speed that his coat streamed straight out behind him. He beat the elevator to the ground floor and was waiting when the door opened and the girl came out.

She had forgotten his admonition, and was rushing at a rate of speed a full hundred times faster than that of the average pedestrian in a hurry. Open-mouthed spectators stood frozen in motionless surprise as she whizzed by them. Then, as she gained the street, they seemed not to see her at all, so rapidly did she move.

Swift followed her, and emerged from the office building into a strange world.

Automobiles barely crept along the street. Even the noise and confusion of the city had been toned down until it sounded as a hollow boom of slow noise, low-pitched, almost inaudible. Hurrying pedestrians seemed standing upon one leg, their feet almost motionless. Their swinging arms were held at grotesque postures. A newsboy crying his wares stood for seeming minutes with his mouth open, a queer, rattling sound slowly emerging from the throat. A paper being waved in front of a passing pedestrian seemed utterly motionless; one corner, fluttering in the wind which whipped down the street, was barely moving.

Swift followed the girl, keeping well behind her, swinging his way between other pedestrians as though they had been inanimate figures, bunching on the sidewalks for purposes of ornamentation.

No use to take a car or cab. Walking at a rate of speed that seemed painfully slow, the atmosphere whipped his garments until it seemed they would be torn to ribbons. The girl's short skirt streamed and fluttered, flapped and blew, whipped and skirled. Her hair came out from under her hat and streamed back of her head. She was exerting her every ounce of strength to fight against the wind caused by her rapid progress through the air.

Swift figured they were walking at a rate of speed that would ordinarily have taken them two miles an hour. Now, multiplied a hundredfold, that speed of two hundred miles an hour caused the terrific rush of air to threaten to tear their clothes off their backs.

He felt his coat whip and slat into a ripping tear. He slowed his speed still further, noticed that the girl's skirt was coming off, saw her stop to adjust it. Yet it seemed several long minutes before it ceased its fluttering.

During all of this time the street traffic seemed barely crawling along; the wheels of the automobiles hardly moved in their slow revolutions.

The girl resumed her pace. She was walking more slowly now. A man standing at the window of a store, apparently engrossed in the display within, seemed vaguely familiar to Swift. As he glanced for a second look, he saw the girl was approaching him. She put her hand on his arm.

The man started what was evidently intended to be a swift whirl. To Art Swift it seemed to be but a slow motion picture of a slow motion picture. After an interval of what seemed seconds he had his eyes telling more than his ears, for the two were gazing at each other, and the man was Nick Searle of the *Star*.

The girl was talking. Swift could see her chin move, see the lips opening and closing. Searle was trying to talk, but the slow, drawling sounds which issued from his leisurely lips were nothing the girl could wait for. Her eagerness to impart her information made her pour out a torrent of sound at top speed.

Swift wondered how much longer the drug would act, and, even as he wondered, saw the phenomenon happen before his eyes. The girl suddenly became a sluggish replica of her former self. She had started a gesture with her right hand. That gesture slowed in its motion until the hand barely crawled toward the lapel of Searle's coat.

Swift knew then that the drug had worn off. He remembered also that he had taken his drug just a second after the girl had taken hers. That would give him the advantage.

He moved forward, walking as swiftly as he dared, the wind whipping at his garments.

So rapidly did he move that the eyes of the two never faltered from each other. Not by so much as a glance did they see this man who was circling them at a rate of speed which made him almost invisible.

There was a pillar of concrete supporting an alcove, almost directly behind Searle, and Art Swift made for this place of concealment. He wanted to hear what the girl was saying, and he wanted to warn Searle that the girl was in reality one of the gang of crooks that bid fair to terrorize the country.

He leaned forward. The girl was speaking. Her slow words drawled with such exasperating languor that it seemed to take fully half a minute to drag out a word.

The traffic continued to crawl. Noises were as a low-pitched clack of sound, overlapping at times, but hardly audible. And then, right in the middle of a sentence, Swift's ears snapped back to normal. There was a brief period of dizziness as his functions returned to normalcy.

* * *

Of a sudden the traffic resumed its customary rumbling roar and shot past the store. The girl's voice was shrill with hysteria. The words ceased to drawl, but beat upon Swift's ears as the patter of a torrential rain on a tin roof.

"I have some of the drug. He never questioned my identity at all."

Searle's voice was also rapid, fierce in its intensity.

"Could you recognize this man?"

"Of course."

Searle pulled a photograph from his pocket.

Art Swift, crouched behind the pillar, cast about for some way by which he could warn Searle of the identity of the girl, of the danger of being trapped. But the reporter handed her the photograph.

"Why, yes. It's this man, the third from the end."

"Great Scott! Why, that's Art Swift!"

"I can't help who it is. It's the man that gave his name as Dr. Zean."

Swift's mind whirled. What was this all about? He started to step forward.

"Then we'll have to kill him on sight," snapped Searle's voice. "He knows too damn much!"

Swift sank back against the support of the cold concrete.

Searle, then, was the real arch-villain in the whole affair! He had been the one to bring about the deaths of the millionaires. He had been the one to send the letters to the unfortunate men who had attracted his attention.

As Swift turned this matter over in his mind, Searle and the girl moved away.

Swift waited a few minutes, thinking, then moved out into the stream of pedestrians. A chance fragment of a passing man's conversation came to his ears.

"Something whizzed right in between us. It must have been a cannon ball or something. It went so fast I could feel the air tugging at my clothes, but I couldn't see a damned thing.

I'd have thought I was dreaming or drunk, but Roberts felt the same sort of a sensation."

Swift moved away. His senses were reeling. He looked at his watch. It was exactly sixteen minutes past two o'clock. All of this frantic action had taken place in just about a minute.

He thought of the dead doctor, the nurse imprisoned in the closet. He must arrange for the arrest of the nurse, and he must arrange to have Searle arrested.

A sudden drowsiness overtook him. He went to his room in the hotel, telephoned police headquarters, and asked that a detective be sent out to interview him. Then he fell asleep.

The newsboys were crying "Extra!" on the street when he awoke, and some one was pounding on his door. Swift turned the key, instinctively knew the square-toed man who hulked on the threshold was a detective.

"You had a tip an' wanted a man from headquarters?" asked the man.

"Yes," said Swift. "Come in."

The detective entered the room, whirled, swung out a hand. By sheer luck Swift was able to dodge that grasping hand.

"What—" Art began, dodging another fist, and then the detective was on him in a lunging attack.

The very bulk of the man made him clumsy. Yet his charge knocked Swift to a corner. He saw it all, then. This could be no detective, but an agent of the crime ring, sent out to kill him. Fear and desperation gave him strength.

The other was pulling a revolver from his hip. Swift swung a chair. There was the crashing of wood as the rungs slivered, and then Swift saw the man staggering back, slumping to the floor.

Swift ran from the room to the foot of the stairs. A newsboy thrust out an extra of the *Star*. Swift grabbed it, and, to his horror, saw his own features staring forth at him, just underneath the words:

KILL THIS MAN ON SIGHT!

Then followed an article about the identification of Art Swift as the arch-killer, the greatest blackmailer, the scientific wonder who had used his genius to undermine civilization.

Swift stared at it, stupefied. Was it possible Searle was so daring as to hope he could prevent discovery by making a counter-accusation? The idea had merits, particularly as the *Star* argued that the scientific knowledge of the criminal made him immune to arrest and necessitated his being shot as a mad dog would be dealt with.

Swift read the article. To his surprise, it exposed the secret of the extract which speeded up the human metabolism to such an extent that life was lived a hundred times more rapidly than was possible under normal conditions.

The article claimed that Searle had solved the mystery with the aid of a female assistant who had tricked the arch-criminal into explaining the details of the crime to her.

That might have been correct. The girl might have been an assistant. Then Searle would not be the real criminal, but just what he appeared, a reporter. Yet, suppose this was merely a trick? Suppose Searle was so clever he had planned for this all along?

Swift wanted to think it over. He clutched the newspaper to him, started for a taxicab. There was the crash of glass, a bellow of rage, the shrill of a police whistle.

The detective had smashed out the glass of the hotel window, was frantically blowing his police whistle. As men looked up in startled surprise, the detective opened fire.

Swift ducked behind a parked car. The bullets from the detective's gun crashed into the metal, spattered the glass from the door windows, but failed to find their real mark.

Swift realized, however, he was trapped. It would be all right if he had a chance to tell his story. But how about the hysteria of the police? Would they get rabid and shoot on sight as the *Star* requested them?

He thought then of the box he had in his pocket, the rubber capsules that would speed up his body so that he could escape. He slipped the cover from the box.

And just then a burly form catapulted around the corner of the car. Swift had only time to thrust the box back in his pocket. The cover clattered to the sidewalk. A great blue-coated figure swung a club. Swift tried to dodge, but to no avail. He felt the impact, felt a great wave of nausea and engulfing blackness. Dimly, he realized that the thing that smacked him between the shoulders was the cold pavement. He felt the bite of handcuffs at his wrists, and then lost all consciousness.

CHAPTER 5

In a Frozen World

Searle's voice was in his ears when he regained consciousness. There was a tang of jail odor in the air. His form was stretched on a prison pallet and the steel ceiling contained a single bright incandescent, which stabbed his throbbing eyes.

"From the looks of this telephone number, we figured it might be a lead. I got Louise Folsom to give a ring and stall along for information, and the conversation sounded promising, so I sent her up.

"She ran onto this Swift. Of course, she didn't know him at the time. He was merely a certain Dr. Zean. But he proceeded to explain to her just how the murders had been committed and—"

He broke off as there was a commotion near the door.

"We knocked over that office and found a nurse tied and gagged in the closet, and a dead man in the laboratory. Looks like there's hell to pay. Somebody had been in the place and cleaned it out, busted up bottles, pulled out drawers, and raised hell generally." A red-faced sergeant was speaking.

There was the scraping of chairs.

Swift struggled to a sitting posture.

"Can't you understand, you fools?" he asked.

Hands grabbed his coat, jerked him forward.

"All right. Let's hear your story."

Swift kicked with his feet. "Take these handcuffs off."

A clock, clacking off the seconds, pointed to three minutes to four o'clock.

"Leave him with a guard and let's go see the office and the dead man," said one of the officers.

"Triple handcuff him, then," said Searle, "because he's the man who pulled the murders. There's no doubt of that in my mind."

"It was Ramsay," said Swift, striving to be patient. "I blundered on to this Dr. Zean, and—"

"Save it!" snapped one of the officers.

"No, no, let him talk."

Art Swift told his story. The officers looked at one another, incredulity stamped on their faces.

"There's a chance," said Searle, speaking judiciously, "just a chance that he's right. But, Swift, how did you know about the idea of switching cigarettes, the mechanics of the murders? You told Louise just how to go about it."

"Pure deduction, putting two and two together," said Swift.

One of the men clicked a key in the lock of the handcuffs.

"Stand up here and we'll make a search," he said.

Swift moved to stand up, and, as he did so, felt as though a hundred needles were shooting into his hip. He jumped, gave an exclamation, then as it suddenly dawned on him what had happened, he frantically plucked at his hip pocket.

"The capsules!" he exclaimed. "They've spilled from the metal box, and I jabbed myself with them!"

He pulled out of his pocket the crushed capsules. He had given himself a terrific dose of the extract. Nearly all of the capsules were crushed. The extract had penetrated to his blood. Even the big, five-hundred-to-one capsule had discharged its contents.

Men moved toward him.

"Maybe it's a s . . . u . . ."

Searle was talking, but midway in the sentence, his mouth ceased to make sounds. The extract had taken effect, and Swift was speeded up to a terrific rate of activity. The men before him were arrested in mid-motion. One of the officers had been in the act of jumping forward. His feet, Swift noticed, were both off the ground.

Art amused himself by walking around the officer, bending down and inserting his hand beneath the officer's foot. He couldn't feel the foot even moving.

He waited patiently for what seemed seconds, waiting for the situation to change. It remained unchanged. Men remained as they had been, their eyes staring, their mouths open. Every possible expression of surprise was depicted upon the frozen faces.

Swift realized that there was no use spending hours in that jail waiting for these men to dawdle through their slow motions.

He walked to the door.

Even when he walked as slowly as possible, the wind tore savagely at his garments. He knew then that he was speeded up many times faster than when he had taken his first, experimental capsule. He was living at a ratio of at least five hundred to one, perhaps much faster.

He worked his way through the jail doors.

At the outer door a guard was stationed and the officer who sat on a stool on the other side of the door was peering intently through the bars. The door was locked.

Swift reached through the bars, grabbed the guard by the coat collar, pulled him forward. He pulled so slowly that it seemed hours before he had the man against the bars. Yet he noticed even that slow motion was about to jerk the head of the officer from his neck.

He had to reach out with his other hand and pull the head of the guard so that it followed the body. Otherwise he would have broken the neck of the unfortunate man.

He searched the pockets, found the key, fitted it to the lock from the outside, manipulated it with the tips of his fingers, and heard the bolts shoot back.

He pushed open the door.

The guard was as he had left him, but, as Swift watched, he fancied he detected the faintest possible motion of an eyelid, the beginning of a slow flutter.

Swift waited for what was, as nearly as he could judge, five minutes, watching that eyelid. There could be no question of it, it was slowly moving.

"Evidently he started to wink when I grabbed him," said Swift to himself, interested in the scientific aspect of the phenomenon. "It only takes a man around a fiftieth of a second to wink his eye, but I can't even see the blamed thing move. I must be speeded up so fast I whiz like a bullet!"

That thought made him wonder how a bullet would appear. Could he see it leave the gun?

He took the revolver from the officer's belt, pointed it at the steel wall of the jail and pulled the trigger.

Nothing happened.

He waited, watching, his wrist braced for the explosion.

"Something wrong," he said, and lowered the weapon, put it back in the holster of the officer. As he did so, something unusual about it caught his eye. The hammer of the weapon was only halfway back.

"Must have forgotten to cock it, but thought I did," he mumbled, and took it once more from the holster.

Then an explanation dawned upon him. The hammer was descending, ready to fire the shell. But that split fraction of a second which elapsed between the pulling of the trigger and the exploding of the shell was so multiplied by his speeded-up senses that it seemed an interval of minutes.

He looked around the jail for a while, watching the postures of the men who remained as living statues, motionless. Here was a man who had been about to sit down. Now he was suspended in mid-air, his body jackknifed, the weight on his heels.

Swift watched him for a while, then returned and took up the revolver. The hammer was just about to contact the shell. Swift moved to a place where the light was good, pointed the weapon, waited.

There was a faint jar, a slow impulse up his wrist. Then he saw something mushroom from the mouth of the weapon. It was the bullet, propelled by a little mushroom of fire and smoke.

He was able to follow the progress of the bullet from the time it left the gun until it struck the wall of the cell. He could even see it flatten against the steel and start dropping to the floor.

He knew it must be dropping because he could see that nothing supported it. But it remained in one position so long he was unable to detect motion.

He returned the weapon to its holster, walked back to the cell where the officers had been interrogating him. The men all remained in the same position. The officer who had been jumping forward still had his feet off the floor.

Swift turned and walked from the jail, out into the late afternoon sunlight.

The atmospheric conditions bothered him more than any other thing. There was a perpetual shortness of breath. It seemed as though his laboring lungs simply couldn't suck enough air into his system. It was only when he was walking that he could breathe comfortably.

It must be that the rapidity of his progress forced the air into his lungs. But when he walked the wind pressure against his body was terrific. It tore his coat to tatters, and it was a physical impossibility to keep his hat on his head. He had the unique sensation of walking at a rate of speed that seemed to him to be somewhere around one mile an hour, and having the air pressure whip his hair straight out while his garments were torn.

And he was isolated in the midst of a busy world.

The street was crowded. People were starting for home. Street cars were jammed. Vehicular traffic was at its peak. The sidewalks were a seething mass of jostling humanity frozen into rigid inactivity.

Everywhere were people. Yet nowhere was motion. There was no sound. The universe was as silent as the midst of a desert. Occasionally there would be a faint buzzing sensation in Swift's ears, and he realized that this was probably caused by sound waves which were too slow for him to interpret as sound.

He walked across the street, threading his way through traffic, and wondering how long this strange sensation was to continue. He thought of the words of the dead scientist that it might be possible for one to live his entire life in a space of five minutes.

What a terrible fate it would be to be left to go through an entire lifetime without any contact with other people, to go from youth to middle age, middle age to doddering old age, all the time in a city that was suspended in the rush hour of its traffic.

If the scientist had been right, it would be a horrible fate. There was a man getting in a taxicab. It might be that Swift would be an old man before that fellow had traversed the length of the block. He could amuse himself for a year, then come back and find the taxicab just starting; perhaps the cabbie would be in the act of closing the door.

When Swift got to be an old man he could come hobbling back to the corner and find that the traffic signal had changed and that the man in the cab was halfway across the street.

It was an appalling thought.

But Swift was glad he had not been imprisoned in a cell. He might even have been held in a dark dungeon. He paused to think of what it would have meant. He would have had no food or water. He would have starved to death in what would, to the ordinary mortal, have been but half a dozen seconds, perhaps not that long.

The air tugged and whipped at his garments. He crawled painfully along, thinking over the events which had led up to the strange position in which he found himself.

CHAPTER 6

Among Living Statues

Art thought of Carl Ramsay and of how Ramsay would undoubtedly have summarized the situation in headlines. "Time Ticks Tediously," or some such alliterative expression. And, thinking of Ramsay, he suddenly thought of the murders, and knew that he must apprehend the real criminal.

He had unlimited time at his disposal. He could cover all trains, all means of escape. It only remained to walk where he wanted to go. Any form of so-called rapid transportation was out of the question.

One mistake he made. He jumped over the wheel of a machine that stood between him and the curb. The trip up in the air was quite all right. In fact he felt like a feather. Had it not been for the atmospheric resistance it would have been simple. But the rush of air held him down somewhat.

Even so, he jumped faster, farther, and higher than he had intended or thought possible. This was doubtless due to the fact that his strength had multiplied with his ability to speed up the muscular action.

But when he wanted to come back to the sidewalk he

found that he could not do so. He was held a prisoner, floating in mid-air. The force of gravitation was so slow that it seemed he wasn't even drifting toward the sidewalk.

Finally he managed to claw his way along the side of a building, find a projection, use this to give him a handhold, and push himself toward the sidewalk.

He walked for fully a quarter of a mile before a strange pressure seemed to strike the bottoms of his feet. Then he knew that he was normally just alighting from the jump he had made. The force of gravitation had just taken hold.

That very element made it difficult for him to get about. He found that he dared not trust to any jumps, but must keep at least one foot on the pavement; if he made any sudden motion, there was not enough friction engendered by the force of gravitation to give him a foothold.

Altogether, it was a strange world, one in which every physical law seemed to be suspended. This was due, not to any change in the world itself, but merely to a change in the illusion of time. To express it in another manner, it was due entirely to the fact that Art Swift could think more rapidly.

The rate of thought, then, controlled environment.

It was a novel idea to toy with, but he couldn't wait for speculation. He had work to do. He must solve those murders, apprehend the real criminal.

He started with Carl Ramsay.

Undoubtedly Ramsay had been the point of contact for the murders. He had taken some of the drug, diluted so the tempo of living became a hundred to one. He had switched the cigarette Tolliver Hemingway was about to take from his cigarette case, for a poisoned cigarette in which the first half inch of tobacco had been prepared with some poisonous drug.

The millionaire had inhaled that drug with the first puff of the cigarette. Then, when he exhaled the smoke, the other watchers in the room had been able to get the odor. But Hemingway had received the full force of the concentrated gas.

It had been simple.

But Ramsay had grown careless. He had made his substitution when Swift's eyes were upon him. Swift hadn't been able to detect what was going on, but he had been able to see the sudden disappearance of the fast-moving right hand and arm, and then, when he had talked to Ramsay, Ramsay had tried to answer before the drug wore off.

That was the reason those first sounds which came from Ramsay's lips had been so unintelligible. Doubtless they had been words, perfectly formulated. But the sounds had been so rapid that it had been impossible for the eardrums of his hearers to split those sounds into words.

Then something had happened to Ramsay. Either he had planned his disappearance because he knew he would be suspected, or else he had actually been abducted after a struggle.

Swift determined to find out which.

He battled his way against the ever-present roar of the rushing atmosphere to Ramsay's room and took up the trail from there.

The police had combed the room, and had taken every article that might be of value. Yet Swift made a search of his own, going into every nook and corner. He found nothing.

He wondered if he should make an attempt to cover trains, and thought of Dr. Zean's office. He might find something there, and he could drop into the Union Depot on the way.

He walked down the stairs to the street, and suddenly jerked himself upright with an exclamation. A strange sight met his eyes.

The street was frozen into arrested activity. He had grown accustomed to that spectacle. A horse was trotting, and but one foot was on the ground. On his back was a mounted policeman. He had evidently been swinging his club. Now he was like a mounted statue. A taxicab was cutting over on the turn, and the tires on the outside were flattened by the weight of the car. There was not the slightest motion in either wheels or tires.

But that which arrested Swift's attention was the peculiar sight of a man walking casually through the tangled mass of arrested traffic.

The man's coattails were whipped out behind. His hair was streaming. His hat had gone, and he walked with the peculiar pavement-shuffling gait which Art Swift had found so necessary to cultivate.

Here, then, was a man, the tempo of whose life was some five hundred times plus that of other men. Here was a man who must be inoculated with the mysterious extract which Dr. Cassius Zean had discovered. By that same token, he must be one of the outlaw gang.

He carried a suitcase, and the suitcase had been streamlined to make it offer less resistance to the air. He walked like a man with a certain fixed purpose, and he seemed perfectly at ease, confident in his own power.

Watching him, Swift became convinced the man was an old hand at this rapid life. He seemed to show no interest in the strange phenomena of the frozen world where motion had been stilled. He walked calmly, sedately.

And Swift, slipping behind a parked automobile, watched him curiously, wondering what strange errand had caused this man to speed up his life at a ratio of five hundred to one.

The other slithered his way across the street, paused before the door of an imposing edifice. There was a fleshy woman leaving the door of that building, and Swift had noticed her prior to seeing the other man.

She was tugging at the door, one foot stretched out, ready to step to the pavement. Her mottled face was flushed with dark color. Her glassy eyes were staring straight ahead. Her mouth was open. Probably she was gasping for breath, but it would have taken seeming hours for her progress to the place she was going, minutes for the first intake of her breath to be apparent.

Swift realized now that he had no mere five-hundred-to-one ratio in his life tempo. The cumulative effect of the dosage he had taken when several capsules jabbed their contents into his blood stream had given him a much faster rate of life than that. He had no means of knowing just how fast.

The man he followed walked directly to the door out of which the woman was emerging. He ducked under her arm, brushed against her, and entered the lobby of the building. Swift followed.

Once the man turned. By the simple process of freezing into complete immobility, Swift defied detection. All about were the figures of men staring with glassy, unseeing eyes at what was going on about them.

There was a policeman standing at a marble table in the center of the flagged floor. All about were counters, wickets, gilt cages.

Swift realized he was in one of the big banking establishments. The man he followed walked to one of the cages. He took a key from the inert hand of a guard, unlocked the cage door, pulled it open, entered.

There were piles of gold on the counter, stacked up in glittering spheres of coin. The man scooped them into the suitcase. Then he left and went to another cage. Here he repeated the process. Here, also, there were several piles of large-denomination currency. The man scooped these in with the gold.

When he had selected the cream of the plunder, he closed the suitcase and turned toward the door. Swift became stockstill, standing with one foot out and up, as though in the act of taking a step. The man passed within three feet of him. When he had gained the street, Swift followed.

His quarry led him to a corner a block away. Here he sat the suitcase down, right beside a traffic policeman who was in the act of blowing his whistle.

He had left thousands of dollars in stolen gold and currency unguarded, right within reach of a policeman's hand. Yet he was perfectly safe in doing so. No one could move fast enough to pick it up.

The bank bandit shuffled into a jewelry store, selected several diamonds, dumped them into his pocket, returned to his suitcase, bowed his head to the policeman in ironical thanks, picked up the bag, and crossed the street.

Swift followed.

The man walked as rapidly as the air resistance would allow. He seemed intent upon reaching a certain destination as quickly as possible.

He turned into an alley. A truck was standing there, motor running. The suitcase was tossed into the truck. There were more suitcases there, all of the same general design.

As Swift watched, another figure came around the corner, walking in the same pavement-shuffling manner, carrying a suitcase. He tossed this upon the truck, paused to speak with the man Swift had been following.

Then the two turned and came directly toward Art Swift.

Once more he froze into immobility. They passed close to him. One of the men stopped.

"Say, I've seen this guy before. Who the hell is he?"

Swift remained motionless, one foot reaching out as though taking a step. Yet he knew there was something different in the studied balance of his pose from that of the other men who were caught in arrested motion.

"Never lamped him," said the second man. "Come on. We've got work to do."

But the man Swift had been following wasn't so certain.

"I'm telling you there's something funny about this guy. He stands funny, he looks funny. I've seen him before. I think he was standing in the bank I frisked. Let's go through his pockets and see who in hell he is."

"Aw, forget it. We got no time to be pulling all the funny stuff. That newspaper gave the whole show away, Doc Zean is croaked, and we ain't goin' to be able to get no more of the stuff. We gotta work fast and make a clean-up while the getting is good."

They moved away. Swift heard the man he had followed fling a final comment.

"When we come back we'll see which way he's walking and what he's got up his sleeve. He looks off color to me."

The men reached the mouth of the alley and turned away.

Swift started for cover, and, as he approached the place opposite which the truck was parked, saw a swirl of motion at the opposite end of the alley.

He adopted his usual expedient of standing absolutely still.

Two men, loaded down with suitcases, came into the alley. One of them stopped.

"Say, that guy wasn't there last trip!"

"What do we care? He couldn't do anything."

"Yeah, but he might be stallin'."

They set down their suitcases, walked with quiet menace directly toward Art Swift.

Then Swift caught sight of something else. Another man glided swiftly into the alley. There was something familiar in the posture of that man. He gave a swift glance and found that it was Nick Searle of the *Star*.

In some manner the reporter had speeded himself up so as to get into the game. Art thought of the metal box the girl had received, a box containing a complete assortment of the rubber capsules. Probably Searle had secured possession of that and had injected sufficient of the serum to take part in the strange game which was being enacted.

The two bandits approached Swift. Searle was not far behind.

"Hey, you, what you doing here?" asked one of the men, pausing before Swift.

Swift endeavored to keep his face entirely devoid of expression. He fixed his eyes upon distance, and held his breath.

"Aw, he's all right," grumbled one of the men. "Just some poor mutt that strayed into the alley and we didn't notice him the other trip."

"The hell we didn't," insisted the more suspicious of the two. "He just wasn't here, and if he wasn't—"

He moved his hand in a swift gesture, directly toward Swift's eye.

"If he's on the up-and-up, we can stroke the eyeball," said the man.

Involuntarily Art blinked.

"Ha!" exclaimed the bandit, and jumped forward, his fist swinging in a terrific uppercut.

Art sidestepped, jerked his head back to dodge the blow, and shot out a straight left.

He found the atmospheric resistance slowed his punches somewhat, but the superior strength which had come to his muscles with the speeding-up process largely overcame that. It was his clothes that suffered most.

As he launched that straight left, the resistance of the air held his coat sleeve stationary. He had the peculiar sensation of feeling his sleeve peeled back from his arm, and the bare arm flashed forward in a quick punch which connected.

But the second man was busy. He swung a slungshot, and only missed Swift's head by a matter of inches.

"The damned spy!" yelled the man who staggered back under the impetus of Swift's punch.

Art knew he was no match for the two men, and jumped to one side, hoping to get where he could have his back to the wall. But they understood his maneuver and closed on him from different angles.

He ducked, caught a punch on the back of the head, felt his stomach grow cold as a fist landed in the solar plexus, and dropped to his knees. He flung out his arm, reaching for the legs that sought to kick him in the face, caught an ankle, jerked it, and had the satisfaction of seeing the man go down.

CHAPTER 7

The Man Who Mastered Time

With a roar Nick Searle joined the conflict.

That was the determining factor. The men had hardly expected an equal battle. Having Swift down and getting ready to knife him was one thing; having that wiry young man on hands and knees grabbing at their ankles while another man swung lusty fists was quite another.

It took but four punches to decide the battle. The two bandits sprawled on the cement.

Swift was still on hands and knees, writhing in pain. But he had managed to tackle both of his adversaries with groping hands which had kept them from doubling up on Searle.

"Hurt?" asked Searle.

Swift made a wry face, gasping for breath.

"Wind—knocked—out."

Searle helped him to his feet.

After a few seconds Swift got over the temporary paralysis of the diaphragm which had been induced by the blow he had received, and gave a wry grin.

"How'd you get here?" Art asked the reporter.

"Took some of the serum and started out. Found I wasn't hopped up enough, so I put half a dozen of the small capsules into effect all at once."

"How did you know you weren't hopped up enough?"

"Because of the way things were whizzing by me. I tried to follow a man, and I might as well have tried to follow an express train. I figure we are living right now at a ratio of around three thousand to one." Searle seemed awed as he said the words.

"Not that fast."

"Mighty near it."

"The girl?" Art demanded.

"You mean Louise Folsom?"

"Yes."

"That's what worries me. They've managed to get her somehow, and they've carried her off. This looks to me like the final blow-up. The exposé in the *Star* has broken a lot of their power . . . You'll forgive us for jumping at the conclusion you were the mysterious scientist who was at the head of the thing? Tell me how you got into it—but first let's get these two chaps tied up nice and tight and see if we can't locate where they were going."

Swift nodded.

"There's some rope on the truck. I'll tell you the story while we truss 'em up. And I think I know about where headquarters are."

"What truck? This one?"

"That's the one. You'd better be careful with those suitcases. They're all loaded with money and gems."

"What?"

"Fact. They've lost their power to terrorize the nation and make the big executives bow to their will, but they still have their power to rob without the victim's being able to guard against it. They're stripping the city."

"Humph. And there's only two of us," commented Nick Searle, as he trussed up one of the bandits. "Guns any good?"

"None whatever. The bullets could be dodged, and it takes forever and a day for the hammer to explode the shell. If we wanted to shoot one of these men when he broke loose, we'd have to start shooting the gun now. Then we could go about our business for a while, come back and see if the man had got the knots untied, and, when he did, trust the explosion of the revolver would happen somewhere along about that time."

Searle laughed.

"You paint a gloomy picture."

"It's almost that bad. Notice the truck is backed up to a

cellar. I have an idea that cellar is of some importance. Let's explore in it a little."

"Suits me. What'll we do with the men?"

"Drag 'em in . . . Look out! Here come another couple! Lord, there are two more. Four of 'em. We've got to hide here in the truck, and when we start hostilities we've got to work fast. There's a couple of stakes that'll make good clubs."

Swift crouched behind a pile of the strangely streamlined suitcases. Four men appeared, laden with loot. They called a greeting, started for the truck.

"Look out!" yelled one. "Somebody's hiding here!"

"Let's go!" shouted Art Swift.

The young scientist and the reporter got into action.

One of the outlaws, doubtless forgetting the uselessness of the weapon, pulled an automatic from his pocket, leveled it, and pulled the trigger. Then he dashed it to the ground when the weapon failed to explode.

Two of the men had knives. One climbed on the side of the truck, the other tried the rear.

Thud, thump sounded the clubs, and the men drew off, one of them with a broken arm.

"Let's go!" yelled Swift, for the second time, and they charged.

It happened that the two men had chanced upon the most deadly weapon available. Knives were limited as to range. Guns were of no use. Clubs, swung with terrific speed and force, were bone-breaking instruments of destruction.

Apparently these outlaws had never encountered resistance in the time-plane upon which they had learned to function. They had never experimented with various weapons, and the futility of their guns, the limited efficiency of their knives, left them helpless before the onslaught of the two men armed with clubs.

Searle surveyed the sprawled figures, grinned at Swift.

"Looks like a good job. Do we tie these up?"

"Sure thing."

"How about headquarters?"

"Let's investigate."

"Attaboy! Better keep that club. We'll probably run into some more trouble."

They lowered themselves into a cellar, pushing themselves down the stairs because the force of gravitation was too slow to function, felt their way along a passage, and emerged into a lighted room.

A man sat in this room with telephone receivers clamped to either ear. He was tall, gaunt, dominating. His eyes held a restlessness that seemed unclean, unhealthy. The thin lips were compressed into a single razor-blade slash that cut from cheek to cheek. His jaw was bony, determined.

On the third finger of his right hand gleamed a ring of interlaced triangles. He glanced at the two men, looked at their clubs, half rose from the chair.

"Mr. Zin Zandor, I presume," said Swift.

The restless eyes snapped to his face.

"So?" rasped the man, and fumbled beneath his desk.

"Stop him," shouted Searle, and made a wild leap forward.

Swift lowered the point of his club and launched it through the air like a lance with every ounce of force of which he was capable.

At the same instant he became aware of a sickening sweet odor which permeated the room.

Zandor tried to duck. The hurtling club caught him on the forehead as he lowered his head, cutting an ugly gash, sending him staggering back.

His right hand flashed up. It held a sort of gas mask, which he tried to raise to his nostrils. But the impact of the blow had dazed him. His hands seemed to function uncertainly. He turned half purple in the features as congested blood mottled the skin.

"He's holding his breath," shouted the reporter, quick to grasp the situation.

Swift whirled. Together they fought toward the door, holding their breath, the sickly-sweet odor seeming to constrict the muscles of their throats.

Behind them they heard a peculiar scraping sound. They turned for one last look.

Zin Zandor was clawing at the top of the desk. The poison gas had got him now. His features were distorted, his mouth open. Even as they looked he went limp, and apparently remained suspended in mid-air.

"Dead and falling," said Swift as he dragged his companion into the passageway, out to the open air.

They sucked in great lungfuls, feeling strangely dizzy.

"The girl!" cried Searle.

Without an instant's hesitation, Swift turned and led the way back into the passageway.

"Take a deep breath and we'll try for her. Probably the gas rises. Keep your head near the floor."

They dived down and crawled along the floor. The sickening sweet odor was in their nostrils. At the corner of the desk, inclined at an angle of almost forty-five degrees, was the form of the man who had signed himself Zin Zandor. He was falling to the floor, and the force of gravitation was so slow, compared to the speeded-up life forces of the two men who watched him, that he seemed to drift downward with hardly perceptible motion.

There was a door to the left of the desk. Swift took a deep breath, reached upward, turned the knob. The door opened; they scrambled into the inner room.

Here was a Remington typewriter, doubtless the one upon which the blackmail letters had been written. Here, also, was stored great treasure, gold coins, currency, gems. And here they found the girl who had posed as messenger. She was bound hand and foot, gagged—Louise Folsom, captured, doomed to die.

Her eyes stared straight up at the ceiling of the room. She made no move when they entered.

"Living at a normal rate. Can't see us," said Searle.

He drew a knife and cut the ropes. Even then she did not move. They watched her anxiously. The closed door was shutting out many of the poison fumes. But there was a chance she had already inhaled too many of them.

Searle reached out and gently touched the eyeball with the tip of his finger. The lid gradually—very, very slowly—commenced to droop.

"She's alive," said Swift.

The girl's lips moved with such slowness that the motion was hardly perceptible.

"She knows we're here, trying to talk."

Searle nodded.

"We've got to get her out of here. That gas, you know."

"The door's closed. Remember, it disperses quickly. It takes a concentrated dose to produce death. He probably had it in the ring. He intended to liberate the gas from the poison ring and fill the room with it. Then he was going to put on some sort of a gas mask."

"Yeah. Your blow with the club got him groggy, and he sucked in a mouthful of the concentrated gas before he knew what he was doing."

"How about getting the girl out?"

"Let's try to carry her. But pick her up gently or we'll jerk her to pieces, and we'll have to stop easy like or—wait a minute—I'm feeling queer!"

At that same moment Art Swift felt a peculiar sensation at the pit of his stomach.

"The gas!" he exclaimed.

"No," said Searle. "We're coming back to normal!"

There was a brief spell of vertigo, and then, of a sudden, things were normal.

The girl's eyes were blinking; her lips were forming words.

Beyond the door that led to the other room something crashed—the body of Zin Zandor, just falling to the floor.

The girl's rapid words rang in their ears.

"Hoped you would come. They were planning to make this the day of the big clean-up. They had all their men ready to bring on a reign of terror, and they were going to kill me."

Swift pointed to a door that opened from one side of the room. He picked up a chair, crashed it through one of the panels.

"Let's get out of here!"

They felt the tang of fresh air upon their faces, saw the street roaring with the busy life of a rush hour. The noise burst upon their ears. In the alley, motor running, was the truck, filled with the strangely shaped suitcases. Sprawled just inside the door, where the two adventurers had dragged them, were the bodies of the unconscious bandits, tied hand and foot.

There was no traffic in the alley, but the street just beyond was filled with activity.

"Load 'em in and start for headquarters," said Searle, and grinned.

The girl climbed into the driver's seat.

"I can handle the truck."

They struggled with the men, got the inert figures into the truck.

"Let's make a good job," said Searle.

Swift caught his drift and grinned assent.

They returned to the cellar. The fumes of the deadly gas had dispersed. There remained only an odor, something like that given off by orange blossoms. The dead form of Zin Zandor sprawled on the floor.

They carried it to the truck. Then they loaded the stored treasure. Then they started the truck.

"Go to the *Star* office," Searle called to the girl. "We were the ones to blacken Swift's character, and we might as well be the ones to laud him to the skies as the hero who saved the country."

The girl flashed him a smile.

"Scientist Saves Day!" she said.

"That reminds me, where do you suppose Ramsay is?"

"Suicide," said Searle. "We found him just before I met you last. He had blown his brains out and left a typical note—poor chap: 'Reporter Reaps Ruin—Rum Ruins Ramsay!'"

They were silent for a moment.

"He was in on it from the beginning, of course?" asked Swift.

"Yes. He was the contact man. He actually switched the cigarettes. He faked an attack upon himself to divert suspicion."

Swift sighed. "Man, but I feel sleepy!"

"Effect of the drug. We've been living rapidly, perhaps more than a year in the last few hours. It's gone out of our lives."

"A year in a day," laughed the girl.

Swift caught her eye.

"Then I've known you a year, Louise," he said.

Her answering smile contained no trace of offense.

"We can call it that, Art."

"A heck of a fast worker," said Searle. "That goldarned scientist doesn't need to have any one pep him up with a lot of extracts to make him work fast!"

All three joined in a laugh as the truck with its strange load swung to a stop before the *Star* office, the biggest scoop in a half century delivered at the very door of the newspaper.

THE MAN WITH PIN-POINT EYES

CHAPTER 1

Victim of a Vampire Mind

If you are going to understand this story, you have got to visualize his eyes as I saw them there in that Mexicali dance hall.

I have gazed into the eyes of a swaying rattlesnake. I have seen the eyes of a mountain lion reflect a phosphorescent green from the darkness beyond my camp fire. I have watched the eyes of a killer, crazed with the blood lust, his hand clawing for the holstered weapon at his side.

But I have never seen eyes that affected me as did the eyes of the man who sought me out there in that place which is known as "Cantina Gold Dollar Bar."

His eyes were gray, but not the gray of the desert. It was as though his eyes had been washed with aluminium paint. They glittered with a metallic luster, and they seemed to be all the same color—if you could call it a color.

When he got closer, I saw that the pupils were little pin-points. You had to look close to see them. And the whites of the eyes had that same metallic luster, the same appearance of having been coated with aluminium paint.

Those eyes gave me the creeps.

He looked at me for three or four seconds and said nothing. I couldn't help watching him, couldn't keep from staring into those funny eyes. It was then I saw the pin-point pupils for the first time.

They looked as though they were turning around and around rapidly, but they always kept the same size. I've seen the pupils in a parrot's eyes do the same thing, only a parrot can change the size of its pupils. This man's eyes were always the same, always black pin-points against aluminium.

He got on my nerves.

"Well," I said, "spill it!"

He didn't speak right away, not even then, but his eyes kept boring into mine. When he finally spoke, his voice was the sort I'd expected, one of those deep, resonant voices.

"I know all about you," he said.

I thought then he must be doped up. I'd seen those little pin-point pupils before when men were all hopped up. And I'd seen gun-play start awfully fast under those circumstances, so I began to humor him along.

"Sure," I said, "I could tell that as soon as I saw you. How about a drink?"

He shook his head, not a shake back and forth the way most people would shake their heads, but a swift, single shake of his head.

"No," he said. "You don't think I know about you. Let me tell you. Your name is Sidney Rane. You had two years of college in medical school. Then your health broke down and you came to the desert. You got a job as guard for the gold shipments out of Tucson, and you've been hanging around the Southwest ever since. You are reported to know more of the desert than any man living."

He stopped then, letting his words soak in.

I glared at the pin-points.

"Who the heck are you?" I asked, and my tone must have showed irritation.

"Emilio Bender," he said, and put out his hand.

For a second or two I thought I wouldn't take that hand, but I couldn't keep from looking at those strange eyes of his, and finally I put out my hand and shook.

"Now," he said, "we'll have a drink," and led the way to the bar. We drank.

That was a hot afternoon. Flies droned about the place, or circled over the damp spots on the sticky bar. A perspiring bartender dished out the drinks as they were ordered. Half a dozen Mexicans lounged about. There were a couple of drab girls who got checks for promoting drinks. There was little tourist trade. Mostly the tourists went to the fancier places.

Bender waited until I had finished with my glass and had half turned toward him. I knew that his pin-point eyes were staring fixedly at me, trying to catch mine.

It irritated me, and I kept looking away. Finally the silence became awkward. I glanced up and his eyes locked with my gaze and held it.

"Shoot your story," I said, and knew my irritation was showing in my tone.

He lowered his voice.

"I'm a hypnotist."

"Don't try it on me," I told him. "If you want some one to practice on, go hire a Mex."

He shook his head, that single swift shake of negation again.

"Listen," he said, and led me over to a dark corner of the bar. "You've had an education. You're not a fool like some of these people. I've got something that bothers me and I want you to look at it."

He waited for me to say something. I didn't say a word.

"Hypnotism," he went on, "is something they don't know anything about; and medical science is afraid to try to learn anything about it. From the time when poor Mesmer sat his patients around a washtub, their feet in water and an iron ring for their hands, up to the time when science proclaimed that hynotism is nothing but suggestion, science hasn't learned one thing about it."

He waited again.

After another interval of silence he said abruptly, "Do you know anything about multiple personalities?"

I'd read a little something, but I shook my head.

"They're encountered once in a while in dealing with a hypnotic subject. A woman will suddenly become some other personality. There'll be times when one personality dominates, then times when the other personality is in control."

I nodded and let it go at that.

As a matter of fact I'd heard of cases like that. Hypnotism would seem to bring out some hidden personality from the dark places of the mind. Science has recorded half a dozen instances.

"I want you to come," he said.

I kept staring into those pin-point eyes.

"Where?" I asked.

"With me," he said and started for the door.

I waited a minute, and then curiosity or the effect of suggestion or something got the best of me, and I followed him.

By that time the afternoon crowd of tourists was flowing in a stream across the United States border. The A.B.W. Club was doing a rushing business. You could hear the whir of roulette wheels, the click of chips, the clink of glasses.

I rather expected we'd turn toward the border, but we didn't. We headed down the side street which runs into the native part of old Mexicali.

It was a 'dobe house he stopped at, and it wasn't much different from the other 'dobe houses around it.

There were some dirty, half-naked children playing around in the yard. They all had drooling noses and black, questioning eyes. Their mouths were sticky from eating, and more dirt had gathered at the sticky places than on the rest of their faces.

They looked at the man with pin-point eyes, and then turned and ran, just like a bunch of quail scurrying for cover when the shadow of a hawk flits across the ground.

The house was just a square, boxlike affair with small windows and some green stuff growing in the front yard. There was a pool of surface water that smelled sour, some peppers hanging on the wall, and a door that was half open.

Bender and I walked into the house.

There were three people: an old, old woman who had a nose that looked like a withered potato, a fat woman who looked hostile, and a Mexican of the *cholo* or half-breed class. He had a low forehead, black eyes, thick lips and looked surly.

The man with pin-point eyes walked in just as if he owned the place.

"Sit down," he said to me in Mexican.

I sat down. It was a funny adventure and I wanted to see how it ended.

The fat woman snapped a shrill comment in the language of her race.

"Again!" she said. "Why don't you leave us alone?"

"Shut up," said the man with her, in a surly voice. "He is a friend."

The old woman chattered a curse.

I caught the eye of the fat woman. "*Señora,*" I said to her, "if I intrude I will go. I beg of you a thousand pardons." I spoke to her in Mexican Spanish, letting her know I was a friend.

She smiled at me, after the manner of her race, one of the most friendly races on earth—when you take 'em right.

"You are welcome," she said. "It is the other. He has come from the Evil One."

"Shut up," said the surly man again.

The woman turned to me and shrugged her shoulders.

"You see how it is, *señor*. He has sold his soul to the devil!"

I said nothing. The man with pin-point eyes said nothing.

It was warm there in the 'dobe house, close with the closeness which comes from many people sharing the same room on a hot day. Yet it was hotter outside, and the sun tortured the eyes. In the 'dobe it was dark and soothing.

CHAPTER 2

The Past Breathes

I sat and waited. Every one seemed to be waiting for something. One of the children came in the door. I motioned him over and gave him half a dollar. His eyes grew wide, and he thanked me in an undertone, then scampered out.

One by one, the other children came in and got half a dollar each. They muttered thanks. They didn't ever look toward Emilio Bender, with the aluminium eyes.

The splotch of bright sunlight from the west window moved slowly across the floor. No one said anything. They all sat and waited. I sat and waited. It was a queer sensation, like being plunged into the middle of a dream. It was all unreal.

They seemed to be watching the Mexican.

He sat in a chair, stolid, indifferent, after the manner of his race. He rolled a cigarette and smoked it, flipped the stub to the floor, looked around him with eyes that were black and inscrutable in their stolid stupidity, then rolled another cigarette.

The splotch of sunlight slid halfway across the floor.

There was a rustle. The old woman was muttering something and making the sign of the Cross. The fat woman rocked back and forth. "He comes," she said, and crossed herself again.

The man with pin-point eyes was looking at the Mexican.

I watched him, too.

I could see something was happening. The Mexican began

to sit a little more erect in his chair. His head came back, and the chest was thrust out. There was something military in his bearing. The surly air of stupidity slipped from him. The dark eyes flashed with spirit. The lines of his entire face became more sensitive, more intelligent. His nostrils dilated and he got to his feet.

When he spoke his words were in a Spanish tongue, but different from the slurring idiom of the Mexican. I had to listen closely to follow what he said.

"I tell you there is a fortune in gold there! Why don't we start? Are you a coward?" he asked of the man with the aluminium-paint eyes.

Emilio Bender smiled an affable, ingratiating smile.

"We have to get our army together, my friend. It takes time."

The Mexican laughed, and there was in that laugh a note which no peon ever yet achieved. It was the laugh of a man who laughs at life.

"*Dios!* Pablo Viscente de Moreno has to wait for an army to reclaim that which is his? Bah, you make me laugh! What are you, a soldier or a coward? Bah!"

He spat out the words with a supreme contempt.

"We need provisions," said the man with pin-point eyes.

"Provisions!" said the Mexican. "Did we wait for provisions when the brave general Don Diego de Vargas went into the desert to reconquer those who had massacred our countrymen? I can show you the spot, *señor*, where we camped by the foot of a great rock, and I watched while the brave general wrote upon that rock with the point of his knife.

"I can tell you the words: '*Aquí estaba el Gen. Do. de Vargas, quién conquistó a nuestra santa fé y a la real corona todo el Nuevo Mexico a su costa, año de 1692.*' "

I translated mentally, "Here was General Diego de Vargas, who conquered for our holy faith and the royal crown all of New Mexico at his own cost, in the year 1692."

The Mexican laughed again, that laugh that was a challenge to the universe:

"It was by camp fire that he wrote that message, and I stood beside him as he wrote. That day we had killed many Indians. We carried all before us. Those were the days! And now you babble about armies and provisions. Lead up my horse! Damn it, I will start alone! Get me my blade and dagger, give me the gray horse. He is better in the desert than the black . . . Come, let us away! I tell you there is gold to be taken!"

He whirled toward me and and transfixed me with an eye that was as coldly proud as the eye of an eagle. His head was back, his shoulders squared.

The man with pin-point eyes got to his feet and made passes with his hands.

"Not now," he said soothingly. "Not now, Señor Don Pablo Viscente de Moreno; but shortly. We shall go back into the desert. To-night, by the light of the moon I will come again and we shall start. Peace. Sleep until to-night at eight. Then we shall start."

A cloud came over the proud eyes of the Mexican. The chest drooped backward, the shoulders hunched forward. The head lost its proud bearing.

The old woman swayed backward and forward in her chair, chanting a prayer. The fat woman crossed herself repeatedly.

Then the Mexican was no longer a proud soldier, but a *cholo* once more. He looked at me with dark eyes that were stolid in their animal stupidity.

"It is hot," he said, and rolled a cigarette.

Emilio Bender took me by the arm.

"We will go," he said. "Later, we will return." And he led me to the door.

There was no word of farewell from the women. The man grunted the formula which the hospitality of his race demanded. The children scuttled from the front yard and hid in the greenery at the side of the house.

I took a deep breath of the afternoon air.

"What," asked the man with pin-point eyes, "do you think of it?"

I was careful of my words.

"The rock he speaks of is known," I said. "It is a great sandstone cliff and is known as El Morro, or as 'Inscription Rock.' It was by the old trail of the Spaniards who sought the Seven Cities of Cibola. They camped there, and because the sandstone offered a fitting place to inscribe their names and the date of their passage, they carved inscriptions. The first starts with Don Juan de Oñate in 1605. After that many expeditions left their marks.

"There is not one person in a thousand who knows of this rock. But it is a great cliff that looks like a white castle. And there is a message from General Don Diego de Vargas upon it."

The man with the curious eyes took a deep breath.

"Then," he said, "we will start. I was not sure. They told me you could give me more information of the desert than any other man. I know now we will find gold."

"Wait a minute," I protested. "Do you think this man is at all genuine, or is he a slicker trying to promote something? Or is he hypnotized?"

Emilio Bender shrugged his shoulders.

"You have seen," he replied. "The man who talked to us is Pablo Viscente de Moreno, a soldier who marched with General Diego de Vargas when the country was yet young. I know not the history; but I gather from what the man has said on other occasions that there was a massacre, and General de Vargas was then reconquering the country."

"But," I argued, "how could a man who marched in 1692 across the desert with General Diego de Vargas speak to us in a 'dobe house in Mexicali in 1930?"

The man with pin-point eyes shrugged his shoulders.

"Do you believe in reincarnation?"

I made a gesture with my hands and answered him in Mexican: *"Quién sabe?"*

He nodded. "All right," he said; "that's the answer."

We went back to the Cantina Gold Dollar Bar and had another drink.

"We leave at eight o'clock," he said, and fastened his metallic eyes upon mine.

"What's in it for me?" I asked.

"Fifty-fifty," he said.

"The Mexican?"

"He doesn't count. We'll give him what he has to have."

I laughed at that.

"Be sure you have the half-breed personality on deck when you make the division, and not Pablo Viscente de Moreno, the soldier. You might have difficulties in getting even a cut out of the soldier."

He nodded, and his pin-point eyes seemed whirling around in spiral circles, emitting little glitters like a whirling wheel reflecting the light.

We had another drink and then I went to roll my blankets. It was adventure, even if it wasn't anything else. And how could a soldier who marched with General Diego de Vargas in 1692 talk to us in a 'dobe house in Mexicali in 1930?

It just couldn't be done.

CHAPTER 3

Warrior Without a Sword

But I rolled my blankets and met the man with pin-point eyes at eight o'clock. We went back to the 'dobe. The women crossed themselves, and the children ran and hid. But the Mexican decided to go with us.

He had another of his surly fits on, and he seemed a little groggy as though he had been asleep and hadn't fully waked up.

Emilio Bender treated him like a dog. He put him in the back of the touring car with the rolls of blankets and cooking stuff.

"Sit there!" he snapped.

"*Si, señor,*" said the Mexican.

The car started with a lurch. The old woman crossed herself. The fat woman watched us with apathetic interest. The children were hiding in the shadows cast by the full moon. I couldn't see one of them.

We crossed the border, headed east toward Yuma. It was a hot night and a still night. The rushing ribbon of road and the drone of the motor made me sleepy. The man with pin-point eyes did the driving until we got to Yuma. Then I took the car and made Phoenix.

The Mexican slept as well as he could, what with the jouncing around on the washboard road between Yuma and the Gillespie Dam. Then we hit paving again. I gave up the wheel at Phoenix, and Emilio Bender took the car over the black cañon grade to Prescott. It was getting warm by that time, but out of Prescott we did some climbing and it was cool and nice by the time we got to Flagstaff.

Back of Winslow the road changed again to sage country, and we stopped the car in the shade of the last of the stunted cedars and had a siesta. We were on our way again by the time the moon got up. We weren't letting any grass grow under our feet.

The rock known as El Morro in New Mexico is off the beaten trail. Not many tourists get to it. It's where a mesa juts out into a valley, and a couple of cañons run together. The mesa plunges into an abrupt drop to the level of the valley. It's over two hundred feet straight down from the top to the bottom, and the sandstone sides gleam in the sun.

They've protected it from vandals. For a while people wrote their names and addresses on the rock, scratching out the messages of the early Spaniards to leave their own names. Why they did it I don't know. But they did.

We made a camp. The Mexican looked to me as though he were about half conscious. His head lolled around and his black eyes were utterly expressionless in their stolid stupidity.

"Wait," said the man with the aluminium-paint eyes.

So we had a siesta, cooked some beans, and warmed up some *tortillas* and waited for the moon.

It came up over the desert, casting long, black shadows. In the places where there weren't any shadows the desert gleamed like silver, and the inscription rock was like some huge castle.

We sat and watched the Mexican.

Once or twice Emilio Bender made passes with his hands and crooned low words. The Mex seemed groggy. I figured the whole thing was going to be a flop.

I don't know just what time it was, but the moon was up a good two hours and the camp fire had died down to a bed of coals before I noticed anything.

The Mex was sitting all humped over, as motionless as the rock that had weathered the countless ages, and which cast a great blob of shadow in the moonlight.

I saw his shoulders twitch and his head come back. The chin stuck out and the eyes glanced around the desert. The flesh lost its heavy look of sordid animalism and took on the fine lines of the thoroughbred. I glanced at Emilio Bender, but the man with the pin-point eyes was staring unwinkingly at the Mex.

It happened all of a sudden.

The Mexican sprang to his feet, and looked all about him. The moonlight caught his eyes, and there seemed to be fire in his glance. He looked at me and jumped back, his hand flying across his body to his left hip, groping for the hilt of his sword.

"Who are you?" he shouted. "Friend or foe? Speak, before Pablo Viscente de Moreno slits your gullet with a blade of Damascus!"

And then he frowned as his groping fingers failed to encounter the hilt of his sword.

"*Dios!* I am disarmed!" he roared. "And whence came these clothes? What witchery is this? Where are the sentinels? How about the horses? We are in hostile country! The horses are more precious to us than gold. Where are those horses?"

He whirled and fixed the man with pin-point eyes.

"You!" he bellowed. "I've seen you before—a sniveling scribe, a hunchbacked, round-shouldered, driveling devil who is learned in something or other. Who the devil are you?"

Emilio Bender said nothing, simply continued to stare with his pin-point eyes, and the moonlight glinted from them and made them seem more than ever as though they had been coated with aluminium paint.

"Speak!" roared the Mex, and made a swift imperious stride toward the hypnotist.

Bender faltered in his glance. I mean it. He shifted his eyes quickly as does one when he is afraid. It was the first time he had ever lost that positive, unwinking stare, that incisive power.

Once more the Mexican's hand groped about his left hip.

"If I can find the devil who stole my sword I will spit him like a rabbit and leave him to writhe on the sand in the hot sunlight of to-morrow . . . Where's the commander? Where is General Don Diego de Vargas?"

He paused, waiting for an answer; and as he stood there, the moonlight clothing him with a silver aura, he seemed like a man of fire. Gone was the stolid Mexican who was a peon, a *cholo*. In his place was this imperious man of fire and courage, a soldier who had made a profession of soldiering when carrying arms was not merely being a cog in a military machine.

He took a swift step toward Emilio Bender, then halted.

"*Carramba!* We have few enough men as it is, even if you are a devil of a scribe. The general would like it none too well if I should run you through. But show me where my sword is, or by the Virgin I will spit you to the gills!"

Emilio Bender made a few passes, muttered soothing words, but the passes were without effect. The Mexican turned to me.

"Crazy," he said. "It is the heat of the desert, and the constant watching for raids from the savages. I have seen men so before. Tell me, comrade, where is my sword, and how come I by these clothes?"

I met his eyes, feeling a strange fascination for this man of fire.

"You left your sword and your armor at a cave where you stored much gold plunder. Have you forgotten?"

He shook his head as a swimmer shakes his head upon emerging from the water.

"Damn it, you tell the truth!" he said. "I had forgotten about that cave. It seems that I have been in a long sleep. Things are not as they should be. There is much that has intervened.

"*Bien*, we will go to the cave. Let me get my blade in my fingers once more and I will be myself. But how quiet it seems! Where are our comrades? Where is the general? Where are the horses?"

"They, too, are at the cave."

He glared at me.

"If you are lying you will be spitted like a bird!"

I shrugged my shoulders.

He looked around him at the desert.

"Strange!" he muttered. "The moon was well past the full. Now it is but turned on the wane . . . This must be the rock. Surely, this is where the general carved his name and the date of his passage. But last night it was. And to-day seems a haze. I must have had the fever. Tell me, you scrivener, have I had the fever?"

The man with pin-point eyes nodded.

"Yes," he said, "you have been sick."

The Mexican said no further word but strode across the sand toward the white silence of the glittering rock. The moonlight sent a grotesque shadow, as black as a pool of ink, accompanying him. And I trotted after.

Following me came the man with the aluminium-colored eyes, and he had to trot rapidly to keep up.

The Mexican went directly to the place on the rock where the autograph of General Vargas has been protected from vandalism by the fence. He stared at the fence.

"Done to-day!" he exclaimed.

We said nothing. He raised his eyes to the inscription on the rock and nodded.

"I had thought it was more clear. Perhaps it's the moonlight. Perhaps it's my eyes that have become dim with the fever; but it's the inscription all right."

His eye caught the yellow pasteboard box in which a roll of films had been brought to the spot by some tourist.

"What the devil?" he exclaimed, and stopped to pick it up.

We waited. He turned it over and over in his fingers.

"*Cascaras!*" he exclaimed. "There is magic in this thing, or else it is the fever."

"It is the fever," said Bender.

The Mexican glared at him. "Speak when you're spoken to, scribe. Tell me, how do we join our comrades? Which way do we go?"

"Where is the cave?" asked Bender.

He pointed toward ancient Zuñi. "It lies in that direction, a march of two days."

Bender nodded.

"Come," he said. "We have a new chariot."

And he led the way toward the automobile which had brought us.

The Mexican's breath hissed in astonishment as he saw it.

"What a chariot! But how are the horses fastened? And why make it so cursed heavy? But it has good lines; only it would do ill in battle. Mark you, my man, there is not proper arm room in which to swing a sword, and that may betray us to these savages.

"A good chariot should have a grip for the left hand so that one may lean out and swing the sword in a complete circle, free of all obstructions. But look at this! There is no grip! There is no place to lean out, and that step which runs along the side will prevent a free swing of the sword.

"But we only talk! Talk is for scriveners and women, not for men of battle. Bring on the horses and we will start."

Emilio Bender fastened the aluminium eyes upon the man.

"First," he said, "you must sit in the chariot. We will all get in, and then the horses will come."

CHAPTER 4

An Old Battlefield

When the Mexican swung into the car, I noted that the heavy awkwardness was gone from him. He was as graceful as a race horse. I got in the back. Emilio occupied the driver's seat and stepped on the starter.

The car whirred into life and lurched forward.

The Mexican leaped out into the desert in a long arched vault of such surprising swiftness that it could not have been anticipated.

"*Madre de Dios!*" he exclaimed, and crossed himself. "It

is magic. It shot at us from under that place in the front and it moved. I swear that it moved! Look, you can even see the tracks in the sand where it moved! And there were no horses!"

Emilio Bender got out and fastened the pin-point eyes upon the Mexican, made passes, muttered soothing words.

"It is a magic chariot. We have come from those who are powerful to take you to your comrades. We must make haste. You must enter the chariot and go with us."

The Mexican shook his head.

"No. I travel either with my horse under me, in a chariot that I can understand, or on my two feet."

"Surely," taunted Bender, "Pablo Viscente de Moreno is not afraid of a chariot that can be driven by a poor scrivener!"

That gave the Mexican something to think about. I could see his face writhe and twist in the moonlight.

"He is not!" he said, and climbed back in the car.

Bender stepped on the starter, slammed in the gears. The car lurched into motion, gathered speed, started skimming over the moonlit road.

The Mexican gazed about him at the flying landscape with eyes that seemed to bulge out beyond the line of his bushy eyebrows.

"*Car-r-r-ramba!*" he muttered. "Wait!" he yelled at Bender. "Such a pace will tire out the chariot within the first two miles. I tell you it is a two-day march!"

For answer Bender slammed it into high and stepped on the throttle. The Mexican tried to say something, but the words would not come. He sat on the edge of the cushioned seat, gripping the windshield support with a grip that showed the white skin over his knuckles drawn taut and pale. The car hurtled through the moonlight.

After half an hour the Mexican recovered his faculties sufficiently to glance about him for landmarks.

"This road," he said, "has no business being here. But

perhaps the magic chariot makes its own road as it goes? That mountain over there is where we camped the first day's march, and the distance from here to the cave is not great. The first march is short."

Then he became interested in landmarks and seemed to forget the novelty of his means of transportation.

"There," he said, "is where we lost two men only last week. There was a scouting party of the savages. But we routed them. I charged three of the Indians over against that rock. Their bodies are there yet, if you care to go and look."

The car roared onward.

"Wait!" yelled the Mexican. "You are turning away from the direction. Over there against that hill is where we are to go. Just under that mesa that sticks up into the moonlight!"

Bender slowed the car, turned it into the native desert. The wheels bit deep into the sand, and he shifted to second.

The Mexican nodded sagely.

"I knew it could not stand that pace," he remarked. "Mark you, charioteer, you are not accustomed to these desert places. I can tell that from many things. You have probably come from Spain within a fortnight. You will soon learn that things are different here, and the greatest distance is covered by him who makes the less speed at the start."

Bender said nothing. He was pushing the car through the sand, dodging clumps of sage and greasewood.

I said nothing. It wasn't my funeral—not yet.

The car ground its way toward the base of the mesa. As the ground got higher it got harder and the laboring engine gave us a little more speed. I knew the radiator would soon be boiling at that rate. Personally, I'd have given the car a rest.

Not Bender. His greed was getting the better of his self-control, and he was pushing the car to the limit.

We covered about five miles before I could smell the motor overheating. Then it fumed like rancid butter poured on a hot stove.

"Better cool her down," I suggested to Bender.

He nodded and slowed.

The Mexican pointed to the rugged skyline of the mesa. "There to the left and down at the base. There is the entrance to the cave."

"There is much gold?" asked Bender.

"As much as two horses could carry," said the Mexican casually. "We have made these savages pay for their rebellion and the massacre of the priests."

Bender got ready again and his foot jammed the throttle to the floor boards. The wheels lurched and jumped in the sand, the car gathered momentum.

We were way off the road now, out in the desert, away from the line of sane travel. We might find anything here. I watched the line of the mesa grow larger until it loomed above us.

Then the motor halted for a second. Something clicked and from the mechanism came a clatter—clatter—clatter. The wheels ceased to spin and the car slowed.

"Connecting rod bearing," I said.

"The gold," commented the Mexican, "is but a little distance."

And Emilio Bender slammed his foot back on the throttle. Rod bearing or no rod bearing, he was going to get to that gold.

The motor lost power. The rod clattered and banged. I looked for it to thrust through the bottom of the crank case at any moment. But the wheels bit into the sand and we crawled ahead.

For several minutes the car pushed forward. Then there came a terrific noise, a hissing of hot oil on the sand, and the motor froze tight as a drum.

"Busted out the crank case," I said, not that there was any need for the comment, but I just wanted to remind him that I'd warned him.

Bender cursed, then jumped from the car. "Come on! We'll walk."

The Mexican was out of the car before the words were well clear of Bender's tongue.

"*Carajo!* It was great magic while it lasted!" And he was striding toward the wall of the mesa, his feet crunching into the sand, his black shadow marching beside him, a mere black blotch of squat darkness.

We followed as best we could. Greed was giving excessive strength to Bender, the hypnotist, and I noticed he didn't pant or tire, but jog-trotted through the sand at a steady pace, keeping almost up with the fiercely striding soldier.

We arrived at the base of the mesa. The Mexican found some long forgotten trail, and we started up.

It was a hard climb. Cloudbursts, wind and sun had done things to the trail, and the Mexican cursed from time to time.

"The Indians have been here, I tell you. We shall find where there has been a great battle. Strange I do not smell the blood or that we do not see corpses piled along the way. I tell you they are cunning. They have cut away this trail as though it had been done by a hundred years of time. Only an Indian could do that.

"Forward, my comrades! Who knows what we shall find within the cave? I wish I had my blade. It would be most awkward to be attacked now." But he kept pushing up the side of the mesa until the sheer wall frowned above us.

He stopped and pointed. "Look you at the cunning of the Indian. He has put these trees and bushes at the mouth of the cave, and he has made them look as though they had been here for years. I am afraid this means that he has conquered our men. But how could a horde of savages conquer trained soldiers?" And he looked from one to the other of us.

I shook my head and said nothing. It was Bender's party and Bender could handle the explanations.

Bender fastened those pin-point eyes of his on the Mexican and said quietly, "Who are we to fear a few savages?" and pushed aside the brush.

"Charioteer, you are a man of courage!" said the Mexican.

He reached out, grasped Bender by the shoulder and jerked him to one side. "But it is the part of a soldier to go first. Only I warn you, these redskins are fiends for torture. They gouge out the eyeballs and grind hot sand into the ears. They cut the skin off the soles of one's feet and press cactus thorns into the flesh. They heat little splinters of wood and stick them into the body. They are devils when they capture one."

Bender grunted. "Never mind that stuff. Let's go ahead and get the gold."

CHAPTER 5

Dust

Moreno shrugged and marched forward, going unarmed into a cave that he thought was filled with savages, who had been dead for three hundred years. It was the act of a brave man.

There was a narrow entrance. We had to stoop to get into it, but that entrance widened out within the first twenty feet. The cave went down on a sharp incline, but there were stone steps, worn smooth by many feet, and I groped my way in the darkness.

"There should be flint and steel here, a little tinder and a candle," said the Mexican, pausing and groping.

Bender took a pocket flashlight from his coat and sent the beam flashing into the darkness.

The Mexican jumped back with an oath.

"*Cascaras*, charioteer, but you have magic of sorts! What kind of thing is that?"

"A magic light," said Bender.

The Mexican regarded it for a moment with admiring eyes. Then he reached out and took it.

"It's like the other magic: fine at first, but it may tire. I

344 Science Fiction of Erle Stanley Gardner

prefer the dependable light of my fathers before me. Here's the flint and the steel, but, there's no tinder. Surely that dust can't be . . . *Dios!* It is!"

He looked at me, and I could see his eyes gleaming in the reflected light from the flash.

"There is too much magic around here," he said. "I left that candle and the flint, steel, and tinder here on this rock shelf but last week. Now look at it. A hundred years might have passed, yes, two hundred years!"

And he scowled at me with an expression I didn't like.

"You," he said, "are the one who says but little. Yet you are never surprised, and you seem to know more about these magic things than this charioteer with the funny eyes. Speak!"

I smiled at him. "Better wait to argue about the magic until we find what has happened to your brave comrades. We waste time in idle talk. It seems to me you are better at talking than at rescuing comrades."

The words snapped him out of it. He whirled.

"Right. First we will rescue those who need to be rescued. But you shall pay for those words! Blade to blade and foot to foot you shall make them good or eat them. To call Pablo Viscente de Moreno a coward, one must fight!"

And he was off down the stone stairway.

By the light of the flash I could see that it had been rounded by years and millions of feet. The very stairs had been worn in a deep passageway that bare feet alone had grooved into the rock.

"It was always here, this stairway," said the soldier, as though he could read my thoughts. "But there is much that is strange. I will be glad to see my comrades, but I fear they are trapped by these savages.

"There must be treachery somewhere, and I will smell out the traitor and have his heart spitted with my blade. I remember something now of this place. It had to do with the feeling of sickness . . . There was a fight. Hundreds of savages came pouring down into the cave. I remember that which followed— Wait! It was off here to the right. The Indians crowded me into that little chamber. There were hundreds of them. I fought them and hacked them, and they shot their arrows at me, and there were spears. I was wounded. I remember a darkness that came over everything. My torch ceased to give light and I felt a drowsy feeling. At the time I thought it was death.

"But that must have been but a swooning, for I woke up at El Morro, the rock of the inscriptions. Let us see what happened here."

He darted the beam of the flashlight into the interior of a round chamber which opened off from the main slope of the cave.

I caught the glimpse of the light on something white, and then he jumped back.

"Damn!" he cried. "I remember it now!"

For a moment he stood there, then he crossed himself and strode into the chamber.

There were skeletons there, and the floor of the cave was littered with bone dust. Bits of grinning skulls turned to dust when we touched them. There was a pile of bones in one end of the chamber from which there emerged a strip of glittering steel, reflecting in the beam of the flashlight.

The soldier leaned forward, grasped the blade from the bone heap and drew it toward him.

"*Carramba!*" I heard him hiss in a whisper. "It is my own. But my blade is rusted with blood. Look you, charioteer, at the incrusted blood upon it!"

He held it out and turned the light on it.

It was a wonderfully well balanced sword of finest steel. The hilt had been ornamented and incrusted with gold. There was a coat of arms upon the upper end of it.

In the shelter of the cave, in the dry climate of the desert

country the blade had kept in splendid shape, almost as it had
been laid down there some three hundred years ago. And who
had laid it down? To whom did those bones belong?

The same question was in the mind of the soldier.

"Look you," he said. "I was left here to guard this cave
and this gold. There were two other men. The general was
out making a raid, and meanwhile the savages swarmed down
the stairs to attack us three. That is all I remember, that fight
here. I went to sleep, or I swooned from loss of blood.

"And then I woke up at the inscription rock. I am still
confused on the time. It was more than two weeks ago that
I stood by my chief while he wrote his name upon that rock.
After that came the fight. That is the last that I remember
until I awoke by the rock.

"But now I am unwounded. When I swooned I had a hundred wounds. The blood poured down my arm until the hilt
of the sword slipped in my fingers through the slime of my
own blood. There were dancing savages grinning at me, shooting arrows at me . . . Now I wake up two days' march away
and am unwounded. What sort of magic is this?"

And he glared at Bender, with the pin-point eyes.

Emilio Bender did some tall lying, and did it fast.

"I am glad," he said, simply and in a low tone of voice.
"We were in the desert and we heard the cries of savage Indians. We knew that they were torturing white men. We
sneaked our way toward the place from which the cries came,
and we saw little fires, and there were white men who were
lashed to a heavy stake, and the fire was eating its way into
their flesh.

"You were lying unconscious on one side. Your turn for
the torture was to come, and my friend and I rescued you.
There was a great fight with the savages. And we would have
been caught had it not been for the magic chariot. But we
loaded you into the chariot and took you to a safe place in

the mountains. There you recovered your health, but you could not remember how or when you came there or where you had been.

"We took you back to the rock so that the sight of the inscription might bring back your memory. Your wounds have healed, and the savages now have gone."

With eyes that were clouded with thought the Mexican looked at him.

"Then," he said, "you are no charioteer at all, but a brave soldier who rescued me from the savages."

Bender nodded.

"That is right," he said.

The Mexican clapped him on the shoulder.

"Ha!" he said. "A soldier!" And his eyes glittered. He turned to me. "Then you, too, are a soldier?"

I sensed trouble coming, and I wasn't going to lie about it.

"No," I said. "I am what you'd call a charioteer. Civilization has decayed my courage and spoiled my fighting trim. If you want to list Bender as a soldier that's all right. I'm a charioteer."

He stepped back, whirled the sword in a glittering arc, made a thrust or two.

I've seen fencers in my time, but I have never seen any one who could get the things out of a sword blade that man could. The muscles seemed to have been oiled and greased, made especially for sword handling.

"But the gold," Bender was prompting him.

"My comrades!" snapped the soldier. "Is it too late to rescue them? How long was it since you found me?"

The man with the metallic eyes glittered his magnetic gaze straight into the pupils of the soldier.

"It has been more than a month," he said.

"More than a month!" repeated the Mexican in wonder.

What would he have said if he had known it had been more

than three hundred years more than a month? Perhaps nothing could have surprised him very deeply after his ride in the
magic chariot.

So I was treated to the spectacle of a man picking his three-
hundred-year-old sword from the bony hand of his own skeleton and starting out to avenge the fate of two comrades who
had been dead for a third of a thousand years.

CHAPTER 6

A Monster

I got Bender off to one side.

"You've found the cave now. But you'd better do some of
your hypnotic stuff and bring this fellow back to earth. There
are natives all around here, and if I have any accurate knowledge as to where we are I'd say there was an Indian pueblo
within a few miles of here. This is quite a cave, and we're
likely to find the Indians are familiar with it.

"If this chap runs onto some Indians down here, you can
figure what's going to happen. Better snap him out of it and
we can find the gold somehow or other."

Bender looked at me, and for the first time I caught a
greenish glint of panic in his aluminium-colored eyes.

"I can't hypnotize him any more," he told me. "I've tried
it half a dozen times. He's dangerous, but there's nothing we
can do about it. The primary personality, Ramon Ayala the
Mexican, I can hypnotize any time I want. But this secondary
personality has too strong a will. I can't do a thing with him."

"Where," I asked, "did this secondary personality come
from?"

"It must be evidence of reincarnation," he said. "I have always believed in it. This proves it. The individual is made up
of hundreds of thousands of personalities. The channel from

the conscious to the subconscious is well developed, and the experiences of the conscious mind are transmitted faithfully. But the channel from the subconscious to the conscious is not developed. That is why we don't see the tangible evidence of reincarnation in—"

He was interrupted at that point by a roar.

"By my sword!" swore the soldier. "The man who has left his bones here is a robber and a thief. He has even stolen the gold chain and cross from around my neck. Look, I tell you! It is mine, and look at the shape it is in. It is blackened, the links of the chain are corroded. He well deserved slaying.

"But, mark you, my comrades, there is some foul miasma here which rots bodies quickly. For these are the bones of Indians whom I slew myself with this very sword, and but a little over a month ago. You are sure of the date?"

Bender nodded easily.

"Certain," he said. "But let's go find the gold."

"Gold!" bellowed the Mexican. "Let us go find my brave comrades, or let us avenge them."

"You are but one," tentatively suggested Bender.

"Two!" snapped the Mexican. "You forget that you are also a soldier. Two soldiers and a charioteer. *Diablo!* What more do you want? We will avenge our brave soldiers who have died the death of the Indians' torture!"

And he was off down the main slope of the cave, brandishing his sword in a glittering arc.

Bender leaned toward me. "I left my revolver in the car. Have you a weapon?"

I shook my head. I had nothing except two fists and a jack-knife.

We followed the soldier, hurrying to keep up with the circle of illumination which was cast by the flashlight. There was no time for conversation, little for thought. Bender was worrying about the gold. I was worrying about what was going to happen. Perhaps it was a presentiment, perhaps it was the uncanny atmosphere of trailing around after a warrior who had been dead for three hundred years, but there were cold chills racing along my spine.

For we couldn't control this soldier. I knew it. Bender was going to find it out, if he didn't know it already. With the passing of every single minute the strange secondary personality that was the individuality of Pablo Viscente de Moreno, a soldier who had campaigned the deserts under General Don Diego de Vargas, and who had been dead three hundred years, became more firmly ensconced in the body of a *cholo* Mexican named Ramon Ayala.

And the personality of that soldier was something to be reckoned with. Civilization has done things to us. We have become weaklings, the whole race, believe it or not. It isn't so much the physical strength that has ebbed from us, as it is the spiritual courage which we should have. Here was a man who had lived by the sword and had died by the sword. He was one who had lived his life, enjoying its every moment. His vitality showed it, made us seem as sick shadows.

Here was a man who had been raised at a time when one must be able to preserve his life in order to live. He couldn't call a cop or rely on an injunction if his neighbor got crusty. He had to stand and fight, and that was the life he enjoyed.

We talk proudly of our hardy forbears who went westward across the plains in Eighteen Forty-nine. But how of those soldiers who campaigned the deserts in Sixteen Hundred-odd? Those men were traversing trackless wastes whose very nature and extent they knew nothing of. They didn't have covered wagons and sturdy oxen. They didn't have a green and fertile goal at the end of their march.

No, they simply headed their horses into the dry and burning desert, surrounded by hostile tribes, armed only with the weapons of ancient warfare, and knowing not what was before them.

Such was the man who strode in front of me, whirling his sword in a glittering arc for the very joy of life and combat.

And in the chamber behind me were the bones of this very man, dead three hundred years.

Is it any wonder that the cool air of the cave made the perspiration on my forehead seem dank and clammy?

We came to a place where the cave widened out into a great chamber. The flashlight couldn't penetrate the darkness far enough to disclose all the walls; only a stray outthrust of rock here, or a bit of lowhung ceiling there.

The soldier stopped and sent the beam of the electric flash in a long circle.

"I have got to look for landmarks here," he said. "I was only here a few times, and it has been over a month ago, and I have been sick in that month . . . Wait! There should be a branch of the main cave over here to the left." And he walked confidently forward into the darkness.

"If anything happens we'll have a hard time getting out of here," I whispered to Emilio Bender.

"There is gold here," he said, and his voice quavered with eagerness.

I said nothing further. I could take my chances with the rest. I had been taken along to see the thing through, and that was what I was going to do.

The flashlight hit the walls again, and there was an arched opening.

"This is the place," said the soldier, and started to run.

We followed.

When he stopped short we almost ran him down. The beam of the flashlight was glittering from something white again, and I knew what it would be.

"*Madre de Dios!* Another fight. More bones. *Carramba*, there is another blade, and it is the sword of Juan Bautiste de Alvarado!"

And he stooped and picked up another red-incrusted blade of finest steel.

"Here, soldier," he said, as he thrust the hilt into the limp hand of Emilio Bender. "Here is the sword of one who was brave of heart and steady of hand. Take it and bear it well and with honor."

He took another step forward and stooped to the floor of the cave. He presently turned to me with another blade, dulled with three hundred years of disuse.

"Here, señor charioteer, take this. You are unworthy of it. It is the blade of a brave man, but it is the fortunes of war, and you may have to stand shoulder to shoulder with us before you quit the place.

"Remember that a cut is faster and more terrifying, but a thrust is the means of piling a corpse at your feet to make a partial barricade. But, when you thrust, be sure to thrust true and be careful to pull your blade out before the weight of the falling man jerks the hilt from your hand . . . Come."

And he started forward again, his feet grinding the bones beneath him to a powder.

"There is some horrid miasma about this place," he muttered. "Think of bodies that are only a month old turning to dust!"

I said nothing. Bender had started the explanations. He could finish them.

CHAPTER 7

A Medieval Raid

The room opened out into a wide circle, then narrowed again. There was the sound of running water, and my nostrils fancied they could detect the odor of wood smoke. I spoke of it in a whisper to Bender, but he shook his head.

"Gold," he said in a hoarse whisper, and hurried on.

We came to a little alcove which had been carved out of the cave by the action of prehistoric waters. The soldier walked into this alcove, then stopped and swore.

"Here it was," he said. "Now look!"

We crowded at his shoulders to look.

We saw the remains of a stout chest, bound with hasps of iron, bolted with some strangely designed bolts. The chest had been battered and splintered. It was empty, save for several inches of dust.

Bender pushed his eager fingers in the dust, fished around with them for a few moments, then uttered a cry. He withdrew his hand, and there, in his fingers, was a great ornament of gold.

The Mexican nodded casually.

"There were hundreds more," he said.

The man with pin-point eyes slipped the golden ornament into the pocket of his coat, where it bulged out the pocket and sagged the garment. Then he started groping once more in the dust. When he had finished he knew that there was no hope of additional loot. The chest was empty.

He sat down on a rock. I thought for a moment he was going to swear.

"Where would they have taken it?" he asked.

"Back to their villages. They were, for the most part, ornaments which adorned the temples they erected to their heathen gods . . . But hold. There was a private store of gold. This was the treasure chest which all were to share in; but there were some ornaments, some melted gold in bars, some of their turquoise jewelry which was mine. I hid it in another part of the cave. Perhaps they were not so fortunate in finding that. Come with me."

Bender needed no second invitation. He was on his feet and striding forward.

I thought the light from the flash was getting just a trifle more dim.

"Better turn off the flash for a minute or two and save the battery," I warned.

"Later," said Bender. "Hurry on."

And the soldier hurried on.

With us trailing after, our strange guide went back to the main chamber, ran along the dust-covered floor which sent his footfalls thudding back at us in muffled echoes, and shot the beam of the flashlight toward the west end of the chamber.

There was nothing here but wall.

The soldier muttered, sent the beam along the wall, up one side, down the other, stepping back a few paces, muttering to himself.

"It should be here," he said. "See you, there is the head of a lion in the stone, and that to the left looks like an old man . . . Ha, now I remember! It is off to the left."

And he strode confidently to the left. There seemed to be nothing but solid rock, but as we approached nearer a little vault opened out.

"This is the place," he said. "We must stoop."

We stooped, and as we got our heads near the floor of the cave there was a gentle draft of air which smote my nostrils with the unmistakable odor of wood smoke.

But the others either did not smell it, or if they did, gave it no heed. Eagerly trailing the three hundred year old secret, they entered the chamber.

It was really an entrance to another cave, or to another branch of caves shooting out from the main chamber. I could see that there was a long passageway, and then an arched roof, and I thought I could detect a glint of light coming from some faintly discerned opening in the distant darkness.

"It was in this little cleft to the right of the opening," said the Mexican, and turned the beam of the flashlight.

I saw a long cleft some little distance away, and I saw also that the beam of the flashlight was weaker now. The light was no longer a brilliant pencil of white light, but was taking on a reddish hue.

Emilio Bender ran forward, getting his shadow so that it danced along the wall in a grotesque blob of ebony silhouette.

"To one side," yelled the soldier. "I cannot see."

And, at that instant, the light went out.

"More of your damned magic that gets tired!" shouted the Mexican, and dashed the flashlight to the floor of the cave. There sounded the tinkle of broken glass and then darkness was about us, a soul-chilling darkness that seemed as tangible as a smothering blanket thrown about our heads.

"Fool!" ranted Emilio Bender.

But his ranting did no good. The flashlight might have recuperated enough strength in the battery to have given us a few flashes that would have enabled us to find the gold and make our escape from the cave.

"I can't even find the cleft where the gold is," whined the man of the pin-point eyes.

"Bah!" scoffed the Mexican. "Are we men or are we babies? Why whimper about a little darkness? I have seen darkness before. Doubtless I will see it again!"

"Come back, come back! We must get the gold!" yelled Emilio Bender.

"It is my gold, not yours. This is a private store of my own plunder. I do not share it with soldiers who are cowards. There is much more gold in the Indian temples. Go to them and get your own store of plunder. As for me, I am going to go to the other cave."

And I could hear the Mexican's feet ringing on the stone floor as he strode away.

"How many matches have you got?" asked Bender of me, and his voice was wheedling.

"I have a number, but we need them to get out of here," I said.

"Strike one, just one that I may see where we stand."

I struck just the one, and as I did so knew that I had made

a mistake. For the light of that match showed me the greenish glitter of those aluminium-colored eyes staring into mine from the dark background of the cave.

"Hold that match, steady," said the man.

I wanted to shake it out. Some inner voice told me to dash it to the floor of the cave and step on it. But I hesitated too long.

The pin-points of the eyes became rapiers, thrusting long tongues of flame into my brain. The whole side of the cave seemed to be a fathomless depth of aluminium-colored darkness from which radiated twin streamers of lambent flame.

"Give me the matches."

The voice was low and vibrant, and I could feel my hand starting toward his with the matches. But I brought all my will power to my aid, and held them back.

Once more came the command.

"Give—me—the—matches!"

The pin-points of the eyes seared the volition from my brain. I did not know that I was holding out the matches. I knew only that I was no longer master of myself.

The next I knew, the match I was holding had burned my fingers, and a cold hand had closed about the box of matches I was holding out toward Bender.

The darkness was welcome, but I was still haunted by the memory of those pin-points in their aluminium-colored background.

The next I heard was the scrape of a match on the rock wall, the sputter of flame, and the dancing of grotesque shadows as Bender moved the light slowly along, nursing the flame between cupped hands.

In a little while he found the place in the cleft where something had been thrust into a hole in the rocks. He lit another match, put in his hand and pulled out a bit of what had been cloth. Now it was but a few rags of scattered remnants. But from the openings gleamed the unmistakable yellow of gold.

"Gold!" he cried.

Then, as though it had been an echo to his shout, the cave reverberated with a blood-curdling scream which came from the distant darkness.

Emilio Bender jumped back.

"What was that?" he asked of me.

"A woman's scream and a man's yell mingled together," I said.

We waited, tense, listening.

Something was coming toward us. I could see the little flickers of ruddy light which were cast by a moving flame. The woman screamed again. I could hear the pound of shod feet.

Then, from a distance, there was a bedlam of sound.

Around the corner of a passageway came the flicker of a smoking torch, and there was the Mexican, holding to him the screaming form of a young woman.

He was laughing, and there was blood on his face, marks of where her nails had raked down the skin. In his right hand, held with his sword, was a smoking wood torch, a pine knot that was filled with pitch. The girl was Indian, young, attractive, and frightened. She was held in his left arm so that her feet barely touched the floor of the cave, and the soldier was laughing, the happy carefree laugh of an adventurer.

"Forward, *amigos!*" he cried. "There are other women to be had for the taking, and then there will be a splendid fight. The warriors are coming in force. This is life! And I have been as one dead for over a month!"

And he laughed again.

The woman was kicking, squirming in his embrace like an eel fresh from the water. Her lithe body was a beautiful nut-brown. Her well-turned legs writhed and twisted like twin snakes as she sought to get some purchase from which she could add to the efficacy of her struggles.

"Go," said the soldier, and threw the torch from him in a long arc of whirling fire. Then the pitch knot hit the floor of the cave and rolled along, bouncing, giving off red embers of fire.

And the soldier was gone in the darkness with a mocking laugh.

CHAPTER 8

Battle

Ahead of me I saw a barrier of grim shadow outlined against the light of that pine knot, and then heard the sound of naked feet pattering upon the floor. A torch gleamed from around the corner of one of the passageways, and I saw a young buck Indian, almost naked, running swiftly, low to the ground, a spear in his hand.

He saw me as soon as I saw him, and flung up the spear.

I am no swordsman, but desperation stirred dormant cells of dead instinct in my brain. I acted without conscious skill, but I swung that sword at just the right angle to parry the thrust.

Then we were at it, the Indian thrusting with the spear, my sword seeming to bite through the darkness and ward off the thrusts as though it was the sword that guided the arm instead of the arm that must have guided the sword.

There were half a dozen torches, now, and there were others coming on the run. Arrows whizzed about me, and the cave reverberated to the thunder of a rifle. A bullet fanned my cheek and spatted against the wall back of me.

Another Indian was on my left, and I caught the gleam of a dagger as he struck. Out of the corner of my eye, I could see Bender standing against the wall, his sword glittering in a mad frenzy as he fought off the Indians.

Then came more men and more torches. The red flames gave a weird illumination to the scene of battle. The black smoke went up in streamers until it clung to the distant roof of the chamber. And something thudded against my sword arm with numbing force. I tried to raise the blade and the muscles refused to function.

I sensed a hurtling body coming through the air, and the sword clattered to the rock floor. I swung my left. The fist connected and the man went down. Then the half darkness fairly seemed to rain hurtling brown shapes that ran forward in close formation. Naked arms shot around my knees and I was dragged down. Something hit me on the head, and my brain exploded into a flash of light.

For an instant or two I was unconscious. When I knew anything again I was being bound swiftly and securely. I could hear groans from my left where Bender was lying, two Indians banging his head on the rocks.

There were shouts from one of the side chambers, and my captors, finished with their job of binding me, ran toward those shouts.

I raised my head, and for a few seconds saw such a battle as few living men have seen.

Our soldier had dropped the woman now, and his teeth were gleaming in the light of the torches as he fought and laughed. They did not shoot him because the very press of Indians about him prevented a bullet's being placed with any accuracy.

But they crowded upon him with grim and relentless fury. There were hunting knives that glittered red in the torchlight, and there were spears that were thrust forward by lean brown arms that rippled with wire-hard muscles.

And moving with effortless ease, his glittering blade flashing in a swift circle of defense, the man held them at bay and laughed at them.

Never had I believed it possible that a slender bit of steel could move with such bewildering speed, or could offer so perfect a defense against pressing numbers.

A swift circling cut, and a man jumped back, his right arm dangling, a knife clattering to the rock. A pointed thrust that made of the sword a mere glittering tongue of naked steel, and a savage cried out in pain and toppled forward to join the piled bodies that were slumped in a half circle around the soldier's feet, forming a barrier which hampered the movements of those who sought to attack.

The sword glittered with red for a second or two, then as it whirled in its hissing circle, it cleared again and the light reflected from the smooth steel.

It was a rock that got him, a rock expertly thrown. At that there must have been an element of luck in it, for the rock was thrown by the young girl who had crawled to the outer edge of the circle of combatants.

It arched over the heads of the warriors, and dropped from the half darkness, squarely upon the top of the soldier's head.

He would have shaken off the daze in a few seconds, but he was too hard pressed to stop even for an instant. The sword wavered for a moment in its glittering speed, and then they were on him like a pack of brown wolves dragging down a wounded buck. The whole place became but a swarming mass of seething bodies, and then the motion gradually subsided.

I moved my arms, testing the bonds which held me to see if there was any chance of escape. There was none. My arms might as well have been gripped in a vise.

Then the circle of red figures fell apart and I saw our warrior raised to his feet. His head was bleeding heavily from the cut the rock had inflicted. His arms were circled with cords, and there was still the half-dazed look in his eyes I have seen in the eyes of prize fighters when some unexpected blow has caught them with deadly force in the middle of conflict.

But he was still laughing, and I could see the gleam of his teeth.

*   *   *

About us gathered the enraged Indians. Many had wounds and they were in a deadly humor.

"Explain to them. Otherwise they will put us to death," chattered Emilio Bender.

Explain! As well have tried to explain cold-blooded murder to twelve men in a jury box. All the smoldering enmity of these Indians against the white man had been fanned to life. They had captured us in the act of raiding them in their sacred cave. All we could hope for was that the end would be merciful. But that was a vain hope. They had been too careful to catch us alive.

If our Mexican could throw himself back three hundred years into some past incarnation under the influence of hypnotism, then these savage Indians could throw themselves back under the influence of rage until the traditions of millions of years of ancestors swayed them in what they were to do.

They jerked us together, tied the three of us with a rope which went around our necks. Many of them had nasty wounds from which blood was flowing in veritable rivulets. But they paid them no heed. Their obsidian-like eyes were glittering with a deadly rage.

The voice of the swordsman rang out. He was fully conscious once more.

"What sort of soldiers are you?" he cried at us. "Why didn't you hold them here? You two should have had no trouble holding off the tribe. But you didn't hold one. You let the whole band come down upon me. Soldiers! Bah!

"Where are the circles of dead bodies that should be in front of you? Not a body. You are both tied like a couple of rabbits being taken to the spit! Bah, you have disgraced the swords you carried!

"You, charioteer, did the best that could be expected of you. But how of you, soldier? Soldier indeed! You will answer to me for that falsehood! You are not a soldier. You are not even a charioteer!"

He would have said more, but they jerked on the rope which circled our necks, and we perforce shuffled forward in the half darkness.

Behind us, men looked to their own wounds, or gave treatment to the wounds of others. Ahead of us, some half dozen of the Indians jerked on the rope and took us forward at a half run.

"Don't stumble," I warned Emilio Bender, "or they will drag you to death, and the weight of your body will strangle us all."

I knew something of Indian methods, and knew how hard it was to rush at a half trot through the darkness with hands tied.

Bender yammered some reply, but I could not catch it nor did I care greatly what it was. But he did not stumble.

I did not warn the Mexican. He had heard my warning to Bender, and he was not the sort to stumble, that soldier of a distant past, come to life to plunge us all into a conflict which mocked at history.

We came at length to a lighted chamber. There was a big fire in the center and the walls were black with smoke. This must have been the council chamber of the tribe for countless centuries.

They lined us up against a wall and there were iron loops driven into the solid rock of that wall. They tied us to these loops, and I could hear the laugh of the Mexican as the rope bit into his flesh.

"These are the loops we put into the wall to tie our prisoners to. Now they have turned the tables!"

I found nothing to laugh about, nor did Emilio Bender.

CHAPTER 9

The Magic of Gold

The Indians squatted in a circle to hold a conclave, and they talked in low tones.

"Will they kill us?" asked Bender.

"Ha!" chuckled the soldier. "Will they kill us! My white-livered scrivener, who talked like a soldier and fought like a coward—they will kill us by inches! Look you to the lofty walls of the cave. From those walls your screams of agony will echo back to you before another twenty-four hours have crossed the pathway of time."

The remark got on Bender's nerves.

"Yours, too!" he snapped.

"No," said the soldier, simply. "I will not scream."

I spoke to Bender in a low voice. "I have heard of a tribe which dwells in a secret pueblo. They come in to Zuñi to trade; and once or twice when I have been in Zuñi I have seen members of what I considered a new tribe. This is their secret: They make headquarters in this cave. If they are ever surprised on the outside, they pretend to be the ordinary run of Pueblo Indians. How savage they are I don't know. Perhaps when they have had time to cool off I can barter with them. Remember, we know where there is a store of golden plunder which doubtless they consider sacred ornaments. For the present, our hope is that they will save us and not put us to immediate death."

Bender grunted at that.

The soldier laughed aloud. "What a fight it would have been had the comrades of my army been with me!"

I turned to him. "Whatever possessed you to grab that girl?"

"Because I wanted to," he said promptly enough. "I could see that there were not so many men but that three soldiers could hold them at bay. But you are a charioteer and would not know the pleasure of battle."

That was, to him, sufficient reason. We stood there in a line against the wall, ropes knotted around our necks, ropes binding our arms behind us.

About the fire squatted the Indians in council. From time to time stragglers, more or less seriously wounded, came into the chamber of the cave. The women were treating those who had suffered the most, and in the distance I could hear that wailing cry of savage sorrow with which primitive people mourn for a loved one who is dead.

As the fire died down, fresh wood was piled on it. I noticed the shape of that wood. Plainly it had been cut short in order to be dragged in through an opening; it would not have been cut in such lengths to be hauled in over the long trail we had used. Nor was there any evidence of the entrance we had used being known to the Indians.

I hoped it was a secret entrance about which they did not know. That would give us a break—if we could find our way back to that hole, and if we had the chance to get loose.

The council droned into the small hours of the night. From what I could hear I gathered that the Indians were worried lest others should know that we had come to the cave. Before they decided what to do they wanted to make certain we were alone.

After several hours of powwow, they seemed to reach some decision, and slept. They left a man to watch us and see that we didn't work loose from the ropes which held us.

But we had been tied by Indians, and there wasn't much chance of working loose.

The guard regarded us with eyes in which glittered a hatred that made chills ripple the spine. It was clear that his sole desire was to wreak vengeance upon us.

"I've got to lie down. I'm weak and the cords are hurting my arms. There's no feeling in my finger tips," said Bender.

I laughed at that. They meant to keep us standing, without sleep. If we so much as relaxed our muscles and slumped forward against the bonds, the rope around our necks would strangle us to death unless they decided to loosen the knot after it had bit into our wind, and save us for a more horrible death. I explained as much to Bender.

He seemed to be thinking things over.

"What about the car?" he asked.

"I don't understand all they said," I told him. "It's a mixture of part Spanish, part Indian, and part of a dialect I've never heard before. But they've set fire to the automobile and covered the wreckage over with sand. They're worried about how we got into the cave. They think we came in past their guards. But they'll trail us when it comes daylight and find the entrance we came in by."

He let his aluminium-colored eyes narrow in thought, and I got an idea.

"Can you hypnotize the guard?" I asked.

He suddenly stiffened to alert attention. "I can try. Talk to him in a low voice. Get his attention on you. Then, when I start to talk, you keep silent."

I told him I would. The Mexican was listening to us with a frown of perplexity on his features.

Soon the guard came close.

"Would you like gold?" I asked of him.

He scorned to answer me, after the fashion of an Indian.

"Gold, lots of gold, a fortune in sacred gold," I told him, and let my voice sink to a droning monotone. "You could be wealthy. You could traffic with the white men and buy all that you desired. You would never need to hunt, never need to work. You could have everything that any one in the tribe could have, and a thousand times more. You would be powerful, you would be chief."

He approached me and spat in my face.

I waited a few moments, then droned again: "Gold, gold, gold, ever the thing of power. There is plenty of gold. You can have sacred gold, precious gold . . ."

And then, from my right, the voice of the man with pin-point eyes took up the refrain.

"Gold, gold, gold," he said, speaking in Spanish. "Gold, gold, gold. Look at me, gaze into my eyes. In them you will see that there is honesty.

"Gold, gold, gold. You are feeling drowsy. Sleep is coming to you. Gold, gold, gold. Always there is the glitter of gold. The firelight on the wall is like gold in the rocks. You see it and the light hurts your eyes. You close them to shut out the sight of the gold, gold, gold."

And I noticed that the Indian was indeed closing his eyes. He fought against the drooping lids, but the fight was a losing one.

"Gold, gold, gold," droned the man with pin-point eyes. "And before you go to sleep you must kill the white men. You hate me. You want to kill me. When I am dead you can sleep. But you must kill me first. Take your knife from your belt, hold it in your hand, ready to cut."

And the brown hand sleepily went to the belt, took out the knife, and looked stupidly at it.

"Gold, gold, gold," droned the voice in its monotone of sleepy intonations. "Gold, gold, gold. The easiest way for you to kill me is to cut my arteries. See, I am tied up with my arteries, and my arteries stretch to the others. They are not ropes, but arteries in which there courses blood.

"Cut those arteries and watch us slowly die in great agony. Then you can sleep. You cannot call out, you cannot stay awake. You have to sleep, and then you will wake up and find gold. Gold, gold, gold."

And I saw the hand that held the knife raise it and start sawing at the ropes. As the first of the ropes parted I could see the expression upon the savage features.

Never have I seen such an expression of horrible blood lust before, nor do I care to again. It was as though I could study, through the lens of a slow-motion picture camera, the face of a man who was murdering me in a burst of savage hatred.

The eyes were maniacal. The lips slavered. The facial muscles writhed with the animal pleasure of torture inflicted upon an enemy.

"I groan, I scream, I cry out in my anguish," purred the man with the aluminium-colored eyes, "and the sound is as music to your ears. Not too fast do you work the knife, but just fast enough to let the blood flow from my arteries and leave me in agony. The warm blood is splashing upon your arms now. You are bathed in it, and you are being revenged. And presently you will sleep, and when you wake up you will find gold, gold, gold."

The words droned on while the Indian cut through the bonds that held us together and anchored us to the wall.

"Now I am dead and you can sleep," said the droning voice. "You will lie back upon the floor and your eyes will close. You will relax your hold upon the knife. You have avenged your tribe. And you will sleep a deep and dreamless slumber. When you awaken it will be to find gold. Gold, gold, gold."

The Indian slumped to the rocky floor, flung one arm under his head and instantly went to sleep.

"What magic is this?" demanded the Mexican.

"Shut up!" I hissed at him in a whisper.

The council fire was some little distance from us, and the men slept about it like logs of wood. I knew the Indian delicacy of sense. They would be almost certain to hear us before we could make good our escape. But every second was precious now.

I sat down on the rock floor and inched my way toward the sleeping Indian, took the knife from his nerveless fingers, and held it rigid in my hand.

By an effort I got to my feet. The aluminium-eyed man

leaned against the blade of the knife and sawed the last of his bonds across it. When they had dropped to the floor he took the knife and cut my ropes, then those of the soldier.

CHAPTER 10

Through the Blackness

Our swords had been taken from us and flung into a corner of the rock chamber. We retrieved them, and I was barely able to restrain the soldier from then and there giving his battle cry by pointing out to him in a whisper that he was accompanied only by a charioteer and a scrivener who were worse than useless in battle. He regretfully agreed, and then we wormed our way silently toward the arched opening through which we had been marched.

In one of the pockets carved in the rock wall by the action of the elements, were stacked some pitch knots to be used as torches, and I gathered up two or three of these.

"You have the matches?" I asked of Bender.

He nodded.

Back of us some one stirred.

"Run!" I whispered.

There was a shout from behind us, but it was the confused shout of one who is not in full possession of his faculties.

Some sleeping Indian, hearing the faint sound of our feet, had doubtless awakened, looked toward the wall and seen that we had gone. But he did not know in which direction.

"Feel your way through the darkness," I cautioned them. "Do not show a light and do not make noise. They don't know which way we have gone."

They followed my instructions, although the Mexican grumbled at being forced to flee from a horde of ignorant heathens.

I had no time to explain to him the development of the modern revolver, or the repeating rifle. I could only urge him to run by warning him that he was with two cowards. It was the only argument which moved him.

I doubt if we could have found our way back to the place where the gold was stored had it not been for the uncanny sense of perception of the Mexican. He seemed able to see in the darkness, and he must have known the inside of that cave as a river pilot knows his stream. For he took us on a swift but silent walk until I could hear the wailing of women, and knew that we were approaching the scene of our conflict.

We had some light here, the light of a distant camp fire in the other chamber of the cave. The women had taken the bodies out into this chamber and built a fire. About this fire they rocked back and forth, wailing their thin chant of mourning.

They were as hypnotized with their grief as the Indian guard had been with the droned words of Emilio Bender.

Getting past them was easy, but we had to use considerable care to keep some of the children from spotting us. It was the older girls who made the trouble. They sat in on the mourning party, but youth is ever unable to concentrate for long upon any emotion other than love; and we could see the slender forms of the girls flitting about the mourning fire, putting on additional wood.

We finally reached the cleft where the gold had been stored. It was still there, intact.

Emilio Bender raked out the gold pieces and struck one of the matches. He devoured them with his eyes. There were golden ornaments, little gold images, even gold arrowheads.

In the greed of that moment, the man with the strange, aluminium-colored eyes forgot himself. He scooped such things as he desired into his pockets.

"This is *my* third," he said, heedless of the fact he had taken a good three-quarters. "You two divide the rest and we'll get going."

It must have been the silence which warned him. It was
the silence which precedes a storm, and Emilio Bender looked
up to encounter the flaming gaze of the man who claimed to
be Pablo Viscente de Moreno, a soldier who had marched
the deserts three hundred-odd years ago.

"So!" yelled the soldier. "You would loot the plunder of
a soldier, eh? You who claim to be a soldier, but are not
even a charioteer!"

And the right hand of the soldier whipped the naked blade
in a hissing arc.

"Arise and account!" shouted the soldier.

There was only the faintest light from the distant camp
fires. They glinted in half reflections from the polished blade,
and served to show the men as half-formed shadows moving
against the chalklike wall of the cave.

"But think," said Emilio Bender in his droning voice, "of
what you can buy with that gold! Think of the sleep you have
lost . . ."

I still believe that if he had surrendered the gold instead
of trying to use his hypnotism he could have saved himself.
But he was flushed by his success with the Indian and em-
boldened by greed.

"Sleep, sleep, sleep," he droned. "You need to rest, to
relax, to let your senses become warm and drowsy. You feel
a strange quiet . . ."

It was then that the Mexican said something which has
puzzled me, and will always puzzle me. Some of what had
happened could be explained through the theory of dual personalities. But this remark tended to show that he knew.

"Quiet!" he shouted. "Sleep, you say! I have slept for
three hundred years. Now look out for yourself!"

It happened so quickly that I could not interfere even had
I wanted to. These two men had come to the final show-down,
and that show-down was inevitable. The hypnotist had virtually created this strange man who was now challenging

him. And the greed of the man with eyes like pin-points was bound to bring about such a conflict, sooner or later. As well sooner as later.

I heard the rasp of steel on steel, and an exclamation from the soldier.

"You would try to slip a blade into my stomach from below, would you? Then stand up and fight, man to man."

"Quick!" yelled Bender to me. "Run him through in the back and we will divide the gold."

I know of no remark that better illustrated the character of the man. It was his last.

There was the whirl of a blade, a cut, a thrust, a groan and something staggered back and slumped to the rock.

"Fool!" grunted the soldier. "You would pose as a soldier and turn out a thief!"

I groped for the pulse of the man with pin-point eyes. There was no pulse. His wrist was limp and already chilling with death.

The soldier saw my motion and laughed bitterly. "Am I so clumsy then that when I run my blade through their hearts you can feel a beat in the wrist? He is dead, I tell you. Come."

He stooped and took the gold from the pockets of the dead man, and he made a rough division with me.

"Thus do soldiers share their spoils upon the field of battle," he said.

I crammed my gold into my pockets.

From the main body of the cave was a terrific clamor of noise. The Indians were loose and on the trail, rushing down the cave toward us.

"Quick, run!" I yelled.

"Run? Why? Are we not two soldiers?"

"They have guns," I said. "We have no chance against them."

I doubt if I could have moved him, but, of a sudden, he spoke in a thicker, slower tone.

"Very well, then, let us run. I know this cave. Follow me."

He ran; and as he ran his steps became more heavy, slower. The body gradually lost the spring and became as the muscle-bound body of a *cholo* laborer.

We ran through the dark, he leading the way.

"Stoop here," he called; and I stooped, felt a low archway graze my body.

"There is another entrance, a secret entrance," he said. "I hope I can find it. I am getting drowsy. Some one is shouting in my ear to go away and leave his body alone. Why should I have some one shout at me to leave my own body?

"*Carramba!* It's all because of that man with the funny eyes. I know now that I must die because I killed him. As his corpse gets cold, so does my own soul get cold. I am paying a price, and yet it is not a price. It is something I have already paid . . . Here, *amigo*, take all the gold. I would rather you had it than the strange man who is pushing me out of my skin. How he pushes! And he is slow and stolid. He could never oust me but for the death of the man with the strange eyes. I can feel an inner chill."

He stopped in his tracks, thrust golden ornaments and turquoise necklaces into my hands.

"Fill—your—pockets . . . *Adios, amigo!*"

And he was gone. I knew instantly when the other came into possession of his body.

"*Que es?* What is it?" he demanded, Mexican fashion, and his tone was dull as the tone of a man who is slowly awakening from a long sleep.

"We are in a cave," I said. "Follow me."

He accepted the statement with the unreasoning stolidity of his kind. I led the way in the same general direction the soldier had been piloting me. It was dark, and yet it was not entirely dark. There was a half light in the air, and a freshness which reminded me of dawn.

We pushed forward, seeing the vague shape of walls and

minarets on our sides. I thought there was an opening overhead and glanced upward. I saw the pale glow of a star,
pin-pointing out before the dawn, and I thought of the man
with pin-point eyes.

Somewhere, we had left the cave and were in a cañon
which towered on either side in great cliffs. The cliffs spread
apart. The floor of the cañon became rough and bowlder-
strewn. We fought our way forward. The light grew stronger,
and dawn smells were in the air.

We found a deer trail angling from the floor of the cañon
to the side of the mountain, around it to the desert plain
below the mesa. I led the way along this. There were no signs
of Indians.

The Mexican looked down at the sword he was using for
a walking stick. It was stained with sticky red, and even
now the flies were commencing to drone about it.

"What is this?" he asked in his thick, suspicious voice, and
raised it to his eyes. Then he flung it far down the cañon. It
clattered upon the rocks. He crossed himself, looked at me
with eyes which were showing a glint of expression, an expression of wonderment.

"It is nothing," I said. "Come."

"Where is the other man, the Señor Bender?"

"He has remained behind. Come."

We struck the shoulder of the mountain, zigzagged to the
plain. The sun came up and tinted us with its reddish rays.
Far off in the distance I saw a cloud of dust and knew that
it was an automobile.

I followed the course of the road, figured where we might
intersect it, and ran down the sloping plain, shouting at the
Mexican to hurry.

He ran with a heavy-footed pace which covered the ground
but slowly. We would have missed it, but the automobile
driver saw us and waited while we covered the last half mile.
He was a bronzed rancher who was inclined to be suspicious,
but he gave us a lift.

I had taken the things from the pockets of my coat, taken off my coat, and rolled the treasure stuff into a ball within the coat. The rancher looked at it suspiciously, but I offered no explanation. He took us to Gallup, and from there we caught a train to Los Angeles.

I had purchased a suitcase for my treasure stuff.

At Los Angeles I secured a car from a friend, and drove the Mexican back to Mexicali.

I deemed it better to transfer a portion of the gold into money and pay him his half in coin. It amounted to more than twelve thousand dollars at the prices I was able to get. Many of the things were museum pieces, even without an authentic history. And I gave no history.

But I did not pay him until I had him back in his 'dobe, and was ready to leave. His women folks commented on the wounds on his face, on the scratch marks which stretched from forehead to chin.

"Where is the evil one?" asked the old woman, when there had been mutually evasive comments on the wounds of the man.

"He remained behind."

She rocked back and forth on her chair and crooned some charm, or perhaps it was a curse. The words were unintelligible.

I shrugged my shoulders.

"He was evil, very evil," she said at length.

"He was a devil-man," said the fat woman.

The Mexican spoke simply.

"He made me very sleepy," he said.

I made no comments. The children came trooping in and climbed all over me. I gave them a *peso* apiece. Then, when I was ready to go, I took an envelope from my pocket and handed it to the Mexican.

"Señor," I said, "I have the honor to wish you good day,

and to express regrets at the parting and appreciation for the association."

He muttered some formal courtesy. It was the fat woman who opened the envelope and saw the crisp five-hundred-dollar bills that were in it. I heard her scream as I left the door.

From the sidewalk I could hear her voice through the open window. She was explaining the amount of the money to the more stolid and ignorant husband. The old woman was keeping up a shrill chattering of words and phrases which had almost no meaning, although once or twice I caught the expression "Devil Man."

I have no explanation. I have given you the facts as they happened; but to understand them you must be able to visualize the eyes of the man as I saw them there in that Mexicali dance hall, aluminium-colored eyes that had pupils that were mere pin-points.

If you had seen those eyes, the story would have seemed but the natural sequence of events, rather than something bizarre. Strange things happen on the border desert; strange whispers seep through the ear-aching silence of the desert spaces.

But never again have I seen a man with eyes like those—only the once. And that is enough. Emilio Bender lies asleep in a cave of death beneath a mesa in New Mexico. Perhaps, if there is anything in the Buddhist law of reincarnation and repayment, some hypnotist of three hundred years hence will disturb his rest and summon him back to the land of the living.

Personally, I do not know.

THE SKY'S THE LIMIT

CHAPTER 1

The Mysterious Inclosure

Click Kendall realized that there was something almost impersonal in the antagonism of the man before him.

"Do I understand you refuse to make any statement?"

That question had been effective with many another tough customer. But this man answered it with a single explosive word.

"Yes."

Click Kendall played his trump card. With a happy smile suffusing his features he whipped a notebook from his pocket.

"Then I shall quote you as saying that!" he exclaimed, and wrote meaningless words rapidly. "I have your permission to quote you as having used those words! Now your further plans are to—"

But the man at the gate did not weaken. His black, glittering eyes looked directly at Click Kendall, yet seemed focused upon some distant point.

"You may quote me as having said that you had better withdraw your foot from that gate!"

The words were a monotone of calm irritation.

Click Kendall hastily jerked back his foot. The gate

slammed shut. The sound of a lock clicking into place terminated the interview with conclusive finality.

Kendall sighed, turned, walked a few steps, then looked back.

The sun illuminated an unpainted board fence, ten feet high, surmounted by a triple barrier of barbed wire. What lay behind that fence could only be surmised. It stretched for a hundred yards without so much as a knothole, and the cracks had been covered with strips of batten.

Climbing into his battered flivver, Kendall gave one last, longing look at the fence, yellow in its unpainted newness, then wrestled with the steering wheel as the car jolted over the dusty highway.

He had failed, and the editor of the *Bugle* wouldn't take kindly to that failure. He had been ordered to find out, and he was returning as ignorant as when he started.

Professor Wagner was a nut, to be sure, but there was a good story in him and—

Click snapped to abrupt attention.

His car, jouncing around a curve in the road, rattled full upon a scene of conflict.

A low-hung touring car was crowding a roadster to one side of the road. Three pairs of hands, stretched out from the touring car, were literally lifting a struggling figure from behind the steering wheel of the roadster.

Even as Click gasped his incredulous astonishment, the figure was jerked clear. The roadster careened, skidded, and headed directly toward him. The touring car ripped into a tearing charge that billowed a vortex of swirling dust behind.

Click dodged the roadster, tried to jerk the wheel in time to avoid a collision with the touring car. Failed. A jar tingled his shoulders. Metal ripped. He was rattled around the inside of his flivver like a bit of popping corn in a popper.

His swimming eyes saw a kaleidoscope of scenery circulating about him, then steadied as the cars came to a stop.

The flivver had locked front fenders and hubcaps with the touring car, bringing it to a stop, half twisted about on the road.

The driver of that car was standing up. The two figures in the back seat were struggling with their captive, and Click saw that that captive was a woman.

For a swift fraction of a second he watched her kicking legs, fluttering skirts, heard her screams. Then he realized that the arm of the driver was extended, pointing something directly at his body.

He flung himself down, over the door. There was a flash of fire. The spitting explosion sounded surprisingly inadequate in the unechoing atmosphere of the hot afternoon.

Click's surprise gave way to an unreasoning red rage. Kidnap a woman and smash his car, would they? Shoot at him as though he'd been a mad dog, eh? He'd show 'em!

It never occurred to him that he was tackling three armed men, that they were desperate, that he was unarmed. He only knew that he wasn't going to stand for such tactics.

Click swarmed over the door of the touring car.

Some one cracked him over the head. The heel of the girl's shoe kicked him in the face. The driver fired again, and a searing pain stung its way the length of Click's left arm.

His right fist crashed upward.

The driver toppled backward under the force of that blow. The edge of the car caught him back of the knees. He flung up his hands in a wild, instinctive effort to regain his balance. The weapon flashed from his hand, whirled in a glittering arc, and landed in the brush. The man tottered for a moment, then plopped into the dust.

Click jumped in the back of the car.

One of the men raised an automatic. The girl was frantically beating the other man with a barrage of puny-fisted blows that served only to tire her.

Click lunged for the automatic, missed, heard the spat of powder, swung, missed, stopped a blow on the jaw, swung again. This time his fist thudded home. The man staggered back. The girl wrenched herself free, vaulted the car, and sprinted.

Click heard a curse from the driver's seat.

Instinctively he ducked, twisting his head as he did so. The dust-covered figure of the driver, one leg crooked over the back of the seat, held a wrench aloft. The wrench descended, and then nauseating darkness engulfed Click.

There was the sensation of falling endless miles. Hot dust stung his nostrils. He could hear the sound of profanity, repeated with mechanical regularity, an utter lack of tone expression.

The roar of a speeding motor, a sickening smell of gasoline, and the car was gone, leaving behind it a swirling cloud of dust. Click realized some one was bending over him.

He struggled, sat up, spat, and tried to speak. The dust gritted in his teeth, clogged his nose.

"Thanks," said a feminine voice.

"Don't mention it," muttered Click with an attempt at humor.

The girl muttered a single explosive word. It sounded remarkably like "damn."

"Yea?" prompted Click.

"We've got to get in the brush. They thought I'd kept on running. They'll be back as soon as they can turn the car. Can you walk?"

Click rolled to hands and knees, straightened, and gave a wobbly grin.

"Let's go," he said.

Down the road came the roar of a motor, the clash of shifting gears.

"They're coming!"

She half dragged him into the brush.

From the other direction could be heard the sound of an

approaching motor. Then the touring car ripped into motion.

"Another car scared 'em off. Sit still."

The girl's voice was calm, confident, given in the manner of one who is accustomed to command. Abruptly Click became conscious that she was beautiful.

"Don't say a word. They're slowing to look at the wrecks. Keep quiet!"

Brakes squeaked upon dry drums. The sound of excited voices came to his ears. "How could it have happened?— nobody hurt—roadster must have gone out of control—better take the numbers—couldn't have been long ago—"

Click watched the girl's face.

She was sitting, as alert as a crouching lion, peering through the screen of the brush. Her lips, slightly parted, were full but nicely shaped. Her eyes a deep violet, nose small, slightly upturned. There was about her something indefinable, the aura of one who is accustomed to take care of herself, who is playing with big events.

"Can I look?" asked Click.

She shook her head without even lowering her eyes to his face.

"Lie still. They're going. Now, quick. They've gone!"

Click rolled over, found that his strength was returning rapidly, got to his feet.

The violet eyes regarded his sleeve.

"You're hit?"

He looked at the red-stained cloth.

"Guess so."

She pulled up his coat sleeve.

"Humph, just a flesh wound, but it's got to be bound."

Click said nothing. Somehow he resented that tone of minimizing disinterest.

"Think you can walk to the house? It's not a quarter of a mile."

"The Wagner place?"

"Yes. I'm Professor Wagner's daughter. You know him?"

"Just met him. I was sent out from Centerberry to interview him for the *Bugle*."

She paused, regarded him with appraising eyes.

"Do you know, I think I could hate you most cordially. Reporters are snoopers who pry into other people's business. But I can't let you bleed to death. I've got to take you inside, so come on."

"And in reply to your cordial hospitality," snapped Kendall, "permit me to remind you that I'm a reporter, on official business, and that I'm going to publish any information I can get."

"That's to be expected—of a reporter!" And then she laughed. "Do you know, we're not behaving in the conventional manner? I should be thanking you for having saved my life; and I really should have developed a sprained ankle or something so you could have carried me to the house. Come on, let's forget that you're a reporter and act human. After all, it's not your fault."

As a reply trembled on his lips, Click stopped dead in his tracks, his unbelieving eyes staring at the upper portion of a shed which showed over the top of the board fence.

That shed disintegrated into scattering lumber. A pointed dome of glittering metal thrust itself above the ripping roof, hesitated for a moment, then shot into the air.

The glittering dome became the tip of a huge beehive affair, made of some highly polished metal. And that great beehive drifted placidly through the tumbling ruins of the wrecked shed, ascended some forty feet in the air, and hung there, poised, shimmering like some gigantic soap bubble.

For a space of swift seconds it remained suspended, then dropped swiftly, paused, drifted, and jolted to earth. Only the upper portion remained showing.

The girl made a few swift, running steps, then paused, turned.

"Oh, I hate you!" she flared.

"Hate me?" asked Click, dazed.

"Yes, hate you! You did have to come right at this time! He's solved it. I tell you he's got the thing he's been working for; and I've got to take you in there! That's what I get for being a woman. If I'd been a man I'd have been better prepared for those thugs. But no, I had to play the part of the poor, helpless damsel in distress; and you had to come along as the rescuing hero, and had to get shot so you require attention; and I've got to take you inside."

Click Kendall drew himself up. A sudden ringing was in his ears. She seemed rather far away, surrounded by a dark border of flickering darkness.

"I assure you you won't need to—to—I can—look out—"

He noticed that the violet eyes widened in alarm.

"Don't faint, don't faint!"

And then her arms were around his neck.

"Please, Mister Man, don't faint. Oh, I'm sorry! I was rotten selfish. But you can't understand. Please hold up until we get to the gate. Try. Fight. It's life and death, more than life and death."

And Click, hating himself for the momentary weakness, wishing that he hadn't been hurt so he could have raised his hat in a very dignified gesture and walked wordlessly away, was forced to lean upon her and fight to keep his consciousness.

The entire world seemed suddenly a sort of Alice in Wonderland place, where strange beehives floated around in the afternoon skies; where beautiful girls supported him with firm, muscular arms, begged him not to faint, laughed, sobbed, praised his spirit, and then grunted maledictions at an unkind fate that had thrown a helpless man on their hands.

His feet worked mechanically up and down. But they seemed to cling to the earth with each step. And there was no feeling of contact. It was as though he floated, yet was bogged down in a sticky marsh.

He saw the outlines of the board fence before him, heard the roar of a motor car behind him. Fancied there was the rattle of shots, and fainted.

CHAPTER 2

Attacked

A thin, reedy voice was piping meaningless figures and formulae. At first the sounds meant nothing to Click Kendall except a source of irritation. Then he gathered that these sounds had meaning, that they were words. The words seemed to formulate in his brain, independent of the sound, yet connected in some way with the reedy voice. He tried to open his eyes, but was too weary.

"Light varies inversely as the square of the distance," rasped the reedy voice. "Magnetism varies inversely as the square of the distance. Gravitation varies inversely—"

Click Kendall opened his eyes. The reedy voice snapped to an abrupt termination. A pair of wide, violet eyes were gazing into his. Over the girl's shoulder was the face of the man who had slammed the gate in his face earlier in the day.

Click tried a smile.

"Professor, I was sent out to get an interview. There's been a rumor floating around Centerberry that you were experimenting with an anti-gravitational contrivance, and were planning an exploration of the moon."

The girl's hand clapped to his mouth.

"Dad! Mr. Kendall's a reporter. And he refused to come to a truce. He's going to publish what he learns."

And then she leaned over him, placed a small glass of excellent brandy to his lips.

"Drink this," she said kindly, and then added with swift rancor, "and shut up!"

Click gulped the stinging liquid, felt it coursing down his gullet, leaving a welcome trail of warmth, bringing new strength.

"When are you leaving?" he asked.

The professor's black eyes snapped.

"Here, drink this," crooned the girl.

Mechanically Click opened his lips. Another jolt of fiery liquid shot down his throat. He realized that the girl was deliberately attempting to get him drunk so that he could not utilize the advantage his injury had given him.

He scowled at that, then smiled. After all it was a pretty good world. A rosy hue permeated his thoughts. Beautiful, violet-eyed young girls, beehives that floated, black eyes, pre-war brandy. Oh, it wasn't so bad! And he had the nucleus of a nice story! He felt better now.

Click smiled.

"Do I get another drink, Miss Wagner?"

"You do not!" she snapped.

"Thanks. No harm in asking. But, Professor, if I may ask you a question—"

The question was never asked.

There was the sound of crashing lumber, the splintering of boards, a tearing of metal. Hurried footsteps sounded without the door. A frantic banging of fists caused Professor Wagner to fling it open.

A man, armed with rifle and revolver, gestured toward the fence.

"They've driven their machine right through the fence, sir, and are trying to get to the bell!"

Wagner's dark eyes glittered with cold fury. He snatched a rifle from over the desk, made the door in two great strides. Nor was his daughter far behind.

Click Kendall jumped to his feet, felt a great wave of dizziness, groped for a chair, and stood, swaying. His eyes could see the running figures through the open door. There was a length of smashed fence, a wrecked automobile, running men as they deployed toward the metal shell.

One of them raised his arm. A revolver spat viciously. The professor flung up his rifle. It cracked forth a high velocity bullet that sent the rushing man tumbling to the ground in a search for cover. Another figure on the left ducked behind a pile of lumber, opened fire.

Click saw the bullets kicking up dust near Professor Wagner's feet. He saw the girl pleading with her father, leading him toward the great metal beehive. Out in the road a passing motorist had stopped. The passengers gawked in open-mouthed wonder.

Click tried a feeble, wobbling run.

The professor gained the metal bell. The girl was behind him. Then the enemy rushed.

Professor Wagner threw his rifle to his shoulder, then suddenly spun half around, and lurched against the girl.

The running figures held their fire, pressed grimly forward. The man who had given the warning, apparently a watchman not overburdened with intelligence, fired an indecisive shot or two, then lowered his rifle, standing uncertainly.

Click passed him, snatched the revolver from its holster.

"Hands up!" he yelled at the foremost figure.

His answer was a singing bullet that wasped its way past his ear. Click fired once, then held his fire, fearing to hit the girl. He reached her side almost at the same time as did the running enemy.

A single lucky swing of the revolver, and he felt the impact of the barrel on the man's skull. Then he realized that there were struggling figures about him, that the girl had clubbed the rifle taken from her father and was swinging it. There was a spatter of shots. The enemy withdrew, apparently nonplused by the unexpected strength of the defense.

The entrance of the polished metal beehive was before them.

"Inside," piped the professor in a weak voice. "It's bulletproof."

Click helped the girl get the professor in the open door. She slammed it shut.

"Dad, are you badly hurt?"

"Nothing much; caught my shoulder an awful wallop. The shock was the worst. Guess we can bandage it up. We're safe from bullets here."

He got to his feet, explored his right shoulder with the tips of his left fingers.

"It'll be all right," he said.

Click Kendall looked about him eagerly.

The bell was not over twenty-five feet high, but was more than thirty-five feet in diameter. Within the shell was a cone of what appeared to be silver. It furnished a rounded mirror in which the reflections of the little group flickered in weird distortions. There was a metal table, a glass case containing various instruments, a clutter of boxes and barrels. And there were windows in the metal sides of the shell, little round windows in which three-inch plate glass was set in what appeared to be live rubber.

Breathing heavily, still weak from his loss of blood and exertion, Click pressed his face against one of the windows, wondering what had become of their attackers.

He saw two men grouped in ominous conference, saw a third bringing up an oblong box. Click recognized the label. It was dynamite.

"Quick!" he called. "They're going to blow off a side of the metal. Is there a loophole through which we can fire?"

And his words brought Professor Wagner to his side.

"Yes, we can and will. Those men deserve to be killed."

"No, no, Father. There must be some other way!"

Click noticed the men dart their alarmed glances to the left, noticed also a sudden ripple of panic in their attitude, and turned his own eyes.

He saw a red machine, filled with grim men, swinging in from the road. A siren was fastened to the front of the car, just below the radiator.

"Here comes the sheriff. It's all right!" Click exclaimed.

And the three, setting down the case of dynamite, sprinted for the gap in the fence.

"All right nothing!" moaned the professor. "We'll have to testify, go through all sorts of red tape, be photographed, held for a trial—"

He staggered to the metal table, lurched into the chair.

"You put in the provisions, Dot?"

"Yes, Father."

Professor Wagner pulled a lever. Then Click Kendall gasped his utter incredulity.

For the sheriff and his companion drifted down and away. There was no sensation of motion. It was merely that in place of watching the striding figure of the sheriff he suddenly saw the top of the broad-brimmed hat, then caught the oval of an upturned, open-mouthed face.

"Good heavens!" exclaimed Click. "What's happened?"

He saw Professor Wagner at the table, crouched over, studying the instruments. He wanted to see what was going on, ask him what was happening.

He took a swift stride, and then found himself shooting up toward the pointed dome of the shell. Frantically he waved his arms, kicked his feet. All to no avail. He drifted up until he touched the roof.

He pushed his hands against the metal to ward off the impact, and found himself descending, squarely for the professor's head.

Click tried to avert that collision. His efforts availed nothing. He saw that he would fall squarely on the man's head.

"Look out!" he yelled.

Professor Wagner looked up. As he did so, Click fell directly into the upturned features.

To his surprise there was no shock of collision. The professor did not crumple to the floor, crushed beneath the weight of the falling body. Instead Professor Wagner brushed Kendall away with his uninjured hand as one might brush off a fly.

And Click Kendall found himself floating through space until he fetched up against the far side of the shell.

"Watch out where you're going!" snapped Professor Wagner. "You might interfere with my instruments!"

Click Kendall was too astounded to even attempt an answer.

It was the girl's voice that gave him the explanation.

"You see there isn't any gravitation up here," she said. "There's a window in the floor. Take a look through it. Dad, do let me take a look at that shoulder. You're losing blood."

The man gave the instruments a final adjustment.

"All right. We're safe here. I just got the missing factor in my calculations this morning, and I'm not exactly certain of the coefficient of balance and repulsion. But we can keep an eye out. Kendall, keep your eye to the window in the floor. If we start drifting down warn me at once. All right, Dot. I don't think it's serious, but I can't afford to lose any blood. I think the collar bone's fractured. You'll find the medicine chest under the table; but no opiates. Must have my senses clear."

Click dropped to the floor.

"Call me if I can help," he said, then looked through the glass window.

What he saw made him believe he was dreaming.

The shell hung suspended at about a thousand feet. Below him, the fenced portion of the ranch stretched in a square, a square that was rapidly filling with moving figures.

He could see the winding glitter of dusty road, the thicket of brush, could see the hills beyond, then the shimmering ribbon of placid river. Far over to the right was Centerberry with its smokestacks, its clusters of trees, white houses. But the elevation of the shell was hardly high enough to give him other than a hazy view of the place.

Click glanced again at the grounds below.

To his surprise they seemed to have moved to the right. But he could see the road, see, also, the sudden increase in traffic as automobiles came crawling along to ascertain what it was all about. Click thought how weird the shimmering metal beehive had appeared when he had first beheld it floating like a bubble in the air, and realized how much more of a spectacle it was now, a thousand or fifteen hundred feet up in the air, glittering in the slanting sunlight of mid-afternoon.

No wonder that automobilists, glancing upward, suddenly turned from their course to come tearing along the branch highway, jolting and rattling along the last few dust-covered miles.

The roadway around the fence was blocked. Black automobiles parked before the torn section as thick as iron filings clustering to the ends of a magnet.

Kendall looked up.

"We seem to be drifting to the southwest," he said.

Professor Wagner, stripped of shirt, was watching his daughter's skillful fingers as she packed antiseptic lint into the puncture in his shoulder.

"That's the wind, a gentle northeast breeze. I don't care about that. It's the height. How are we staying up?"

"I should say we were holding our elevation pretty well."

The lines of the scientist's pain-tortured face relaxed a bit.

"Mathematically we should be rising a trifle. The heated air must have an up current. And there should be a slight drift to the westward. That is, the motion of the earth should not entirely be counteracted by the motion of the atmospheric blanket. However, we'll take a look at that presently. In the meantime, we've got to complete our preparations."

"Keep a sharp watch," snapped the girl.

Click resumed his station.

His mind seethed with a tumbling confusion of thoughts. It was impossible to concentrate. Try as he might, no single line of thought could shut out the overwhelming influx of new sensations.

He knew the country well. He could recognize many of the ranches as places where he had hunted. Now the country seemed strangely new, viewed from this angle. It was so different from riding in an airplane. Here was no roaring of motors, no shrieking of wind, no altering perspective. Nor was it quite the same as being in a balloon.

A drifting shadow came scudding over the ground. Click wondered what was causing that shadow. A rushing shape screamed past his window, just below. The bell rocked and spun with the twisting air currents.

"There's an airplane come to look us over!" yelled Click.

Professor Wagner muttered his irritation.

"I'll attend to them," he snapped.

Click returned to his window, located the shadow, then peered from one of the windows in the side.

He knew that plane. It was Bill Savier, an old-timer in the game, and with him was a helmeted individual who fairly screamed "newspaper reporter" to Click's trained eye.

The Graflex camera covered with a wooden shield to protect the bellows, the whipping coat, the grease-stained collar, all told their own story. Here was a reporter snatched from a desk and rushed aloft by a frantic editor.

The plane banked so the reporter could get a better picture. The lens of the Graflex glittered darkly as it was pointed at the bell.

And then, suddenly, the plane vanished. It simply wasn't. Click saw blue sky, unbroken by any flitting plane as it banked and wheeled.

He looked down at the window in the floor, and gasped.

The plane was far, far below, a mere speck, zooming upward with all the power of its mighty motor. And it actually seemed to be falling, so rapid was the ascent of the bell. There was a bursting sensation in his eardrums. A sudden nausea gripped him.

He felt weak, tried to shout, but was unable to do more than make a few squeaky noises in his throat.

The ground below that had been so plainly visible, seemed

mantled by a haze. The timbered hills had flattened out until
they were only a dark stretch of green. The winding ribbon
of the river had become a thread so fine as to be almost invisible. There was a rushing scream of whipping air skidding
past the pointed dome of the bell, a strange rocking sensation.

Centerberry, which had been far in the distance, seemed
right below. It was not possible to see individual buildings.
The entire city showed as a mere cluster of checkered squares,
and those squares, as fine as the meshes of a tea strainer, Click
knew were, in reality, full city blocks.

CHAPTER 3

Defying Gravity

The professor was shouting.

"I didn't do that. We're out of control, falling upward!"

"Falling upward?" asked Click, suddenly having recovered
his voice.

"Falling upward. Something's happened—no, wait. Look
at those controls. Quick, the gun!"

Professor Wagner, his bandaged shoulder bare, his suspen-
ders flapping about his scrawny legs, made one swift reach
for the revolver, approached the inner shell, and flung open
a door.

"Come out!" he shouted.

Click realized, suddenly, that his laboring lungs were crying in vain for life-giving air. He was weak, dizzy, seeing
things as in a dream.

He saw a man come staggering out of the inner shell. He
noticed that this man's face was warped in a smile of triumph.

"The oxygen tanks, Dad!" shouted the girl. "They're
jammed, won't open."

Professor Wagner gave Click the gun.

"Keep him covered. Be careful how you move. When you walk just tap the tips of the toes gently on the floor."

Then he backed away.

Click realized why he had the dreamlike impression of objects when he saw the manner in which Professor Wagner backed away.

He merely tilted backward, slowly, as though he were making the motions in a slow motion picture camera. Then he tapped a toe gently on the floor and sailed through the intervening space to the table. He thrust over a lever, slid the button along the grooved guide.

Click was panting for air, suffocating. He saw that the man on whom he trained the gun was in as bad a way. He staggered about as though he would have fallen had it not been for the suspended power of gravitation. As it was, he wobbled weakly back and forth, swaying like a bit of seaweed swinging to the ocean currents. His face was the color of putty.

Then, as Professor Wagner pulled the slide over, there was a sudden tug of gravitation. Click felt his legs buckle under the quick pull, braced himself, felt that he would give much for a single breath of air, then crashed to the floor.

Almost instantly he felt light again, felt a peculiar sense of ease. He saw the professor swimming in the air above him, approaching the inner shell. He heard the rasp of metal, and then the professor came plunging out, like a trout darting through a shaded pool.

"He—had—the other set of controls. Had one of the windows open—oxygen escaped—air rarefied, cold. We're falling now. Won't be long, better air—turn that compressed air cock."

Click saw the face of the girl. It was a purplish hue of convulsed agony. He saw her turn a valve, heard a hissing stream of escaping air, felt his eardrums swell until it seemed they would burst, and then his lungs sent great gulps of life-giving air into his blood.

Professor Wagner had stood the ordeal the best of any,

notwithstanding the shock of the wound in his shoulder. And he was cool, alert, vigorously watchful.

"All right, Kendall. Feel better now? Watch through that floor window. I'll watch the instruments. We're falling with gravitation accelerated a thousand per cent. We've got to watch out."

Click pressed his face to the window.

The earth was leaping up to meet him.

"Too fast!" he yelled.

Professor Wagner flipped his wrist.

It seemed that ten thousand crushing hands pressed Click's body to the floor. He tried to move, couldn't. It was all he could do to breathe.

In an agony of suspense he watched the rushing ground.

He felt a slight ease in the pressure, caught a breath, turned, and saw Professor Wagner's face set in taut lines.

"Something's wrong," gasped the professor. "Shouldn't act like this. Some factor overlooked! But we've got to stop. Hold fast!"

His wrist twitched. The lever moved.

It seemed as though a ton of water pressed Click down and down. The very metal of the floor seemed to bulge out with the pressure.

The ground was still far away, but it was rushing up rapidly. They were almost over Centerberry now. The buildings rushed into view. The squares were like those of a checkerboard, grew until they were as patterned linoleum.

The terrific pressure increased. The ground hesitated in its mad upward rush. The pressure upon Click's chest relaxed enough so he could breathe.

Click could see the streets, the people scurrying about like ants, the moving automobiles, the belching smokestacks, the tangle of tracks in the railroad yards, the spires of churches, the roofs of buildings.

Closer and closer came the ground. The pressure was terrific. The buildings zoomed up, seemed rushing into his very face. He couldn't breathe. The air that had been in his lungs whooshed out. He felt that he would rather die a thousand deaths than suffer such agony.

He felt a relief in the cruel pressure and managed to raise his face. A welcome flood of air was in his lungs. He gave a great gasp.

Then suddenly every bit of pressure was relieved. He was as light as he had been before. He saw Professor Wagner draw the back of his left hand over his head while his injured right arm dangled at his side.

"A close squeak, a mighty close call. We developed too much acceleration falling through the rarefied upper atmosphere," rasped the professor. "I threw it back to stop it, but even with gravitation accelerated to twice normal falling speed the check was so great that it nearly crushed us with momentum. I'm afraid there's some factor that's escaped my calculations. But we managed to check ourselves, and just in time, too. Look out and see where we are and what happened."

Click glanced downward, gasped.

He found that the shell had finally come to a stop not more than a hundred feet above the tops of the office buildings in the main business district of Centerberry.

Just below him were the intersections of Main Street, First Avenue, and Center Square. And those intersections were thronged with people. Every face was upturned. They had detected the strange metal container as it hung poised above them.

Traffic had stopped. People stood exactly as they had paused to look up. Some were halfway across the streets. Some were entering stores.

Then people began to swarm out of buildings, into the street. Even stalled automobiles debouched their startled passengers.

The shell drifted gently downward. The tops of the buildings became closer. Then the metal actually dropped into the cañon between the buildings, drifting over the heads of the people as a drifting soap bubble. People became panicky, ran for shelter, trampled and jostled in a squirming mass.

"We're getting lower and lower," shouted Click, and turned to see if Professor Wagner was aware of their danger. To his consternation he found that the professor had fainted, that his daughter was bent over him solicitously.

The shell was down below the seventh floors of the buildings now, drifting ever downward. It got closer to the north side of the street, finally brushed against the windows of the building. Those windows were black with packed humanity.

Click could see their faces, see the startled eyes, big with wonder, could even see their lips moving in shouts. But no sound penetrated to the interior of the shell.

The man on the floor, who had become unconscious when the oxygen content of the air had been sucked out through the open window in the interior shell, stirred.

As lightly as a bit of thistle down blown by a gentle breeze, the metal shell rubbed along against the office building. Click saw that it was the McKinstry Building, even recognized one of the stenographers who stared with popping eyes at the shell.

And the strange metal structure was settling lower and lower. People ran screaming from its path. A policeman had drawn his revolver, was pointing it upward threateningly. The beehive was trapped in the cañon of city streets. The wind held it against the north side of the street, plastered it against the buildings.

Click jumped to the metal table. There was a lever and a slide button in a metal groove. He didn't understand the function of the lever, but he saw on the grooved slide the figures which had been etched into the metal.

GRAVITATION GAUGE: + 64, 32, 16, 8, 4, 2, 0, − 2, 4, 8, 16, 32, 64, 128

Click noticed the button. It was almost at a point marked with a zero, but it was not quite on the line. He pushed on the button, gingerly shoved it until it was exactly on the etched line opposite the zero.

"Father's in bad shape. Too much strain, too much shock. We've got to get him to bed," said the girl.

And then, as Click moved to help her, she picked up the unconscious form by the simple expedient of pinching her thumb and forefinger in the waistband of his trousers.

For a moment Click could not believe his eyes. Then he remembered the sliding indicator with the button set at "Gravitation zero."

"May I help?" he asked.

"No," she said. "I can manage all right. You keep your eyes on that fellow on the floor. You can't take any chances with him."

The inner door slammed.

CHAPTER 4

A Good Newspaper Man

Apparently the girl had failed to notice that they were drifting down the main street of Centerberry, creating a veritable panic of interest.

Click thrilled to the opportunity. Busy with her father, nursing him, getting him safely in bed, seeing that the bandaged shoulder was made comfortable, the girl wouldn't notice the motions of the shell. It was a chance for Click to experiment.

He glanced once more at the figure on the floor, then suddenly awoke to his original mission. The shell was holding its elevation now, rising very slightly on the warm currents of air that shimmered against the sides of the office buildings.

But the offices of the Centerberry *Bugle* were only a block down the street, and the wind was drifting the metal shell against the buildings, almost directly in line with the newspaper offices.

There was paper and pencil in his pocket, and Click fell to scribbling rapid notes, printing the letters large so the notes could be held against a window and read.

> Kidnaped. Thugs attack professor and daughter. Stowaway held captive. Gravitation overcome by some theory of neutralizing etheric vibrations. Trip to planets planned. Professor and self wounded, but not seriously. Have ascended over twenty miles above earth.

He looked out. The *Bugle* offices were but a matter of windows away. Click rushed to the round loopholes.

The wind brushed the shell against the building. It bumped, bounced, rolled and bumped again. Then the windows of the *Bugle* loomed before him. He looked squarely into the eyes of the city editor. That individual's face ran a gamut of emotions. He yelled an order over his shoulder.

The shell drifted lightly by the window, came to the next. Here were men, packed to the frame, gawking outward. There was a rustle of motion and the men cleared from the window as though by magic. Click held the message against the three-inch plate glass. Would they copy it? What was the matter?

A round lens was thrust up against the office window frame. He could see a photographer focusing his camera upon the message.

It was a clever idea. They'd photograph the message, it would be quicker than copying. Click wished he'd said more.

But there was no time. The photographer nodded, jerked out a plate holder, ran to the next window, tried again, nodded.

Click crossed to the metal table, pulled the button over to "— 2."

There was a lurch, a scraping of the building against the

metal of the shell, and then the windows of the structure shot past with the smooth velocity of an express elevator.

Click realized that the shell went upward with an accelerating velocity, equal to the acceleration of a falling body.

A hundred, five hundred, a thousand feet up shot the metal container. Click moved the sliding button to zero. The ball continued to go up. Then Click realized that the momentum of the shell was taking them on up. It would be necessary to overcome that momentum.

Click pulled the button over to plus two.

Instantly things happened.

There was a peculiar sensation of arrested motion. His heart gave a few panicky beats, but there was no sliding toward the roof as he had expected. Instead, everything remained as before, save for that peculiar sensation of arrested motion.

He looked about him, rubbed his eyes.

Then it dawned upon him. Gravitation had taken hold of everything alike. But weight had returned to his body. His blood weighed twice as much. The strain of lifting it was that much more of a burden on his heart; but only for a few beats. Then the new gravitation had compensated itself.

Had the shell been stationary, his body would weigh twice as much, but the shell was floating in the air. If it fell, his body fell equally fast. It was only when the motion was checked that gravity had a chance to tell.

Of a sudden Click remembered the trouble Professor Wagner had encountered in stopping the falling shell. He looked out. Not only had their upward motion ceased, but they were falling.

He moved the control.

The door slammed open from behind him.

"What are you doing?" snapped Dot Wagner. "Is this any time to experiment?"

"We were drifting down into the street," he explained, but

did not bother to tell her of how he had taken advantage of that fact to get the greatest scoop of the century to his newspaper.

She grunted. "Get over and tie that man up. I'll try the controls."

She tossed him a bit of rope, and Click tapped his toes upon the floor, propelling himself toward the stowaway.

"Who is this fellow?"

She shook her head. "Ask Father."

Click tried another question. "Where are we going?"

She pointed upward. "The sky's the limit."

"Let's go."

She sighed. "Do you know, I'm commencing to like you. You've got adaptability, and—"

"Yes," prompted Click, "and what?"

"And nerve," she snapped. "Got that man tied up?"

"After a fashion. It'll hold him from doing anything rash."

The girl looked about her, touched the lever.

The cage whirled, wobbled back and forth in a swing, for all the world like a compass needle swinging toward the magnetic north. Then, when it had steadied, she pushed a button.

Instantly the ground below began slipping by, not at a very rapid rate of speed, but at a smooth motion that was constantly accelerated.

She moved the gravitation control to negative two, watched the ground below for a second or two, then slipped the button back to zero. The ground drifted and dropped until the shell was over two thousand feet. Then the girl eased over the button so gradually that the shell swung smoothly along at a constant elevation.

She smiled up at Click's puzzled frown.

"Magnetism," she said. "You might as well know something about it. Magnetism is the least known force in the world, and the most universal. The world's a magnet. Even living organisms are magnetic. Also remember that all electricity is, is a force induced by cutting magnetic fields with a wire. We multiply that force by wire that's in fine coils rotating rapidly. But you can imagine what would happen if a properly energized, properly constructed apparatus suddenly cut the magnetic lines of force about the earth."

Click waved his hand.

"Whoa there! You're getting too deep for me. I've seen the thing run, and the fact that we're up here's proof enough that it works. What I want to know is, when I'm going to get back on my job, and what we're going to do with his nibs over there. I don't mind tying up a man to accommodate him; but I don't want to get mixed up in a kidnaping charge."

She frowned thoughtfully for a minute, then moved closer, lowered her voice.

"I'll tell you this much. This man is a dreadful menace; and he's a murderer."

Click glanced at the man on the floor.

"He doesn't look so bad. Those gimlet eyes of his are a little disquieting; but I wouldn't take him for such a hard case. Looks a little too thoughtful to be a crook type."

She gave her head an impatient shake, placed a hand on his arm in an earnest attempt at conviction, realized what she had done, and jerked the hand away.

"He's a scientist. That is, he'd call himself one. He worked in a laboratory, has a good grasp of magnetic sciences and astro-physics. But he's unscrupulous, a fanatic—and—and—and a murderer."

"Yes? That's twice you've used that term."

"Well, it's not my secret to tell. But his name's Badger. He worked in one of the laboratories where Father had certain parts of his equipment manufactured. He was shrewd enough to find out what Father was up to. And he realized something of the possibilities of this thing, which is more than many people did. Father had a partner, a young assistant, a frightfully keen chap. He had tuberculosis; but he wouldn't take any sort of care of himself. He got so worked up over this idea he worked on it night and day. Father trusted him, told him a lot. Badger kidnaped this man, held him out all one night, threatening all sorts of dire things if the man wouldn't talk. As a result he caught cold and died."

The man on the floor raised his voice.

"I don't know what she's telling you, but I know it's false. I'm merely an innocent stowaway, searching for a thrill. I demand that I be given my liberty."

The girl paid no attention to him.

"You have no idea what this invention means commercially. Father is interested in it purely from a standpoint of scientific investigations. Commercially it's worth millions and millions.

"You saw the three men who tried to kidnap me. When they knew Father had achieved success they would have stopped at nothing. They planned to hold me captive, and force Father to ransom me by giving them a share of the profits, or else to force Father to divulge his secret to them.

"I tell you, there's so much potential wealth in this thing that murder becomes a mere nothing to the men who want to solve the secret."

Click turned her words over in his mind.

"What'll you do with this chap? Drop down and turn him loose?"

"Certainly not! He knows too much now. He had an opportunity to study the mechanism. He'd ask for nothing better than to be put out. By the time we returned he'd have the whole invention exploited for all it was worth."

"Well, what, then? Will your father call off his trip of interstellar exploration?"

"You should know Dad better than that. He warned me not to give him an opiate, but I did it just the same. He'll sleep a few hours. When he awakes, no power on earth can keep him from starting on his journey. You understand that money and glory mean but little to him. He's after scientific data."

"But," protested Click, "this man Badger will be a menace to him when your father returns."

"We'll handle that when the time comes. But you must remember the chances are about a hundred to one against our returning. And if we do not, we aren't going to leave our secret behind us, in the hands of an unscrupulous scoundrel."

Click Kendall rubbed his chin.

"Well, then, how about me?"

"Why, you're going, too, of course. We couldn't leave you behind to publish what you've found out."

"And I'm not to be allowed back on earth, not even to send messages?"

She smiled, and shook her head.

"Of course not, silly! That's just what we don't want you to do—send messages."

Badger stirred, attempted to sit up.

"You'll pay for this," he croaked.

The girl paid no attention whatever to him, but glanced at the terrain below.

"This is a good place," she remarked, and manipulated the lever and slide. Instantly the car slowed to a stop, wobbled back and forth like a gob of wax on the end of some invisible string.

Then it slowly settled.

Below was a wild, wooded country. There was no sign of habitation. The level rays of the setting sun showed dark green foliage, winding rivers, occasional meadows. There was no sign of any road, no house, no fence.

Dorothy Wagner flung open the door, thrust out her head.

"Come and look at it. It's delightful. We're only about a thousand feet up. You can even smell the pines."

Click joined her at the door. The balmy air was soothing to his nostrils. Over the country lay the calm hush of a warm twilight.

"What do we do now?"

"Wait."

"For what?"

"For Father to wake up."

"And then?"

She did not answer in words, but pointed her finger up at the darkening sky.

Badger struggled with his cords, flung himself about on the floor, but was unable to gain his freedom. At length he subsided, muttering rumbled threats.

The last rays of the sun were swallowed up by the golden horizon. Dusk gave place to darkness. In wordless silence the two in the doorway drank in the scenery.

Each engrossed with thoughts, they watched the stars silently appear, swing upward. Below, the world lay black and mysterious. Once there was the flicker of a light. Far to the north a camper built a small camp fire which sent its red light flickering over the tree tops. Away to the east a glow in the sky marked the location of a city.

After an hour the eastern horizon glowed, lighted, and the rim of a moon climbed into dazzling sight. Within a few minutes it hung suspended, clear of the mountain rims.

CHAPTER 5

Into Space

There was the sound of a door opening. Abruptly, lights came on, flooding the place with eye-aching brilliance. Professor Wagner stood in the doorway of the cone, his eyes glittering with hectic intensity.

"Dot, you gave me an opiate."

She met his accusing gaze.

"I did what I thought was best, Father."

He pointed toward the circle of the moon.

"Do you want us to get tangled up in the gravitational field of that moon?"

"What would it do, Father?"

"Do? It would delay us hours, days, perhaps trap us in the cold clutch of a dead satellite! No moons for me! I want to get out and see something of the solar system. I want planets, life, atmosphere. Quick! Let's go!"

Badger again flopped about in struggling panic.

"It's kidnaping, murder!" he cried.

"Close that door, hold everything!" snapped Professor Wagner, and placed his thumb upon the sliding button.

The lights clicked off. There was a sensation of sudden motion, and then the scientist's exulting voice pealed forth a cry of triumph.

"We're off!"

Click looked through the window in the floor, then recoiled in surprise.

The shell was hurtling upward with such terrific speed the earth seemed to contract upon itself, wither into a shriveled shell. The boundaries of the forest were not apparent. Clusters of lights showed as bordering villages. Those pin-points of lights crowded closer together, became merged in a single blob of brilliance. The larger cities appeared, swept below in an ever narrowing circle.

"What's that in the west?" he exclaimed.

Before his question could be answered an arched tip appeared over the western circle of earth, grew in size and became a flaming ball of fire. Yet around it was no glow of blue heaven. There was a ribbon of radiance, then black sky. And the ball of fire speedily welled to white, eye-blistering heat.

The sun was rising in the west!

Dorothy Wagner was at his side, watching the spectacle in silence.

Higher and higher came the flaming ball. The earth showed as an arc now, and on the side nearest the sun was a growing ribbon of light.

Click tore his gaze away, turned to her.

"How come?" he asked.

"The sun," she exclaimed. "It seems to be rising in the west because we're ascending above the rim of the world. You can see the motion of the earth below us. Look at that range of mountains. See them glittering in the sun. And the earth seems to be slowly revolving. That's because we're overcoming some of the momentum with which we were thrown to one side by the envelope of air and the centrifugal force."

Click could see the earth, showing now as a suggestion of a great ball, outlined against a black void, slowly turning.

"But why is the sky black?"

"The air acts as a light diffuser. If it wasn't for our atmosphere, the sun would be a ball of fire in a black sky. There would be dazzling light on one side of an object set in its rays, and intense blackness on the other side. You get something of that same effect on the high mountains where the atmosphere is more rare. Ever notice how much blacker the shadows seem, how much more dazzling the light?"

Click nodded. It was just occurring to him that there were a good many physical phenomena he had been taking for granted.

"What's the strip of sunlight to the west?"

"That's late afternoon on the Pacific Coast. The sun is just setting there. Later on we'll be able to see the Pacific Ocean. Then the motion of the earth in its revolution will become more apparent as we get farther away and gradually overcome the force of our outthrust from the rim of the wheel. You see our anti-gravitational force is acting as a centrifugal force resistant."

"How fast are we going?"

She shrugged her shoulders.

"What keeps us from being cold now that we've passed the atmosphere?" asked Click.

"You've seen a thermos bottle?" she countered. "Well, this is made on the same principle; and remember we are surrounded by a vacuum."

Sighing, Click relaxed himself to a contemplation of seeing the earth through the eyes of a solar wanderer. He was out in the solar system, tickling the edges of the universe, and something of the terrific, mind-paralyzing nature of infinity was beginning to permeate his brain.

Below him the earth showed as a mighty sphere. The sun glowed as a white-hot ball of fire against a perfectly black sky, raised some twenty degrees from the arc of the earth's crust.

The motion of the earth was now readily apparent. It swung in a long sweep of increasing speed. The Sierra Nevada Range was now being swept into the twilight zone. The glittering sweep of Pacific Ocean showed as a long expanse. The shore line of Lower California and Mexico was sharply marked. To the north, where Oregon and Washington merged into the coast line, there were fogs which reflected the dazzling light of the sun in eye-bewildering brilliance.

It was sunset in California. Deserts, mountains, orange groves, plateaus, fertile river valleys were all being swept into the curtain of dusk. Over to the east was midnight. Yet the moon illuminated the earth with enough light to make certain features of the crust apparent.

The Atlantic coast line showed as a dim glow. Click fancied he could detect a difference in the illumination that must represent the big cities of the seaboard, New York and vicinity. But he was not certain that that which he mistook for brilliance of illumination was not really caused by a local fog.

Professor Wagner switched on the light, beamed about him.

"My children, this is the happiest moment of my life."

Badger croaked hoarsely.

"Well, make the most of it, because it's about the last of your life. I could have taken this invention and made something out of it. We'd have been millionaires. But you had to go and start this crazy expedition. Now your secret will perish with you."

The professor shrugged his shoulders.

"That may be. But I have had the thrill of going where no

mortal has ever ventured before. Oxygen tanks working perfectly. Compressed air releasing smoothly. Temperature constant, speed accelerating. Wonderful! Who could wish for any greater triumph to crown a life of hard work?"

Click interpolated a comment.

"But can we get back?"

The professor waved his hands, palms outward.

"Back! Who wants to get back? It will take us a lifetime to explore the universe, and then we'll only have touched one or two highlights."

Badger groaned.

"Oh, Lord, he's crazy as a bedbug. Mister, you and I are trapped. Our only hope is to overpower him and take the machine back."

Professor Wagner whipped a revolver from his belt, using his unwounded arm with swift grace.

"Badger, you've murdered, you've robbed, you've stopped at nothing to steal the secret I've worked out. Now I warn you, if I catch you so much as lifting a finger to interfere, I shall shoot you as I would a dog!"

Cowed, Badger lapsed into surly, menacing silence. Click turned away, repressing a momentary shudder of apprehension. He looked out of the floor window.

The shell had developed terrific speed, with no atmosphere to retard it. And it was an awesome spectacle. The globe still subtended a great arc, but it showed as a rotating ball, shadowed with seas, glittering with continents. Majestic mountain ranges billowed in reflecting clouds, or raising glittering snow-capped mountains.

Click looked upward.

The moon was getting larger. Their constant acceleration had piled up a most terrific momentum.

"What time is it?" he asked.

Professor Wagner laughed, flipped a hand toward the rotating globe below.

"Time? My boy, there is no time! Time is merely an arbitrary division of the period of rotation of that ball below you. You are now in the depths of infinity. There is no clock that can measure infinity. The birth of universes are as but the ticking of the clock of infinity. And that clock measures a something that is beyond measure. We are accustomed to think of eternity as something vague and intangible that comes into existence after our individual deaths. You are in eternity now. It is all about you. You are a part of eternity. Time indeed! There is no time."

Professor Wagner took out pencil and paper, did some rapid calculating. Then he approached the lever.

"It's about time we were building up some side speed. We're going to have to keep clear of the moon. If we get too close to it we'd either be stalled or flipped off in space like a comet. Let's see. That lever gives us a side speed of east to west. That should be away from the moon, toward the inferior planets. Now Venus is about twenty-two million miles away in round figures. I believe this is the proper adjustment. I'm going into the inner room with my daughter. We'll do the navigating from there. You two better get some sleep.

"Look at the earth. See that brilliance it's throwing off? That's earthlight, just as we call the moon's reflected light moonlight. Rather weird, eh? Badger, I'm going to leave you tied up. Kendall, I'm trusting you. Get some sleep, both of you."

The inner door slammed.

"Good night—Click," called the girl's voice.

Badger grunted.

"Crazy as a loon, him and the girl both. Mister, you and I have got to get control of this thing and take it back."

Kendall laughed.

"Don't count on me for any treachery. A ship can have but one skipper. I don't know where I'm going, but I'm on my way; and I'm not going to turn you loose. So shut up and get some sleep."

And, rolling on his side, Click Kendall stretched his length on the floor of the weird craft and went to sleep with the light of a half full earth in his eyes.

CHAPTER 6

A New World

Hours later Click awoke. It was a sensation of spinning vertigo that brought him to his senses. He found himself suspended in mid-air. The shell was wobbling, twisting, and turning in spinning confusion.

He rubbed his eyes, started to swim through the atmosphere within, found drowsiness again sweeping over him, and dropped off to peaceful oblivion, his limbs gloriously relaxed.

Again he slept. Voices in his ears brought him to. He found himself lying against the floor of the shell. Through the thick glass window in the floor he could see the round surface of a globe.

At first he thought it was the earth; then he realized it was vastly different.

The surface showed a mass of piled-up clouds, and the reflected light from those clouds was such as to dazzle the eye. Through the tops of the cloud masses could be seen the snow-capped peak of a single towering mountain. But for miles and miles the clouds extended in tumbled masses.

Professor Wagner stood at the switchboard control and upon his face was a smile of serene tranquillity. The sun was about quartering, and a portion of the dark side of the planet could be observed.

The girl's sparkling eyes regarded him with crisp enthusiasm.

"Oh, you're awake. Lord, how you slept! It's lucky the navigation wasn't intrusted to you."

"Venus?" asked Click.

"Venus," answered the professor.

"Where's Badger?"

"Asleep. I gave him an opiate. He was too much of a nuisance."

Click glanced at the planet again.

"Why all the clouds?"

Professor Wagner squinted at the periscope image.

"Always clouds. That makes it seem logical that it's inhabited. There's water vapor in the atmosphere. There's a high reflecting power. It's scientifically known as the albedo. The albedo of Venus is 0.76. In other words, the light that is reflected is almost three-fourths of the light received. It's just about the reflecting power of new snow."

He flipped the lever, manipulated the slide.

The surface of the billowing clouds came up toward him, dazzling with their brilliance. Then a swirling streamer of cloud stretched misty tentacles toward the shell, swirled about it, and they were enveloped in a white mist.

Darker and darker became the mist. The eyes slowly adjusted themselves to the greater darkness after the white brilliance of the reflecting cloud banks. Lower and lower went the shell, but its progress could only be told by the slithering clouds of moisture which slipped past the sides of the shell.

"Keep a sharp watch for obstacles," called Professor Wagner. "If you see anything, shout at once."

Click pressed his face against the floor glass, watched below. There was nothing but fine drifting mist, and through that mist a strange, unreal light penetrated.

And then a bit of mist seemed to congeal, take color.

"Hold everything!" he yelled.

The girl saw it at the same time.

"Something dark below."

The professor held the shell motionless, then joined them at the floor window.

"Humph," he said. "The top of a tree. Watch it. We'll try to avoid the branches."

He returned to the controls. The shell settled lightly, down, down. The top of the tree slipped past to one side.

"Great heavens! It's got a diameter of over ten feet right near the top, and some of those branches are regular trees in themselves," said Dorothy.

Suddenly Click gave a shout. "Life!" he exclaimed. "A bird fell out below and flew away. It was an enormous bird, bigger than our eagles. And it looked as though it wore spectacles."

Professor Wagner chuckled.

"If some of our contemporaries on the earth could only be with us! But that bird's flying is a wonderfully favorable sign. It shows that the atmosphere must be equally dense with that of our earth. Gravitation we know is about the same. Ah, here's another tree to one side. We're going down between them, and look. Here's the ground!"

The shell dropped rapidly, checked itself, fluttered to the ground as lightly as a snowflake, then was quickly sent up.

"It's a regular morass!" exclaimed Click.

"We'll bounce up and try it over a little farther. Watch out for trees, but I'll have the gravitation at zero and the speed down to three or four miles an hour. There won't be much momentum. Here we go."

The shell drifted through the forest. Overhead the luminous sky reflected dusky light through the ever present mists.

The great trees stretched up in long spires of green. The shell was about twenty-five feet above the ground, floating along like a great soap bubble.

Dorothy gave a shriek.

"A man! Watching us from the tree. Quick, look!"

And there, perched on the limb of a small tree, regarding them with unblinking solemnity, was a man, some four feet in height, clothed in some peculiar texture which seemed a species of silk.

In appearance he was very like an earth man, save for the eyes. Those eyes were apparently without lids, were so large and protruding as to dominate the entire face. The pupils alone were almost an inch in diameter, and they regarded the drifting shell with an owl-like scrutiny of expressionless contemplation.

Professor Wagner guided the shell closer, brought it to a stop, lightly drifting against a tree branch.

The strange creature slipped from the branch, caught a twig with fingers that were somewhat like those of a monkey, and dropped to another branch, hit the trunk, went down it with an agility that no earth human had ever possessed, and disappeared in deep ferns.

Search as they might, they could find no sign of him. He had vanished.

The professor reluctantly set the shell in motion again, drifting at a slow rate of speed. Within half a mile the forest abruptly thinned to a clearing. Bare ground, hard and brown, cleared into a huge circle, was beneath.

"That is undoubtedly the work of man," said Professor Wagner, and dropped the shell to the ground, brought it to a rest, slipped the gravitational control over to normal, and opened the door.

Moist air came pouring in, air that smelled of mists, dripping green stuffs, decaying wood. Dank, yet warm and pleasant, the air seemed to bathe them as a lukewarm shower.

"All out for Venus!" yelled Professor Wagner.

Click got to his feet, sighed, took a step, and then held back. For into the clearing had suddenly debouched a row of men, marching gravely from the fern-rimmed forest.

"Ah," sighed Professor Wagner, and stepped to the ground of the planet.

The line of men advanced.

"Look here," insisted Click, "I don't like their looks. We've got some weapons inside. Let's get them ready. We may have to fight."

"Bosh! That is the way hostilities start. Think you we are

going to come here and depart without stopping to investigate these inhabitants? We must investigate their flora and fauna, take motion pictures, learn their language, their tribal beliefs, their family life. We can't do all that by starting a fight.

"Their clothes look like silk. Do you know, I believe those eyes can penetrate the fog. You'll notice there's a reddish tinge to the light. The violet rays are absorbed in the upper layers of atmosphere.

"That's the chief there in front. He's coming this way. Hold up your hands, palms outward. Hang him, can't he tell a gesture of friendship? And look at their joints. See how they bulge. That's probably caused by generations of rheumatism. Gradually they've become immune to it, probably, but the joints are remarkably enlarged. They average about four feet. Almost dwarfs, but—"

The line swung at the ends, became a half circle, swept about, darted inward, and the trio found themselves crowded out from their entrance, walled in by the little creatures who surveyed them in austere silence.

"Hello, howdy. We come for a visit."

Professor Wagner smiled, waved his hands, bowed.

The circle made no motion.

"More men coming out from the forest, Professor," warned Click in an undertone.

"They're our friends," said the professor, and smiled again.

A man stepped forth from the circle.

"That will be the chief. He's an old man, yet there's no wrinkling of the skin. Notice how they all appear to be of about the same age," muttered the professor. "But the chief has certain unmistakable indications of age. He has knotted veins in his temples, and the teeth are worn down. Then there's his neck. The neck glands are almost invariably deficient in aged persons. Why, look out—the beggar's hostile!"

"Look out, Father!" shrieked the girl.

For the chief's lips had twisted back from his gums. He opened his mouth, barked a single shrill word, and lunged forward.

The circle closed. Hands reached out.

Click swung a terrific blow.

To his surprise, the little man side-stepped that blow with an agility that would have done credit to a monkey. Strong hands darted forward, seized his wrists, and Click knew then that these men were incredibly muscular, for the hands bit deeply into his skin, held with a grip of iron.

A twisted strand of some light substance appeared from nowhere, was looped about his hands and twisted over his neck.

From behind him he could see the others were being similarly treated.

The chief opened his mouth again. Another single sound issued forth. And, with that sound, he turned abruptly. Some of the men remained behind with the shell. The others accompanied the chief. And the captives followed, persuaded by a single jerk of the rope that had been placed around their necks.

"We're going to be taken into the forest. Now we shall see how the men live," purred the professor.

CHAPTER 7

Captives on Venus

"Has it occurred to you that they show no surprise at our appearance?" asked the girl abruptly. "They should be surprised at the color of our skins, at our eyes, at our clothes, at our height. But they take us for granted."

"By George, that's so!" agreed the professor. "Ah, here's where they have their village. Notice the manner in which the trees protect them from surprise attacks from above. What enormous trees they are! That one is thirty feet in diameter. It must stretch up for five hundred feet, perhaps more.

"And here are the women. Ugh! How ugly! Evidently

they're closely allied to the animals of our globe as far as sex beauty is concerned. The males have the beauty."

Click made no comment. His startled eyes surveyed the drab spectacle in the cheerless, dripping forest. Little huts had been made, thatched with broad leaves, lashed with thongs. Overhead a tangled mass of branches dripped globules of moisture in endless cadence upon the echoing leaves.

Ferns had been cleared away to make a little circle before the houses. About this circle the women had gathered. They were even smaller than the men, and their appearance was startling.

They showed as squat, dish-faced creatures, thick of lip, dark of skin, round of eye, low of forehead. Their faces were expressionless, and they made no sound. But Click noticed a peculiar twitching of the nostrils, as though they were sniffing some faint odor.

The chief led the way to a hut. The dwarfs who pulled the prisoners followed. They led the trio inside, gave a deft loop of the neck rope about their ankles, knotted it, and backed out.

There was no sound of conversation coming into the hut from those who clustered in the village. Occasionally a sound of motion, the thud of bare feet on the ground, a hacking cough, would attest to their presence, but there was no conversation.

Professor Wagner closed his eyes, sighed. Click tried to sleep, and could not. There was an atmosphere of tense waiting about the place that was as omnipresent as the everlasting fog.

Steps sounded without the hut.

"I wonder," began the professor, then suddenly broke off. For to the ears of the men came a strange sound, the sound of a human voice talking as men on the earth talked, although the words were indistinguishable.

"Good heavens!" snapped the professor, and struggled to a sitting posture. "That's the German language, or I don't know it when I hear it. What's this? What's this?"

"I told you," reminded his daughter, "that they didn't show any curiosity. They've seen people like us before."

"Tut, tut," snapped the professor. "We're the first earth mortals ever to set foot on Venus."

But his voice lacked assurance, and made up in irritability what it lacked in conviction.

The door darkened with moving bodies, bearing a shuffling burden. They swayed and tottered with the weight of it as they formed a congested group in the doorway.

Then they crowded through.

They carried a species of stretcher made of saplings across which had been stretched a network of cords. Upon that stretcher a huge form reclined, heaving restlessly, grumbling.

They up-ended the stretcher, and Click found himself gazing into the face of a man, pop-eyed, blond, frightfully obese, the skin bleached of color.

The man sputtered a stream of German at them.

Professor Wagner rattled a reply in English.

"We don't speak German. Do you speak English? How did you happen to arrive here? When did you arrive? How? What are these people? Do they have a language? Do you speak it? Are you a captive, or are you treated as a guest?"

The fat neck rolled the huge head from side to side.

"Nein, nein, nein. Ach Gott, nein!"

"Can you speak any German?" demanded Professor Wagner.

Click Kendall shook a reluctant head. It was a language of which he knew nothing. And that ignorance seemed in a fair way to shut them out from all understanding with the strange creatures who held them captive.

"The man evidently isn't held as a captive. He's treated with some respect," muttered Click.

"Crippled with rheumatism," added the professor. "Notice the enlarged joints, the peculiar posture of the fingers. It's a bad case, and the heart is evidently impaired. You can see the blue lips, the discolored finger nails. Truly this is a great disappointment, to think that our remarkable voyage has been anticipated by other scientists, and that these scientists are of another nation."

"Look, Father! He's trying to make signs."

The man on the stretcher slowly and laboriously raised an arm. He tried to make a gesture, but broke off in a groan. Perspiration stood out upon the forehead. The pop eyes puckered in agony.

With a sigh the man collapsed back to immobility. He shook his head, groaned, gutturaled another sentence in German, then smiled a wan smile.

The squat men clustered on either side regarded the scene in unblinking silence. Their eyes, looking like twin lenses of a huge camera, turned from time to time as they exchanged glances.

"I'm afraid it's hopeless. Was there ever such a tantalizing situation?" exclaimed Professor Wagner.

Again there was a commotion before the door of the hut, and then two of the squat natives entered bearing between them a human burden. It was Badger, bound hand and foot, his face gray with fright, his vest-button eyes fixed with terror.

"You speak German?" shouted the professor.

Badger nodded.

The pop-eyed man on the stretcher saw that nod, interpreted it correctly. His blue lips parted and rattled forth a long string of conversation.

And Badger settled the question of his linguistic ability by replying in smooth German, speaking rapidly, making gestures from time to time.

"Ah!" sighed Professor Wagner. "At last we have solved our difficulties. Ask him if these men intend to do us harm, Badger."

But Badger paid no attention to the command.

* * *

For more than fifteen minutes the two chattered on. The little men sat hunched about, apparently without curiosity. Their huge, lidless eyes remained motionless. Their breathing was deep and regular. They showed no emotion, gave no faintest flicker of facial expression.

Then it became apparent that the conversation had drifted to the three who lay listening with such eager curiosity.

Badger pointed toward them, indulged in a rattle of conversation. The German nodded, looked at the three, and his eyes clouded with hostility.

Again he looked at Badger.

"Treachery!" snapped Click. "That bird's double crossing us."

"Hush!" whispered the girl. "We have got to make him our ally. Otherwise we won't have any means of communicating with these people."

The German rolled his head, turned his pop eyes upon one of the natives, and muttered a single sound. It was one of those crisp, explosive words such as the chief had used.

The native got to his feet, left the hut without a word of reply.

Badger turned to the others.

"Well, I guess you folks are wondering what it's all about," he said. "You see, it's this way. This chap, Carl Gluckner, was working on a new type of aërial warship during the World War. He discovered a peculiar ray that had remarkable properties, but he couldn't control that ray. At length he made himself a metallic house somewhat similar to ours, made it airtight, constructed it to withstand terrific pressure from within, and determined to explore the upper atmosphere.

"He's a little indefinite about it, and I think he's perhaps trying to confuse me on the nature of his invention. That's only natural, anyway. But he, and four companions, started out. They tuned up their ray, directed it beneath them, and found they were ascending with such terrific velocity that they lost all control of the car. Gluckner says he was unconscious because of being thrown against the floor, the acceleration was so great.

"They were in the interplanetary regions for seven days. Then they managed to control the ray somewhat, and, by using it in short intervals with a greatly reduced current, were able to effect a landing. But the machine was pretty badly smashed when they landed. They came down not far from here, and the natives tried to capture them.

"They had rifles, and turned loose, killing more than a hundred. But the little beggars don't seem to have any great fear of death. When they start to do a thing, they do it. Sheer force of numbers told the story, and they overpowered the expedition. They killed Gluckner's companions, but held him for purposes of observation.

"He's managed to learn their language. Says it's a simple affair that's like certain of the primitive African tribes. He's sent for the chief. Here comes the chief now."

The little man entered the hut, stood for a moment before Gluckner, regarding him in unwinking gravity. Then he muttered a single word.

Gluckner answered slowly, laboriously. He used five separate words, rolled his eyes, waited, then put together a slow, halting sentence, hesitating between each word as though to let the brain of the chief absorb the expression.

The chief turned his camera eyes to Badger, took from his robe a huge diamond that had been shaped into a knife, and slit Badger's bonds with a single stroke of the razor edge.

"Good heavens," exclaimed the professor; "that knife is a diamond; unpolished, but a diamond, nevertheless."

The chief approached the others, bent over the girl, cut her bonds, then straightened and put the knife back in his girdle.

"But how about Father and Mr. Kendall?" asked Dorothy.

Badger shook his head.

The chief grunted again.

Two men armed with spears entered the hut.

The men each took an arm of the girl, led her outside the door.

Click glanced at Badger.

That individual was smiling, a loose-lipped, crafty smile.

The girl's steps died away. The steady drip, drip, drip of the mournful forest rattled on the leaf roof of the hut. And then that fog-filled air was knifed by a single piercing scream.

Click struggled frantically with his bonds.

"The girl. She's in danger. Quick, turn us loose, go see what it is!" he told Badger.

Badger went to the door of the hut. His manner was that of one who strolls casually. For an instant he stood within the entrance, then vanished. His feet could be heard on the ground, running.

Click struggled with his body, writhing, twisting, trying to get free, hardly conscious of what he was doing. One of the guards arose, picked up a spear and thrust the sharp end against Click's throat.

Click glanced up into the expressionless eyes, jerked his head toward the doorway.

"Can't you let me go to help her?" he asked, forgetting that the man could not understand his language.

His only answer was a tightening of the pressure where the spear pushed against his throat.

Click subsided. The spear had punctured his skin, was pushing against the tender spot of his throat. He concluded that he was to be murdered in cold blood.

"*Nein, nein,*" warned Gluckner.

The pressure relaxed. Shod footsteps came strolling along the packed ground outside the hut. Badger's grinning face appeared in the doorway.

"She just saw a snake," he remarked. "Said to forgive her for screaming."

And then he turned to Gluckner and rattled off a long discourse. Gluckner shook his head once, then talked swiftly for more than a minute.

* * *

Badger yawned, stretched, nodded, turned to the professor. "Pity you don't speak German. Some of this information is well worth hearing. He says the heat on the central portion of the illuminated disk is unbearable. That no one lives there except a race of people that are close kin to the things we call apes. They're hairy and live in the trees. This tribe represents about the highest order of civilization he's seen; but he hasn't made a complete exploration of the planet.

"The same face is always turned toward the sun, just as the same face of the moon is always turned toward the earth. That means there's one side that has perpetual night. There's a peculiar sort of mushroom growth that attains gigantic proportions in the night zone. And the borderland is peopled by a race of ferocious warriors.

"They use a sort of blowpipe and have a missile that's got some toadstool preparation on it. It causes a painful death within about three hours of the time it's absorbed into the system.

"These people aren't very warlike, but they have a certain callousness to all forms of pain or suffering. They're something like wild animals of a low order of intelligence. Yet they're human all right. It's what Gluckner calls 'undeveloped soul ego.' There's a German name he uses that's hard to translate.

"Well, I'm going out and walk around and see if I can make better friends with these natives. So long."

He strolled to the door, muttered a sentence in German, and then went out.

Gluckner regarded the bound pair for a moment with pop eyes that seemed to contain some element of doubt. Once more he sought to raise his hand and make motions, but the effort was futile. The rheumatism had made his joints almost immovable. He sighed, barked a single explosive order, and the natives took hold of the stretcher, bore him outside.

There remained three guards watching them with unblinking camera eyes. About them the fog swirled. The trees dipped their mournful protest against the dismal environment. The reddish glow of waning light gradually began to tell on Kendall's nerves.

Perspiration slimed his body from the effort of his struggles. The thongs bit into his wrists, and Click noticed that they developed a slime as the perspiration came in contact with them. There was a gelatinous something in the substance that softened in water. An idea seized him.

He worked his hands back and forth—up and down—sliding one over the other, trying to slip his bonds over his wrists, seeking to get as much perspiration on them as possible.

He noticed that the reddish light was becoming less bright. There seemed to be a pall settling down. Things lost their color, became drab. It was harder to see. The air seemed quivering with suspense.

"Thought it didn't get dark here," he said to Professor Wagner.

"Most strange. It cannot be night as we know it. Yet there is undoubtedly some obscuration of the sun. Perhaps there is an eclipse caused by some minor satellite. After all, the question of a small satellite for Venus has caused astronomical arguments at various times."

The guards became restive, uneasy. The darkness grew more profound.

Then came a terrific crashing noise in the forest. It sounded as though millions of feet were tearing through the foliage, smashing branches.

CHAPTER 8

Horror in the Dark

"Rain!" exclaimed Click.

And it was rain, such as terrestrial residents never experienced. More like a thundering cloudburst it came. The trees bent and swayed. The beating drops, larger than any Click had experienced, came hissing through the foggy air, spattered upon the soggy ground.

The guards peered out of the door, turned their great eyes upon each other. Click could see them as shadowy outlines vaguely visible against the curtain of pouring water which covered the doorway.

Then came other forms. The doorway was blocked with struggling figures that paused long enough to make explosive remarks, single syllables of alarm.

In the confusion Click managed to plunge his arms in a pool of water which seeped through the wall of the hut. The water softened his bonds, made them as slippery as so much wet seaweed. He slipped his arm down until his right hand could grasp his knife which had been left in his pocket. A few seconds and he was free.

He rolled over to Professor Wagner.

"I'm cutting your ropes," he hissed in a shrill warning, audible over the crash of the storm.

Click slit the ropes. "Come on," he ordered.

The professor arose, followed.

The two fugitives slipped out into the darkness. Instantly they were drenched to the skin. Yet the rain was warm, almost tepid. The fog still swirled through the moisture. The trees steamed, and the darkness was that of a foggy night.

"I believe these fellows can see in the dark," said Click.

"Better keep to the shadows. Let's try ducking into the first shelter we can find."

A doorway loomed before them. So dark was it that they were almost upon it before it became visible.

They dived inside.

"Here's where I find a spear," promised Click, as he groped about.

Of a sudden his groping hands touched clammy human skin. He jumped back, bracing himself for attack.

There was a guttural exclamation from the darkness.

"Gluckner!" exclaimed Click.

"*Ja, ja,*" came eagerly from the darkness.

A sudden inspiration seized Click; perhaps the man spoke French. And Click knew a little something of that language. His execution was atrocious, but it had served to get him by before.

He tried to bring his mind to work upon his slender vocabulary. The result was a few stuttering words that ventured upon the darkness and were abruptly swallowed in an enthusiastic burst of voluble French from the German.

Click gave a sigh of relief. Why hadn't he thought of French before? But the events had been so exciting, so unusual, and Badger had been so ready with his flow of German that it had entirely escaped his mind that the German would very probably know French.

Click interrupted the rapid flow of words and ordered the man to speak more slowly.

"Ask him what is the trouble," said Professor Wagner.

Click tried to frame the question.

Gluckner caught the idea and answered it slowly in simple words.

"Rain. Once a month it comes; sometimes oftener. It is in those times that the people from the dark side attack. They have eyes that see well in the dark. The natives of this side see but indistinctly. I see not at all. These men see through the fog, but not the darkness. You understand?"

Click gave a swift translation.

"Yes, yes," purred the pleased professor. "Now ask him about the satellite. Is it true there is a small satellite? And ask him—"

Click interrupted. "How about the girl? Where is she?"

The German grunted.

"The girl? You do not know? The wife of the man Badger? She was the ransom price given to the chief for the liberty of that man."

"What?" yelled Click.

The German repeated. "She becomes the wife of the chief. Otherwise he could not have her for a wife. He could take her, but that is against the law. Captives can be slaves, but not wives. So the man Badger sells his wife to the chief for his liberty. It is not that which one should do, but—"

From the rain-soaked darkness without came a fierce yell of wild menace. There was the sound of rushing bodies.

"The night people! They come. It is bad."

A body staggered against the doorway. A huge shape blotted out what little gray light seeped through this opening.

Click could hear the sound of a blow, a mortal groan. Something slumped to the floor.

He had a vague sense of something rushing toward him.

He hurtled forward, driving his right in a swing, slipping his knife in his left hand.

The right connected. There was the jar of impact, a *whoosh* as one who has had his breath knocked from him, and then great hands clasped the wrist that held the knife. The weight of a body was thrown against him.

From the darkness he heard the German's voice.

"They are big men, these people of the night. Beware their fangs. They tear throats with their teeth, these night men."

Click sensed the warning, flung himself backward.

In the darkness there was the gnashing sound of fangs clashing together. Hot breath was on his throat, steaming in his nostrils.

He flung his right across and over. The blow landed on the creature's jaw, staggered him. Click tried to free his left, and then felt himself beaten to the ground.

Rushing shapes swept through the hut as football players thunder down a field.

The inert bulk of his adversary fell on him, shielded him. He could hear spears thudding into the ground, heard men falling to their death. The smell of blood was in the steaming air. The rattle of dying men sounded above the pelting roar of the rain.

Click squirmed, twisted, finally worked his way out from under the enormous body that had covered him. His hand encountered a spear thrust into the ground. He pulled it out, staggered to a corner of the hut, braced himself for attack.

But the conflict had swirled out of the hut, gone on to a more remote portion of the village.

"Professor," he called cautiously.

There was no answer. The interior of the hut was silent.

Click felt his way forward. His feet encountered a body. His hand stretched out in exploration. Instinctively he knew it to be one of the night people. The body was huge, cold, clammy. A spear was driven clear through the breast, well into the ground.

His hand encountered another body; this time it was the night man he had knocked out with his swinging punch. The man stirred slightly.

Click's hand went over the features. He shuddered as he felt the moist slime of wide open eyes, staring straight up, unconscious. The eyes were as big as the palm of his hand.

He pushed on. His hand encountered the side of the stretcher. He felt for the German. He encountered the outlines of the huge body, the gnarled limbs with their twisted joints. He felt for the head, and drew back in horror.

Evidently it had been some species of war club that had finished Herr Gluckner. But he was finished, completely and conclusively finished.

A sudden horror rippled Click's spine.

"Professor! Professor!" he called, raising his voice, shouting as loudly as he could.

There was no answer.

His feet stumbled upon a body. His exploring fingers encountered clothes. It needed but a second to complete the identification. It was the body of Professor Wagner, and he was quite dead, the entire top of the head crushed by a terrific blow of a war club.

Then, over the pelting of the storm, over the hissing sound of the rushing water, the rattling leaves, the swaying, groaning branches, came a sound that was unmistakable. It was the crisp crack of a rifle. Again and again it sounded. Then there was silence once more.

Click flung himself out into the pouring darkness. Water sloshed about his ankles. The green slime of the forest had washed down to the ground, turning it into a soggy mass of slush upon which his feet slipped.

There was nothing to give him the faintest sense of direction except the general idea which he had of the location of the rifle shots. About him in the darkness there was a vague sensation of rushing forms. Occasionally he could hear grunts, groans, blows.

A spear hissed through the darkness, thudded into the bole of a tree. That spear could not have missed his body by more than inches.

From behind him sounded a wild yell, running steps. Instinctively he ducked forward, half spun, collided with a tree trunk, flung himself around it.

There was a puff of explosive sound and something spattered the tree trunk with a peculiar suggestion of vicious force. Click realized it must be a mushroom-poisoned missile from a blow gun.

He whirled, made for the dense forest, then cut in a zigzag, floundering through wet ferns, crashing into slimy trees, constantly inundated with the torrential downpour that emptied itself from the black heavens.

His slithering feet found the slimy mud of the immense clearing in which the shell had landed. He had no very good idea as to his location. Was he on the near side or the far side of that circular clearing? He had no means of ascertaining other than to keep exploring in the hope that he would stumble upon some clew. And stumble upon it he did, for he literally fell over the body of a man.

Swift exploration with his questing fingers disclosed that this was one of the night people, that a bullet hole had accounted for his death. The bullet had torn through his heart and the man had died in his tracks.

The direction of that bullet hole, the way the body was facing, all served to give Click a general idea of the direction he wanted to take.

Of a sudden he realized that it was growing lighter. There was a faint margin of visibility creeping out from the surrounding circle of darkness.

Then to his left, hardly fifteen yards away, there again sounded the deep-throated roar of a rifle. A running figure barely visible in the rapidly increasing light, jumped high in the air, flung up its arms, fell forward, twitching, jerking.

Click saw the outline of the shell, sitting upon the muddy field, the polished sides streaked with moisture, the base spattered with mud. The door was open, and standing just without the door was Badger, the rifle at his shoulder.

Had Badger lowered that rifle and turned, it must have been certain death for Click Kendall. But the cruelty of his nature was too strong. It was not enough that he had merely disabled the runner, Badger wanted to kill him. And so he waited, squinting down the sights of the rifle, his entire face twisted with a ferocious blood lust.

The native struggled to hands and knees, tried to stand, but was unable. He dropped, began to crawl. Badger slammed in another shell. The gun roared forth its summons. The native crashed to the ground, splashing water and mud in a death agony.

Badger lowered the rifle and stepped within the shell. His arm reached to the door, slammed it over.

And Click Kendall managed to just thrust a foot in that door to keep it from slamming shut. His shoulder thrust against it, sent it crashing inward, and charged. His head crashed into the pit of Badger's stomach. For a moment they hung, locked, poised, then they crashed to the floor.

Badger whipped over his arm, tried to obtain a strangle hold. Click gave no thought to guarding, but sought rather to smash to his objective. He sent his fists in short, jabbing rocking blows, thudding home with all of his shoulder muscles behind them.

His wounded arm sent little shoots of agonized pain racing up his shoulder, stabbing into his very brain. But he persisted.

Badger rolled over, squirmed free, got to his knees. He swung with all his force and the blow caught Click as he came in.

Click felt the nauseating blackness of that blow, but fought grimly to keep his senses. Blood poured from his nose. His eye was swelling. He caught the other off balance, sent his right straight for the chin, a blow that carried momentum behind it.

The fist crashed straight to the button. Badger's head snapped back. He flung up his hands, crashed over backward. His head thudded against the metal floor of the ship.

Click scrambled to his feet, weak, dizzy, wet.

He floundered to the door, swinging upon its metal ball-bearing hinges. The rain clouds had vanished. The same rosy-hued fog was filling every nook and cranny of the steaming world. Water glistened everywhere.

CHAPTER 9

Disaster

Click moved to the control table. Had the little men placed the shell out of control? He pushed the slide over to gravitation zero, felt the same sensation of lightness which enabled him to drift about the shell, and sighed his relief. He had a chance, just one chance in a hundred, but he was going to take that chance.

He moved the slide control into the negative segment. The shell slipped upward, bounced from bole to bole, swung from branch to branch as lightly as a bit of thistle. Click possessed himself of the rifle, snapped a shell into the barrel, and searched the unconscious form of Badger.

He found a couple of boxes of shells, found also several rough diamonds of the type which the natives fashioned into knives. Click found a bit of rope, proceeded to tie the man's hands and feet. Badger fluttered his eyes, groaned.

"Where's the girl?" demanded Click.

Badger's swollen lips twisted in an effort to speak.

"Find her!"

Click picked up one of the great diamonds, its hard edge fashioned into a razor edge, held it over Badger's throat.

"If she's come to harm—"

The man's face turned livid with fear.

"No, no. In the inner cone, locked in!"

Click gained the inner door, found it barred, flung it open. Dorothy Wagner was stretched on a cot, bound hand and foot. Her eyes rolled toward the door in an agony of hopelessness, found his, then lit until they were as twin stars.

"Click! You escaped! You came! Father, where's Father?"

Click would have broken it to her gently, but she read

correctly the expression on his face. Tears welled into the eyes.

"Cut me loose, Click. There's a whole box of those diamond knives there on that table. Badger traded me off for them and his liberty. He told the natives I was his wife. Then he killed my guards and brought me here."

Click saw the box. The diamonds were unpolished, in the rough, but they caught the light and sent it glittering in brilliant reflections. They were large, some being three inches in length.

He grasped one, cut through the cords which held the girl, assisted her to her feet.

"Could we—Father's body?"

He shook his head.

"It was in the thick of the fighting. And it's getting light now. The storm's over."

"Where are we?"

Click Kendall led the way to the outer room.

He turned to the window in the floor, began a minute study of the ground below.

Little men were rushing about, splashing through the mud. The ground was carpeted with dead and wounded, showing where the brunt of the fight had taken place, and most of the victims were of the dwarf tribe.

Click had an opportunity to study one of the night men who had been taken captive. He was tall, well over six feet, splendidly muscled. The skin was pale, and the forehead seemed to be all eyes. They were astonishingly large and the man continually kept his crooked arm over them, shielding them from the rays of the sun as these rays filtered through the envelope of mist.

"I think," said Dorothy, "Father would prefer being left here. It's his planet, you know."

And her tapering finger firmly slid the control button to negative gravitation.

Like a rocket hissing through the air, the shell darted

through the warm moisture of the fog-filled air, shot past towering trees, and suddenly seemed enshrouded with white radiance. For only a fraction of a second did the white radiance grip the atmosphere, and then the shell, gathering speed with every foot of travel, shot out into the clear open air.

The blazing sunlight seemed the promise of a new world. The blue of the sky, intense, brilliant, deep; the piling billows of cloud below, all seemed clean, an augur of a more happy existence than the life of the fog-drenched planet.

Faster and faster they went. Click moved the lever. The car swung into lateral motion, went skimming over the top of the fog.

The dark rim of twilight loomed before them, showed a crescent of eternal darkness.

"The earth should be about above us now," said the girl.

Click slammed the control over to extreme negative gravitation, and the car shot into accelerated motion. The planet below began to show the motion of its diminishing perspective, and the outer air grew dark with the darkness of interplanetary space.

The girl twisted a valve. Compressed air hissed into the car. She opened another valve.

"Oxygen," she said, "and there's a valve control to exhaust the foul air. Let's go back in the inner room. There are controls there. I don't like to be out here with Badger."

Click followed her into the inner shell.

"These controls are arranged in series now," she said. "We can handle the car from here."

Click nodded.

"You get some sleep. I'll keep it moving until we get somewhere's near the earth."

She nodded, patted his hand.

"Good old Click!"

He got her to lie down on one of the beds, started an alcohol stove, brewed her a hot milk drink, saw her head nod with utter exhaustion even as she drank it. He eased her form back on the pillow, covered her with blankets, then turned his attention to the problem of navigating the car through space.

It was not easy, yet it was not so difficult as he imagined. He could see the disk of a bright star which he knew must be the earth. He moved the control over to a more easy rate of repulsion so that their speed would not be entirely beyond control.

His own head nodded with fatigue, but he grimly fought off the warm drowsiness. The clean sun beat with dazzling splendor upon the metallic sides of the car. The universe showed clean and sparkling, gems set in jet black.

Click improved his time by taking stock of the contents of the inner shell. It touched the outer shell only upon one long seam. There was a window at the top where it joined the top of the other shell. Click could see that this window was made to open inward. The glass was set in live rubber, under terrific pressure. This was to prevent the window blowing outward in space with the pressure of the air in the shell. And there were complicated levers and screws by which that window could be swung into place.

It was out of this window, then, that the life-giving air and the pressure necessary to sustain existence had leaked on that first wild plunge into the upper regions of the atmosphere.

Click inspected the bookshelf with its tables of planetary positions, its gravitational formulae, then turned his attention to the other equipment. There was a telescope, well made, mounted upon a folding tripod. There was a bulky package hanging from the wall. Inspection showed that it contained two parachutes of the type worn by aviators.

Evidently Professor Wagner had placed them there for use during his earlier experiments. They offered him a way back to earth should the shell prove unmanageable.

Click set up the telescope, unfolded the tripod, and swung the objective toward the window in the top.

The glass was crystal-clear, yet gave some distortion to the image, a species of haziness that prevented really clear perception. But Click was able to pick out the earth, almost directly above them. He could see the whirling continents, the seas, the cloud areas, those places where the sun beat down with glittering light upon shimmering deserts. The shadows of a mountain range loomed plainly.

Click saw they were approaching with terrific speed. He had made no effort to calculate speed other than by the unaided estimate of his eye. He felt reasonably sure of coming somewhere within the influence of the earth's gravitation. He didn't need to hit it at all close, a hundred thousand miles in either direction would still enable him to fall into the earth.

And then sheer exhaustion levied her toll. Click slumped to his side, pillowed his head on his arm, and slept. Hours later he awoke with a start. He could see that the car was somewhere above the Pacific Ocean. He caught a glimpse of Australia, China, then shifted his gaze to the east. Late afternoon mantled the shores of California, Oregon, Washington, Mexico, South America. He could see the mighty mountain chains casting long shadows to the east. And the car was whizzing its lateral motion with constant acceleration.

The girl was awake, at the controls. She smiled at him. "We're getting there," she said.

Click rubbed his eyes, peered through the window.

It was a breath-taking spectacle. The girl prepared a meal while they watched the panorama below. The great black disk of the earth, illuminated by the moon, the flaming stars, the mighty disk of the sun itself, blazing in white-hot splendor.

Then the sun was obscured by the earth. All about them reigned darkness save for the pin-points of flaming stars. Click groped for the light switch, set the lights going. He and the girl ate in anxious silence.

"Let's see where we are," said Dorothy, and switched off the lights.

Below them a luminous haze seemed to bathe the floor.

"Moonlight on the earth, being reflected back at us," she remarked.

They sat in awed wonder, watching the spectacle. Click reached over, took her hand. Nor did she make any move to withdraw it. Hand in hand they watched.

At length there was a ribbon of light, a great horn that grew in volume.

"We're swinging clear of the world," she announced. "Now to check our lateral speed and start falling again. Leave the gravitational indicator over at about half gravitation. I'll shove the lateral speed back and we'll see how we come."

Click moved the controls.

"I'd better see how Badger's getting on," he said, smiled at her in the light that was streaming into the shell from the sun's disk as it swung around the edge of the world, and flung open the door.

He stepped into the outer shell, saw a little wad of rope lying on the floor; just the rope, nothing more.

"How did that get there?" he asked, and, of a sudden, knew the answer. Badger had slipped from his bonds. Where, then, was he?

Click turned, saw the huddled shape of menace, caught the outthrust rifle as it held upon him, steady as a rock, and gave one wild leap.

The bullet spattered squarely on the edge of the door, glanced, and hit the control box. Click slammed the metal door shut, snapped a bar into place.

"He's in command outside. We're cooped up in here like rats in a trap," he said.

Dorothy Wagner nodded. "Lucky we've got the controls here, though. We can land almost where we want to, and we'll land him f.o.b. Police Station at Centerberry."

Click grinned at her.

"S'pose they'll believe the story we tell by way of complaint?"

It was her turn to smile.

She advanced to the controls, glanced down at the earth.

"We seem to be coming in all right. Guess I'll let it check a little bit."

She pushed at the indicator.

"It doesn't work. His bullet must have smashed the control wires. We're out of control, falling into the earth, and we'll pick up speed. I don't think we're over a hundred miles away, and our lateral speed has checked a lot."

They exchanged glances.

"Can we make some sort of repairs? After all, we could come to a truce with Badger. He'll realize that we're all threatened by the same danger."

She shook her head.

"The last discovery, the last experiment that gave the missing link in his invention was perfected by Dad while I was away. Then you know what happened. Dad never had a chance to explain it to me. Even if we could get out there, I couldn't fix the controls, I'm afraid."

Click scratched his head.

"And this box is entirely out of order?"

She had been experimenting with the keys.

"No-o-o. It isn't quite wrecked. But it seems to have lost about nine-tenths of its control effectiveness."

"Then," remarked Click, "there's nothing to do but to wait."

Wait they did. Once more their hands touched, held.

"Dot," said Click, his voice choking. "Now's no time to say what I want to say, but if anything should happen, I want you to know—"

She raised her face to his, smiled at him with deep eyes, half parted lips.

"Yes, dear. I know, have known ever since I saw the look on your face when you came to rescue me."

She gave him her lips. For a long minute they stood clasped together. Then they separated and looked destiny in the face.

The earth showed as a vast curved plain now, and the tumbled sea of water below seemed endless, sparkling in the rays of the morning sun.

Click opened the outer door a crack.

"Badger, throw down the gun. I want a truce. We're in a bad situation."

A taunting laugh was his only answer.

"Bluff!" snapped the man. "You've got another control in there."

And the roaring of the gun punctuated his comment.

Of a sudden, as Click slammed the door and bolted it, he noticed a peculiar sound that had been gradually springing up, gathering force. It sounded like a weird whistle, long drawn, wailing.

He glanced at the girl.

"Atmosphere," she said. "We're getting into the air of the earth, and it's whirling around at a speed of perhaps a thousand miles an hour, following the motion of the earth."

Louder and louder shrilled the whistling air. The shell had been lagging behind the motion of the globe. Now as the air caught it, the shell was hurtled ahead, constantly increasing its velocity. And, as the air grew more dense, the atmospheric pressure became more pronounced.

The girl worked the lateral lever, easing the strain as much as she could. Closer and closer came the globe. And the sun ceased to sweep across the heavens, the globe ceased to whirl below them, spinning at terrific speed. Instead, the world became more fixed, and the sun resumed an orderly march across the heavens.

Minutes lengthened into anxious hours. Night enveloped them. They were within some twenty miles of the earth's surface now, falling, but not rapidly.

Then the girl made a discovery.

"Look, the positive side of the gravitation is almost intact. Not that it does us any good except that it might facilitate landing. It's the negative side that's broken."

"Don't work that side, then," warned Click. "There'd be nothing to check us."

She nodded. "I wonder where we are?"

"There's the moon. Looks different down here, doesn't it? Look, look, that's land!"

She followed his finger. Far to the east was a dark shadow lying upon the golden reflection of the waters.

"Looks like it, all right. It's land unless it's a fog bank. Get the telescope."

They set up the telescope, gazed through one of the windows.

"Yes, yes, I can see lights. It's a coast town!"

Click pressed his face against the window.

"And we're drifting toward it."

For minutes they watched. The lights came closer and closer, finally swung below them.

"S'pose it's an island?"

She shook her head. "No. Look to the south and east. See the airport? See that whole ocean of lights looming up. I'll bet that's Los Angeles, and this must be Santa Barbara down below. Look, you can see a drive along the ocean front there, and there are palm trees along it. Here, use these night glasses."

Click took the glasses, saw the city, the buildings, the mountains, quiet and serene, saw moving lights where automobiles crept along.

"We'll be down soon," he said.

She nodded.

"And we've got too much downward speed. My experimenting with the downward scale of plus gravitation increased our falling speed."

They remained silent for another spell. Click noticed that the side speed of the car was increasing.

"Yes," she said when he pointed it out to her, "it's functioning somewhat, and it's getting acceleration. It's a good thing to have side speed. It'll soften the bump."

"Mountains?" asked Click.

"Below us," she said. "We're still five or six miles up in the air."

Again they drifted on and down.

The lights faded away. Great pools of darkness showed ahead.

"The desert," she said.

"We don't want to come down there."

"We'll have to, I'm afraid. The car's settling rapidly. I'm afraid we've got a lot of down speed."

And then Click's mind snapped with a sudden recollection.

"Parachutes!" he yelled. "I saw a couple of packed 'chutes. Can we get out?"

And she rippled into a laugh.

"How foolish of me not to have remembered. Yes, we packed a couple of emergencies. Here, I'll get them out. You put some of the diamonds into your pockets. You can't tell. Badger may manage to clean us out of what we leave."

Click nodded.

The bright moonlight, flooding through the window, showed them what they wanted. They strapped on the 'chutes.

"Know how to work them?"

He nodded.

"Served on an observation balloon once. How do we get that window open?"

"I'll show you. Give me a boost. That's it. There it comes. Doesn't that fresh earth air feel good. How much better a place this is than that wet, miserable, soggy planet of hopelessness!"

CHAPTER 10

The Crater

Click walked softly to the inner door, eased off the bolt, tied the knob with a bit of heavy rope. Then he opened it a crack and called to Badger.

"Badger, we're going to jump. You can come in when we leave. I've tied the door with rope. It'll take you a minute or two to cut it. You can bring it down, but the control's broken. You can't come down any slower than it's going now. We'll jump when we see a settlement, and we'll send a search party out after you."

His answer was a curse.

"Boloney!" went on the cursing man. "The control's no more broken than I am. Try getting out! I'll send this shell dashing after you, crush the life out of you. Got some 'chutes, eh?"

"Yes, we have, and don't experiment, either!" snapped Click.

"Oh, Click," called the girl. "Here's a cluster of lights out here. It looks like a desert town."

"Coming," he said. "You jump and I'll follow. Don't forget to have your hand on your rip cord as you leave."

She waved her hand.

"See you later, dear."

And then she tilted backward and plunged into the night. Click opened his knife, slithered it out into the room.

"Cut the rope, Badger. We're off."

And he jumped to the table, caught the upper edge of the vertical window, slipped outside, and turned for a last look inside the shell.

He saw the flash of a knife blade. The lights switched on,

brilliantly illuminating the interior. He saw the rope part, the door swing open, Badger come running in with a rifle in one hand.

A quick look and he saw Click, clinging to the edge of the window.

Cursing, Badger sprang for the controls, slammed the slide over, despite Click's warning shout. Straight up he pushed the slide, then, as there was no response, pushed it clear over the other way.

Click's hands felt the shell jerked from them as though he had been trying to hold a rifle bullet. He was left suspended in the air.

For a moment he thought he was shooting straight up at terrific speed, for the light of the shell slipped into the moonlit night below, became but a speck.

Then he realized what had happened. The shell was dashing toward earth, and there was no control that would check it.

Air that was grippingly cold rushed past him, whipped his garments. He remembered to jerk the rip cord. There was the crackle of cloth. Something white streaked up into the moonlight above him. Then the harness tugged at him. The 'chute opened with a crackling report.

He swung back and forth in a sickening arc. He looked below to see what had happened to the shell.

As he looked, it struck, struck the desert with such force that it seemed a volcano must have opened. There was a white spot of incandescent heat, a burst of flame as oxygen ignited, then nothing but a single glowing coal that melted away finally into nothing.

Far to one side, higher up, he could see the girl's parachute, swinging in the white moonlight like a gigantic mushroom.

Down he drifted.

The surface was farther away than he had anticipated. It

took them an appreciable length of time to come down. And a desert wind whipped them far to the east.

At length Click saw the ground, a white blur, coming to meet him. He braced himself, struck, tugged at the 'chute to spill the wind, and then wrestled with the harness.

The 'chute swung over, crackled in the wind, was whisked away. The silence of the desert gripped him.

"Oh, Click," he heard a voice, and his ears had never heard a more welcome sound:

"Here, dearest," he answered.

They found each other, melted in a single affectionate embrace. Then they began their long walk.

Somewhere to the north a coyote howled.

The moon bathed them with mellow benediction. The lights of the town twinkled in the frosty desert air.

Then there was the sweep of a searchlight. An automobile blared its horn. Another came down from the north. They could see the path of the lights, see them come to a stop, see shadowy figures moving about.

"Let's go there. We can get a lift," said Click.

She nodded, increased her stride.

Yet it was an hour before they reached the place, and by that time a circle of machines had gathered.

"By George, I believe—yes, it's where the shell struck!" said Click.

They joined the throng, unnoticed.

A deep crater was in the sand. About it the sand itself had been melted by the heat of that which had happened. A twisted lump of discolored, seared metal was out on one side of the rim.

"Meteor," explained one of the spectators. "They seen it strike an' been digging for it. Just found it. Funny it ain't bigger. Looked like she weighed ten ton when she come down. You folks goin' to town? Guess the show's all over here."

Click nodded.

"Thanks. We'll ride," he said.

The desert man piloted a rattling flivver, covered with white dust, over the desert roads.

"Lookin' for mines?" he asked.

Click shook his head.

"Looking for a preacher," he remarked.

The girl started, squeezed his arm.

"Aren't you rather abrupt?" she asked.

Click nodded. "Bet your life I am. We've got to see a preacher, and then we've got to see a gem expert and cash in a few thousand dollars' worth of gems. After that? After that we've got to learn to keep quiet about where we've been and what happened. Let the Wagner shell remain one of the unsolved mysteries."

"Yes," she said after a while. "It's better so. We're in a new country. We'll just begin life here and forget the other."

The desert man looked back at them curiously.

"Elopers, eh? Well, you're gettin' a good start. See that bright star over there in the east? That's Venus, the star of lovers. It's the mornin' star these days. Be daylight in coupla hours."

The two turned, joined the gaze of the desert man in looking at the bright planet. But he would have been surprised could he have fathomed their thoughts at that moment.